"Make love to me."

She felt the rawboned power of him, knew the sheer intensity of energy, and in her discovery of Cole Slater she nearly forgot herself . . . until, with a rush of molten fire, she flamed beneath him and her cry mingled with his on the night air.

"I never knew," she whispered running a hand over his chest.

"What?" he grunted without opening his eyes.

"How it is between a man and a woman."

He rolled away from her, away from the dreamy expectancy in her eyes, away from the soft alluring touch of her hand.

"How much?" he asked tersely.

"What?" The breath tightened in Kansas's chest. Her eyes were wide and luminous and vulnerable as she stared up at him, but he refused to look at her. He refused to see.

"How much do you usually get for your services," he asked digging into his pocket. . . .

Also by Peggy Hanchar:

Desire's Dream
Renegade Heart
Creole Angel
Golden Promises
Tender Betrayal
Tomorrow's Dream

THE GILDED DOVE

Peggy Hanchar

A Fawcett
Published by
Copyright © 1991 by Peggy Hanchar, Inc.

All rights reserved under International and Pan-American Copyright Conventions. Published in the United States by Fawcett Gold Medal, a division of Random House, Inc., New York, and distributed simultaneously in Canada by Random House of Canada Limited, Toronto.

Library of Congress Catalog Card Number: 90-93373

ISBN 0-449-14715-7

Printed in China

First Edition:

FAWCETT GOLD MEDAL • NEW YORK

A Fawcett Gold Medal Book
Published by Ballantine Books
Copyright © 1991 by Peggy Hanchar

Library of Congress Catalog Card Number: 90-93479

ISBN 0-449-14715-0

Printed in Canada

First Edition: February 1991

Author's Note:

Legendary characters abound in the history of the old west. Scarlet women and lady gamblers were a welcome addition in any mining town. They added color and style to a lonely miner's entertainment.

Kansas McKay is loosely based on Julia Bulette, a soiled dove who made an enormous fortune in a few short years and died under mysterious circumstances. Julia's generosity in helping others earned her the love and admiration of the rough miners of Virginia City. "Her skin may be scarlet," they declared, "but her heart is white." Thus are legends made.

Chapter 1

"*H*ERE SHE COMES!"
Abe Scoby slid down the flagpole and came to rest on the roof of the hotel porch. Cupping his hand to his mouth, he called to the man in the street below. "She's a' comin'. Best let Mr. Slater know."

"Sure thing," the cowhand hollered back, and quickly entered the hotel. In no time, the empty street filled with people peering eagerly in the direction Abe pointed.

The Butterworth noon stage came rolling across the prairie leaving a plume of dust trailing behind. The brightly painted coach appeared almost gaudy against the dun-colored prairie grass and pale sky. Legs churning, mouths foaming, the team of horses made a final effort as the driver applied his whip. He always liked driving into town with a bit of dash. It made folks appreciate the stagecoach a little more.

"Looks like Web's pushin' it some," Scoby said, coming to join his boss in the street. "Reckon he had some trouble?"

Les Slater squinted his eyes against the searing white light of the noon sun and rubbed his clean-shaven jaw. He'd just removed a three-day stubble and he still missed it. Rocking up on his toes he let his weight settle back four

1

square on booted feet and waited a moment more before
answering. When he finally spoke, his voice was deep and
slow, as befitted a man of his position and authority.

"It's just Web showing off for the townfolks," he said
disapprovingly, for he never could understand a man mis-
using his horses. His feeling was not born out of consideration for the beasts, but from a successful rancher's
understanding that a used-up horse was of little good to
anyone—and time and a bullet had to be wasted to shoot
him.

Slater glanced along the main street. People had left the
shaded interiors of stores and saloons to watch the stage
come in. Their easy smiles bespoke their anticipation. The
stagecoach's arrival broke up the monotony of their every-
day lives.

Even the gamblers and dance hall women had trickled out
to welcome the arrival, their eyes blinking against the unaccustomed brightness of high noon, their gaudy satin
dresses and heavy makeup garish in the Texas sunlight.

Molly McKay and some of the other girls at Moody's
Saloon leaned over the railing of the second-floor balcony,
their loose hair streaming over their shoulders, their low-cut
dresses gaping to show the plump white wares they offered.

Quickly Les averted his gaze, pretending not to see Molly
wave at him. His lips thinned in irritation at her boldness. It
had been some time since he'd been up to see the town
whore. She'd grown fat and careless over the years, and
he'd moved on to a younger, more imaginative partner, for
those rare times he needed a woman.

His frown deepened as his gaze settled on a slim reed of
a girl standing at the corner of the saloon porch. The blue of
her ill-fitting dress was faded from numerous washings. Her
cracked shoes and trim bare ankles were clearly in evidence
beneath the skirt's short hem. Without proper petticoats, the
limp material hugged her slender hips and trim rear. But her
attire wasn't what caused Les to frown. It was the way she

carried her slim, young body, with shoulders thrust back so the small feminine mounds of her young breasts drew a man's gaze. Thick, honey-gold hair tumbled around her shoulders and down her back, nearly brushing the rounded curve of her buttocks.

Kansas McKay! The spitting image of Molly when she first came to this town. She was trouble, and no doubt about it. Even now, half the men in the street were watching Kansas instead of the stage. Kansas appeared not even to notice, nor was she looking at the stage. Les followed the direction of her gaze and swore softly under his breath.

Cole Slater, his youngest son, stood on the porch across from the saloon, his hat pushed back to reveal his lean, tanned face and the dark curl of hair across his forehead. He was a big man like his father, broad-shouldered and slim-hipped. His young body was well muscled and hardened by his hours in the saddle. Now he slouched against the post, his dark eyes pinned on Kansas and his wide mouth curved in a crooked grin. With one hand he sent the girl a small salute and shifted his lanky frame restlessly. He paid no attention to the approaching stagecoach.

"Cole," Les growled, glaring at his son. "The stage-coach's comin'. Get on over here."

Cole Slater straightened, his glance darkening as he glared back at the old man in the middle of the dusty street. Les knew he didn't like to be spoken to in that manner, especially not in front of other people. He had half a mind to turn on his heel and walk away, leaving his father to look the fool in front of the whole town. But this was a special day for Les Slater, and father and son had acknowledged an uneasy truce. An old friend was coming from the Oregon Territory to visit for a spell, and Les wanted to show off his sons and his ranch. Swallowing his ire, Cole stepped off the porch and strolled over to join the Bar S hands.

Kansas watched him walk away and wished she felt brave enough to join the crowd in front of the hotel, but she'd long ago understood that one side of the street was for one kind of people and the other side for another, and never the twain shall meet—except in the upstairs rooms at Moody's Saloon. She pushed away her doleful thoughts and concentrated on watching Cole walk toward his father. She liked to watch him move in that lazy, easy saunter that belied the amount of distance he could cover in a hurry. She'd never seen him look so handsome. Instead of his usual cotton shirt, denim pants, and bandanna, he was wearing a suit today. The jacket fit across his broad shoulders like a soft glove and draped easily over his sloping back and slim hips.

Tugging impatiently at the too-short waist of her gown, Kansas wished for the thousandth time she had a new dress to wear. Not that Cole would notice. When he came around the saloon kitchen, he usually came to play cards and never seemed to notice anything particular about her, no matter how hard she tried. At least today she had a ribbon in her hair, a blue ribbon to match the color her gown once had been.

The thunder of horses' hooves and the rumble of wheels signified the stage was drawing near. An excitement pervaded the townspeople. Smiles grew wider, eyes brighter, and everyone moved forward a few steps as Web Porter brought the stagecoach into Webster with a flourish.

"Whoa, whoa," he called to his team, rearing back on the brake with all his weight.

"Damn fool," Les muttered. Cole grinned at his brother Neil.

"I was starting to worry," he said. "The old man hasn't been upset with anyone yet today. I was afraid he was going soft on us."

Scoby sent him an answering grin. Les Slater might intimidate his ranch hands, but he'd sure failed with his son. Cole was a hellion all right, rebellious and impatient, but he was always fair and hardworking and most of the men would rather work for him than the old man. Somehow Cole got the same job done as Les, but with a lot less fuss and hard feelings. Men who would have ridden out long ago stayed because of Cole. In spite of his youth, he had a way of winning and keeping a man's loyalty. The cowhands around the Bar S ranch respected Cole; they resented Les. Too bad the old man couldn't take a lesson from his son.

"How about it, Scoby?" Cole asked under his breath. "You boys want to get together later for a few hands?"

"Your pa's already given us strict orders about card playing while his company's here," Scoby said reluctantly.

Cole shrugged. He and Les had been butting heads ever since he could remember. He'd long ago given up trying to win his father's approval . . . or letting his opinion dictate what Cole wanted to do.

"Besides, ain't none of us got any money till next payday. You done took it all," Scoby was saying.

Cole tugged at his hat and shot his father's foreman a grin before turning his attention to the stagecoach. It thundered to a stop in a cloud of dust. His thoughts weren't on his father's guests, however. He was remembering how pretty Kansas had looked with the sunlight in her hair.

"Got some company for you, Mr. Slater," Web called, climbing down from the high seat and walking around the side of the coach. Pausing for effect, he glanced around at the eager faces, enjoying his moment, then with a rough flourish opened the door and set the heavy wooden step in place.

A nattily dressed gentleman with gray-streaked hair and beard alighted and glanced around. Then he reached inside the stage to lend a hand to another passenger. The onlookers seemed to be holding their breath, which they let out with a little sigh of approval, as a young lady stepped down and stood in the dusty street looking around with bright, expectant eyes. Her hair was dark as the gentleman's must once have been. Her skin was a pale ivory. Her gown was finely cut and obviously expensive, with more velvet trimmings and lace rosettes than the simple townfolks could have imagined. The full skirt was held wide by a hooped petticoat. Beneath the hem peeked elegant embroidered boots, while on her head perched a cream-colored straw bonnet adorned with black velvet ribbons and lace and a bird's plume.

"Oh, Father, how charming!" the girl said in a ringing voice. One small gloved hand brushed dust from her immaculate skirts, and then she immediately opened a small lacy parasol and held it so it shielded her face from the sun. Longingly Kansas watched the vivacious girl, studying every aspect of her beautiful clothes. One day, she thought, she'd have a dress just like that one.

"Oliver Howard?" Les Slater asked, stepping forward, hand outstretched. "Welcome to Webster."

"Les, you old son of gun," the newcomer answered, shaking hands warmly. "I wasn't sure if I'd recognize you, but I sure would have your son." He pointed to Cole Slater. Les introduced Cole, who stepped forward to shake hands.

"I'm afraid my wife couldn't make the trip. She's been ill of late. This is my daughter, Claire," Howard said, with obvious pride. The girl laughed up at her father and turned a dazzling smile on the two Slater men, charming each one of them in turn.

Jealousy shot through Kansas as she watched the way Cole leaped forward to take Claire's dainty hand. He looked absolutely puppy sick, Kansas thought in disgust, and turned in a huff back to the saloon. If she were Cole, she certainly wouldn't stand out there in the middle of the street letting the sun boil her brains while she made calf's eyes at someone like Claire Howard. Picking up a broom, she set to sweeping the saloon floor, not even noticing the dust that rose in swirls around her. As she worked, she couldn't help thinking about Claire. Even her name sounded elegant. She could never understand how Molly could have named her Kansas, even if it did remind her of a happy time in her life.

"Whooee! What've we got here, a windstorm?" Odie

Tibbs asked, making his way back to the bar. "Looks like Kansas has got herself into a snit. What're you upset about, honey?"

"I'm not upset about anything, Odie!" Kansas snapped. "I've just got work to do." She applied the straw broom with more vigor than before. Sweat rolled down her brow and into her eyes and dirty runnels formed on her cheeks. Still she didn't slacken, letting physical exertion ease the tight pain around her heart at the thought that she could never be like Claire Howard—and the even more frightening thought that a lady like Claire was just what Cole wanted.

"Looks like ol' Cole's got hisself a new girlfriend . . . and whooee, what a looker she is, too!" Odie echoed Kansas's fear. "Don't that make you just a little bit angry, Kansas?"

"Why would it?" she snapped. "Cole is not my beau."

"Funny, I thought that was who you was saving yourself for," Odie said, and made a grab for her. His arms wrapped around her from behind, pinning her arms to her sides while his coarse hand closed over the front of her dress.

"Let go, Odie. I'll tell Ma, and she won't have a thing more to do with you," Kansas cried, struggling in his embrace.

"I don't need Molly with a cute little heifer like you around." Odie laughed and pumped his pelvis against her backside in an obscene gesture.

"I said let go!" Kansas cried. Her face had grown flushed with anger as she twisted and brought her foot down on his instep. Odie's arms loosened so she could bring up her elbow and gouge him in the ribs. Other men had entered the saloon now and stood laughing.

"Hold on to her, Odie," they called. "She's gettin' away from you."

Egged on by his friends, Odie tried to regain his hold on Kansas, but she'd twisted enough now to bring up a knee and, although she missed her intended target, it was warning enough to Odie. He released her and turned away with a gesture of disgust.

"Ah, what would I want with a scrawny kid," he growled, and waved to the bartender for another drink. "Give me Molly any day. Someone with a little meat on her and right accommodatin', so a man don't have to waste hisself fightin' for it."

Kansas didn't hear the rest of his discourse for she'd sped out of the saloon, leaving the broom and a pile of dirt on the floor. Clutching a torn sleeve with trembling fingers, she paused in the kitchen and drew a shaky breath. These playful attacks of Odie's had become more frequent of late, and his hands always seemed to be touching her in places they shouldn't. She felt a horrible dread building inside her.

"What happened, Kansy? Odie been at you again?" one of the girls named Rose asked, crossing to the stove to fill a cracked cup from the blackened coffeepot.

Kansas wiped at a small tear that had escaped at the corner of one eye and held the pieces of her sleeve in place. "Uh-huh." She sniffed in a rare moment of self-pity. "I don't know why he keeps doing it. I'll never go with him. Never!"

"You can't blame a fellow for hoping. He just wants everyone to know he's first in line."

Kansas's head jerked up. "What do you mean?" she demanded.

Rose stirred her coffee and studied Kansas with a measuring look. "Maybe you'd better ask your momma," she advised, not unkindly.

"I will!" Kansas snapped "Where is she?"

"Oh, I wouldn't bother her now," Rose warned. Kansas paused. She'd been taught long ago never to bother her mother when she was with a customer. "She ain't with nobody, but when the stage came in she went to her room—

and she's been in there drinkin' ever since. Charley ain't goin' to like that none. She's been warned.''

"Maybe I can do something with her," Kansas said, and resignedly climbed the back stairs to the rooms above.

Molly McKay sat before a dressing table littered with jars and vials of cheap perfumes and coarse powders. The cracked and wavery mirror above it gave back the distorted image of a face that had once been beautiful. Self-indulgence had slackened and coarsened the features and age had begun its irreversible damage to the jawline and neck. Only the hair retained something of its former glory, although in truth it was growing a bit thin, for Molly sat for hours plucking away the graying strands. Now she stared at her image in the mirror, while a monotone of sound, barely recognizable as a song, escaped her lips.

"Momma?" Kansas said tentatively, peering around the door. Her wide gray eyes were troubled as she approached Molly. She was never sure what her reception would be, for her mother often swung between moods of violent resentment and stony indifference toward her daughter. Now the drunken woman raised a pudgy finger and pointed it at Kansas.

"Jush the girl I wanted to sh-see," she muttered. "C'mere." She waved Kansas forward.

"Are you all right, Momma?" Kansas asked, moving closer. She always felt as if she were cringing when she was in her mother's presence, as if expecting a blow, and indeed there had been blows aplenty in her youth. "What is it?"

"Look here, my fine girl," Molly said, holding out a gold locket Kansas had often seen her wear. It was of a rare design and heavily scrolled. Obviously it had cost a good deal of money, and Kansas had often wondered about it.

"Here, thish ish for you," Molly said, thrusting it away from herself as if it were distasteful to her. "C'mon, take it, I shay. It's from your father."

"My father?" Kansas's eyes were enormous as she stared at the locket dangling from its chain. Molly had never mentioned her father before. She'd always remained mysteriously silent in response to Kansas's questions.

"This is from my father?" Kansas asked incredulously, reaching out a hand to take the locket. She held her breath as if caught in a spell. Dust motes danced in the yellow light, streaming through the dirty windowpanes, and the locket gleamed with a magical sheen. Her fingers closed around the gold chain and she could feel the heat of the metal, as if Molly had just taken it from around her neck.

"Shure, it's from your father. What'd you think? You didn't have a father? You're jush as good as that highfalutin piece of baggage that climbed off the stage out there. Jush as good . . . and you got a father, too." Molly nodded her head with satisfaction and reached for her glass. Her unaccustomed interest in her daughter had waned, and now she sought the solace she'd found the most effective.

"Oh, Momma, it's beautiful," Kansas cried, fastening it around her neck and letting it fall forward onto her bodice. It looked elegant and rich, finer than anytbing she'd ever possessed. Her slender, sensitive fingers rubbed the shiny surface, tracing some of the etched scrollwork. Then the pleasure on her face dimmed somewhat as she made her way to her mother and knelt beside the table. "Momma, tell me about my father. What was he like? Was he handsome? Was he tall?"

Silently Molly stared at her daughter until Kansas feared that once again she wouldn't answer. Then Molly's eyes took on a dreamy faraway look. Her features softened, looking younger and more vulnerable. "He was the handsomest man in the whole world," she said. "I ain't never seen a man since as handsome as he was. And he was kind and gentle, too. Tall and strong. Why, on the wagon train, he used to—"

"Molly, you in there?" A loud knock at the door interrupted Molly's reminiscences. "It's Odie, and I got me a powerful need, honey."

Molly's eyes hardened, and casting a resentful glance at Kansas, she got to her feet. "Your father wasn't no one special. He was just a man, a customer, and I ain't ever sure which one at that. Now you go on and get out of here. I got to work."

"But, Momma. You said this locket came from him, that it was a present from him."

"I was just funning with you. Give it back to me." Molly held out her hand.

"No!" Kansas cried, backing up. Her eyes gleamed with unshed tears.

"Molly, you in there?" Odie hollered, and pounded on the door again. "If you are, you'd better open up or I'll get Charley."

"All right, you can keep it for now," Molly said ungraciously, moved more by Odie's threat than she was by the pain on her daughter's face. Stalking to the door, she threw it open. "What's your hurry, Sugar?" she said to Odie, with syrupy sweetness.

Mollified now that she'd opened the door, he strolled in and grabbed hold of the prostitute. "I told you I needed me a woman in a hurry," he said, wrapping his arms around her and planting slobbery kisses over her face and neck.

"Wait a minute," she protested, pushing against him. "I got to get rid of the kid first."

"Don't pay me no never mind if she wants to stay and watch," Odie said, swinging toward the bed. He flopped down and swung his booted feet onto the covers. Grabbing hold of his crotch, he hooted with laughter. "I got enough here for both of you," he bragged.

"Are you sure about that, Sugar?" Molly asked, motioning Kansas out of the room. "You know Molly always takes real good care of you all by herself." Remembering her torn sleeve, Kansas picked up her sewing box and headed toward the door.

"That's a fact," Odie agreed, sitting up to pull off his boots. One spur caught in the covers and came free with a tear. "When're you going to make Kansas start workin' like you and the rest of the girls?"

"Let's not talk about Kansas," Molly purred, sliding the loose silk cover off her shoulders and standing before him in her corset and stockings. Kansas averted her eyes from her mother's plump backside and hurried out, quietly closing the door behind her.

Odie's last words tore at her peace of mind . . .

"When you put her to work, I want to be the first," he declared.

"You will be, baby. I promise, you will be," Molly answered. The springs protested as she slid into bed beside him.

With their rhythmic creaking ringing in her ears, Kansas made her escape to the kitchen, where she sat at the wooden table and mended the sleeve Odie had torn. She strove to quell the anxiety raised by Odie's words and thought instead of all the things her mother had told her. Her father had been very handsome, the handsomest man in all the world. Kansas could well believe it. She'd expected little else. He'd been kind and strong and he'd come out West on a wagon train, so he'd been brave as well. No doubt he'd fought hostile Indians and outlaws. What if her father were dead? What if the Indians had killed him? She'd had no chance to ask Molly. Perhaps he'd died fighting to protect her mother and her.

In her innocent yearning to belong to someone, her musings gained substance and became reality. Tears formed in her eyes and she wept for the brave father she'd never known. But he'd left her this locket to remember him by, and she'd always cherish his memory. Kansas rubbed it with her skirt until the gold gleamed. Then she examined each minute tracing on it, opened it to check for pictures or a lock of hair, but there was neither, examined the hinge and, finally, carefully closed it and let it fall against the bodice of her gown once more.

The weight of it was pleasant around her neck, reminding her with every move she made that she had a father. He must have been very rich to afford a piece of jewelry as fine as this. She fell to dreaming of what would have happened if he had lived. He would have taken care of Molly and her and seen to it that they had plenty of food to eat and a fine house and lovely clothes, like that girl from the stagecoach. Perhaps he would have persuaded Molly to call her something else besides Kansas, something like Evelyn or Victoria or Claire.

And maybe then Cole Slater would notice her and bow over her hand the way he had Claire Howard's. Kansas gathered up a fold of her worn skirt and sashayed around the drab kitchen. She sketched a graceful curtsy, or what she guessed a proper curtsy might be, and held out her hand, batting her eyelashes. She could almost feel Cole's lips pressed to the back of her hand. Her bosom swelled with emotion, but she quickly hid it, smiling coquettishly.

"What a charming boy," she said in a simpering voice.

"Don't tell me you've turned into a fancy fluff-duff, too," a voice said disgustedly. Kansas whirled and looked into the teasing eyes of Cole Slater.

Openmouthed, she stared at Cole. She hadn't expected to see him tonight, not with the Howards at the ranch.

"If you leave your mouth open long enough, you'll get a bug in it," he teased, and slung a long leg over the back of a chair. One large boot was planted on the seat. His hat was pushed to the back of his head and strands of glossy dark hair fell across his broad, tanned brow. His wide mouth curved into a grin and his eyes sparkled with mocking humor.

"Ready to let me win back some money?" he asked, taking out a deck of cards and seating himself across from her.

"I didn't expect you tonight, seeing as how you had company," Kansas said archly. When he looked puzzled, she rushed on. "I saw her . . . them come in on the stage-coach."

"That's some of Pa's friends."

"One looked awfully young to be your father's friend," Kansas said, and hoped she didn't sound as jealous as she felt.

"Maybe," Cole grunted, and shuffled the cards. "Want to play vingt-et-un tonight?"

"All right," Kansas agreed, and gripped the gold locket for courage and wisdom. "She was awfully pretty."

"Who?" Cole had laid aside his hat and lit a cheroot. Its smoke encircled his head.

"Clai—your guest. I mean the whole town couldn't help but notice her hair and clothes. She seemed quite the lady." She paused, but Cole was busy studying his cards. "You must have found her very attractive," Kansas persisted. "I mean, how could you help it? . . . The way she looked and all . . ."

"I swear, Kansas, you got more lip than a muley cow tonight." Cole leaned back in his chair and regarded her with some surprise. "If you weren't such a kid, I'd swear you were jealous of Claire Howard."

"Jealous? Me?" squeaked Kansas. "Why on earth would I be jealous?"

Cole studied her a moment longer while he tried to fathom what went on behind those bright, intelligent eyes. She kept her gaze level and innocent. "Beats me," he said, and shifted his attention to his cards. He didn't want to talk about the Howards. He'd already found the beauteous Claire vain and silly. He'd quickly lost interest in her. "Your play," he said impatiently.

With ill-concealed irritation, Kansas picked up her cards

and looked at them for the first time. In the next half
hour, conversation was sparse and concentrated solely on
the game. Kansas played with a vengeful skill that soon
had Cole emptying his pockets. She was never quite sure
how they'd come to play for money or how it was she
always won. Cole was good, exceedingly good. She
knew, for she'd heard Odie and some of the other
men talking. Cole had started teaching her to play some
years before, when he was too young to frequent the saloon. Somehow playing cards with Kansas had become
a habit, one that Cole had graciously kept up even after
he was deemed old enough and man enough to join the
others.

Cole had been her friend when no one else had. She'd
been grateful for the time he spent with her on his trips into
town from the Bar S, for her childhood had been a lonely
one. The kids in town had often picked on her for her
ill-fitting and worn hand-me-downs, taunting her about her
mother. Kansas had fought back, pummeling them with
her small fists, sometimes inflicting damage, usually receiving more than she gave, and always bringing Molly's wrath
down on her head, for invariably, the fathers of her tormen-
tors complained to Molly about her ruffian daughter. Molly
was not about to have her business affected by her daughter's behavior.

One day three boys ganged up on Kansas—and she was
taking the worst of the fight—when a white horse halted
close by and its rider leaned forward to lift away one of her
assailants by his shirt collar. Though only a youth himself,
Cole Slater had carried an air of easy authority that most of
his peers followed cheerfully. Now the boys fell back and
stared at him with scared expressions.

"I don't think too highly of men who fight defenseless
girls," he said, and his voice was already deep in spite of
his young years.

"Heck, she ain't no girl, Cole," the other boys scoffed.

"That's just Kansas McKay. Her mother's a whore over at Charley Moody's saloon."

"She looks like a girl to me," Cole had said, alighting from his horse and holding out a hand to help her to her feet. "My friends are real sorry for their behavior, Miss McKay," he said, doffing his hat as if she were a fine lady instead of the dirty-faced urchin she resembled. Kansas glared at him, certain he was making fun of her.

"Miss McKay!" the younger boys snickered. He quelled them with a glance. Kansas looked up at the tall, rangy boy and thought she'd never seen such a handsome or kind being in her whole life. Instantly she fell in love. She'd loved him ever since. He never seemed to notice her as anything but a friend, and that had been fine with Kansas at first, but lately, she'd taken to imagining what it would be like if it were he who kissed her instead of Odie. Her cheeks flamed at the thought of Cole touching her breasts the way Odie did.

"Come on, Kansy," Cole chided now as she sat with her cards still in a pile on the table. "You're sure not interested in playing cards tonight."

"I'm sorry," she said, gathering up her cards and fanning them in her hand. "I've just got a lot on my mind."

"Problems?" Cole asked instantly, and she knew whatever problem she might have he'd do his best to solve it for her. But what would he say if she told him the problem was him, that she wanted him to look at her with the same lovesick expression he'd worn when he met Claire Howard that afternoon?

"No problems." She sighed. "I'm just feeling a little sad. Today is the anniversary of my father's death."

"Your father?" Cole echoed. He'd never thought Kansas knew who her father was, but he forbore to tell her that. She was just a kid, and people picked on her enough as it was. "How did he die?" he asked instead.

"He died fighting off a band of Indians who attacked our wagon train," she said, elaborating on her dream, spinning it into a reality. Who was to say it wasn't so? "We were on our way to Oregon—Molly, my father, and me. We were going to have a wonderful life together, but . . ." Her voice dwindled away sadly. "Before he died from his wounds, he gave this locket to Molly and told her to give it to me one day . . . so I'd know how much he loved me."

"It's beautiful," Cole said, not knowing what else to answer. He studied the gold locket and the girl who fingered it lovingly. Her long golden lashes swept downward against the rose-hued curve of her cheek, then flashed upward, and he found himself staring into the clear gray-blue depths of her eyes. He'd never noticed before how the gray-blue held gold flecks, or that there was a darker ring around her iris. He found himself drowning in a well. Suddenly he was noticing other things about Kansas McKay, things he'd always known were there. But now he was seeing them in a different light. He was touched by the soft smattering of freckles across her small, well-shaped nose, mesmerized by the soft pouty curve of her mouth, and suddenly and intensely troubled by the sweet mound of her breasts beneath the faded blue bodice. He saw and felt every part of her, the texture of her skin, the heady sweetness of her breath, the fragrance of her hair, and he wanted to touch, hold, and taste Kansas McKay.

His chair scraped against the bare plank floor as he hastily got to his feet. "I—I . . ." He swallowed convulsively. "I've got to go," he finally got out.

"But we haven't finished our game," Kansas protested.

"I—I've got a bust hand," Cole gasped. "You win the pot." He raked the money toward her and grabbed up his hat. "I'll see you around."

"All right, Cole," she said, and he could hear the hurt in her voice. He couldn't do anything about that now. There was a pressure in his groin that alarmed him. He had to get away from her so he could think clearly. God almighty, the thoughts that had gone tumbling through his head!

He stomped out to his horse, mounted, and spurred it toward the ranch at a hard gallop. He kept his head lowered so the wind streamed around the wide band of his hat. Fiercely he concentrated on the flash of racing hooves and the pale line of the roadway below. What had be been thinking of? She was a kid. Kansas McKay? Molly McKay's daughter? one part of him jeered. A kid who'd had the misfortune to draw Molly as her mother, he reminded himself. A kid who'd been treated badly in one way or another by nearly everyone in town. He didn't need to add to her woe by acting like a randy bull in her presence. She looked on him as a brother, someone to protect her. Who was going to protect her from him?

He should have stayed in town with one of Charley's girls, he scolded himself. Molly McKay perhaps, another part of himself sneered. Not Molly, someone else. Rose maybe. She'd been his first woman. He remembered her fondly. But Rose was dark haired and Kansas was . . . Kansas was fair, with long blond strands that his hands itched to feel. Her mouth was soft, her body . . . He shut off his thoughts, cursing himself for every kind of fool.

Chapter 2

"*I* HEARD SOME damn fool come galloping his pony into the corral last night like the devil himself was after him," Les Slater said the next morning over a breakfast of flapcakes and salt pork. His dark eyes studied his son. "That wouldn't have been you, would it, Cole?"

"Yes, sir," Cole said, feeling a dull flush stain his cheeks. Les could have taken it up with him personally instead of in front of Oliver Howard like this. He supposed he should be grateful Claire Howard hadn't come down for breakfast. She'd chosen to stay upstairs, resting after her long journey. Not that Cole cared a lot about her opinion of him. No, thoughts of Claire Howard hadn't tormented his sleepless night. It was Kansas, in her simple blue dress with the sunlight in her hair, who haunted him.

"Well, where were you?" Les demanded. Oliver Howard cleared his throat to remind his host of his presence, but Les ignored him. Cole's eyes darkened with anger. It was going to be one of those dressing-downs by his father—regardless of who was present. "You know I don't like you riding off to town like that to drink and carouse at Moody's Saloon."

"I wasn't at Moody's!" Cole flared, his vow to remain

calm forgotten in the face of his father's commanding tone. "Leastways not in the saloon part."

"Don't tell me you were with one of those whores?" Les roared. His full face had grown red.

Cole remained silent and defiant.

"Well, boy?" Les persisted.

Cole's chair scraped loudly as he shoved it back and got to his feet. "The men are waiting for me."

"Let 'em wait!" Les bellowed to Cole's departing back. Red-faced he heaved his bulk out of the chair and followed his son out to the porch. "I asked who you went to see!"

"Kansas KcKay!" Cole called over his shoulder. He stepped down into the dusty yard and gathered up his reins.

"Same as a whore," Les snapped.

Cole's hands clenched into fists as he faced his father. His features were rigid with barely controlled anger. "She's not a whore," he said, with deadly calm. "She's a decent kid who's been treated badly by the people in Webster."

"She's the daughter of a whore. One day she'll be a whore herself, if she's not one already. I forbid you to see her again," Les ordered. His loud voice carried around the yard so the cowhands near the corral glanced around. Then, smothering a grin, they went back to saddling up their horses. The old man and the kid were locking horns again. They'd seen and heard it all before. The funny thing was Cole was a good kid, a son any man would be proud of, but if Les kept riding him that way, he'd turn Cole mean.

"You can't keep me from seeing her if I want to," Cole said in that same quiet, stubborn voice that should have been a warning to Les. "I'll work your ranch, Les"—Cole pointed a finger at his father to emphasize what he was saying—"I'll round up your cattle, mend your fences, and ride your range, but when the work's done, my time's my own, the way it is for every other hand out there, and you can't stop me. If that's not good enough, I'll ride out now."

"Then ride out," Les growled, then, as if realizing what he'd said, he backed down. "Ride out to the south range and gather up them cattle for the branding iron." Then as if sorry he'd weakened for even a moment, he glared at his son again. The vein in his temple throbbed. "Check the fences while you're at it."

Cole stared at his father as if looking for some softening, some sign that he felt as bad about their fight as he did, but Les's face remained cold and forbidding. Cole could never remember it looking any other way. Cole broke their impasse first, springing into his saddle with a quick, fluid motion. Without glancing back at the impassive-faced man on the porch, he heeled his mount into a canter. One by one the other hands fell in behind him. Then, and only then, did Les Slater's expression change. He knew he was hard on Cole, but the *land* was hard—and a man had to be what he had to be in order to survive.

"I'm sorry for the ruckus, Howard," he said, going back inside to join his guest. He motioned the Mexican cook forward to refill their coffee cups.

"Think nothing of it," Howard said expansively. He was impressed by the magnitude of his friend's spread and the well-appointed, two-storied ranch house. He liked Cole Slater. "He's just sowing a few wild oats. You did that yourself in your day if I disremember correctly."

Les chuckled. "We both did," he said. "You're right, though. Cole's a fine boy. If only I can keep him away from that little dove in town . . ."

For the next three days, Cole was kept too busy to think about riding back into Webster, but not too busy to think about Kansas. She was everywhere—in the brightness of the sunlight, or the yellow buttercup he found growing along a creek bed. He thought of her waking and sleeping, when he was eating, or when he was cursing the dust that clogged his nostrils as he rounded up the cattle. By Saturday he was in a fever. Rising early, he washed himself in the horse trough, donned a fresh shirt, and headed into town before the other hands were even up.

Cole had a very clear idea of what he intended to do. He was going to see Kansas—to see if she was as pretty as he remembered, or if all the feelings he'd been nursing were just a passing fancy. He hadn't the slightest notion of what he'd do if they were real. He couldn't think that far ahead.

But once he rode into Webster he lost momentum; instead of heading directly for Moody's Saloon as he'd planned, he rode out of town a piece to a creek that ran down along the back of the stables. Tying off his horse so it could graze, he plopped down on the bank and skipped stones across the water while he tried to sort things out. He might have stayed there forever if a flash of yellow hadn't caught his eye.

Silently he watched as Kansas came into view. She was barefooted and her hair hung free about her shoulders, swishing across her back saucily as she walked. She was humming a little tune under her breath. She hadn't seen him yet. Seating herself on a large flat rock, she slid her feet into the water and groaned with pleasure. Lifting her skirts, she tucked them into her waistband and waded into the creek, pausing now and then to pick up a rock and raise it to the light to study. Cole couldn't take his eyes off her. The picture of a pretty girl, the sunlight on the water, and the idyllic calm of the day was such that he could only sit and enjoy the spectacle.

A bird, startled from its perch, flew across the creek. Kansas dropped the rock and looked up. "Oh!" she cried when she caught sight of Cole, then her features relaxed into a smile. "Hello!" she called, and waded toward him. "Why don't you take off your boots and join me? The water's nice and cool."

"I believe I'll just stay here on the bank and watch you," he answered. "I've never seen a wood sprite before."

Her eyes sparkled with laughter. "A wood sprite?" she repeated, pleased with the image he'd evoked. Aware of his steady, warm gaze, she blushed unaccountably and turned away. "Shouldn't you beware of wood sprites?" she called over her shoulder. "I've heard they're mean-tempered."

"Not you. You're too beautiful. You must be a fairy princess." His words caught Kansas off-guard and she whirled around to stare at him in consternation.

"Are you making fun of me again, Cole Slater?" she demanded, hands on hips. Her gray eyes had grown stormy, her small chin set.

His laughter rang out, rich and deep and somehow intimate in the hushed air. "Would I be foolhardy enough to make fun of a wood sprite?" he asked. "Especially one so fair of face?"

"You *are* making fun of me!" Kansas cried, and kicked a spray of icy water at him.

Immediately Cole sprang to his feet. Kansas squealed and turned to run. Heedless of his boots, Cole was after her. She gained the other bank, but Cole was there, his long arms snatching her back against him.

"I'm sorry I splashed you, Cole," Kansas cried, unable to free herself for her laughter.

"I've heard it's good luck to catch a wood sprite," he said, easily subduing her. Suddenly Kansas stopped struggling and stood still in his encircling arms. The laughter died from her face as she looked at him. His expression was different, darkly smoldering and dangerous.

"I wonder what would happen if I kissed a wood sprite?" he whispered huskily. His dark gaze swept over her as if to discern everything there was to know about her.

"You might be turned into a toad," Kansas said, trying to regain their former teasing mood. Suddenly she felt frightened of this new Cole gripping her so tightly, more tightly than Odie ever had. She could feel the thud of his heart against her shoulder . . . and now he turned her, his eyes nearly black with a desire she'd never seen there before.

"Cole . . ." She whispered a denial for the things she saw in his eyes, but the name turned to a soft moan of yearning. How could she deny what was in her own heart?

Slowly his dark head lowered until his lips brushed across hers. "Kansas . . ." He sighed, then increased the contact of their lips. Waves of heat washed through Kansas. "You're so beautiful, so sweet." His large hands spread wide across her back and hips, molding her young body to his. His lean hardness felt solid, implacable, all consuming. Her knees trembled and she leaned against the hard strength of him. His tongue tasted the texture of her lower lip, his teeth nibbled, and she heard a moan, low and earthy, and wasn't sure if it was his or hers. His tongue delved into the flowerlike sweetness of her mouth. Now his hands moved upward, tangling in her hair, smoothing the silken mass. There was no need to hold her against him for she clung to him, pressing her eager young breasts flat against his chest.

"Oh, Cole, I love you," she whispered, raining kisses across his jaw and neck. Her fingers came up to pluck at his shirt buttons, to move the soft material aside so she could press kisses deep in the V.

Need, hot and pulsating, washed through him, and he lifted her knees and laid her on the mossy grass, his lips holding hers captive. She pressed upward, protesting the loss of contact between them, and he lowered his weight onto her, feeling once more the brush of her firm young breasts. His hands came up to touch the soft mounds, his long, sensitive fingers brushing enticingly across the tips, eliciting a moan from Kansas. Her long skirts were still tucked into her waistband, so her long, slender legs were bare. At the pressure of his knees, her legs fell apart, and he felt the searing heat of her even through his heavy trousers. He ground his hips against her and heard her answering whimper of response.

His mouth claimed hers again, barely giving either of

them time to breathe. Her arms were entwined around his neck, her eyes were closed, lashes thick and luxurious against her cheek.

"Oh, Cole! I never knew you loved me, that you wanted me for your wife," she whispered, and laughed deep in her throat. At her words he drew back, his expression growing troubled.

"Cole, what's wrong? Did I do something wrong?" Kansas asked.

"No, no. You did nothing wrong," Cole said, sitting up and propping his arms on his raised knees. He held his head and sat staring at the ground.

"I'm sorry. Whatever I said or did, I'm sorry," Kansas whispered, her face stricken at the thought she might have done something to make him withdraw his love.

"Shh. I'm the one who's done something wrong, Kansas. Me, not you. You're the same sweet Kansas I've always known, but I'm the one whose changed. These past few days—I don't know—I couldn't seem to stop thinking about you, about doing just this to you, about doing more. I'm sorry. It was wrong of me."

Kansas's face was suffused with shame, for she'd wanted him to kiss her and touch her. "I know I'm not like Claire Howard," she began stiffly. "I'm Molly McKay's daughter, and people think I'm like her. They speculate that one day I'll work upstairs at Moody's Saloon, too. You probably think I'm not good enough."

"It's not that," Cole said quickly. "I'm the one that's not good enough. You're fine and good, Kansas. I see how hard you work, how you keep yourself clean and neat, how bright and clever you are. And here I am treating you like one of Charley's whores. You don't deserve that from your friend."

"But I don't want you to be my friend," Kansas blurted out miserably.

"I don't blame you after my behavior here today."

"I didn't mean it like that," she whispered. Tears filled her eyes and rained down her cheeks.

Gently Cole raised her chin and gazed into her eyes. His dark eyes were warm and caring. "Can you forgive me, Kansas?" he pleaded.

"There's nothing to forgive." She hiccuped and raised her eyes to his in a perfect frankness that was heartrending in its honesty. "I wanted you to kiss me."

"I wanted to kiss you, too," he answered, and smiled, wanting to take away the tears, wanting the happy sunshiny girl in the yellow dress she'd been only minutes ago. "I want to kiss you again," he continued, "but I won't, not like I did before . . . and not if you don't want me to. I want to treat you like a lady."

"A lady?" Kansas asked tremulously. Her face was radiant, like new sunshine after a rain. "Don't ladies like to be kissed? Because I liked it very much."

"Oh, Kansas." Cole laughed, a feeling of joy coursing through him at just being near her. Then he sobered as he looked into the clear gray eyes. "May I kiss you again, Miss McKay?" he asked softly.

"By all means, Mr. Slater," she answered seriously, and pursing her lips, held them up for Cole.

Studying her face, with her eyes tightly closed, her face bright and giving, Cole thought he'd never seen anyone more beautiful or more innocent-looking. Desire coursed through him, but he pushed it down.

"There you are, Miss McKay," he said, dropping a light kiss on her nose and getting to his feet. "If you'll find your shoes, I'll walk you home," he ordered, pulling her up. With a pout and a flounce, Kansas straightened her skirts and collected her shoes, carrying them in her hand as she fell into step beside him.

"Do you suppose your momma'll mind if I come courting you?" Cole asked as they followed the creek back to the stable.

"Momma never pays attention to anything that happens to me," Kansas answered simply, "so I don't expect it will matter."

Cole took hold of her hand. "Good. I'll come every chance I get. That is, if you want me to . . ."

"I want you to," she answered, and it seemed her heart was too full to say another word.

They had left the creek and followed a footpath along the side of the stables to regain the main road. Moody's Saloon lay just at the end of the street. Kansas's feet dragged. Soon her time with Cole would be over, until the next time he came to town. Who knew how long that would be?

"Cole!" The name was a mighty roar that caught the attention of most everyone in hearing distance. Les Slater, mounted on a gray stallion, galloped toward them, drawing to a halt in a rain of dirt and pebbles. Neil was close behind.

"Pa!" Cole said, and Kansas could hear the tightness in his voice.

"Just like I told you, Pa," Neil said, pointing an accusing finger at Cole and Kansas. "I saw them down by the creek."

"I told you to stay away from that girl!" Les shouted. His face was red with fury. Folks gathered on the sidewalks and in the street to watch the scene. It was not a new one. They'd seen Les and Cole butt heads before. But this time it was over Molly McKay's girl.

They'd seen it coming. Funny, Les hadn't noticed sooner. For years they'd been watching as Cole grew to manhood, strong-willed and rebelling against his father's iron hand. And Kansas—well, every man there could tell you how she'd blossomed into a young beauty so tantalizing she made a man's brain go soft and his groin go hard. They'd watched the two young people as if awaiting a thunderhead building on the edge of the prairie sky. The day of reckoning was at hand.

At Moody's Saloon, some of the women came out on the

balcony to see what the commotion was about. Kansas could see her mother and wished Molly had taken the time to pull her dressing gown together before she stepped out.

"Didn't you hear me, boy. I told you not to be seen with this harlot."

"Don't call her a harlot!" Cole shouted. "You don't know anything about her."

"I know enough. If you wanted to bed her so bad, why didn't you pay Charley a dollar and be done with it? Now get on back to the ranch where you belong."

"She's not one of Charley's girls," Cole rasped, his chest heaving with anger. "And I'm not coming back to the ranch until you apologize to Kansas."

"Apologize!" Les roared. "I ain't ever apologized to the likes of her and I ain't startin' now."

"Then I'm not coming back to the ranch, ever," Cole flared. He stood with feet spread, his dark head held high in defiance. The onlookers quietly placed bets as to which man would back down first.

"By God, you'll come," Les shouted, and dug his spurs into the stallion's sides.

Cole flung Kansas to one side, but had no time to leap out of the way himself. The stallion brushed against him, knocking him to the ground.

"Cole!" Kansas screamed.

Cole rolled over several times and got to his feet. His face was pale. His clothes were covered with dirt. A trickle of blood ran from one corner of his mouth. Defiantly he faced his father.

"Are you coming back to the ranch now?" Les yelled. The stallion tossed his head and whinnied nervously.

"Are you going to apologize to Kansas?" Cole asked quietly, his gaze unwavering.

Fury distorted Les Slater's face as he once again spurred his horse toward his son. Cole threw himself clear, rolled over, and huddled on the ground shaking his head. Kansas screamed, and he looked up in time to see the stallion galloping toward him again. There was no time to leap aside. The deep-chested horse hit him hard, knocking the wind from him. Les jerked the reins to bring the rearing horse to heel, then vaulted from the saddle and ran toward his son.

Horrified, Kansas watched as Les reached down to grasp his son's shirtfront and pull him upright. One balled fist landed with a sickening crunch against Cole's jaw. Cole's body jerked and went slack, but the big man continued to beat him around the face and head.

"Stop him!" Kansas screamed. "He's killing him!" She launched herself at Les Slater, her small fists pounding ineffectually. Slater tossed her off as if she were no more than a kitten. Kansas rolled in the dust and lay sobbing.

Alarm spread through the other cowhands and Abe Scoby stepped forward. "Mr. Slater, you'd better stop. He looks hurt pretty bad."

Les stopped the relentless pounding and looked around as if dazed. Chest heaving, he glanced down at the bloodied face of his youngest son and released his shirtfront. Unconscious, Cole slid back into the dusty street.

"Load him into the wagon and take him back out to the ranch," Slater gasped. His belligerent gaze swung around to Kansas and he raised a finger to point at her. "You don't bother my boy no more, you hear me, girl? You ain't no better than the dirt in this here street. You stick with your own kind."

People began to disperse. The fight was over. Swinging into his saddle, Slater turned his horse toward Moody's Saloon. Sitting in the dusty street, Kansas watched the wagon bearing Cole's battered body roll away. She paid no heed to the tears making tracks down her dirty cheeks or the speculative glances cast her way.

Chapter 3

MOLLY MCKAY STOOD on the balcony of Moody's Saloon and watched Les Slater ride toward her. She had little doubt he was coming to see her or about what he had to say. She studied the powerful figure on the magnificent stallion and for a moment allowed herself to remember a younger day for them both, when there had been laughter and passion between them. The fact that when he finished he always left a ten-dollar gold piece on her dresser didn't seem to matter. Nor did all the cowboys who came to her in between Les's visits. It was their Saturday nights together that she'd looked forward to. She'd felt giddy and hopeful back then. She'd still believed in dreams. Dreams that he'd marry her and take Kansas and her back to his fine ranch, where they'd both live like ladies.

When his marriage to the widowed Etta Kent was announced, Molly had been genuinely hurt. The other girls had poked fun at her, but she'd held her head high, pretending he'd been just another cowboy to her. Two years later, when Etta Kent Slater died in a riding incident and Les started coming around again, Molly was smart enough to know that dream could never be resurrected. The ten-dollar gold pieces left on her dresser grew sporadic and, finally, quit altogether as Les moved on to someone else.

The first time Molly had learned he'd chosen another girl, she'd sat at that same dressing table and watched as the face reflected in the mirror grew distorted by rage and the mask of makeup was eroded by silent tears. She'd loved Les Slater almost as much as she'd once loved Kansas's father. But both men had abandoned her. She'd never shed a tear since.

Now, as she watched the man rein in his stallion and raise his eyes to meet hers, she knew at last revenge had come to her, a worse revenge than she could ever have devised—and best of all, she'd had to do nothing. It was something that had just naturally evolved between two handsome people. Les hadn't been smart enough to figure out that his disapproval and high-handed manner with his son had only fanned the flames. But she, Molly, was about to tell him that and more, much more. And when Mr. Les Slater left her room today, there would be more than a ten-dollar gold piece lying on her dresser, much more.

Slowly Kansas became aware of the curious, derisive glances cast her way. Wearily she picked herself up from the dusty street and brushed at her yellow dress. The hem was still wet from the creek and mud clung to it. Gathering up her shoes, she made her way down the back streets to Moody's Saloon. In one short hour she'd known more joy and despair than she'd ever thought possible. Cole Slater loved her and desired her, not like the cowboys who made their way to Molly and the other women in the back rooms, not with lust. Oh, there'd been desire, and how willingly she would have succumbed to that seductive flame, but Cole hadn't wanted that for them. He wanted to come courting as if she were a real lady. For a moment, caught up anew in the wonder of his love and protective attitude, she forgot her misery, then it came sweeping back as she remembered Les Slater's fury.

Was Cole all right? she wondered, and paused in the alley

to lean against a building and give way to the sobs she'd not allowed to escape before this. They came deep and wrenching and when she was finished, she used a clean spot on her yellow dress to wipe away her tears. Even here, she saw, there was no privacy, for nosy old Mrs. Edwards was peering over her fence. Straightening, Kansas hurried down the alley and let herself into the saloon kitchen.

All the old familiar smells of stale whiskey and cigarette smoke, unwashed bodies and rancid grease, rose up to her delicate nostrils. Kansas swallowed to keep from gagging and looked around in utter hopelessness. What promise life had seemed to hold for her in Cole's arms; now it lay before her bleak and uncertain.

"So there you are," Molly snapped, coming into the kitchen. Her face was raddled, the complexion coarse. She was puffing from her exertions. Why, Momma's getting old, Kansas thought, seeing her clearly for the first time. As if reading her daughter's thoughts, Molly plopped down on a rickety chair. It creaked a protest at her weight.

"What took you so long to get back here?" Molly gasped, one chubby hand pressed against her chest as if she were having trouble breathing. Two bright spots of color stained her cheeks and her eyes glinted with anger and something else—triumph—Kansas thought.

"I—I went for a walk along the creek," Kansas answered, uncertain if her mother had seen what happened.

"Walkin' wasn't all you was doin' this morning," Molly snapped, and Kansas's heart sank. She might have known. Her mother knew everything that transpired in this town and the ranches around.

"That's not true," she answered. "Cole just came along when I was wading in the creek and—and we talked. That's all. It's not like Mr. Slater said."

"Ain't it? Molly asked, studying her speculatively. "If that's so, then Cole Slater sure ain't the man his father is." Kansas turned away, unable to watch the lascivious look on her mother's face. She'd always been disturbed by the open, frankly lustful comparisons the women made about their customers. Now to think of Les Slater with her mother only cheapened what was fine and good between Cole and her.

"Ah, so Les was right," Molly said, a dangerous gleam in her eyes.

"No!" Kansas whirled to face her mother again.

"Don't you lie to me, girl," Molly said, rising from the chair, letting her bulk intimidate the girl. "Have you been giving away free what I deliberately saved back to up the price a bit?"

"What do you mean?" Kansas asked, her cheeks reddening. Her eyes widened with horror as the realization came of what her mother had in mind for her. "Surely you can't mean you intend me . . ." She couldn't say the words.

"Surely I do," Molly said. "I've just been waitin', lettin' the interest in you build. I've got all kinds of men waitin' for you to start workin'. They're standin' in line."

"I won't do it!" Kansas cried.

Molly's hand slashed out, leaving a red mark across her daughter's cheek. "You'll do as you're told or else," she shouted. "I'm tired of supportin' you. I was younger than you when I started in this business, but I gave you more time out of consideration for your father."

"My father's alive then?" Kansas asked, grasping at straws.

"He's alive, all right," Molly said, "but he won't be any help to you. You're on your own, just like I was years ago when I told him I was expectin' you. He just left me, left me off at the fort like one of them boxes of china people left behind on the trail when they got to be too much to carry. Well, I learned how to survive, Kansas, and you'll learn, too." She glanced at Kansas's stricken face and, remembering her own pain and humiliation those many years ago, she softened. "It ain't a bad life, really," she offered.

"Most men treat you nicer than they do their wives, so you're probably better off."

"Momma, I can't," Kansas sobbed.

"I need you to, Kansas, baby," Molly wheedled. "I'm gettin' too old. The men don't want me now like they used to. I'm losin' my customers."

"I'll get a job. I'll become a teacher. Mama, I always wanted to be a school teacher."

Molly hooted with laughter. "Do you think folks in this town are goin' to let you teach their young'uns, especially after that little exhibition out there in the street today? No, baby, folks in this town expect you to work at Moody's Saloon with your momma." Silently Kansas shook her head in denial. Tears rained unchecked down her face. "It ain't so bad. Some of those men want you real bad. Odie Tibbs for one, and Jim Nolin. Even Old Man Richards, my best customer, has asked about you. I'll bet even Les Slater would come . . . And every Saturday night you could save just for Cole." Kansas moaned as if in pain. "It's time, Kansas. You can clean up in this town."

"I won't!" she cried, and her tone was adamant.

Molly's face reddened with anger. Leaping forward, she grasped Kansas's long hair, making a fist around it. "Then you won't be doing anything else," she threatened, and yanked her daughter forward by her hair. Kansas stumbled and fought to keep her balance, but Molly gave her no time to recover. Through the kitchen door she dragged Kansas, and out into the backyard toward a small wooden shed. Kansas dug in her heels and tried to resist, but Molly's grip on her hair only tightened. "You'll stay in here until you've decided to mind your momma for a change," she shouted, shoving Kansas so hard she was propelled into the dark, dusty interior. The door swung shut behind her.

"Momma, no," Kansas shouted, regaining her balance and rushing toward the quickly dwindling patch of light. Molly had often used this form of punishment for Kansas as a child, and now the girl had a fear of closed-in places. "Momma, please," she pleaded, but the door closed implacably upon her cries. She could hear a bar being shoved into place. "Momma, let me out," Kansas begged, pounding on the wooden door, but there was no sound on the other side. "Momma?" Kansas whimpered.

Cole would come, she told herself. He would be all right and he would get on his horse and ride right back to town to take her away. They'd never be separated again. She alternated between pounding on the door and sitting crouched with her back against it, staring with terror-filled eyes at the shed's black interior.

Slowly her eyes adjusted to the darkness and she began to make out vague shapes, which only added to her terror, for she couldn't discern what they were. Only by burying her head against her raised knees and losing herself in daydreams of Cole and her father was she able to withstand the stress-filled hours. Sometimes in her fantasies, her father and Cole ran together and became one and the same, until she thought of their time by the creek. Then her heartbeat grew calmer and her fears subsided.

This moment would pass, she told herself, and Molly would set her free. She always had before. Then Kansas would make plans for this never to happen again. She'd run away from Molly. She'd go to Cole. He was like a beacon of strength lighting the darkness in her heart.

Several times throughout the afternoon, Molly returned to the shed to see if her daughter was prepared to cooperate, and each time she closed the door on Kansas's pleas. The sun had climbed the heavens and was sliding downward again, its angling rays heating the shed to an unbearable degree. Sweat poured down Kansas's face and into her eyes. Dust from the street, and now from the shed floor, rose in the air with every movement and settled over her, making her skin itch and burn. Her mouth grew dry and cottony. She longed for a drink of water, but Molly had given no thought to such essentials. Kansas lay on the dirt floor gasping for air.

Up in her room, Molly waved a brightly colored paper fan before her blotched face. On her dressing table were spread stacks of gold pieces and paper bills. Slowly, with great enjoyment, she counted her hoard. Les hadn't paid as much as she'd demanded, but anything added nicely to her little savings. It had been accumulated slowly, painstakingly, over the years and represented services rendered to countless men. She'd added considerably to her pile by engaging in a little pilfering when her customers had proven too inebriated to know what was happening. Oh, she was always good old Molly, understanding and tolerant if a man needed to doze off a bit to relieve a spinning head from too much whiskey. But unknowingly they'd paid. She'd never been greedy about it, had never taken too much or they would have guessed and complained to Charley. Molly knew too well what Charley would do if he found out she stole from the men. She'd be out of a place to work from, and that wasn't in her plans. Not yet, anyway.

Carefully she counted the money before her and calculated how much more was needed. If she worked Kansas for six months, maybe only three, for she'd bring a prime price at the beginning, Molly would soon have enough to quit Moody's. She'd take Kansas and go to another town and open her own place. Kansas would be her star attraction. At first she'd even claim Kansas was a virgin again. It could be done. Molly cocked her head as the faint sound of pounding came to her. Kansas should be ready to listen to reason soon, Molly decided. She'd leave her out there for another hour or two, just so she learned her lesson well. Molly ran her fat fingers over her money again and continued with her daydreaming.

Kansas could tell when dusk fell, for the darkness in the shed deepened. The evening coolness hadn't reached the shed yet, so she sat sweating and faint, desperate for water and freedom. Cole hadn't come, or if he had, Molly must have sent him away. Kansas was left to her own devices. She must think what to do. She held her throbbing head with trembling hands and tried to still the dizzy, sick whirling. Molly would never let her out of here, unless she agreed to what she wanted. She couldn't become one of Charley's girls, but she could pretend she would—and at the first chance she'd run away.

The streets rang with the noise of Saturday night revelry as cowboys hooted drunkenly to one another and the town in general. The life of a cowboy was a hard, lonely one, so few blamed him for whooping it up come Saturday night as long as he didn't kill anyone or get killed himself. Kansas listened intently, identifying some of the merry-makers by their voices. The distant laughter and rough talk made her feel less lonely.

Suddenly the door swung open. "Well, Kansas, what's it going to be?" Molly loomed in the opening, hands on her hips.

Kansas leaped to her feet and put a hand on the door. "Don't lock me in here anymore, Momma. Please," she whispered.

"Are you going to do what I say?" Molly demanded unrelentingly. Her blue-gray eyes seemed to gleam in the dark. Kansas knew her mother would never back down. She must be the one to do so.

"All right, Momma," she said, hanging her head. "I'll do what you say."

"That's a good girl." Molly gloated, a big grin on her face. She moved away from the door. Quickly, Kansas stepped out of the shed. "You'll see it ain't so bad," Molly went on. She could afford to be magnanimous now. "You hurry on in and get cleaned up now. I got somebody waitin' for you."

"Who?" Kansas asked, hope spiraling through her. Cole

had come after all. He'd talk to Molly, make her see how wrong she was. "Who is it?" she asked again.

"Just Odie and some of the other boys. They're right anxious to be with you tonight."

"Tonight?" Kansas asked, blanching beneath the dirt covering her face. "I—I thought I'd have more time to get ready."

"There ain't much to gettin' ready for these boys," Molly advised. "Just wash up a little. I left a new dress for you on the bed." When she saw Kansas hesitating, her mouth tightened. "Don't be thinkin' about runnin' away," she warned. "I got Odie and the others keeping an eye out for you. Now just get on inside."

"All right, Momma," Kansas said, and slowly walked into the kitchen. Her thirst drew her to the bucket of water sitting on the side table. Picking up the dipper, she drank until the water dribbled off her chin.

"You better drink a little slower or you'll bloat like a cow," her mother warned unremorsefully. "It'll be uncomfortable with a man layin' on top of you."

"Yes, Momma," Kansas answered, and continued holding the dipper to her mouth without drinking, while thoughts spiraled through her mind. On the edge of the window sash was a sharp knife, left there from the last time she peeled potatoes. Thirst assuaged at last, she turned to face Molly.

"Mmmm, you'll have to clean yourself up more than I thought," Molly said, observing Kansas's condition in the harsh light from the kerosene lamp. "Best get a bath."

"All right," Kansas agreed, with more calmness than before. She'd come up with an idea that might buy her a little time. Taking out a kettle, she placed it on the stove and filled it with water, then added more wood to the coals.

"What's so funny?" Molly asked suspiciously, seeing her daughter's amused face.

"I was just thinking," Kansas answered, letting the smile

grow on her face. "Charley'll have to get another girl to cook for him."

"That's right," Molly said, glad to see Kansas looking at the brighter side of things. "Hurry up now. I got customers waitin' for you." She headed up the back stairs. On a Saturday night, she'd have customers waiting as well.

When her mother was gone, Kansas took down the tin bathtub and filled it with the heated water, then, making sure the door was bolted, she peeled off the dirty yellow dress, picked up the sharp knife, and stepped into the warm water.

Molly was back almost before she'd finished, bearing a simple dress of blue calico. It had once belonged to someone else, obviously. The bodice had been altered and one sleeve was mended, but it was clean.

"You get into this now," Molly said, "and comb your hair real pretty. Then we'll have you sashay out through the saloon for all the boys to get a gander at what's being offered."

"Momma, I can't."

"Kansas, we ain't going through this again."

"It's my bleeding cycle," Kansas blurted out, forcing her gaze to meet her mother's unflinchingly.

"Are you sure? You ain't lying about this, trying to get out of working?" Molly demanded. "I want to see some proof."

Kansas was prepared. She brought out a blood-soaked rag.

Molly sighed. "I guess Odie and the others'll have to wait a few more nights," Molly grunted finally. She threw the new dress over her arm. "You won't be needin' this. I'll tell Charley you'll be doin' the cookin' for tonight."

"Yes, Momma," Kansas answered, hiding her relief. When Molly was gone, she put the knife back on the window ledge and placed a clean rag over the cut on her thigh. The cut throbbed, but the pain was well worth it. Now she had to be careful not to arouse Molly's suspicions until she could get away.

In the next week, Kansas began to despair it would ever happen. She was never left alone one second during the day, and at night, when the saloon closed down, Molly made Kansas sleep in bed with her. The door was locked and the key safely tucked beneath Molly's pillow. In the meantime, Molly worked the men into a fever pitch, reminding them often of Kansas's virtues. Kansas slashed her leg again and left the bloodied rag conspicuously in evidence. Saturday rolled around again and Molly took matters into her own hands, deciding that the dreaded monthly curse had surely ended by now.

"Tonight," she said stiffly, eyeing the cuts on Kansas's bare thigh. "It's Saturday, and all the hands are in town." Kansas knew her reprieve was over. "Mr. Richards will be your first customer; I owed him that. And Odie will be your second. I made him pay extra. Besides, we can fool Mr. Richards that you were a virgin."

"I am, Momma," Kansas said, but the words went unheeded.

"The poor old fool gets hisself so lickered up he hardly knows what he's doin', anyway. I figure Odie'd be harder to fool. He'd notice the fresh cuts on your leg." Kansas looked away from her mother's level gaze. Molly crossed to the pegs that held an assortment of clothes. Taking down the blue calico gown she tossed it across the bed. "Get dressed and come on downstairs."

Kansas watched her mother leave the room and looked at the blue calico dress. Despair washed over her. She couldn't give in, she thought, hastily pulling the gown over her head and tugging at the low-cut bodice that exposed too much creamy skin. Shrugging in defeat, she crossed to the window and studied the balcony. It would be a long drop. She might break a leg, but she was willing to risk it.

"Are you ready?" Molly asked from the doorway, and Kansas turned to face her mother.

"As ready as I can be," she answered.

"It won't be so bad, honey," Molly said, feeling more kindly now that she'd won. "Just remember the things I told you. Men ain't so bad, even old fools like Elroy Richards. Now smile. You ain't goin' to a wake."

Silently Kansas followed her mother downstairs to the smoke-filled saloon. She'd often been here in the evenings to clean up after the cowboys who'd gotten drunk and spilled things, but tonight was different. Smoke hung in the air and waves of ribald laughter and shouted obscenities washed over her.

"I said smile," Molly ordered, and Kansas took a deep breath and pasted a sickly grin on her face.

"Boys, here she is," Molly said. She'd stuck a gaudy plume in her hair and her red satin dress was too tight and slightly soiled. Next to her cheap finery, Kansas might have seemed dowdy as a dove but for the fineness of her features and the glorious wealth of her hair, which she wore in a coronet braid around her head. She held herself so regally she might have been a queen viewing her subjects. None guessed that beneath the icy calm, her palms were sweaty and her heart pounding.

"Whooee," Odie called. "That's some piece of fancy, and I got me some time with her already, boys. You'll have to get in line behind me."

Elroy Richards gazed at her with bleary eyes, his mouth slack and moist, his head wobbly on his narrow shoulders. "You're a fine girl, a fine girl," he crooned, taking hold of her hand. His rough fingers fumbled, twining themselves through hers. Kansas shivered.

"You'd best get her on upstairs, Elroy, if you're going to. I'm about to bust my britches right now," Odie shouted, and the other cowboys hooted encouragement.

"Are you ready, girl?" Richards asked, with mock stern-
ness. He had trouble focusing his eyes.

Numbly Kansas nodded.

"Well, go on then," Molly said, giving her a shove
toward the stairs.

Elroy Richards got to his feet and stumbled behind. Kansas cast a last desperate glance over her shoulder, but Molly
was holding aloft a whiskey glass in a toast with Odie and
some of the others. None of them would help her, Kansas
realized. They'd expected her to come to this, as had Les
Slater and all the so-called decent folks of Webster. Not one
of them believed or cared that she wasn't like her mother.
Only Cole. The thought of him gave her heart.

Slowly she made her way up the stairs, her mind racing,
looking for an escape. Richards followed happily, drunkenly, behind. At the door of the room she shared with
Molly, Kansas turned to face her would-be customer. "Mr.
Richards," she began, but he was weaving unsteadily.
"Come on in. You're about to fall down," she exclaimed,
and lent him her shoulder to lean on. With some difficulty,
she got him to the bed, where she let go. Silently, almost
gracefully, he fell on the bed, his loose limbs sprawling
wide.

"Mr. Richards?" Kansas said, peering at him. "Mr.
Richards?" Only a snore answered her. Cautiously Kansas
glanced around. Now was the time. Molly wouldn't dare
come up here while she was with Mr. Richards. How long
did she have? An hour? Less? Hastily she grabbed up a
cloth bag and stuffed a clean dress and petticoat into it.
There was pitifully little else. A comb and two hair ribbons.
On top she put the gold locket her father had given Molly.

Frantically she looked around, suddenly fearful of leaving, knowing she couldn't stay. She would need money
until she could find a job. Tentatively she crossed to Molly's hiding place and pulled out a square tin that held her
savings. She was surprised at how much was there. She

thought bleakly of all the years she'd longed to have a dress that hadn't belonged to someone else first—and of the way she'd pleaded with Molly to send her on to advanced school so she could get her teacher's degree. On both accounts, Molly had claimed not to have the money.

Defiantly Kansas reached into the tin. Taking only a few dollars, she put the box back in place and turned toward the window overlooking the balcony. It was so ridiculously easy, after all. She had only to drop from the balcony to a rain barrel and she was free. She'd given no thought of where to go once she was away from Molly. Now the answer just seemed clear and right that she go to Cole. He'd said he loved her. She believed him with all her being.

The street was dark, except for lights spilling out of the saloons. Cowboys wandered along the street, and from somewhere came the wheedling voice of a man and the giggling acquiescence of a woman. Sneaking along the front of the saloon, Kansas chose a red-brown gelding that she knew belonged to Odie. She'd have Cole send it back to him in the morning. He probably wouldn't even miss it, for it was his habit to spend the night at Moody's if one of the women would accommodate him. Guiding the horse back to the alley, Kansas used the rain barrel to mount and turned south out of town, heading for the Bar S ranch. She hoped she could find it in the dark.

Although the evening was young, stars thickly dotted the black sky. The road lay like a white ribbon in the full moonlight, so she had little trouble finding her way. Nearly two hours had passed since she shinnied down from the balcony, and still no sign of the gate posts of the Bar S. Just as she was about to give up, she saw them looming ahead. She followed the drive toward the ranch house, pulling the horse to a stop some distance away. Lanterns had been hung in the trees and the scrape of a fiddler came to her, while people whirled and pranced in the yard. Les Slater was having a party. Dismounting,

Kansas tied the reins to a post and made her way around the fenced corral and stood in the shadows of the barn to watch. Everyone who was anyone in Webster was there, and from the way they gathered around Oliver Howard, Kansas could tell he was the guest of honor.

At first she didn't see Cole, and when she did, her heart lurched with happiness at just the sight of him, then settled into a dull thud when she saw he was dancing with Claire Howard. Claire looked like a princess in a light gown of white-sprigged muslin. The wide skirts were trimmed in bands of blue and flared enticingly as Cole spun her around the floor. Unconsciously Kansas's hand smoothed down the faded blue calico she wore.

"Scoby?" she called softly to a lanky cowboy who lurched by. He staggered closer, peered at her with a comical expression on his face.

"Howdy, Kansas," he called jovially. "What are you doing out here all alone? Come and join the party."

"No, I—I don't have much time, Scoby. Could you get Cole for me? Tell him I'm waiting here for him?"

Scoby hiccuped, then laughed at himself. "Shure thing, Kanshas," he said, and staggered away. "Cole," he bellowed.

"Don't tell anyone else I'm here," Kansas called after him, but feared he hadn't heard. Anxiously she watched his unsteady progress across the yard toward Cole and Claire. For a moment the two men stood talking, slapping each other on the back and laughing. Scoby pointed back toward the corral where Kansas stood waiting. Cole's head came up as he glanced in her direction, then Les Slater called to him and he turned away. Kansas felt hope dwindling away as Cole helped some of the cowhands roll out new barrels of beer. What was she to do? Scoby was talking to Les Slater now. The rare friendly smile disappeared from his face and he stamped across the yard in her direction.

"What in thunderation are you doing here?" he demanded. His hand was rough on her shoulder as he hauled her inside the barn, out of sight of his guests.

"I—I came to see Cole," Kansas stuttered, trying not to let him intimidate her with his size and bearing.

"I thought I made it clear to you and to Molly back in town last week that you're not to come around my boy!"

"M-Molly?" Kansas said, feeling the old familiar taste of defeat. It had always been the case that Molly would side with her customers against Kansas, and Kansas well remembered when Les had been one of Molly's customers. Molly had been kinder then, happier.

"Molly doesn't tell me what to do anymore," Kansas said, asserting her independence for the first time.

"Well, she God almighty took my money fast enough with a promise to do just that," Les snapped. "And I ain't paying anymore."

"Molly took money from you?" Kansas asked, thinking of the money she'd found in Molly's cash box. She wished now she had taken it all. How she would have loved to fling it back in the face of this superior, disapproving man. "I'm sorry, Mr. Slater," she said instead, and her tone was sincere, though no longer humble. Proudly she raised her head and looked him in the eye. "I can't answer for what my mother has said or done. I know how you feel about me, but you're wrong. I'm not what you think."

"Didn't your momma put you to work at Moody's Saloon last week?" Les demanded, his voice harder than the granite expression on his face.

"She tried," Kansas stammered, her confidence waning in the face of his implacable condemnation. "I'm trying to tell you, Mr. Slater, that I'm not one of Moody's whores." Her voice ended on a high pleading note. How long? How long must she fight this town's misconception of her?

"I ain't heard nothing to make me change my mind, girl. If you're not one of Moody's whores"—the curl of his lip showed he plainly thought she was—"it's only a matter of time before you will be. Either way, I don't want you around my boy. Now you git on out of here before I have my hands show you off my place."

"No!" Kansas cried. She could see the recoil of surprise on Les Slater's face. He was used to being obeyed. "Not until I've seen Cole."

"Is something wrong?" A gentle voice sounded from the doorway, and Kansas whirled around. With a smile sweeter than anything else Kansas had seen, Claire Howard glided across the barn floor. Her slender hands had gathered her full skirts on either side and she held them up a few inches from the dirt and hay-strewn boards. Dainty slippers peeked from beneath. Her dark hair had been pulled high on the back of her head and long glossy finger curls danced around her ears and temple. As she approached them, Kansas caught a whiff of flowers.

Claire smiled again, her dark eyes bright and expectant as she stared at Kansas. Kansas keenly felt the contrast between them, she with her wind-blown hair and plain calico gown, its limp skirts soiled by the foam of her horse's mouth as she had pushed him too far and too fast. She clasped her hands in front of her, twisting her fingers in agitation.

"There's nothing you can do here, Miss Claire," Les Slater said, and his tone was at once deferential and patronizing. "You just run along back to the dance."

Claire ignored him, her bright gaze taking in every detail of Kansas's attire. "You're the girl from town, aren't you?" she asked gently.

"Yes, ma'am," Kansas said respectfully, although Claire was about her age. Kansas was touched by the kind demeanor of the other woman.

"You're very pretty."

Kansas said nothing, but her face flamed with embarrassment and surprise. Claire Howard, with all her fine gowns and dainty ways, thought she was pretty. Kansas was flattered, but she realized she was being sidetracked.

"I've been trying to explain to Mr. Slater that I—I need to see Cole," she stuttered. "Could you tell him I'm here?"

"No!" Les thundered.

"He knows," Claire said.

"Where is he?" Kansas asked, relief washing through her.

"He doesn't want to see you." Claire answered in the same even tone she'd used before. "I'm sorry."

"You're wrong," Kansas insisted, glancing toward the barn door. "I need to speak with him. I need to tell him that—that I've left Molly. I've run away from her."

"I speak for Cole when I say he doesn't want to see you again, ever," Claire said, and her light voice held a trace of steel. "You see, Kansas"—she said the name as if it were outlandish—"Cole has asked me to marry him and I've agreed."

"No," Kansas whispered, her eyes grown enormous in her pale face.

"Well, now, that's good news." Les Slater grinned. It faded to a frown as he turned to Kansas again. "It's pretty plain Cole don't want to see you." He delved into his pocket. "Look here, I'll give you some traveling money." He pulled a roll of bills out of his pocket and peeled off several. "But you have to promise you really are leaving . . . and that you won't come back."

In her misery Kansas didn't hear him. Her gaze was fixed on Claire Howard's smiling face. She enjoyed telling me that, seeing me hurt, Kansas thought in a daze. She's not nearly as nice as she pretends to be.

"Cole wouldn't have asked you to marry him," she said out loud. "Because he already asked me." She whirled to face Les Slater and was unaware that tears streamed down her cheeks. "That day down by the creek . . . He didn't make love to me—because he said he wanted to court me proper and ask for my hand in marriage as if I were a real lady." Her words died in a whisper.

"But we all know you're not a lady," Claire said sweetly. "And Cole"—she shrugged delicately—"Cole has come to regret his encounter with you down by the creek. He says you tried to seduce him and trap him in a marriage. He's embarrassed by his association with you, Miss McKay."

"No, he loves me. He said so."

Claire smiled knowingly. "Men will say anything in the heat of passion," she explained as if to a child. "Cole is the son of a rich and prosperous rancher. He has a standing in the community that must be upheld. He needs a wife who can run his home and entertain his guests. Someone he can be proud of to have standing at his side, not a woman who's been whispered and sneered about."

Claire's voice quietly continued, each word perfectly pitched and precisely pronounced, each word piercing Kansas's heart.

"Here, girl, take this." Les held out the wad of money, and when Kansas failed to respond, he shoved them deep into her worn bag. "This'll help you get started on your own."

"Cole loves me," Kansas whispered brokenly.

Claire's bright gaze and wide smile never altered. "Not enough," she answered.

If she'd denied it, Kansas thought, she would have known the other girl was lying. But Claire's simple words struck home with more clarity than any denials. Cole might love Kansas, but not enough to make her his wife, not enough to suffer the ridicule and snickers of the decent folks in town.

"You'd best get on your horse and get on out of here, girl," Les Slater said, and his tone was so scathing, his condemnation of her so complete, that Kansas's fragile ego couldn't withstand any more.

Biting her lips to keep from crying in front of the two of them, she whirled and left the barn. Reaching the gelding, she climbed into the saddle and kicked at its sides. Startled, the horse whinnied, raised his front hooves in a short rear that nearly unseated Kansas, then lit out over the moon-dappled prairie. Kansas was blinded by her tears and pain, so she paid no heed to the commotion behind her. Kicking the gelding's belly once more, she galloped away, the cry of her name lost in the hoofbeats.

Back in the barn, Les Slater turned to Claire Howard. "Girl, is what you said about Cole and you marrying true?" he demanded.

Claire studied his expression and slowly shook her head. "Not yet," she admitted. "But with Kansas McKay gone, it soon will be." she let a triumphant grin light her face. Les Slater chuckled approvingly, then sobered when he heard the commotion outside. Cole's hoarse cry could he beard. "Come on," Les said. "We've got some more convincing to do."

"Kansas!" Cole shouted.

"She's gone, boy," Les Slater said heavily. He'd come out of the barn, and Claire Howard stood slightly behind him, her face bearing a look he couldn't quite fathom.

"What did you do to her?" Cole asked his father. His face was wild and desperate-looking.

"I wished her well," Les answered calmly. "She's leaving Webster. Goin' on to greener pastures, she said."

"Why didn't you tell me she was here?" Cole felt Claire's hand on his arm, but he shrugged it away. "She came to see me, didn't she?"

Les eyed his son, saw the taut stance, the clenched fists, and suddenly he felt old and ineffectual. If a beating couldn't persuade Cole, what could? Slowly he shook his head. "She came to see me," he answered. "She wanted money. Said she'd never come around you again if I gave her five hundred dollars."

"That's a lie," Cole flared.

"It's true, Cole," Claire said quietly. "I was here when he gave her the money. She just kind of laughed and said it was easier money than she'd been making at Moody's Saloon.''

"I don't believe you!" Cole shouted.

Les straightened his shoulders. "Well, don't, boy. But it's the truth. You didn't see her turn around when you called. She got what she came after, and she don't want you no more." Les glared at Cole, then turned back to his guests. Cole stood with his chest heaving as if he'd just outrun a stampeding herd, his shoulders slumped in defeat.

"Cole?" Claire placed her soft hand on his and pressed closer. "I'm sorry about your friend, but she seemed a dreadful girl."

"She's not," Cole said, snatching his hand away as if her touch had burned him. "Kansas is—Kansas. You'd better get on back to the party. Your father will be looking for you."

"I don't care," Claire said softly. "I want to be here with you, alone in the moonlight." Quickly she placed her cool lips against his. Her sweet scent filled his head, but all Cole could remember was the warmth of Kansas's lips and the way her slender body had molded itself to him. Gently he pushed Claire away.

"Good-bye, Claire," he said, and headed for the barn. He saddled his horse and, without a backward glance, rode away from the Bar S ranch.

Chapter 4

*T*HE SILVER SPUR Saloon was one of the nicer establishments in the ragtag, booming gold town of Virginia City. Like most of the other buildings, the saloon was newly raised and still raw, but the beginnings of elegance had crept in by way of damask drapes and a Brussels carpet over the splintery floor. A new mahogany bar had been installed and an ornate gold-leaf-framed mirror hung behind it, reflecting the light and giving an impression of more space than the bar actually possessed. A piano, having been abandoned once long ago from a wagon train and rescued by one of Nevada's early Mormon settlers, now sat in regal splendor in one corner. A thin man with a small mustache thumped on it without even looking at the keys, a fact that awed some of the bar's rough patrons. The tune was loud and lively, prompting several miners and dance hall girls to prance around the floor with considerably more enthusiasm than skill.

The saloon was packed with men, all of them waiting for the card game to begin. Bets had been laid and now loud debates broke out as to the skill and luck of the two players. This was a challenge game, a duel between players who'd found out that Virginia City wasn't big enough for both of them. The loser would leave on the next stagecoach. Excitement was at a fever pitch, smoke hung in the air, choking the lungs and tearing the eyes, but not one man thought of leaving.

As if on cue, the players entered the saloon from opposite doors and at the same time. Conversation died away, the thump of the piano was ended in midtune. The dancers looked around bewildered, then joined the others who pressed forward. A path opened for the two gamblers to make their way to the table in the center of the room. The players looked around the room, one of them smiled, the other remained somber, grim, and intent.

"Anyone feeling lucky tonight?" the smiling player asked lightly, and the miners chuckled and shuffled their feet.

"Let's play!" the other gambler growled, and the two sat down.

A new deck was broken, cards dealt, bets placed. The smiling player won easily. Cards were dealt again. Smoke rose in a blue haze over their heads, dimming the lantern light. The room grew warm from the press of bodies and still the game continued, one hand after another. The pile of money in front of the players grew higher for first one and then the other. The midnight hour drew near and passed. The rest of the town grew quiet. The press of onlookers increased as others heard of the game and came to place their bets on their favorite winners.

Quill Ramsey, owner of the Silver Spur Saloon and one of the players, shuffled the cards for yet another hand. "Five card stud, imperial joker wild," he decreed. "A hundred dollars ante."

The room buzzed at the higher stakes. Thousands of dollars lay on the table in front of the players. Men shifted from one foot to the other, their gazes never wavering from the players. Somehow they sensed this might be the final hand, the telling hand, and once again excitement rose.

Quill offered the deck for a cut. The offer was declined.

Shrugging, he picked them up and began dealing. Eyes narrowing, he raised his tense gaze to his opponent, looking for any hesitation, any chink in the cool armor. If he'd expected Kansas McKay to show any strain of the long hours of tense play, he was disappointed. Head thrown back, lashes half lowered over clear luminous eyes, soft mouth set in the amused smile she'd worn ever since the game began, she gazed back at him with such assurance, he felt his stomach muscles tighten. He'd underestimated her from the beginning.

When she'd first arrived in Virginia City, he'd been surprised at her youth and ladylike ways. Like others before him, he'd made the mistake of thinking her a helpless female. No one knew much about her past. She'd just appeared in Virginia City one day, and she'd been an instant hit. She wasn't the only lady gambler. Several women had chosen to make their fortunes with the turn of a card, but she'd done it with considerably more skill and style than the others.

Quill had thought the miners' tales just exaggerations. Perhaps they had been telling the truth. Quill watched her through narrowed eyes and thought of all the things he'd heard. She'd set up a gambling table in her own room back in the hotel. She didn't frequent saloons. Every man had to bathe and wear clean clothes if he wanted to sit at her table. No tobacco chewing, spitting, or swearing was allowed. Quill looked at the beautiful face, luminous gray eyes, and glorious gold hair twisted into its elaborate coiffure. Her gown of lace-trimmed, gray-blue silk was of a modest cut that covered her bodice and shoulders yet hugged her young breasts so there was little doubt she was a comely woman. Even after hours of play, she sat tall, her slim back firmly straight, her eyes alert.

She was a good player, he acknowledged to himself, though he'd never say it out loud. She'd handled what cards he'd given her with extreme skill, and when she had a bad hand, she'd bluffed her way so convincingly, he'd folded and brought the miners' gleeful ridicule down on his head.

"Ho! She put the saddle on you for sure that time," they ribbed him.

But this time would be different. There would be no bluff to save her. He was going all out.

Kansas placed a hundred-dollar bill in the center of the table and discarded. "I'll take two cards," she said coolly, and Quill dealt them for her.

"She ain't runnin' a blazer this time," the men chortled.

"Dealer takes one," Quill said, and dealt himself a king from the bottom. Fanning his cards, he barely glanced at the four kings he'd given himself. The tip of an ace of spades shown behind the kings. Just as he'd intended. He had an unbeatable hand. He'd dealt her the other three aces as a teaser, but without the ace of spades she couldn't beat his hand. When these dirty miners talked about Kansas McKay from now on, it would be to tell how Quill Ramsey had beat her and sent her packing. "I'll raise you one hundred," he said, not wanting to tip his hand too soon. He wanted to milk her for every penny she had.

"I'll see your hundred and raise you two hundred," Kansas said serenely.

She's bluffing, Quill thought, and his lip curled in a sneer.

The betting was brisk. The atmosphere in the saloon grew quiet then tense. Quill could feel the sweat run down the inside of his pants leg. The pile of money in the center of the table grew. Kansas shoved several stacks of gold and silver coins onto the pile.

"I raise you five hundred more," she said quietly.

Quill counted the remainder of his money and felt a dull flush sweep over his face. His cheeks were shiny with sweat.

"The bid's up to you, Mr. Ramsey," Kansas said clearly, her blue-gray eyes guileless.

Quill cleared his throat and drummed his fingers nervously. "I . . . uh . . . don't have any more money," he admitted finally.

"Are you throwing in your cards, Mr. Ramsey?" Kansas asked tersely.

"No, no, of course not," he snapped. "I'll have to write you a note for the rest."

"No notes," Kansas said, with exaggerated pleasantness. "You yourself made that stipulation."

"That was meant for you!" Quill flared. "Everyone knows you'll be on tomorrow's stage."

"I hadn't planned on leaving Virginia City anytime soon." Her tone was even, her smile amused. "On the other hand, how am I to be sure *you* aren't planning to leave on tomorrow's stage without paying your note?"

"Me?" Quill blustered, color suffusing his face. "I'm not a fly-by-night. I own this saloon. Why would I be leaving?"

"Ah, yes, the Silver Spur," Kansas mused, pointedly assessing the building and its accoutrements as if she might be considering buying it. "How long has it been since you won it in a poker game? A month?"

Quill's eyes were a blue blaze of anger. "Riley!" he snarled at the fat bartender, who hurried to his irate boss's side. "Bring me that tin box out of the safe," Quill ordered.

"Yes, sir," the man answered, and scurried away to return in short order with the specified box. Taking out a key from his waistcoat pocket, Quill opened the box and extracted a sheaf of papers. "My deed to the Silver Spur Saloon," he said, laying it on the table. A smirk of triumph distorted his thin, handsome face. "I figure it's worth five thousand dollars." His glance dropped to Kansas. "Now, Miss McKay. Will you be meeting the bid . . . or are you dropping out?" He stared pointedly at her empty money bag.

Kansas stared at him a full minute, letting the tension build, giving the miners a chance to place new bets. She knew Quill was already seeing her on the afternoon stage. She let him relish his moment of victory, then languidly raised an arm to motion to Otis Clemons. A miner down on his luck, Otis had been her friend, bodyguard, and advisor ever since she arrived in Virginia City, and she trusted him implicitly. As Otis made his way to her, Kansas sat studying Quill Ramsey. He was something of a dandy, and only a middling poker player, but she'd never considered him a fool. Now she sat wondering what had made him risk everything on one hand as she was about to do. Perhaps she was the bigger fool.

"How're you doing?" Otis asked at her shoulder. His voice was low, meant only for her ears and meant to advise caution. He knew she was gambling high stakes and he hated to see her lose. He'd grown fond of the clever and beautiful lady, thinking of her as a daughter, although their relationship was far more formal. Still, he felt pride in her every accomplishment, sorrow for her setbacks. He alone knew about the lot she'd bought high on the hillside at the other end of town. He alone had listened to her plan to build a great gambling mansion there. And he alone guessed at her deep need to settle down and belong somewhere. He'd sensed the sadness in her, sensed the loneliness and aching loss, but she'd never spoken of her past, and out of respect he'd never asked. Now he bent to whisper in her ear.

"Watch it!" he cautioned. "Quill ain't much of one for taking chances. If he'd go this far, he must have something big."

"Trust me," Kansas whispered back. "Give me the rest of my money."

"If you lose this, you ain't goin' to build that fine gambling house you been jawin' about." He handed over the bag she'd given him earlier that evening.

"If I lose, it won't matter," Kansas whispered back.

"Needing a little advice, Miss McKay?" Quill needled, and Otis drew away. Kansas turned back to her opponent.

"I'll call," she said, laying the last of her money on the pile.

Quill's smile was elated, triumphant, and condescending all at once. "I'm afraid you've lost, Miss McKay," he said, laying down his hand and wrapping one arm around the pile of money and papers. His glance never left her face. He wanted to see her humiliation, to savor her defeat. The onlookers pressed closer. A murmur arose as they noted his four kings.

"I hope you enjoy your trip tomorrow," he smirked.

"Like I said before, Mr. Ramsey. I'm not planning on going anywhere," Kansas answered, and laid down her cards.

Slowly the realization came to him that she wasn't looking alarmed or defeated. Exclamations could be heard around the room as the men saw what she'd laid down. "Four aces! An unbeatable hand!" they cried.

Kansas sat watching Quill's smile fade. He seemed not to understand. "I believe I've won," she said quietly, her expression one of amusement.

"You can't have four aces," he cried. "You've cheated! I have the ace of spades." His frantic fingers shoved the four kings apart so the final card was more fully revealed. "You see! I have—" He paused. An expression of horror washed over his face as he stared at the card he'd thought was the ace of spades. "The imperial joker!" he gasped.

There was a dead silence around the table, then men began to whisper and then to laugh outright. "She outfoxed him, all right!" someone said, and pointed at the table.

"No. I beat her. I had an unbeatable hand."

"The cutter, man," a fellow gambler cried. "You forgot you were playing with a fifty-three card deck. The cutter looks like the ace of spades. You have to look close. Any beginner would know that."

The laughter grew around the saloon. Kansas's face was

bright with humor. "I expect you'll have a safe journey
tomorrow," she said, reaching for the deed. Otis was already gathering up her winnings.

"No, you don't," Quill said, drawing a small derringer
from his waistcoat and leveling it at them. "The money and
deed are mine. I won them, I tell you."

"Let it go, man," the gambler advised. "You lost. She
beat you fair and square. Move on, Quill. You're finished in
this town."

"I'll move on, all right, but I'm taking the money with
me," Quill answered, his eyes fever-bright with anger and
greed. Nervously Kansas fumbled with her bag. "Just move
back from the table," Quill demanded. Kansas motioned to
Otis to comply. No one else tried to intervene. It was a
policy of nearly everyone not to become embroiled in gambling disputes. Otis shuffled backward, his hands high and
in plain view. He didn't need to get shot up by some half-
mad gambler.

Satisfied that no one would stop him, Quill grabbed up
handsful of money and began stuffing them into his pockets.
While his attention was diverted, Kansas moved, her arm
swinging up, her hand still encased in the small cloth bag
she'd carried.

"Hold it, Quill," she said. "Put the money back on the
table. I have a gun in my bag, and I know how to use it."

Quill looked at her in surprise, then snickered in disbelief. He swung around, leveling his gun at her, but before he
could fire, a shot rang out, a bullet ripped through the sleeve
of his coat, spinning him around. His nerveless hand
dropped the gun. Blood welled on his sleeve.

"That's the second time you've underestimated me tonight," Kansas said, pulling the small .22-caliber pocket
derringer from her ripped bag. "Don't try for a third. Put
my money back on the table."

Quill looked around the room, but found no sympathy or
support. There would be none. He'd been a poor loser and

tried to steal what he'd lost. No one here would ever sit at a poker table with him again. Quill saw the condemnation in their eyes and his face contorted with hatred for the calm, beautiful woman who stood facing him. He would have launched himself at her except for the shiny bore of the pistol. Though no more than three and a half inches long, the gun was deadly at this close range. Nursing his wounded arm, Quill emptied his pockets, then staggered toward the door. Wordlessly a path was made for him through the crush of bodies. At the door, Quill turned back to face Kansas McKay.

"You haven't seen the last of me," he snarled, then he was gone, out into the dark of the night. The saloon was silent; the mood tense and uncertain.

Kansas glanced around at the throng and pocketed her derringer. "Drinks are on the house," she called, and the silence was broken. The men gave an exuberant cheer. Few of them had liked Quill Ramsey; he'd cheated them too often. Now they jubilantly pressed to the bar to toast his downfall.

Otis walked back to the table and began gathering up Kansas's winnings. "You beat all I've ever seen," he said. "Where'd you learn to shoot like that."

"Someone taught me long ago," Kansas answered, and for a heartbeat the past, with all its bittersweet memories, rushed in on her. With an effort, she pushed it away from her. Long ago she'd stopped thinking of Cole Slater. He was dead to her, as was her past, and there was no reason to dwell on it. She had the present and the future to worry about.

"Well, Otis, what do you think?" she asked, deliberately forcing a bright smile to her lips. She waved at the pile of money that nearly filled his beat-up hat. "Do you think we have enough money there to build a gambling casino?"

"Yes, ma'am. I expect we have enough money here to do just about anything you want to."

"Then let me buy you a drink," Kansas offered, looping an arm through his.

"Let's not forget this," Otis said, picking up the deed for the saloon. "You're already the owner of one of the best saloons in Virginia City."

"No, let's not forget that," Kansas cried gaily, tucking the deed in her bag. It rested there with surprising weight, and for a moment she felt a premonition that the saloon would only bring her grief, as it had all its previous owners. Then she banished the thought and, with Otis at her side, pushed her way through the sweating, unwashed bodies to the bar.

Chapter 5

COLE SLATER KICKED dust over his campfire, packed the rest of his gear on his mule, mounted the bay he'd traded for in Sacramento, and headed down out of the mountains to the Great Basin below. His lean body sat the saddle with easy familiarity. He'd been moving around the country for three years now, and he'd never stayed in one place for very long. When it seemed he might have found a likely place, the next town called with a promise of some elusive youthful yearning. Only he wasn't young anymore, except in years. He was twenty-six and looked older—and he felt older than he looked. The past three years hadn't been kind ones.

He'd started out looking for Kansas McKay, but he'd long since given up the search. Somewhere in the cattle towns and gold camps he'd let the memory of her slide away. For a time he'd sought her face in the saloons and whorehouses, dreading the day he'd find her, driven to keep up the search. He couldn't say just when he'd stopped searching, when he'd admitted to himself he didn't want to find her. He didn't want to see her beauty and innocence tarnished. She'd chosen a way of life and was forever lost to him. He would have to accept it. But in the accepting, he'd grown bitter and hard.

61

Maybe it was the solitude of the days and nights in the mountains, or riding the flat prairies when loneliness had bayed at his heels like a hungry coyote. At times he was driven to seek what comfort he could find in the arms of the whores who waited in every saloon in every town. At first, when he'd closed his eyes he'd tried to imagine the small, warm body beneath his was Kansas's, that the soft, clinging mouth was hers, that the laughter and glowing eyes held the same promise as hers had, but just as he'd come to realize a whore's whispered endearments were a lie, so, too, were his memories. Once he'd accepted that, the ache around his heart had eased, but not the restless wandering search for some elusive dream. He couldn't go home. The ranch held nothing for him. Once he'd dreamed of running it, but that dream was no longer important to him—only the next town, the next bend in the road.

He wasn't the same man who'd ridden away from the Bar S. Three years of wandering around the country had changed him inside and out. His slim body had hardened, the muscles growing leaner, tougher. The easy slouch was still there, but the cat-quiet sureness of his step made some men uneasy around him. His wary self-contained air only seemed to restate the lean danger of his wiry body. Every man sensed the retribution of which he was capable if pushed too far. Some had learned that lesson the hard way and died.

Along the way he'd earned a reputation of fairness and ruthless courage. No one had ever known him to back down from a fight. Those who'd seen his speed with a gun never wanted to challenge him. Yet he'd been known to withdraw from a fight himself, and his reputation had been none the worse for it. He wasn't a man with a thirst for blood. He just wanted to be left alone, and maybe that was the one reason that made him vulnerable to every hotheaded young gunslinger and every killer who crossed his path. They'd sensed he had no stomach for killing, and they'd mistaken it as a weakness—until they stood facing his gun and learned their lesson too late.

He'd gotten so he avoided the towns, going in just when he needed supplies and when desperation drove him to seek out the sound of another human's voice. Now was such a time. There had been too many soul-aching days alone in the mountains with just the sound of the wind soughing through the timber. If he stayed much longer, he'd get to be as loco as some of those old mountain men wandering around up there. Cole guided the bay down a steep incline. Pebbles rattled beneath its hooves. Below lay Virginia City. He had little doubt what he'd find there. By tonight he'd be sick of the sound and stench of other people, but now they drew him as surely as any Eldorado drew a gold-fevered miner.

About midmorning he became aware of someone following him. The careless fall of an iron-shod hoof against loose rock alerted him and he pulled the bay to a halt, sitting still in his saddle, straining to hear the sound again. The fact that he didn't told him more than he wanted to know. Whoever was back there didn't want him to know they were trailing him.

The sudden hee-hawing of a jackass broke the tense silence. The bay started. Cole tightened his grip on the reins, his lips thinning, his nostrils flaring slightly, as if to sniff out this new danger. The sound had come from the side of him. Someone was trying to outflank him. Quietly he led the bay and packhorse off the trail and into a grove of sugar pines. Dismounting, he tied off the reins to a thin sapling. Here beneath the pines, the world was shadowy and cool and he was reminded briefly of how hotly the sun had beat down on him. From the dim recesses of the woods, he studied the trail behind him, taking his time, knowing in the long run his patience would pay off better than any headlong flight down the steep trail. He needed to know how far back his pursuers were.

The minutes crept by. His pulse drummed in his ear, sweat formed on his brow beneath his hatband. He made no move to wipe it away. His gaze never wavered from the ridge above. Finally he found what he sought. Sunlight flashed against a rifle butt, then was gone. A pebble was dislodged from the trail above and tumbled downward. Whoever was back there was careless. They wouldn't reach the pine woods in much less than an hour. Time enough to take care of the men on his flank.

Drawing his gun, Cole made his way through the thick trees, angling slightly downhill from the direction of the mule's cry.

Except for that one outburst from the mule there had been no other sound, but Cole wasn't deterred. Mules were useful, sociable creatures. It was unlikely wild mules would be this high in the hills. The sound of someone cursing under his breath gave Cole pause. Then stealthily he moved downhill toward the noise, keeping well hidden behind the thick trunks and silvery needles of the pines.

"Dad-burn it, Willi!" An exasperated voice berated a small gray mule. "I tell you this ain't no time to be gettin' cantankerous on me. They's somethin' about to happen up there and we got to get away from here if'n we don't want to get caught in the crossfire. Come on, Willi."

Cole shifted his weight slightly, and now he could make out from behind the branches a scruffy little man who tugged impatiently on the mule's reins. The little man halted suddenly, as if aware of Cole watching him. His scraggly beard quivered and he threw the reins aside.

"Stay here then," he said in disgust, "and get yourself shot." He ran down the trail a piece and darted beneath an overhang of rock, scrunching well back so he wasn't visible from the trail. With a mighty snort and screech, Willi tossed her head and ambled down the trail after him, pausing beside the old man's hiding place.

"Go on, get outta here," the mountain man cried, flapping his hat at the mule. But Wilhelmina twisted her mouth, pulling her lips back from large yellowed teeth, and set the air to ringing with her loud complaints.

"Go on. Shoo, you ornery bag of bones!" The old man cussed and flung a rock at the mule, who only pranced out of the way and set up a louder caterwauling.

Cole could barely repress a grin, but he remained cautious as he used the distraction of the mule to move down trail to the ledge. "Come out of there with your hands high over your head," he ordered, and after only a moment's hesitation, the old man stepped from behind the boulder.

"Who are you?" Cole demanded, patting the man's sleeves and shirt for the bulge of a gun. There was no gun belt strapped to the old man's waist, and the only rifle in evidence was still in the pack on the mule's back.

"Now, son, there ain't no need for you to go gettin' trigger-happy," the man said placatingly. His hands were straight up in the air and his beard quivered furiously. "I ain't the man you're lookin' fur."

"How do you know who I'm looking for?" Cole demanded, standing back to examine the old man.

It was obvious this shriveled little man posed no threat. He was too typical of the mountain men who still roamed the Sierra ranges. Once, they'd explored great uncharted regions of mountains and prairies, living off the land, making friends with the Indians, but their time had come and gone. Now it was left for the old ones to carry on as best they could. Unable to come down out of the mountains and live in the prairie towns, they roamed the hills like restless ghosts whose moments of glory had forever dimmed. Occasionally they came down to cadge a drink or two at a saloon while they regaled a derisive audience with their exploits and the wonders they'd seen.

"My name's Tobias Gabriel Wright; my friends call me Toby. I tell you, son. I ain't got no fight with you, nor you with me. I was just comin' down the mountain, followin' along behind you thinkin' I might meet up with you for a noon meal, then I picked up on these fellows followin' you. I jest figured I'd get myself on round you since it waren't my fight."

"How'd you know they were following me? Maybe it's you they're after," Cole said, watching the old man's expression closely.

"I been roaming these mountains purt near most of my life," Toby answered simply. "I don't own nothing anybody'd want, except maybe Willi here, and if'n anyone wanted this stubborn mule, wal, I'd just give her to 'em. I ain't killed no one recently, leastwise not that I recall. Just ain't no reason for someone to come after me."

Cole holstered his gun and stood looking at Toby, his hands on his hips. Toby was aware the big man's hands never strayed too far from his holster.

"So you've got it all figured out, have you?" Cole said, with some humor.

"Just about," Toby agreed. "The only thing I didn't know for sure was whether that's a posse chasing you or someone else. Willi and me pondered on that some before deciding not to warn you. I figured whoever you was, you'd pick up on them men following you soon enough." His glance dropped to the gun holster riding low on the slim hips. "You a gunslinger or a sheriff?" Toby asked.

"Neither," Cole said sharply, and glanced back up the trail. "Just a man wanting a little peace, but I see I'm not going to get it today."

Toby nodded. "That's a fact. They's more of them than you. I figure they's four of 'em." He noted that fact didn't seem to bother the big man. "Who might I be speakin' to, just in case you don't make it?"

Cole swung his level gaze back to the old man. "I'll make it," he said calmly. "But the name's Cole Slater."

"Cole Slater," Toby repeated. "I've heard tales about you. They say you don't . . ." He paused at the cold lights flaring in the big man's eyes. "Well, ain't no never mind. Willi and me'll just mosey on down the trail."

"I can't let you do that, old-timer," Cole said thoughtfully. "I know these men. They're mean—and wouldn't hesitate to kill if they thought you'd seen them. You don't have enough time to get away from them."

"Willi and me can give it a try," Toby said, grabbing the mule's reins and giving them a tug. As usual, Willi's ears laid back and she dug in her hooves stubbornly.

"You might if Willi would cooperate," Cole said, then the glint of humor left his eyes as he glanced around. "This looks like as good a place as any to make a stand. How good are you with that rifle?" He nodded toward Willi's packs.

"I used to have me a pretty good eye," Toby said. "I can still pick off a jackrabbit at a hundred paces."

"Better get it and your ammunition and find cover," Cole said. "I'm going to get my horse." He climbed back up the steep incline, his long legs churning, his broad shoulders hunched forward slightly. In no time he was back, leading the bay and the packhorse back down the incline. The horses didn't like the steep path and voiced a protest, but Cole gave them no time to balk. They half ran, half slid down the slope amid a shower of small rocks.

"Hellfire, you made enough noise," Tobias complained as Cole settled down in some rocks nearby, his rifle and gun, along with an extra belt of ammunition, laid out before him. "Why didn't you just send them an invitation?"

"I did," Cole said. "I marked the trail so they'd know where to look for me."

"Why'd you do that?" Tobias demanded. "They might have ridden on by without finding us."

"Not these men," Cole said, and took out a cigar and lit it.

Tobias marveled at the steady hand that held the match. "Sounds like you know these men," Tobias grunted, wiping his sweaty palms against his pants. It'd been a long time since he was involved in a shoot-out. Part of him was fearful and part of him felt exhilaration.

"I do," Cole said. "I killed their brother some time back in a dispute over cards." His voice sounded regretful. "I tried to reason with him, offered to split the pot, but he was spoiling for a fight. He was all liquored up. It was a fair fight. The sheriff let me go. Most folks in town were kind of glad to see him dead. He'd shot up the town and killed several men, but once I'd done their dirty work, they wanted me gone."

"Can't blame 'em, if'n he had brothers to come gunnin' for you."

"Yeah, that's how I figured it."

"Who was the man you shot?"

"Someone said his name was Elliott Wheeler," Cole said, pulling on his cigar.

"Wheeler?" Tobias's eyes bulged. "You mean them's the Wheeler brothers tracking you up there?" He leaped to his feet and half slid back down to the trail where Wilhelmina still waited, cropping lazily on a clump of sparse grass.

"Where're you going?" Cole called.

"I ain't fightin' the Wheeler brothers," Tobias yelled, jerking at Willi's reins. "Come on, you ornery mule."

A shot rang out, hitting a rocky outcropping nearby. Wilhelmina snorted and jumped nervously, jerking the reins from Tobias's hand. With a final squeal of terror, she bolted down the mountainside.

"Come back here, you no good—" Another shot rang out, cutting him short. He dove for cover. Above he could hear Cole Slater returning fire. Tobias was in a vulnerable position, he realized, with little cover. Cautiously he began crawling back up the incline to the boulder where he'd left his rifle.

"Look out behind you," Cole yelled, and fired. Tobias swiveled in time to see a man fall forward off a rocky ledge where he'd hidden. "Come on, get back up here," Cole shouted, and began firing rapidly to cover him. Tobias scrambled to safety, picked up his rifle, aimed at nothing at all, and fired in absurd relief that he was alive.

"Thanks," he called.

"Save your bullets. This may take awhile," Cole answered, and Tobias forced himself to ease back on the trigger. No sense to fire wildly.

The sun rose higher in the sky. Without trees or rocks to shade them, they soon began to feel the burning heat. Cole showed no discomfort. He remained alert, hat brim pulled low over his face, eyes squinting into narrow blue slits that studied the dark line of trees on the slope above. With deliberate care, he took aim and fired. A man cried out in pain, then tumbled head over heels down the incline, sliding to a stop halfway down, where he lay silent and unmoving.

"Tommy?" A voice called from the pines. "Tommy! Hank, he got Tommy!"

"Shut up, you idiot," Hank growled, and Tobias guessed he was the leader of the Wheeler brothers.

"That's two down, Hank!" Cole needled. "How many left to go? One? Two?"

"You bastard," Hank cried. "Ned, Wylie . . . let's get him."

"Watch it! Here they come," Cole said, and braced himself.

Tobias sat up and looked around, his gun ready. But no one came running down the slope; the hillside remained empty in the hot afternoon sun. A sound made Cole whirl, instinctively bringing his gun barrel up to fire. One man went down. A second man charged up the hillside without pausing. Cole pulled the trigger again, but it hammered down on an empty chamber. Tobias's rifle roared, and the second man fell at Cole's feet.

"Thanks," he said briefly, and turned his attention back to the pines. Hank Wheeler had made his move, and even now he was charging them, his gun blazing death.

"Come on, you coward," he challenged. "Come out and meet me like a man."

Bullets bounced off the rocks around Cole. He huddled down, his fingers working feverishly to reload his gun, but there was no time. Hank Wheeler was on him. One shot spun the half-loaded gun out of Cole's hand, another bit deep into his shoulder, spinning him around on impact. Hank Wheeler had gained the outcropping and now he paused, grinning evilly when he saw Cole's useless arm. Slowly he moved around Wilhelmina, one large dirty fist automatically landing on her rump to move her out of the way.

"You're going to die, Slater," he sneered, "slowly, inch by inch, so you remember every one of my brothers and wish to heaven you'd never heard of the Wheelers." Hank sighted along his barrel and pulled the trigger. Cole's body jerked as the bullet hit his thigh. Laughing, Wheeler pulled back the trigger and took aim again.

"Willi!" Tobias called, and the mule cried a screeching hee-haw, reared up on her hind legs, and squarely planted her back feet in Hank Wheeler's backside. Wheeler cursed as he was kicked sideways. His gun flew out of his hand and went sliding across the rocks. He recovered immediately and launched himself after the gun, grabbing it up and aiming all in one smooth motion. But Cole Slater wasn't where Wheeler had last seen him. He'd rolled downhill and now took refuge behind one of the fallen Wheeler brothers. One large brown hand scooped up the dead man's gun and he rolled to his feet.

"Put down your gun and let's end this, Wheeler," he said, standing upright. His leg ached and he could feel the warm sticky blood running down his thigh. His eyes were steely, his face grim. "There's been enough killing."

"You're going to die for what you did to my little brother," Hank Wheeler said.

"It was a fair fight," Cole said. "He came after me with

a gun. I tried to talk him out of it, but he was liquored up. You've lost another brother and one is wounded. Take the brother you have left and go home.''

"Not before I kill you," Hank called, and in a lightning move brought his gun up and fired. Cole felt the white-hot pain of the bullet entering his side, felt darkness roar over him, but he pushed it back, took aim, and pulled the trigger. The last thing he remembered before his knees buckled was the red flower that blossomed in the center of Hank Wheeler's chest.

Long ago she'd stopped thinking about Cole Slater. He was dead to her, as was her past, and there was no reason to dwell on it. She had the present and the future to worry about. Now she spread her full house on the table and smiled at the miner sitting across from her. "You shouldn't try to bluff, Everett," she teased kindly. "You don't have the face for it."

He threw his cards down in disgust. "That's it. I'm bust," he said, looking around the table at the other men. "I'll see you boys," he said, reaching for his jacket.

"Where you headed, Ev?" someone asked.

He flashed them a good-natured grin. "I've got me an exclusive, dee-luxe room over at the stables. Guess I'll turn in."

"Are you heading back to your mine tomorrow?" Kansas asked, without glancing up. She'd already stacked her winnings in neat piles.

"Yes, ma'am," he answered, without rancor. "I just come down for suppl—" Sheepishly he looked away. "Good night, ma'am."

Kansas motioned Otis to her and handed him a stack of coins with a few whispered instructions. Otis nodded in understanding and followed Everett into the night. No one around the table said a word. Some knew firsthand what was about to happen. After winning all Ev's money at the

poker table, Kansas McKay had sent Otis to give him a little
loan so he could buy supplies. She'd done it more than
once, and the miners were grateful. Word had gotten
around, and not one man had failed to pay her back. Now
she'd started a fund for miners' wives and children and
every miner had gladly thrown in his spare coins.

. Another hand was dealt and the men were deep in play
when Otis slipped back into the room and nodded. Kansas
relaxed and turned her attention to her cards.

"Well, Otis, what do you think?" she asked later as she
counted her earnings and shoved them over to him. "Have
we enough now to build our own place?"

"Yes, ma'am. I expect we have," Otis answered. "Although it don't come to me just why you want to build
another place when you already own the Silver Spur."

Kansas sighed. How could she make Otis understand? "I
lived in a place like the Silver Spur once," she said. "I
swore that once I got out of there, I'd never go back." She
paused as if lost in a pain that was old and deep, then she
straightened her shoulders. "What I have in mind is not a
saloon, but a gambling casino like the great ones in San
Francisco. There won't be any"—she hesitated—"anything
else in my place, just gambling and good food. Do you
think something like that will succeed here?"

"If you're in charge of it, Miss Kansas, I have little
doubt it will," Otis said. He studied the lovely face and
gleaming hair. She seemed lost in her dreams. One graceful
hand held the golden locket she always wore, swinging it
absentmindedly on its slender chain. Otis thought of the
little bit of herself she'd revealed tonight and wondered
anew at the air of sadness that surrounded her.

"I'd best go," he said, getting to his feet. He settled a hat
over his graying hair and turned to her. "What are you
going to do about the Silver Spur?"

Kansas shrugged. "I don't know yet," she said.

Otis went out, closing the door behind him, and Kansas

sat on, pondering what she would do with the saloon. The ownership of it rested with surprising weight on her shoulders, and for a moment she felt once more a premonition that it would only bring her grief. She shivered delicately and rose. She was tired and becoming fanciful.

"Hold still, son. You'll start the bleeding again," Tobias ordered. He bent over the long, lanky form that tossed restlessly in its sleeping bag. Toby had been hard put to get the big form down out of the rocks and onto a flat grassy knoll where he could tend him. Then he'd been forced to spend the last two days seeing Cole didn't hurt himself as he thrashed around in a fever. Toby had gotten the bullet out and cauterized the wound, but he hadn't been able to cauterize the wounds that remained hidden, the ones that made his patient cry out a name to the night wind and thrash about on his pallet.

"Son, you got devils in you I can't do nothing about," Toby muttered as he went to put more wood on the fire. Hunkering down with a cup of hot coffee, he studied the wounded man. By rights, he should have left him for dead. The bullet wound had been serious enough to kill most men immediately, but it hadn't this man—and something about his courage and downright stubbornness had touched Toby. So he'd stayed to patch him up the best he could, and he reckoned he'd stay for the duration to nurse him or bury him, whichever one it took. Cole Slater, the wounded man had said his name was, and Toby spent the long, lonely hours by the campfire contemplating the young man, wondering who and what was back in Kansas. From the increased thrashing and grinding of teeth from the downed man, Toby doubted he'd ever live to see Kansas again.

Banking the fire, he checked his patient a final time and crawled into his own bedroll. The stars above were blue-white in their orbits, the night sky like black velvet. All around Toby lay the mountains he'd spent his life exploring and mining. He sighed contentedly. It had been a good life, lonely at times, but good enough to please a man like him. He could hardly remember the towns and people back East, they seemed so distant and unreal. This was reality, the cold night air, so crisp and fresh a man could breathe it in clear down to his toes. Pity a man like Cole Slater couldn't see the beauty of the mountains. Why would he hanker after the flat plains of Kansas when he was here in the Sierras with the wind soughing over the mountaintops and through the silver pines in a night melody that stirred his heart? Toby figured he was about as close to touching God up here as he ever would be. He drifted into sleep and awoke during the night to check on the wounded man. His fever had broken and he lay still, in a deep slumber.

"You just might make it, son," he muttered, not at all bothered that the man was unable to hear. "You sleep now. That's the best thing for you." He hurried back to the warmth of his bedroll. Once more he gazed at the star-filled sky. "I reckon we must be closer to God up here," he mumbled. "Otherwise, son, you just wouldn't have made it."

Chapter 6

"**Y**OU BETTER GIT over to the saloon, there's a heap a' trouble goin' on over there," Otis said, standing in the middle of Kansas's hotel room.

"What is it?" Kansas asked in alarm.

"I can't rightly say what got them gals stirred up, but everyone's shrieking at the top of their lungs." Otis looked disgusted.

"I'd better take a look," Kansas said, her voice reflecting the same disgust as she picked up her bag and shawl and headed down the stairs. Otis loped along behind. "No one ever told me how much trouble it would be to own a saloon," she muttered under her breath. "I think Quill may have won that last hand, after all. He must be laughing his head off at me."

She'd gained the sidewalk now. Her stride was long and impatient. Owning the Silver Spur Saloon really was a bigger headache than she was prepared for. Despite its thin veneer of elegance, it was still just a rough gold town saloon and whorehouse. Appalled at what she'd won, Kansas had released the girls from their services at once, but there had been such an outcry by them all, she'd quickly been made to know she would be ousting them from much needed jobs. What on earth was she to do? She had no intentions of earning money on the girls for such services. The thought of Molly and Rose and all the other women at Moody's Saloon back in Webster flashed through her mind and she bit her lip in vexation. She really had to solve this dilemma in which she found herself.

The Silver Spur lay just ahead of her now, but despite the urgency of the moment, Kansas stopped and stared at the hillside at the end of town. Her features softened momentarily as she contemplated the foundations and supporting beams rising against the flat blue sky. Without a roof or walls, it thrilled her just to look at it.

"The Kansas Palace is comin' along, ain't it?" Otis said, pausing to scratch at his unshaven jaw while he squinted an eye against the sun to study the hillside. He'd used the name that most every miner in town had adopted for the large structure. "Yes, sir, it's going to be mighty fine, mighty fine, indeed, when it's finished."

"It's going to be grand!" Kansas said, with pride. She still couldn't believe that the fancy gambling house belonged to her. She stood imagining the Palace when it was completed and furnished with all the fine things she planned to import for it.

Her pleasurable daydreams were interrupted by a loud screech emanating from the saloon and heard clear out in the street. Kansas and Otis exchanged a quick troubled glance and raced for the saloon door.

"What's going on in here?" Kansas demanded before the door had even swung to behind her. Her running entry had carried her to the middle of the room, where a space had been cleared by the cheering miners and two women rolled on the floor, locked in deadly combat. Even as Kansas glanced around, taking in the leering men who egged the combatants on and the other whores who screamed advice to their favorite, one woman drew back a fist and landed it fully on the nose of the other. Blood splattered everywhere, and the injured girl released her hold on the other.

"You've hurt me!" she screamed in outrage.

"Yes, and I'll hurt you some more, Reeny Whittaker, if you ever call me names again, you silly little bitch!" the other woman said, getting to her feet. Her chest heaved as she wheezed in air and she planted her hands on ample hips. Long blond hair, generously shot with gray, spilled over her plump shoulders.

"Get her, girls," the fallen woman cried from the floor, and several of the other whores took menacing steps forward. Outnumbered, the aging whore seemed unconcerned that she might be beaten. Gamely she planted her back against the bar, doubled her fists, and faced her opponents defiantly.

"Ladies, ladies," Kansas said tentatively. No one listened to her. The men whistled and called out when it looked like another fight was about to issue.

"Otis," Kansas called, motioning to him to do something.

Otis pulled out his gun, aimed it at the ceiling, and pulled the trigger. The unexpected sound of a gunshot brought the room to dead silence. All eyes turned to Kansas and Otis.

"Ladies," Kansas said crisply, quick to use her small advantage. "We don't fight in public. Now someone tell me what's going on."

"Maybe you don't fight in public, Miss McKay," the woman at the bar said, "but I ain't standing still for any young snit to insult me."

Reeny got up off the floor, her face smeared with blood. "I wasn't insulting you on purpose, Ellie," she flared, her voice somewhat muffled by the handkerchief pressed to her nose. "I only told you the truth."

"Yeah," another girl cried. "She was only saying what we all think. We elected Reeny to be the one to tell you."

"You're too old and too fat. The men don't want you no more," a slender dark-haired girl said, and ducked as Ellie made a swipe at her.

"We've been carrying you for weeks now, but it's got to stop," Reeny went on. "We can't make a living that way."

"You're all gettin' rich off these miners and you know it," Ellie countered. "If you ain't, then it's 'cause you ain't much good at your job."

The shrill denials of the other whores mingled with the deep bass of the miners, who quickly and gallantly defended their expertise.

"All right, quiet down," Kansas ordered.

Into the silence came a voice shaky and pathetic. "If I leave here, I won't have no place else to go," Ellie said. "I'll be out on the street with the whorin' Indian squaws. I ain't aimin' to stoop that low. I got my pride." But for all her defiant words, Ellie's face had crumbled in despair.

The miners shifted from foot to foot, mumbling among themselves. The mood had changed. Everyone was embarrassed. What had started out as a cat fight to be bet on and enjoyed had turned into a depressing reminder of the tenuous state of women in the harsh West. Shamed, Ellie stood with her head bowed, her gray-streaked, tangled hair nearly hiding her ravaged face.

"Didn't you save back any of your earnings?" Kansas asked gently.

Mutely Ellie shook her head. "All's I've got is a few mine claims the men give me when they didn't have the money to pay."

"And you took them?" the other girls hooted. "We wondered what kept the men coming back to you."

Kansas glared at the women warningly and turned back to Ellie. "Are the claims any good?"

"I reckon not," Ellie admitted, sniffing defensively. "Leastways not to anyone but me. I kind a' hang on to 'em for the memories, you know?"

Kansas found herself warming to the woman. "I know," she said gently, one hand going automatically to touch the gold locket she still wore.

"What should she do, Miss McKay?" Reeny asked, and her voice was not unkind as she shamefacedly avoided looking at Ellie. "You're the boss here. What do you say?"

"We'll discuss this privately," Kansas said, glancing at the avid listeners. "Drinks are on the house, boys. Belly up!"

Placing an arm around Ellie's fat shoulders, Kansas led her to a table in the back corner. The other women crowded to the bar with the men, their laughter shrill and mocking as they cast bright, malicious glances at Ellie. She'd grown old and fat, something few of them could foresee happening to them, so there was little sympathy. Reeny, however, followed Kansas and Ellie to the corner table.

"I'm sorry, Ellie," Reeny said, standing stiffly beside the older woman. Her nose had stopped bleeding and she stood twisting the handkerchief in her hands.

"It's all right, Reeny," Kansas said, liking the young woman. She had a quiet steadfast dignity despite her profession. "Sit down and have a drink with Ellie."

"Eleanor, if you please!" the older woman said, with elaborate haughtiness.

"Eleanor," Kansas repeated good-naturedly, and waved to the bartender to bring them a bottle and glasses. When it came, she poured a glass of whiskey for each woman.

"You're not having any?" Reeny asked.

Kansas shook her head. "I never drink," she explained absently. "Now, can you tell me quietly what was behind all this."

"Yes, ma'am." Reeny began her account.

It was surprisingly fair to Ellie, yet presented the concern the other girls had about the aging woman. As Kansas listened, her respect for the young woman increased. Reeny was obviously intelligent and trying hard to be fair. Ellie, on the other hand, had had her pride hurt too deeply to care what was fair or right.

As Reeny finished her tale, Ellie drew herself up and

rubbed her cheek. "Right cheek, left cheek," she muttered, "why do you burn? Cursed be she that doth me any harm."

"Oh, yes, there's one more thing," Reeny said, casting an anxious look at Ellie.

"Beware," Ellie told the younger girl. "Bleeding from the nose foretells"—she paused dramatically—"death."

"You can't scare me, Ellie," Reeny said dismissively. "You hit me in the nose and that's the reason it bled." She turned back to Kansas. "Ellie casts spells on people, or so she claims. She drives away the men and frightens the other girls with her crazy superstitions."

"I'm not crazy!" Ellie snapped with such outrage that both women knew she wasn't. "My momma passed on things to me, things that I know to be true, and I've tried to warn the other girls, so they can protect themselves. But no more, missy. You'll have to do without my help from now on."

"Ellie," Kansas interjected before another fight began, "is there anything else you could do? . . . Besides—well, you know . . . Can you sew or keep house or cook?"

"I can do all them things," Ellie answered. "I can also sum up numbers and read a little." She looked a little sheepish. "My writin' ain't so good. I make some of my letters backward."

"Well, you see, you can do lots of things," Kansas cried, encouraged. "Maybe you can get another job—like working in the general store or housekeeping or being a maid. Several men have brought their families to town and are building them beautiful big houses. They'll need someone to help keep them clean or to cook for them. Would you be willing to do something like that?"

Ellie glanced back at the huddle of men at the bar. "I'll miss this," she mumbled, and a tear rolled down her wrinkled, plump cheek. Then she raised her chin and straightened her shoulders. "But if no one here wants me anymore, I guess I can just go on with my life elsewhere."

"Good for you," Kansas said, relief washing through her. She hadn't realized how much concern she'd felt for the older woman. Somehow, Ellie reminded her of Molly. Kansas had sent for her mother three months before, but word had come back that Molly had died and was buried in potter's field in Webster. The news had hurt Kansas more than she could have guessed. Molly had been the only relative she'd possessed. Now there was no one . . . unless her father really was alive. Now more than ever she wished Molly had told her more about her father. Kansas realized anew that mother and daughter had never been able to come to terms with old hurts and misunderstandings. Now they never could. Looking at Ellie, Kansas felt compelled to do something for her.

"I'll check with some of the men who have families here," she assured the other woman. "In the meantime, you can keep your room here until we find something for you. You can help Riley behind the bar."

"That's mighty kind of you," Ellie said grudgingly. Her keen eyes scrutinized Kansas's young face. "You've loved a man and lost him," she said, then grasped one of Kansas's hands and bent over the palm. She raised her gaze to Kansas's face. "Don't despair," she intoned. "He's here now."

A chill worked its way down Kansas's spine. "What?" She jerked her hand away, unable to repress a quick glance around the saloon. She wasn't aware of the glimmer of hope that sprang to life in her eyes, then quickly died. "You're wrong. He's married another," she said softly, then shook her head briskly. "Besides, that's behind me. I'll inquire tomorrow about a place for you."

"Mark well Friday night's dream," Ellie said, and mysteriously would say no more.

Kansas wasn't sure whether to shake the woman to have her complete her chant or to laugh at her. She did neither, for Everett Howell, the son of a trader and a young hellion himself, approached the table with two other men. His hat was cupped against his chest.

" 'Scuse me, ma'am," he said, weaving nervously from one foot to the other. He'd obviously been drinking, but his young face shone with good-natured intention. "The—the other men and me—well, we took up this collection for Ellie there. She don't deserve to just be kicked out on the street without a dollar to her name." He thrust the hat toward Ellie.

"Thank you, Ev. You always was a decent young man." Ellie took the hat and counted the coins and bills. She raised a smiling face to his, her eyes sultry, her voice low and intimate. "If you want to go up to my room with me, I'll thank you properly," she said.

"Well . . . uh . . . ma'am, I'd like to," he answered gallantly, "but Reeny and me've already made a deal."

"I'll go wash up and get ready," Reeny said, smiling up at him. "I won't be long." She disappeared toward the stairs.

Disgruntled, Ellie watched her go, then plopped herself back into a chair.

"Are you all right?" Kansas asked.

"Yeah. I'll survive." Ellie sighed and poured herself another drink.

" 'Scuse me, Miss Kansas," Ev was saying. "I was just wondering if you'd honor me with a dance?" The tinny clunk of a waltz came to them. He stood waiting, his body held stiffly erect, his young face eager and uncertain. Kansas guessed he'd had a good deal to drink that day and was on the verge of collapse, but in light of his kindness to Ellie, she could hardly turn him down.

"I'd be pleased to dance with you," she said, rising and following him into the center of the room, where other couples twirled energetically to the desultory waltz. Ev was weaving alarmingly as Kansas went into his arms, but he maintained a clumsy footing. Before too long, he had sagged against Kansas's slender form. Frantically she looked around and spotted Reeny on the stairs.

"Come on, Ev," she grunted. "It's time you went to bed." Leaning heavily against her, the young trapper stumbled toward the stairs.

"Reeny, help me get him upstairs," she called, and the young woman ran down the stairs to lend her support to Ev.

As Kansas wrestled his arm over her shoulder, she chanced to glance back at the roomful of miners. A tall, lean form, with broad shoulders and a natural slouch, was moving toward the door. Kansas's heart constricted and she felt her breath catch in her throat.

"Cole!" she murmured, then blinked as the tall man disappeared without her catching a glimpse of his face.

"What did you say, honey?" Reeny asked, and Kansas shook her head.

"Nothing," she answered.

"You look as if you've seen a ghost," Reeny insisted, her eyes wide and full of caring.

"Just my imagination," Kansas said dismissively, but as she helped wrestle Ev Howell's limp frame up the stairs, she couldn't help remembering Ellie's words that Kansas's lost love was near. For the rest of the night, all the painful memories of Cole Slater could not be denied. They came pressing in on her . . . and once again she was an innocent young girl beside a creek tasting the heady kisses of a first love.

Kansas! Damn her! Damn her all to hell and back. Cole's big fist slashed out, smashing into the corner posts of the saloon porch.

"Take it easy, son," Toby called from behind him. "You ain't healed yet from your other wounds. You ain't got no call to do yourself another injury."

Cole swung round to glare at the old miner, and the look on his face was one of such pain that Toby fell silent.

Cursing bitterly, Cole stalked out into the street. Two miners passed him, the shoulder of one slamming into Cole. He didn't even flinch from the jarring pain. He turned toward the miners, crouching. His fists were clenched into balls resembling sledgehammers, his narrowed eyes mere slits that spat anger and a need for revenge.

"Look, mister, I'm sorry," the miner said, backing up in alarm. "I've had a bit to drink and didn't see you."

"Come on you lily-livered, snot-nosed cowards," Cole challenged. He knew he was baiting them, but his need to fight, to pound someone and be pounded back, was too much.

His words were having the desired effect. The two men exchanged glances, then launched themselves at him. The big man caught the full force of their attack. He did nothing to protect himself, to ward off their blows. He stood with his feet solidly planted in the dusty street, and his fists swung almost methodically.

He hit one miner in the chin and felt the bone give. It gave him no satisfaction to know he'd broken a man's jaw. The pain of his own split knuckles, the smell of blood pouring down his own face, gave him no release from the pain he'd felt at seeing Kansas McKay lead a drunken young cowboy up the stairs to her room. Blows rained on his chest and midsection; blood seeped through the bandages Toby had so painstakingly tied over his wound, and still Cole didn't stop.

Mouth gaping in disbelief at this man's cussedness, Toby watched as Cole battled with the two men. What fool would pick a fight with a miner, much less two? he wondered. Everyone knew miners were a tough lot. Toby watched Cole slugging away, never even flinching at the blows his big body received, and finally understanding that Cole meant to stand there and fight till he was dead, Toby took out his gun and fired it to the heavens. Startled, the men turned to stare at him. Toby leveled his gun at the two miners, though he hated to do it to his own kind.

"Go on, get out of here. Fight's over," he growled.

The two young miners hesitated, eyeing first Toby and then Cole, who only stood in the middle of the street, his head bowed, his shoulders heaving. As if sensing they were watching, he raised his head and brought up his fists, clenching them into weapons of steel. They'd had enough taste of those—and grudgingly they conceded he was a hell of a fighter. They'd never met a man who was still standing after taking on the two of them.

"Git, I said! Fight's over." Toby waved his gun to emphasize his point.

Exchanging glances, the two men shrugged. "He's crazy, anyway," one of them said, and putting an arm around each other in comradely support the two men staggered toward a saloon.

Toby sheathed his gun and walked over to Cole. The big man was weaving in his tracks, and the front of his shirt was soaked with blood from his wound. "Come on, son," Toby said, and hooked Cole's arm over his shoulder. Together they stumbled back to the stables, where they'd rented bed space in a back stall on the fresh hay.

Settling Cole on his bedroll, Toby cautiously pulled away the bandage and looked at the wound. The bleeding had stopped and the blood was coagulating. He grunted in satisfaction. The dang fool hadn't done himself in this time.

"Why you ever picked that fight with those two men, I'll never know," he fussed, dabbing at the blood on Cole's face. The skin was broken over one cheekbone and the skin around one eye was already turning blue. "Were you trying to get yourself killed?" Cole only moaned and rolled away from Toby's administrations. Snorting in disgust, Toby threw down the rag.

"Well, I ain't goin' t' wet nurse you anymore," he declared, and crawled into his own bedroll.

But as he lay thinking back over the evening, his puzzlement grew. Cole had offered to buy him a drink before they parted. Randomly they'd chosen the Silver Spur. Generously Cole had bought a bottle, although Toby was pretty sure it was his last dollar. They'd sat at a back table, washing the trail dust from their throats and enjoying the color and movement of other people. Then those two dance hall girls had started fighting and another woman, just about the prettiest woman Toby had ever laid eyes on, came in and broke it up.

Come to think of it, that's when Cole had changed. He'd been lolling back in his chair watching the fight, and suddenly he was on his feet, muttering something about Kansas. He'd stared at the pretty woman as if transfixed, and Toby had thought nothing of it. If he'd been a little younger and had extra money, he'd have been taken by her, too. Cole had seemed to calm down. He'd sat back down and, ignoring his drink, had spent the rest of the time watching the gold-haired woman as she chatted with the two whores. It wasn't until she'd danced with the young cowboy and taken him upstairs that Cole had gone into a rage. Slowly Toby pieced together the bits of things Cole had cried out in his fever and, finally, he turned to the big man, his expression saying he almost knew the answer without being told.

"Who's Kansas?" he asked the broad back across from him. He had little doubt Cole was still awake. A man didn't lie that tense when he was sleeping. "Was she that woman back there at the Silver Spur?" There was a long silence, and Toby thought he meant not to answer—then Cole took a deep, shuddering breath. His voice was bleak and harsh when he spoke.

"I always knew that someday it would happen just like this." His voice was devoid of expression. "I always knew I'd find her just this way! Her mother was a whore. She couldn't help becoming one herself." Toby lay wondering what kind of woman was this who could bring a big man to his knees when a whole handful of murderers hadn't succeeded. He glanced at the lean man on the other pallet. The wide shoulders heaved. The lanky body trembled as with the ague.

"Damn her! Damn her to hell!" Cole grated. There was so much fury and such pain in the words that at first Toby feared for Cole, then as he lay thinking, he feared for a woman named Kansas.

"I've got a claim up in the hills," he said when Cole's anger had cooled and he lay heaving a long, exhausted sigh. "I'd like it some if you'd go with me. I could use some help, and it'll give you time to heal." There was no answer, but he'd expected none. "We'll leave at morning light." He took the continued silence to be a confirmation. Troubled and sorry for the big man, Toby rolled over and closed his eyes. He guessed there'd be no rest for Cole this night.

Chapter 7

"*H*OW'S IT COMING, Davy?" Kansas called up to one of the men who was swinging his hammer in the rafters of her new establishment.

Davy paused long enough to grin down good-naturedly. He'd grown used to her constant visits and questions. Now he kind of got a kick out of finishing each phase of the building just to see her pretty face light up. "Just fine, Miss McKay," he yelled. "How do you like what we've done so far?"

Kansas took a few steps backward and shielded her eyes with one hand. "It's beautiful!" she cried, taking in the long, clean lines of her new gambling house. "It's much grander than I'd imagined."

"Well, the Palace has got to look like a palace," he said, teasing her about the name the town had already given the impressive structure. "We can't disappoint folks."

"I don't think we will, Davy," Kansas cried happily. "I don't think we will."

Then, reminded of her chore, she gave a final wave and turned down the hillside toward the Silver Spur. In her bag, she carried a sheaf of papers, the same ones that had played such an important role in her poker game with Quill Ramsey. Kansas's bright smile dimmed as she thought about the vengeful gambler.

Contrary to what everyone thought, he hadn't left town. He'd moved down the street and taken up residence in the Bloody Guts, a saloon notorious for its rough reputation. Before long, he'd managed to win that saloon from its hapless owner. Rumors had it that he'd cheated, playing with a marked deck, but few men wanted to confront him with their accusations. Quill's temper was short and murderous. He'd already killed one man who'd had the audacity to challenge him. Quill had hired bodyguards, rough men who were too lazy to dig silver from the ground, but who were not above waylaying unsuspecting miners in dark alleys to relieve them of their earnings.

Kansas shivered, aware of how close she'd come in her dealings with the evil man. Otis had warned her that Quill might yet seek revenge, so she'd taken extra care. Stashed beside the papers in her bag was the little derringer she'd been forced to use at her poker game with Quill. Furthermore, Otis had declared himself her personal bodyguard. At first Kansas had been touched by his concern, then she'd begun to chafe at the restrictions this had placed on her. Lately she'd taken to slipping away from Otis's watchful eye, as she had this morning. Now she'd have to endure his reproachful face the rest of the day. It was worth it, though, she thought, glancing around at the hills and town. This was the best time of day, before the hot sun had blistered everything and people had begun stirring so the dust rose in the streets and hung over the town like a cloud.

Her slender fingers felt the edge of papers in her bag, and Kansas put Quill Ramsey and his thugs out of her mind. She was on her way to the Silver Spur Saloon to perform a most happy task, and she had no wish to sour her enjoyment.

"So there you are," Otis snapped when she pushed through the swinging doors of the saloon. His seamed face

was creased with worry as he looked at the slender young
woman. She wore a gown of plain, unadorned blue, and her
hair, held back by a ribbon of matching blue, hung down
her back well below her waist. The honey-gold curls
gleamed in the bright morning light streaming through the
windows. With her scrubbed face and bright, expectant
eyes, she looked like a schoolgirl—except that her lush
figure testified she was a full-grown woman.

She reminded him of a woman he'd once known long
ago. Today, though, Otis didn't let his pleasure at the sight
of her show. He was worried about her. He'd heard rumors
that Quill had boasted about what he planned to do to her.
Otis had tried to tell her, but she wasn't taking Quill's
threats seriously enough. He scowled at Kansas.

"Don't worry about me so much, Otis," she admonished
him. "I only walked up to the site to see how the builders
were doing." She paused, waiting for him to ask questions.
He was as excited about the Kansas Palace as she was, but
he wasn't going to be deterred today. "It's looking wonderful. You should see what they've done." He remained
silent and reproachful.

Kansas shrugged and glanced around. "Has Reeny come
down yet?" she asked, running her fingers along her bag in
anticipation.

"She was here a minute ago," Otis said. "There she is!"
He nodded toward the piano, where Reeny stood talking to
Ben. He nodded his head in agreement and launched into a
popular ballad that was softer than his usual tinny fare.
"Reeny!" Otis called, and waved her over.

Catching sight of Kansas, the young woman turned toward the bar. She was dressed in a sensible modest dress
of sprigged muslin. Her face was scrubbed of makeup and
her dark hair was braided and wound demurely around her
head. Reeny wasn't like the other prostitutes who fre-
quented gold towns, Kansas thought, wondering where
she'd come from and how she'd happened into the busi-

ness of prostitution. She longed to ask, but was fearful of offending her.

"Good morning." Reeny greeted Kansas quietly, but with genuine warmth. During the past few weeks, since Kansas had intervened with Ellie, she had become friends with Reeny and Ellie as well as the other girls. Now she motioned Reeny to a table and sat down across from her.

"Would you like Riley to bring you some coffee?" Reeny offered, and started to rise again.

Quickly Kansas put a hand on her sleeve. "Stay here," she said. "I don't need coffee, but I do have some wonderful news to tell you."

"What is it?" Reeny asked, settling back in the chair. Her face was expectant.

"I hope you'll think it's good news, too," Kansas said, suddenly shy. This had seemed such a good idea at first; now she worried the dance hall girl might think it charity.

"I can hardly wait to hear it!" Reeny answered, and her normally serene eyes were alive with curiosity. Her face was alight with humor and well-wishing. She had no inkling the good news was for her.

Taking a deep breath, Kansas drew the papers from her purse and laid them on the table. Giving them a shove toward Reeny, she grinned delightedly. "This is for you and the rest of the girls," she said all in a breathless rush.

"For us?" Reeny asked, picking up the sheaf of papers. "What is it?"

"The deed to the Silver Spur Saloon," Kansas said. "Now, it belongs to you."

"I don't understand," Reeny said, stunned by what she was hearing.

"Look, I don't really own this saloon," Kansas said, trying to explain her feelings. "I won it in a poker game. You girls have been here working every night, trying to earn your living. If you don't have to share your profits with anyone else, you'll make more money. The more money you earn, the sooner you can"—she paused, aware of what she'd been about to say and of how it might offend—"retire!" she finished lamely.

Reeny sat studying the papers, unable to believe what she'd heard. "You can't just give away a saloon like the Silver Spur," she said disbelievingly.

"Yes, I can," said Kansas, her tone adamant. "I've already signed it over to you all. Ellie, too. Of course, I've given you a little larger share. Someone has to be in charge. I think you're more than capable and honest. You won't cheat the girls the way Quill did."

Slowly Reeny refolded the papers, her slim fingers carefully creasing each fold, and at last she raised her face to Kansas. "I don't know how to thank you," she said simply. Her dark eyes were suspiciously moist. "Why would you do this for us? The miners say you're not one of us."

Kansas grinned again, happy to hear the miners had at last accepted the fact that she was a gambling lady and not a soiled dove. In the beginning a few hadn't believed her, but Otis had quickly persuaded them. Kansas turned her attention back to Reeny's words, and her grin faded. It was, she realized, time to be perfectly honest. Taking a deep breath she met Reeny's steadfast gaze.

"No, I'm not one of you," she answered softly, "but my mother was." Her expression turned fiercely protective as she continued. "She was crossing on the Oregon Trail. My—my father and she were separated . . . and she had no other way to buy food or housing for us." For the first time, Kansas began to believe that maybe her mother hadn't been able to help her situation, and she felt an easing of the old bitterness she'd felt toward Molly.

"I understand," Reeny answered. "My parents and I came out on the Oregon Trail. They died halfway across from smallpox. The good folks of the train were going to abandon us at Fort MacKenzie, but when I became the camp whore, the men decided they could help us, after all.

Their wives didn't understand at first, and when they did"—she paused, and Kansas could sense the pain—"they wouldn't speak to me anymore. They'd draw their skirts away when I came near as if I'd make them dirty somehow. But they helped with my brothers and sisters. It made them feel charitable, and I thought I could endure anything, as long as I could get my family to safety. Once I reached Oregon, I found a childless couple who were happy to take them in. They didn't, of course, want me." She laughed, a short, bitter laugh.

"You know the funny part about it all? I think those wives on the wagon train were secretly glad I was along. It meant their menfolk didn't make demands on them at night. I discovered something on that trip. We all serve a useful purpose, after all. I decided right then and there, I'd never be ashamed of what I am."

Kansas could see the dignity in the other woman and thought about her own background. How hard she'd tried to maintain her pride in the face of the town's disapproval and condemnation. Suddenly she no longer felt alone. There was a sense of kinship with this pretty dark-haired whore sitting across from her. Impulsively Kansas reached across the table and took Reeny's hand in a warm clasp.

"I think we're going to become good friends," she said, and was rewarded with a shy smile.

"I'd like that," Reeny said. "It's been a long time since I had a good friend."

"How's Ellie making out with Mrs. Simpson at the boardinghouse?" Kansas asked, aware the moment had become too intense.

Reeny, too, seemed happy for the shift in conversation. Eyes gleaming, she shook her head. "Not real well, from what I gather. You know Ellie and her spells."

"Oh, no," Kansas groaned. "I'm running out of places willing to hire her. What has she done this time? Maybe it's not so bad."

"It seems she has this thing about eggs. Mrs. Simpson sent her out back rather late one evening to gather eggs, but Ellie wouldn't bring them into the house because it was already dark. She claims it's a bad omen. Then there's the singing before breakfast. Mrs. Simpson was practicing her solo one morning before church, and Ellie had a fit. Claimed she'd cry before supper. When Mrs. Simpson received word later in the day that her sister had died, she fell to weeping, and you know Ellie. Not being the soul of discretion, she was quick to point out Mrs. Simpson had brought it on herself. Mrs. Simpson says Ellie's a heathen—and right now she's intent on saving her soul."

"Oh, dear," Kansas said worriedly, thinking of the clashes that must be occurring between the highly religious Mrs. Simpson and the superstitious Ellie. "It wasn't a very good match, I'm afraid," she muttered. "But I just didn't have anyone else."

"Ellie's okay for now. Ada Simpson is set on bringing Ellie into the fold, as she puts it. Ellie says she does a fair amount of praying over her. It's a question of who will give up first."

The two women looked at each other, and suddenly the picture of Mrs. Simpson hovering over the recalcitrant Ellie praying for all she was worth, seemed too amusing. They burst into giggles. Finally Kansas calmed herself and rose.

"I must go. I have other errands to run, and then I must prepare for tonight."

"Are you coming back here now that you no longer own the saloon, or will you return to gambling in your room?"

"I'll come here if you don't mind," Kansas said. "What percentage do I have to pay the house?"

Shock washed over Reeny's face, until she realized Kansas was teasing her. Her somber face lit briefly in an answering grin. "For you, nothing," she answered pertly. "You're a good friend of the boss's."

*   *   *

"You feelin' any better?" Toby grunted as a tall, lanky shadow blocked the sun. He didn't have to look up to know who was there. Cole Slater had been chomping at the bit the last few days. With his wound reopened from the fight, infection had set in and a fever had raged through the rangy drifter's body, until Toby had despaired of his making it. But he had, and Toby had just about decided Cole Slater was plumb too ornery to die. Now his big, rawboned body was wasted from fever and his strength was gone. Cole was not a good patient. At first he'd raged against Toby, then against himself and every god that must have lived in the heavens. Only one name was never uttered even in his worst fevers—the name of Kansas McKay.

With grim determination, Cole had spent the past few days dragging himself out to the rock in front of the cave where they sheltered. On shaky legs he'd forced himself to walk the length of level ground that comprised their camp, then he'd climbed down the trails and back up again, sweat standing out on his brow, his whole body trembling from the unaccustomed exertions. Now he stood over Toby, slapping at his pants leg impatiently.

"I'm leaving now, old man," he said. His blue eyes squinted against the sun, scanning the trail below. Toby wondered if he'd ever known peace.

"I was hoping you'd stay some and help me with my claim," Toby answered.

"I'm not much of a digger." Cole picked up some pebbles and rolled them thoughtlessly in his big palm.

"I kind of figured you owed me," Toby said, knowing he was being unfair, yet disappointed that he'd be alone again. He liked this big, quiet man with the troubled eyes.

"I reckon I do," Cole acknowledged, "but I can't stay, old-timer. I'll have to pay you back some other way."

"I'm sorry to see you go, son," Toby said in defeat, not looking up from the shovel he was mending. Behind him a dark tunnel cut into the hillside, its depth disappointingly shallow. "You ought to stay until you're a little stronger."

"I'm strong enough," Cole said dismissively, and Toby forbore to argue with him.

"Where're you headed?" Toby said instead.

"I don't know." Picking up a rock, Cole flung it down the mountainside. His narrowed gaze followed its descent, and his head jerked up as he spied two figures making their stealthy way up the steep path.

"You've got company," he said quietly and something in his voice warned Toby to remain calm.

"Anybody we know?" Toby asked, easing his shovel down on the ground and slowly reaching for his rifle.

Cole grunted. "Looks like your two friends who rode up yesterday and offered to take your claim off your hands."

Toby was surprised. He hadn't known Cole was aware of them. He'd been asleep back in the rocks where they'd set up their camp.

"I told 'em I wasn't selling," Toby said.

"Maybe they're still buying," Cole said, and eased his gun free of its holster. "Reckon they know I'm here?"

Toby glanced up at him in surprise. "I don't reckon they do. They couldn't see the camp from here."

"That's what I figured," Cole said, easing down on his belly. He glanced back at his rifle resting in its case on the pack mule. If he made a move for it now, he'd give himself away. Right now the two men coming up the mountainside expected to find an old man alone. Cole motioned to Toby, warning him to silence, then signaled his intentions to move behind some nearby rocks. Toby nodded in understanding, then settled back on the ground, his rifle conspicuously handy.

Picking up the broken shovel, he concentrated on mending it. He knew he was the bait. From the nearby rocks came the faintest metallic sound as Cole eased back the hammer on his pistol. If either raised a gun to shoot Toby from ambush, Cole would get him first. Toby sat quietly, listening to the sounds of the two men approaching. There was a lengthy pause, then the sound of a lone horse continuing up the trail. A horseman rode into the clearing. He was a lean, wiry man, with his hat pulled low over his eyes. A dark stubble of beard camouflaged his lower face. He had called himself Rod Farley.

"Howdy," he called when he drew near to Toby. In spite of his smile and open manner, there was something stealthy and deadly about the man. Watching from the rocks, Cole studied the man.

"Howdy," Toby answered. "Are you lost?"

"Lost?" The man's lean face registered surprise and wariness.

"I figured we said all we had to say the other day when you was up here." Cole could hear the edginess in Toby's voice and guessed the old man was feeling anxious.

"Oh . . ." The man seemed to relax, although Toby noticed he kept his hand resting on his thigh—not far from his holstered gun. "Sometimes a man changes his mind. I figured I'd just ride up here and see if you've done any mind changing." His lips drew back in what Cole guessed was supposed to be a smile.

Cole swung his gaze away from the smiling man and studied the edge of rocks along the steep path. Farley's friend had to make a showing pretty quick. Carefully Cole made his way down the ridge of rocks until he could overlook the path. "I ain't much on changing my mind," Toby said.

"That ain't a real smart attitude for an old man like you to take," Farley said. "Your friends down the line sold to me, and I kind of figured it'd be right nice to own this here whole mountainside."

"Like I said before, I ain't interested in selling," Toby said. Farley's gun hand twitched, but Toby was too fast for him. He brought up the barrel of his rifle and pointed it at Farley's chest. "I think you better turn right around and ride on back down the mountain, son."

"I'd say you're being kind of inhospitable toward a new neighbor," said Farley, stalling for time. He smiled when a shot rang out, tightening the reins on his prancing horse. The humor died from his face when he saw the old man still sitting on the ground, his rifle steady. There was no sign he'd been wounded. Farley cursed; Ed had missed.

The rattle of stones on the path made him swing around. A tall, rangy man stood on the path, his gray eyes as deadly as the bore of the long-barreled Peacemaker .45 he clutched in his big fist. Further down the trail, Farley could see Ed slumped on the ground, his arms outflung, his eyes staring sightlessly at the sky. Farley felt the sweat form under his hatband and roll down the small of his back.

"Looks like you'd better ride on back down the way you came, stranger," the big man said. His tone was mild. Only those slitted eyes made Farley relax his gun hand and move it away from his holster. Looking from the old man to the big stranger, each of them watching him with a hint of amusement, each of them pointing their weapons at his chest, Farley had little choice.

"You haven't heard the last of me, old man," he snarled at Toby, and spurred his horse. Eyes rolling, the nervous beast whinnied in pain, then broke into a desperate head-long dash down the mountain.

"Dang fool's going to kill his horse if he rides it down like that," Toby observed, coming to stand beside Cole.

"He didn't even stop for his friend," Cole said. "Reckon I'll have to haul him into town myself."

"That was mighty nice of you," Toby said, holding out a hand to Cole. "They was fixin' to kill me. I don't know how I can repay you."

"I owed you, remember," Cole said, and there was a glint of humor in his eyes. He glanced back down the trail. "He'll be back, you know."

"Yeah, I expect he will," Toby agreed.

Cole mounted. "Watch your back, old man."

"Much obliged." Toby watched Cole lead his pack mule down the trail. He was going to miss Cole Slater.

The big man pulled his horse to a stop and looked at Toby. "You need any supplies while I'm in town?"

Toby grinned. "I could use a new shovel," he said holding up the remnants of the one he'd tried to mend. "Better make it two."

"All right." Cole kicked his horse into a walk.

"Better get some more beans and flour while you're at it," Toby called. "And bacon if you've a mind to."

Cole didn't answer, but Toby knew he'd heard him. Grinning, he took off his beat-up hat and scratched his balding head. Hot damn! He had a partner. He turned back to the hillside where he'd been digging. He had a good feeling about this claim. "You're going to make us rich, Silver Sue," he crowed, naming the mine on the spot. "Yes, sir, I'm going to be a rich man. Maybe I'll go into town one of these nights and buy me a spell with a woman." He thought fleetingly of the woman named Kansas and immediately discarded the idea. He pitied any man who spent time with Kansas. He had an idea he'd be facing Cole Slater's guns before the night was over.

"I tell you, he shot him in the back," Rod Farley claimed to the knot of men listening. "Poor Ed never had a chance."

"Are you sure it wasn't you what shot him in the back?" somebody called, and the men around him laughed nervously. Farley fixed the man with a hard look, and the man blanched.

"I was just funnin', Farley," he said, looking around for some support from those that had laughed at his joke. Everyone looked the other way and shuffled away from him.

"Git out 'a here," Farley said, "afore I shoot you." He took his gun from his holster and laid it on the bar.

"I didn't mean nothin' by it, Farley. I swear!" the man mumbled, leaping to his feet.

"Git!" snarled Farley, and the man turned and ran from the saloon, expecting at any moment to feel Farley's bullet in his back.

Farley paid him scant attention. At a nod from Quill Ramsey, he continued with his version of what happened up in the mountains. "I say we can't let those miners up there shoot men in the back. We ought to go up there and hang him. It'll be a good reminder to others who come in here that although we ain't got a sheriff, we've got our own law and order."

"Yeah," the men cried in response.

They'd been well fortified with free whiskey from Ramsey's bar, and now they were feeling camaraderie for the thin-bodied gunslinger who worked for him. Some of them guessed what Farley and Ed had been doing up in the mountains. Rumors had been rampant that Quill's men were scaring miners off their claims—or scaring them into selling for little or nothing of their real value.

"Someone's riding into town," a man called from the porch. "Looks like he's bringing in a body." The men at the bar all scrambled for a spot at the window or door from which they could watch the proceedings.

"That's him!" Farley cried, and grabbing his pearl-handled gun, he took aim.

"You ain't goin' to shoot him from here, are you?" the miners around him asked. It was obvious they found such action reprehensible and cowardly.

Farley glanced at Quill, who was frowning at him. Quill had bought his hired gun, and Farley knew he'd have to prove his mettle. He holstered his gun and moved toward the door.

Cole could feel eyes watching him from the saloon windows, but he looked neither to the left nor the right. Without a town sheriff, he had little idea where to take the body, so he rode through the streets to the stable. By the time he'd dismounted, a crowd had gathered.

"What've you got there, mister?" A man stepped up to the packhorse where the gunman's body was tied.

Cole recognized the man from the general store. "I got a bushwhacker who tried to shoot my partner back up the mountain there." Cole loosened the rope holding the man, and the body slid into the dust of the street.

"That's Ed Walker, one of Quill Ramsey's men," someone said, identifying him.

"You say he tried to bushwhack you?" the storekeeper asked. "Farley's been claiming all afternoon that you shot Ed in the back." The man squatted down and examined the body, noting the chest wound. "Looks like you fought him fair and square," he said, standing up and holding out a hand. "I'm Norm Roberts. I own the general store over there. And this is Fred White. He owns the hotel. We didn't catch your name."

"You!" a voice rang out, and everyone turned to look at Rod Farley. The men surrounding him had heard Norm's words about the chest wound. Infuriated at being proved a liar, Farley was pressing to save face. "I say you shot Ed from ambush when he was unarmed. You murdered him in cold blood."

Cole's face tightened and a white band of anger formed around his mouth. "And I say you're a liar," he said. His voice was low and quiet, but every man there heard him. "You tried to set a trap for my partner. You thought he was an old man alone. Well, hear this, Farley. The next time you come up that mountain, be prepared to die the same way your friend did."

Farley knew he should challenge him, should call him out in a gun duel. That's what the men from Quill's bar expected. That was what the big man himself expected. He stood half crouching, his hands hanging loose on either side of his body. Farley knew he had only to reach for his guns and those big hands would go into action. Was the big man faster than him? Farley'd never worried about that before.

He'd left a string of dead men behind him, dead men who'd added to his reputation as a gunslinger, but now, he hesitated.

Cole saw the hesitation and realized the gunman wasn't going to engage him in a shoot-out this time. His lips curled in a scornful smile and he deliberately turned his back on Farley and remounted. Without a backward glance, he rode out of town.

"There'll be another time," Farley called after him, with false bravado. "Next time you won't ride away." Turning, he made his way through the snickering men back to the Bloody Guts Saloon.

Quill Ramsey stood on the porch, a slim cigar between his fingers, a thoughtful look on his face.

"I couldn't shoot him in front of the whole town," Farley said defensively.

"I don't care how or when you shoot him," Quill answered. "Just get me those claims." With a last warning glance, he stalked back into the saloon.

"You should have seen the fella." Otis and some of the other men were talking in the Silver Spur Saloon. "He shot down Ed in a clear-cut, fair fight, and he faced down Farley as cool as you please. I tell you, he had more guts than you could hang on a fence."

"Do you reckon he'd be willing to act as sheriff for us?" Norm Roberts asked. He'd slipped down to the Silver Spur for a drink after closing his store. He liked Otis, as did most of the store owners in town. Likewise they had a high regard for Kansas McKay. She'd started a collection for a school and a church. By bullying and charming nearly everyone who'd come into contact with her, she'd managed to raise a good bit of money, and rumor had it that a certain percentage of her winnings, which were considerable, went into the fund. New people were moving into town, and not all of them were miners. A newcomer from back East had come to start a bank, and other establishments were going up every day. Virginia City had begun to take on the appearance of a permanent town. Now the citizens wanted some semblance of law and order. The lawless, rough attitude of a year before was no longer welcomed.

"Did anyone get his name?" Otis asked, and the other men shook their heads.

"He was a big man, tall, lanky, good-looking. He looked like he'd been beating the ground some in his lifetime."

Half listening to the men, Kansas thought of Cole. He was tall, lanky, and good-looking. She wondered where he was now. Was he happy with Claire? Did they have children yet? The thought of Cole with Claire was too painful. Why did she keep running it through her mind, punishing herself with images of Cole holding Claire, Cole kissing Claire? That was a lifetime ago. Yet, lately she'd thought of little else. Put it away from you, she told herself, and get on with your life.

Restless and tired of the men's endless rehash of the afternoon's events, Kansas rose and walked to the bar. "How are things going tonight?" she asked Reeny. The dark-haired girl looked pretty in a deep rose-colored dress cut low on her shoulders.

"We're busier than ever," said Reeny, gathering up a mug of beer to deliver to a table of card players. "Everyone's talking about the stranger who gunned down Quill's man. They're tired of Quill's bullying this town." Her words were cut off by someone jostling her. The stein of beer sloshed forward, drenching the front of Kansas's gown.

"I'm sorry," Reeny cried, grabbing a towel and dabbing at the front of her gown.

"That's all right." Kansas held the wet skirts away from her body. "I'll just go back to the hotel and change."

"You'd better not go alone," Reeny cautioned. "Quill's men are all over out there, and they're looking for trouble."

"I suppose you're right," Kansas conceded, looking at

Otis. He was still deeply involved in conversation with Roberts and the other store owners.

"Why don't you go up to my room and change into one of my gowns for now?" Reeny suggested. Her face mirrored her concern and embarrassment over what she'd done.

Seeing her distress, Kansas nodded in agreement. "Thanks, I believe I will." She shoved her way through the mass of unwashed masculine bodies and climbed the stairs.

Sitting in a corner, listening to the talk swirl around him, Cole Slater watched her go, his fingers whitening as he gripped his mug of beer. He'd had to come back, to take another look, to be sure it was her, to be sure he wasn't wrong. He stared into the golden liquid in the glass, and his thoughts went back to that day by the creek. How the sun had sparkled on her hair and skin. How innocent and lovely and desirable she'd been. He'd wanted her that day with a need that was a knife's pain in his gut, yet he'd restrained from touching her because he'd thought her innocent. And maybe she had been that day, but she wasn't now.

His head came up at a movement on the stairs. She'd changed her gown. The sedate silk had given way to a garishly bright satin that showed every curve and left her smooth shoulders and the tops of her high breasts exposed. Cole wanted to tear the dress from her slender body, to feel and see the womanly beauty of her. At the same time, his fingers gripped his buckskin jacket tossed carelessly on a chair nearby. He wanted to fling it around her nakedness so no man here could look at her. Cole watched her descend the stairs, head high, her slim back straight with pride. Before the night was over, she'd be tumbling one of these miners between her long, slim legs—and all for the sake of a pouch of silver. He'd come only to confirm. He had no intentions of talking to her.

Getting to his feet, Cole turned to leave the saloon. By morning he could be high in the Sierras. In less than a week, he could be in California. Toby'd be disappointed when he didn't come back, but Cole couldn't help that now.

"Whoee, Miss Kansas," a man shouted, "I ain't ever seen you look so pretty."

"Thank you, Travis," Kansas answered. Her laughter was light, silvery, a thread that wound inside a man's gut and pulled him to her.

Cole turned and stared after her. Her back was bare in the indecent dress and her shoulder blades looked dainty and breakable beneath the smooth ivory skin. Like a man in a trance, Cole shoved his way through the crowd, guided by the bobbing golden curls ahead of him. When he reached her, he could smell her perfume, flowery and earthy. It filled his nostrils. One big hand closed on her slim white arm and he swung her around.

Her face was a mirror of confusion, anger that any man had dared to touch her in such a rough, intimate manner, outrage and disbelief mingled as the identity of the man before her registered. "Cole!" she whispered.

"Hello, Kansas," he answered.

He wasn't a dream. He was really there. Her eyes took in the breadth of his chest, the deeply tanned face, the creases along his cheeks. All these years she'd been remembering a young man hardly more than a boy . . . and here he stood, a full-grown man, a man who bore the signs of hard living.

"You're bigger than I remembered," she said, and it made no sense to her, but nothing did. Why was he here? She could feel every ounce of blood draining from her head right out the rest of her body. Her knees went weak.

"Cole," she whimpered, and sagged.

His big arm was there, gathering her to him. He pinned her to his chest and shoved through the boisterous men. She was unable to walk or talk or think. Her senses were alive to the sight, sound, and smell of Cole Slater. One slender hand came up to touch his cheek. He felt her touch, feather light and wondering. It left a hot brand on his cheek.

Chapter 8

"**C**OLE," KANSAS GASPED when she could draw a breath. "What are you doing here? How? Why?"

"I don't have to ask the how and why of you being here, do I?" he asked, his gray eyes flinty as they raked over her face and down to the pale bare expanse of skin exposed by the scandalous gown. His gaze flicked back to hers, probing and arrogant. His lips curled with a touch of cruelty that hadn't been there before.

Stunned by his unexpected appearance, Kansas stood within the iron circle of his arms, her breasts flattened against his hard, muscular chest, and all she could think was that this wasn't Cole Slater. This man was a stranger. His shoulders were broader, his face tanned by the sun and furrowed by the wind. There was a rough texture to him now that wasn't there before. Her wide, clear eyes sought the difference, the dark stubble on his chin, the deep grooves in his cheeks, the aggressive maleness of him.

"It's good to see you again," he murmured roughly, just before his mouth seized hers. His lips were dry and firm, his tongue thrust against her lips, forced entry, and then delved into the moist sweetness. The kiss was meant to punish. One tender lip split against her teeth and she tasted blood.

Still feeling the strangeness, she was unprepared for the

thoroughness of his assault on her senses. His tongue rasped along the edge of hers, then swirled deeper, awakening emotions that were strange to her. In protest she shoved ineffectively against those muscular shoulders. His kiss only deepened, the pressure of his mouth demanding she arch her neck so he had better access to her lips. His hands massaged her back, then slipped lower, cupping her buttocks through the thin, clinging satin so he could pull her against him. Her feet no longer touched the ground. Kansas bent her knees slightly, and his broad hand was quick to take advantage, sliding from her buttocks to her slender thigh, drawing her leg up slightly so she fit more snugly against his manhood. She felt the hardness of him and drew in her breath.

Her hands had ceased pushing at his shoulders, and her arms snaked around his neck as she gave herself up completely to his kiss. This was Cole, but not the Cole she'd kissed so innocently by the creek back in Webster. All innocence was past. She sensed the desire and male lust raging through his body, and her own awakening passions answered with a language that was new and exhilarating. She hardly dared guess what would have happened if not for the cheering, applauding men who'd witnessed their wanton embrace.

"Cole, put me down," she demanded against his mouth.

He paid her no heed, once more claiming her mouth in another deep kiss, much like a man who'd thirsted too long and now could not be denied. The feel of his hard, lean muscles beneath her fingertips reminded her of an implacable Sierra wall. Immovable, indestructible! A wave of longing swept over her, but she pushed it away. She'd learned to be indestructible, too.

"Cole! Stop!" she commanded.

This time her words penetrated and slowly, reluctantly, he released her, letting her body slide down the length of his so she felt every hard inch of him. A fire had started deep inside Kansas's soul, and she felt it spreading outward, threatening to consume her, but the noise of drunken, leering men helped her step away from him. He still held her captive, his big hands closing over the tender, pale flesh of her upper arms. Kansas felt her knees tremble. For safe measure she brought her hands up between them and spread them on his broad chest. She could feel his heartbeat, as wild and uncontrolled as her own. She could feel the pulse of him clear down to her toes.

His eyes were nearly black as he gazed down at her. "I never thought I'd see you again," he said huskily, and the timbre of his voice brought back memories of a first love so vividly that she closed her eyes against the well of pain.

"How are you, Cole?" she asked when she could speak again. Her voice was a mere whisper. Her lashes were a dark smudge against her round ivory cheek.

She was different from the other painted women who populated the saloon, Cole saw, and felt his heart swell with pride, then rage. He'd always known Kansas was different. She didn't need rouges and powders to enhance her beauty. There was—and always had been—an earthy sensuality that paints couldn't improve upon. Even now the musky scent of her body and the glow of her skin and hair sent pure lust raging through his frame. He wanted to tear the skimpy, sleazy gown from her body and see the beauty it so scantily, teasingly hid and blatantly hinted at.

A shout of laughter went up as the men jostled around Kansas, casting her lascivious glances, their ribald jests ringing in the air. The thought that even one of these men had enjoyed the sight of Kansas without her clothes on brought him to a rage—and the certainty that some of them had known her intimately, had held her and tasted the sweetness of her, had plunged their sweaty, unwashed bodies against hers—made his fists double.

Poor Hap Groggins didn't have a chance as he stepped close to Kansas, raised his beer mug high in an exaggerated toast. "Whooee, Miss McKay," he began, "I don't believe I've ever seen you kiss anybody like that—"

His words were cut off by Cole's fist. He didn't know what hit him. A beatific smile lit his face and he slid to the floor, his beer mug still clutched aright in his hand. Not a drop was spilled as a man deftly removed it from his hand. Like the Red Sea parting at Moses' command, the men shuffled aside, then closed around their fallen drinking partner.

Stunned at Cole's behavior, Kansas stood silently staring at him. But one miner, offended at what had happened to his drinking partner, doubled up his fist and hit Cole in the shoulder, although the big, rawboned man was a full head taller. Cole glared at him and drew back his arm, his big hand clenched in the biggest fist the miner had ever seen.

"Cole!" Kansas cried, and threw herself forward.

Startled, Cole managed to pull his punch in time so as not to inflict real damage to the delicate feminine body that materialized in front of the miner, but the momentum of the blow knocked her to the floor.

A growl went up from the men around. They might excuse a blow to one of their own, but never to Kansas McKay. She'd become their benefactress over the past few months, giving them a free beer when their pockets were empty, loaning them a grubstake when their mines didn't pay, and even coming out to nurse some of them when they got sick. Even if they hadn't experienced her largesse firsthand, they had heard of her generosity and been touched by it. One day they might need someone to help them, and it was nice to know Kansas McKay wouldn't turn them away. Every man jack there had a soft spot for her, and none would have dared to manhandle her as this stranger had done, first with his kiss and pawing embrace, and now by hitting her.

Of one body they moved toward Cole, but as soon as he'd seen her fall, Cole was kneeling beside her, clutching her slight body against his so he could rock her. One large rough hand gingerly touched the tender, delicate line of her jaw, where even now an ugly bruise was staining the flawless skin.

"Kansas," he called, his voice rough with concern.

Her dark lashes lay in stark contrast against her pale cheeks. Her face had lost all color. She'd never looked more vulnerable.

"Put her down, you lily-bellied coyote," one man spat out, his face twisted in anger.

Cole glanced up at the aging miner. "I didn't mean to hit her," he said. "I was aimin' at that man"—he nodded his head—"and she stepped in the way."

"That's right, she did," an onlooker said, nodding to emphasize his point. Then his eyes turned fierce. "But you had no call to hit Hap. He warn't doin' you no harm."

"No man insults this woman when I'm around," Cole said, and his voice was deadly, his eyes dark and flinty as he glared at the circle of men. They fell silent contemplating his words.

Kansas moaned and rolled her head, then slowly opened her eyes. "Otis, no," she cried as her gaze focused on the giant who towered behind Cole, his gun butt raised, ready to bash down on Cole's skull.

At her cry, Cole jerked around and fixed the old man with a menacing glare. "Better put that away, old man, before you get hurt," he growled. The old man hesitated.

Cole lifted one eyebrow quizzically as he glared around the circle of men. More than one was intimidated by him, but none backed down. They were prepared to defend Kansas McKay.

"It was an accident," Kansas was explaining. With a moan, she sat upright and clutched her chin.

"You shouldn't have leaped in the way like that," Cole said. "I could have hurt you worse."

"You could have hurt old Pete Rayburn, too," Kansas

declared, looking up at him. "Why did you start slugging everyone?" Her gaze was accusing.

Cole felt his hackles rise. "I didn't like the way these men were touching you and talking to you," he answered gruffly. Then, realizing she was all too used to just this kind of treatment from them—and in fact invited it—he hooked a hand around her arm and dragged her to her feet. One arm encircled her waist and held her against him.

"These men have taken no more liberties with me than you have yourself," she snapped.

Cole ignored her irritation. "I want to be with you," he said, his meaning all too clear. "Show me to your room and tell the rest of this riffraff that you're not available for the rest of the night."

"Not available?" Kansas repeated, the blood returning to her head with a rush that made her feel dizzy.

"That's right," Cole snapped, half dragging, half carrying her as he moved toward the stairs. "I'm buying your time for the rest of the night." He dug into his pockets for a coin, then cursed as he realized he'd spent his last money on a bottle for Toby and their supplies. "Where's your room, this way?" he asked, peering up the stairs.

A man and woman were making their way up the stairs. His hand rested on her satin-clad buttocks, and she laughed shrilly at something he whispered in her ear.

"Cole, stop! I'm not—"

"Is there a problem, Miss McKay?" Otis said behind them, and Cole swung around to meet the big man.

Cole's lips tightened in a thin line and his hand swung automatically to the side near his holster in wary readiness. Otis saw the gesture, recognized it as that of a gunslinger, and his belly muscles tightened in fear, but he wasn't about to leave Kansas to the mercy of such a man.

Kansas felt the tension between the two men and quickly pushed herself away from Cole. Reluctantly he let her go, but his gaze never left Otis.

"There's no problem," Kansas said. "Cole's an old friend from my hometown."

" 'Pears to me, folks in your hometown have a funny way of greetin' one another," Otis said, and pulled at his beard. Some of the tension left Cole's body and he relaxed his stance.

"I was just telling Kansas that I'm buying up her time tonight."

"Buyin' up her ti—" Otis began in puzzlement, staring at the tall stranger; then his expression cleared. "Ain't you the stranger that brought in Quill Ramsey's man this afternoon?"

"I brought in a body," Cole answered. "A bushwhacker." His tone was guarded. "I don't know who Quill Ramsey is."

"You're the man who crossed Rod Farley," Kansas gasped. "Oh, Cole, you've made some powerful enemies in Virginia City. Farley works for Quill Ramsey, and both of them are dangerous as rattlesnakes."

"She's right about that," Otis said, "but I ain't ever seen a man who could stop any of Quill's men or back down Farley. Let me buy you a drink."

Otis led the way to a table. Cole, casting a quick glance at Kansas, followed.

"How'd you come to butt heads with Ramsey's men?" Otis asked, pouring a glass of whiskey for himself and Cole. Kansas sank into a chair and listened to the two men. She couldn't bear the thought that Cole might have been in danger.

"Farley and his sidekick tried to jump my partner's claim up at Dry Hole Gulch," Cole said, and explained about Toby and what had happened that morning.

Otis listened quietly. "We've heard rumors they've been doin' that."

"Ramsey's men have been robbing the miners the minute they ride into town; now he's decided to go after their claims,'' Kansas explained. ''Several miners have been killed, most of them shot in the back, nearly all of them unarmed. We've been suspecting Quill Ramsey was behind it, but we can't prove it.''

''That's why we need your help,'' Otis explained. ''We need someone who ain't afraid to stand up to Ramsey's hired gunslingers.''

''I'm not interested,'' Cole said, putting down the empty whiskey glass. ''I'm much obliged for the drink, but I'm just passing through.'' He glanced at Kansas. ''I'll be riding out tomorrow morning.''

''It's best,'' said Kansas. ''Farley will be gunning for you now . . . until he kills you. He has to, or Quill Ramsey will get rid of him. He only wants men who can draw the fastest and have no scruples about killing a man.''

''Or woman,'' Otis said, glaring at her. ''You just remember that, little miss. You ain't out of danger yet.''

Cole's eyes narrowed as he looked from Kansas to Otis. ''Why would Quill be after her?''

''This place used to be his. Miss Kansas won it from him in a poker game.'' Otis grinned at the memory. ''He ain't ever forgive her for it.''

Cole's eyes held a glimmer of humor as he looked at Kansas. ''You always did play a mean game,'' he said softly, and in spite of herself old memories came flooding back of the stale, dark kitchen in the back of Moody's Saloon—and Cole Slater seated across from her as he taught her to play cards. Fast on the heels of these half-forgotten thoughts came the painful memory of Claire Howard and what she'd told Kansas in the barn that night.

Where was Claire now? Back at the ranch tending Cole's children and waiting for his return, while he was here planning to spend the night with Kansas! Kansas sat up straighter, her jaw jutting with stubborn pride as she thought of Cole's attempts to take her upstairs. He'd assumed she was a whore just like Molly. Never mind that she was dressed like one, he had not right to make such assumptions about her. Thinking of how malleable she'd been, how close to climbing those stairs with him, she signaled to Riley to bring her a deck of cards, then turned her attention back to the conversation.

"We could sure use you, mister," Otis was pressing, but Cole sat shaking his head.

"This is not my fight," he said. "I stopped fighting other peoples' battles long ago." His gaze swung back to Kansas. "Are you going upstairs with me?" he asked.

Riley placed a deck of cards at Kansas's elbow. A miner seeing her open a fresh deck squeezed forward.

"Got room for me, Miss McKay?" he asked eagerly.

Otis, regret still sharp on his features, looked from the rangy cowboy to Kansas and an idea formed. "How about if we play a game on it?" Otis said. "If you win, you ride out of town. If we win, you stay for a spell and help us out." When Cole hesitated, Otis rushed on. "Course we'll sweeten the pot some." He pulled some bills from his pocket and laid a hundred and fifty dollars on the table. "If you win, you take the money with you, no strings attached. If I win, that's your first month's pay as our new sheriff. We'll play three hands to determine the winner."

Cole looked at Kansas, torn between wanting to stay and needing to go. He couldn't stay here in Virginia City seeing Kansas sell herself to any man who had the right price. On the other hand, could he ride away now that he'd found her?

"All right," he agreed. "I'll play for it."

Kansas drew in her breath, torn between joy and fear. "What about Claire?" she asked, wondering how he could contemplate leaving his wife and family for months. Perhaps he would bring her here to Virginia City. Kansas couldn't bear the thought of seeing Claire and her children, ready proof of the intimacies Cole had shared with her.

Otis poured him a glass of whiskey, and Cole tossed the contents down without blinking an eye. Otis refilled the glass. "Claire?" One sun-bleached eyebrow arched high as his blue eyes regarded her quizzically.

"Your wife!" she snapped. Had he forgotten Kansas as easily as he seemed to have forgotten his wife?

"My wife?" Puzzlement gave way to dancing imps of humor in Cole's eyes, and Kansas caught her breath. For a moment he seemed like the old Cole, devil-may-care and full of good-natured mischief.

"Never mind," she snapped. "She's your worry and not mine." She picked up the cards and automatically began shuffling them. They'd always soothed her before. Now they did not. Butterflies seemed to have settled into her stomach, and their fluttering made her feel breathless and trembling all at once. She could busy her nervous hands, but she couldn't stop the thoughts from rushing through her mind. Maybe Cole was no longer with Claire.

"Kansas can deal for us, if you have no objections," Otis said, and Cole nodded.

"I've never known Kansas to cheat at cards," he said softly, and something in his tone made her place the deck flat on the table between them. Her eyes sought his, her mind played back the words he'd uttered, looking for the double meaning, for surely one had been intended. Incredulity washed over her. Cole did indeed think she'd followed in her mother's footsteps. Anger claimed her, lifted her small rounded chin, stained her cheeks with color, and set a fire to burning behind the shimmering gray of her eyes.

What was she thinking, Cole wondered, that caused her eyes to turn stormy and her chin defiant? He wanted to whisk her away then and there, to throw her over his shoulder in some primitive display of possessiveness and carry her to a quiet room, away from the noise and leering gazes of these men. He wanted to taste her skin, her mouth, her breasts, and he wanted her to tell him everything about her thoughts and plans, the way she once had when they were young and he was her protector. Old feelings died hard, he reflected, and taking off his wide-brimmed hat, he set it to one side and nodded to Kansas.

"Deal," he grunted, and Kansas had to draw a deep breath to still the wave of emotions that claimed her. It was all so dear and familiar. For a moment it seemed they were indeed back in Moody's kitchen.

"Miss Kansas?" Otis asked when she made no move to pick up the cards.

"Yes, all right. I'll deal." Tearing her gaze from Cole's, Kansas glanced at the deck of cards. They lay faceup, their bright colors mute and mocking. Her hands were slick with sweat as she picked up the deck and clumsily began to shuffle.

"Five card stud, joker wild. Three hands determine the winner," she said.

Cole's unrelenting gaze never left her face as he picked up the cards she'd dealt and fanned them. Then, and only then, did he glance at his hand.

Cheeks burning, Kansas kept her eyes lowered to the scarred tabletop. Her thoughts were churning as she waited for the men to study their hands and place their bets. Had Cole left Claire then? Was his marriage over? Had it ever taken place? The thought shook her that she might have run away from Cole over a lie! Was it possible Claire had lied? Had Cole loved her, after all. He'd come to Kansas once after Claire had first arrived in Webster. He hadn't wanted Claire then. He'd wanted Kansas. Hope lit her face as she began dealing the cards. But it was short lived as she remembered that in the end, Cole had turned his back on her. Les Slater had been there that night and he'd confirmed Claire's claim. And most telling of all, Cole hadn't come after her. He'd not even wanted to see her. Round and round Kansas's thoughts ran, growing more confused. It was hard to follow the game.

Cole seemed to have some trouble concentrating as well. He'd refilled his whiskey glass several times. He lost the first hand. His broad, tanned brow creased in annoyance, he played with the old skill and ruthlessness of his youth and took the second hand. Could he do it a third time?

Kansas shuffled the cards and placed them on the table for Cole to cut. Their glances caught and held. She read many things there in his eyes; impatience, stubbornness, lust, and something more—a sad condemnation of her and what he thought she'd become. In that moment, Kansas knew what she must do.

She'd never dealt a cheating hand, but she palmed the cards from the bottom of the deck, giving Cole three aces. She knew where the fourth one was in the deck and, before the game was through, he'd have that one, too. She'd see to it that he won his hand and the money on the table . . . and she'd watch him ride out of town without remorse. She'd put away girlish dreams of lanky knights with smoky eyes and shining armor. She'd not take them up again. The death of them the first time had been too painful.

Serenely she dealt the cards, deciding the fate of them all, and she felt no sense of power or triumph at what she did, only a tired resignation that this was how it must be. Cole Slater wasn't meant for her or she for him. She was Molly McKay's daughter, the town whore's daughter, and in his eyes she'd come to be the same. So be it.

"I've got two pairs, queen high," Otis said, spreading his hand. "Lay your cards."

Cole sat with narrowed eyes studying Kansas. She refused to look at him. From the corner of her eye, she could see the rough thumb of one big hand stroke the edge of his cards. The whiskey bottle was nearly empty now. With a sigh, he tossed his cards facedown on the table. "That beats me," he said.

Kansas's startled gaze flew to his. His face was inscrutable. He'd known, she realized. He'd recognized what she'd done. Unable to pursue what his response meant, Kansas leaped to her feet.

"If you'll excuse me, gentlemen," she murmured hurriedly. Then her slim legs were moving, carrying her across the room, toward the stairs and the haven of a quiet room above. But it was not to be.

"Kansas." Cole was there, catching her arm in his grip, pulling her against his broad chest. She could smell the whiskey on his breath, and his eyes held a hard, unfamiliar glitter. "Why did you do that?" he demanded.

Refusing to look at him, Kansas shrugged nonchalantly. "I didn't think it was right for you to be trapped into staying in Virginia City because of a mere card game."

"That was a decision for me to make, don't you think?" he demanded. "And since when have you started dealing from the bottom?"

"Everyone deals from the bottom at one time or another in their lives. Haven't you learned that yet, Cole?" She placed one hand on her hip and let her lip curl in contempt as she looked him up and down. "I suppose growing up on your daddy's ranch, you didn't have to learn the same kind of lessons I did."

She jerked free of him, all the bitterness she'd nursed over the years for his betrayal in her contemptuous gaze. "You never had to face life for what it really was, Cole. Oh, you were kind to me, kinder than most back in Webster, but you really weren't any different from them in what you thought about the town whore and her daughter. Well, I am what I am, Cole, and I make no apologies." Her slender arms found the strength to push him away, her wobbly knees trembled as she moved away from the warmth and sheer animal magnetism that was Cole Slater.

"It was good to see you again, Cole," she said, and marveled that her voice sounded so calm, so normal. "Now if you'll excuse me, I have to get to work. Several men have asked for my services tonight." She took a perverse sense of pleasure in seeing the shock of anger that crossed his face. She turned away, her sight suddenly blinded by tears, but her head was held high and proud.

Everett stood nearby talking to a group of young miners. Kansas made her way to him. "Ev, will you accompany me to a room upstairs," she asked in a low voice.

His face flushed with pleasure, then sobered as he looked at her. "Are you feeling poorly, Miss Kansas?" he asked.

"Yes, I—I'm feeling faint." Kansas swayed against him, and automatically his arms wrapped around her slim waist. "I need to get away from someone," she whispered. "Can you help me?"

"Shore, Miss Kansas. It'll be a pleasure," he said, and with a flourish scooped her up in his arms.

Cole's face was a pale blur in her vision. Kansas wrapped her arm around Ev's neck, let her head fall back so her long, slender throat was exposed. Her laughter, teasing and seductive, was a sensuous promise of pleasures to come.

Surprised, the men in the saloon watched as young Ev carried her up the stairs. Some of them tasted bitter defeat, for they'd dreamed of being the one to win Kansas for themselves. None felt as much rage as Cole Slater. His fists clenched, his nostrils flared as he watched Kansas and the young miner disappear upstairs.

"Here's your winning and your badge, Mr. Slater," Otis said, holding them out to Cole.

Cole's big hand swept the money and tin star to the floor. "Keep them," he growled.

His face was grim, his lips narrowed in barely suppressed anger, and his glare hadn't left the door behind which Kansas had disappeared. He didn't need to shove men aside as he started for the stairs. They saw his face and shuffled to get out of his way. When a man looked like that, someone usually got killed.

Cole's long legs carried him up the stairs two at a time. He was breathing hard when he reached the top, but not from the exertion. His chest muscles had constricted and his breath was forced from his suddenly dry throat in great gasps. The whiskey he'd drunk was taking hold of him. His big body shook as he walked along the landing and stopped at a door. Without hesitation, he raised one booted foot and sent the door splintering inward.

"What the hell?" Ev said, swinging around. He had no time for more. Cole's fist caught him under the chin and sent him sliding to the floor in a deep sleep that would last till morning.

Enraged now, wanting to feel his hands around Kansas's lovely throat, Cole looked around the room. A girl in the bed screamed and lurched away from him. Her bright red hair straggled down her chubby face.

"Where's Kansas?" Cole growled.

Too frightened to speak, the girl only stared at him. Cole snarled, his eyes snapping, his lips curling upward, and she was galvanized into action, pointing a shaky finger toward the open window. Cole's long legs strode across the room. With hardly a pause, he stepped through the window out onto a porch balcony much like the one Moody's Saloon had sported back in Webster. His fierce gaze searched the balcony for a slim figure in a red satin dress, but no one was there. Down the street, a glimmer of moonlight shown on golden hair and shimmery dress. Cole shimmied down the porch railing, briefly marveling at Kansas's dexterity and strength. Surely she must have done the same thing—and in that ridiculous dress! He landed with a light thud in the dusty street and started after the moonlit figure ahead.

Chapter 9

THE MOON WAS full, its pale glow lighting the hills above the town and lending the shabby raw buildings an aura of beauty. Breathing deeply of the sage-tinged air, Kansas stumbled up the street to the stark silhouette of her half-finished gambling house. Coming here usually gave her comfort, a sense of pride and purpose, reminding her how far she'd come and what the future held for her. Standing below, Kansas had to tilt her head back to study the regal structure, but tonight there was no comfort and no pride or anticipation. Her future seemed as empty and barren as the naked arches rising above her head.

"Oh, Cole," she whispered, hugging herself while the tears slid down her cheeks. As if the night breeze had called him, he was there, his strong hands whirling her about, his tall, lanky form towering over her in the darkness. "Cole," she gasped, dashing a hand across her face to wipe at her tears.

"Kansas." His voice was rough, aching with need. He shook her slightly, then pulled her against him. His mouth descended against hers, hard and punishing.

"No," Kansas cried, wrenching away from him, one slim white hand going to her bruised lips. "Go away, Cole. I can't go through this again. I can't fight you on my own."

"Why are you fighting me, Kansas?" he asked, and she felt the pain and uncertainty in him. It unnerved her more than his direct assault on her senses. "Why are you running away from me?"

There was a tension in him, like a tightly coiled spring that might snap at any moment, and an answering pulse within her. She moved away from him, going to lean her head against a rough support post.

"I want you to leave Virginia City," she said when she'd gained some measure of control. "Just go back to your family. Go back to Claire, your wife!" Despite herself, the last words ended on a high, wild note and she swung around to face him, her back against the post. "You can't come from your wife to me. I don't want you."

The lie spiraled deep inside her, mocking her, wounding her. She wanted him more than she'd ever thought possible, more than that innocent sixteen-year-old by the creek had ever dreamed of wanting a man. Through all the years of looking for Cole, of glancing up in anticipation every time a door opened, of praying her love and need for him had drawn him over the miles and years, she hadn't realized how strongly the flame of her desire for him had grown. Now he was here, and she feared she might be consumed. Desperately she fought for her freedom from this hold he had over her. She wanted only a surcease of the pain she'd carried in her heart ever since Claire had told of her coming marriage to Cole.

"Kansas, listen to me," Cole said, striding across the damp grass to grasp her shoulders. "I have no wife."

His words barely penetrated the dark core of pain that claimed her. She pulled her tumultuous thoughts together and looked up at him. Moonlight gilded his strong, angular face, casting dark shadows over his eyes and beneath his cheekbones. But she could see his mouth, the flash of his bitter smile, the twist of his lips.

"No wife?" she repeated, as if in a daze.

"No, never," Cole answered gently. "Is that why you've been running from me?"

He pulled her against him, his chin resting on the top of her head. She could feel the rumble of laughter deep in his chest. His arms cradled her, and she gave herself to the comfort of his broad chest, while her very soul took in the wonder of his words. He hadn't married Claire, after all. She'd lied to Kansas.

"You always were a funny kid," Cole said, and lowered his head to place a kiss, chaste and reassuring, on her brow.

"Cole," Kansas whispered, and she saw his expression darken in the moonlight.

His arms tightened, not seeking to give comfort now, but claiming, demanding. His mouth was hard on hers, branding her, possessing her, and Kansas met him halfway, going up on her toes, pressing herself to him, feeling the sweet pain of passion rush through her.

"Oh, Cole. I thought I'd never see you again," she half sobbed between frantic, breathless kisses.

"I looked for you everywhere," he gasped, his lips searing her skin, his breath hot and compelling as the desert air against her cheek, her neck. "I rode through every gold camp, every cow town." His lips claimed hers again. His tongue demanded entrance, danced against hers, stroked, conquered, and seduced all at once. His hands were everywhere, smoothing over her slim back, cupping her buttocks to pull her closer against the hard length of his manhood, stroking the bare flesh of her inner arm, and claiming the tender straining mounds of her breasts. "I looked in every saloon, every whorehouse between here and Webster."

His words sent a shiver of warning across her consciousness, but his insistent hands, his hungry kisses, left her no room to think or feel anything except that which he wanted her to feel. She was drowning in his passion, and she made no effort to save herself. The years had been too long, too barren, and the night was too magical, with the spice-

scented desert air at their backs and the star-studded sky
above.

"Kansas, I've wanted you so long," he whispered, his
big hands tangling in her hair, scattering pins without heed
as he loosened the silken golden strands and buried his face
in them. "I've dreamed of you," he rasped, and his hands
were at her shoulders, pulling her down, down onto the
bare, raw floor of the Kansas Palace.

His hands tore at her dress, impatient with her satin trap-
pings. He pulled the low-cut bodice down, trapping her
arms and exposing her creamy breasts. He breathed deeply,
drawing in the scent of her skin and hair. His moist, hot
tongue rasped across the delicate skin of her neck and shoulders and down to the sweet rise of her breast.

As his hot mouth claimed one tender nipple, Kansas
moaned and rolled her head against the heady spiral of
desire and pleasure that invaded her. She was helpless beneath him, able to bend her arms only at the elbow, but
made more helpless by the claim he made on her senses. He
suckled, sending shafts of delight through her; his teeth
nibbled lightly, and delight turned to pleasurable pain that
made her gasp. As if knowing the exact moment when such
intense feeling could turn to real pain, he laved her nipple
with his tongue, its rough texture bringing another moan,
and then he abandoned that breast, making her know a
moment of shocking bereavement before his hungry mouth
closed over the other breast and she was once again arching
against him, lost in a world of sensual, consuming desire.
Need, and a quick silvery liquid burned with a bright light
in the lower regions of her body, and her legs parted as her
body readied itself.

"Cole, I can bear no more." She sighed . . . and heard
his laughter.

He rose above her, a dark shadow against the moonlit
night. She heard the whisper of clothes being removed, of
boots thudding against the plank floor, then he took her

hands and pulled her up, sliding the dress the rest of the way down her body, until it lay in a red, shimmery pool at her feet.

"God, you are so beautiful," he breathed, and pulled her against him.

Kansas gasped at the first contact of skin against skin. She'd thought his skin would be rough textured, but it was smooth and supple across the hard ridges of muscles. She let her hands slid over him, sculpting the curve of muscle at his shoulders and back, gliding over the smooth, taut mounds of his buttocks, around slim, rock-hard hips, to the heat of his flat belly and loins. Her hands brushed across his arousal and she felt him jump. She paused, startled, awed by him, then she reached again, her slender fingers closing in wonder around the long, smooth hard shaft. Again it jerked in response to her soft hands, and Kansas felt an answering response deep, deep inside her. She gripped him with one hand and deliberately swirled the palm of the other over the hot bulbous end of him.

"You're driving me crazy," Cole gasped, and seized her arms, crushing her to him so her nipples tingled at the first contact with the golden mat of hair on his chest, then her breasts were flattened as his arms tightened. He nibbled at her ear. She could feel his hard arousal against the soft well of her stomach and she wriggled in his embrace, deliberately creating a friction between their bodies. "Kansas, what am I to do with you?" he asked huskily.

"Make love to me," she whispered urgently.

Gently he lowered her to the floor, to the pallet he'd made of his clothes. Her soft breasts, with their sore, throbbing tips, brushed against his manhood and she heard him gasp and felt him stiffen, then he was pushing her back, his knees sliding between her legs, nudging them wider. His hands left her back and seized her pale thighs, raising them, exposing her soft core to him. Briefly she felt his fingers brush against her moist softness, then his shaft, hot and hard,

speared through her, breeching her maidenhead in one
mighty thrust. Kansas cried out in pain as her virginity was
taken from her, then her young body adjusted itself to the
urgent rhythm of his and she moved with him.

She felt the rawboned power of him, knew the sheer
intensity of energy, and in her discovery of Cole Slater she
nearly forgot herself and her own body's pulsating re-
sponses, until with a rush of molten fire she flamed beneath
him and her cry mingled with his on the night air.

The stars had gotten inside her head somehow, and now
they exploded one by one in a thousand shiny splinters
of light before dying out and falling slowly, slowly back
to earth. She became aware of the scent of newly cut pine
boards beneath her and of a heavy warmth at her side.
Her breathing was raspy and quick—or was it Cole's?
She turned to look at him in the moonlight. His eyes
were closed and his chest moved up and down. She put
out a hand, compelled to touch him, to reassure herself
that he was indeed here—and not some wistful dream of
hers.

"I never knew," she whispered, running a hand over his
chest.

"What?" he grunted, without opening his eyes.

"How it is between a man and a woman."

He rolled away from her, away from the dreamy expectancy in her eyes, away from the soft, alluring touch of her
hand. "Come on, Kansas," he said, not sure if his impatience was with her or himself. He should have kept riding
out of town, the way he'd vowed he'd do. Instead, he'd
wanted to see Kansas one last time. Now he felt the soft
web of her femininity closing around him, ensnaring him.
He was in no mood to play games with her. "You're
no innocent to this. After all, you grew up in Moody's
Saloon . . . around Molly and all her men," he said, with
brutal directness.

"Yes, but what I saw and what happened here are not the

same." She paused, and he felt her gaze on him. "At least not for me. I—I'd hoped it was the same way for you."

"What is this place?" Cole asked, sitting up and reaching for his pants. He kept his back to Kansas.

Kansas watched him slide his long legs into his trousers. She bit her lips, trying not to be hurt by his abruptness or his failure to answer her question. Shrugging, she glanced around. "Folks around here are calling it the Kansas Palace," she answered. "I figure it wouldn't do me much good to call it anything else."

Cole buttoned up his breeches and reached for his boots. "Must cost a lot of money."

Kansas shrugged dismissively. "Some, but I've made a lot of money here in Virginia City." She didn't notice the wide shoulders stiffen, then hunch in anger.

"Business been pretty good then?" Cole asked, tugging on the last boot. He sat on the floor, nearby yet somehow unreachable, as he waited for her answer.

"Good enough," Kansas answered. "Cole, there's something I need to clear up with you—" she began, but he reached for his shirt, jerking it with sharp impatience from beneath her hips before scrambling to his feet.

"How much?" he asked tersely.

"What?" The breath tightened in Kansas's chest. Her eyes were wide and luminous and vulnerable as she stared up at him, but he refused to look at her. He refused to see.

"How much do you usually get for your services?" he asked, digging into his pocket. His pockets were empty, and he silently cursed himself for refusing the money Otis had brought him.

Kansas felt the words drive deep inside her, cutting through to some core that had remained free of the pain and humiliation she'd known in her youth. Now Cole had found it and slashed at her more cruelly than anything she'd ever known. She sat still, trying to draw a breath, and her body and mind felt numb. He was drunk, she realized, and hadn't realized she was a virgin. She felt used and betrayed.

Cole's boot heels sounded loud in the quiet night as he stalked across the boards to stand before her. "Kansas?" he said roughly, and, slowly, as if by moving she might make the pain worse, she arched her head back and looked at him. "How much?" he demanded again.

Kansas's fingers curled inward. She felt the bite of her nails against her soft palms as she balled her hands into a fists. She wanted to lash out at him, to feel the impact of her hand against his cheek, but she controlled the impulse and forced a smile to her lips. In the darkness he didn't see the wild, bitter pain in her eyes. He saw only the flash of her teeth and the seductive way she moved her body so her long blond hair swished over her shoulder. One perfectly shaped breast was exposed. She made no effort to cover herself as she swung her knees back and forth suggestively.

"Consider it on the house," she said throatily. She shrugged, and the glistening gold strands slid over her satiny skin. "Congratulations, you're my first customer in the Kansas Palace. Maybe you've brought me luck, Cole, and there will be many more."

He left her then, balling his shirt in his hand as he jumped to the ground and strode away. He didn't see the tears sliding down her cheeks or hear the gasp of pain as the tightly held sobs tore past her tight throat.

"The next time you'll have to pay, Cole," she called after him. "I'm expensive, but I think you'll agree I'm worth it."

Her laughter followed him down the hill, but he never knew the choking, gasping laughter mingled with tears. Kansas watched until he was out of sight, then she lay on the sweet-smelling pine boards of the Kansas Palace and wept for all the years of pain she'd carried in her heart . . . and for the death of yet another dream.

Chapter 10

"**O**TIS, DO YOU have to dog my every step?"

"What's got into you, lately? You're as sore as an old bear. I was just trying to keep an eye on you for your own safety. I heard Quill Ramsey was vowing to pay you back for taking his saloon." Otis's bearded face settled into lines of self-righteous indignation and true concern for her. She'd offended him, and knowing she must make amends only irritated Kansas further.

"You wouldn't have to worry if your new sheriff were doing his job," she snapped. "I haven't seen him around since you gave him his money and badge. Like as not he's on his way back over those mountains as fast as he can go."

Otis's face looked troubled. "I don't think Cole Slater is a man to take somebody's money and not deliver what he promised. Of course, he didn't take the money or the badge."

Startled, Kansas swung around to look at him. The fear that she might never see Cole Slater again had mocked her ever since their night of lovemaking. Good, she'd told herself a thousand times. She didn't want to see him, ever again. He was as snobbish and self-righteous as the rest of the people in Webster. He'd dared to think she was a whore. Yet when she'd caught no glimpse of his lanky, broad-shouldered figure in the streets or at the bar in the Silver Spur, she'd begun to evaluate just what had happened.

Could he really be blamed for thinking her a whore? She was in a saloon where such women worked, and she was certainly dressed as one herself. She still cursed her luck that on that particular night she'd chosen not to go back to the hotel for one of her own dresses. As for her own behavior, she'd deliberately allowed him to believe her a whore, had actually enlisted someone to help her convince him she was. Could she really blame him for believing what was put before him?

Yes, some small part of her cried out. In his heart of hearts, he should have known she would never follow in her mother's footsteps. But perhaps the thing she could forgive him for the least was that when he'd made love to her, he hadn't recognized the taking of her virginity. He'd simply drunk too much—or perhaps he simply hadn't wanted to know. This way there was no need of marriage, no obligation on his part. They had a lot to work out. She must tell him the truth as soon as possible. She couldn't allow him to go on believing she sold her body to any man with the price. Now it seemed she wouldn't have the chance.

"You're right, Otis," she said, and her words sounded hollow, uncertain. "When Cole gives his word, he sticks to it."

"Of course, he may not consider the card game a binding contract"—Otis cast her a sideways glance—"seeing as how you bottom dealt him."

"You knew?" Kansas asked, nonplussed. She'd felt so smug at her skill that night, thinking no one was aware of what she'd done, but both Cole and Otis were on to her. "Do you think anyone else noticed?" she asked, suddenly fearful of her reputation for honesty.

Otis shook his head. "You were slick, Miss Kansas, I'll give you that," he said, and his reassurance gave her little comfort. "I just never figured you for a double-dealer."

"I'm not," Kansas said quickly. "And I'll never do it again. The funny thing is that although I dealt Cole a winning hand, he threw it in. I thought he meant to stay in Virginia City for a time."

Her slender fingers plucked at the skirt folds of her pale blue gown. Her hair was loose, held back with a matching ribbon. The long honey-gold curls hung to her waist. With her scrubbed face, free of the artifice of paint she usually wore in the evening, she looked like a girl of sixteen again.

Silently Otis studied her, wondering where she came from and what had led her into gambling as a way of making a living. Not that she wasn't good at it. She was, and her fortunes had quickly grown here in Virginia City. But a gambling lady was just a cut above the other soiled doves that worked the saloons and bordellos that lined the streets. Otis sighed. Already, "decent" folks were moving into Virginia City, building their fine houses at the other end of town, away from the corrupting influence of the saloons and gambling houses. Even now, a church and hospital were going up, funded in part by the very saloons and gambling houses those folks disdained.

Kansas herself had organized the effort, cajoling and shaming every man jack that came down out of the hills to wet his gullet with a drop of whiskey, gamble away his diggings, or find relief with a woman. Now she sat troubled over some lanky, ragged gunslinger that rode into town and out again—and all they knew about him was his name. Maybe Kansas knew more than she was telling, Otis conceded. He'd followed Cole Slater up to the Kansas Palace that night and he'd seen the tension between the two of them as they argued. They'd known each other before. Otis had stayed until he saw the two shadows merge into one, then he'd made his way back down the hill thinking—hoping— that maybe Kansas McKay had finally found the thing that would erase that shadow of regret and sadness she tried so hard to hide.

"We'll have to look for another sheriff," Otis said now, wanting to get Kansas's mind off Cole Slater. Whatever had happened between them that night at the Kansas Palace, Cole Slater was gone, and whether she wanted it to or not, Kansas's face reflected the naked pain his leaving caused her.

"Damn Cole Slater!" Otis muttered under his breath. His gnarled fingers curled around the tin badge in his pocket. "Guess I'll head over to the general store and talk to Norm. That'll give you some breathing space from me."

Kansas glanced up at him, a wan smile curving her lips, but he caught the brightness of her eyes and knew she'd been trying to hold back tears. "Thanks, Otis," she said, patting his hand. "You take good care of me."

"Just don't you go nowhere until I get back," he ordered, and stepped down off the porch.

Kansas sat where she was on the porch watching the stoop-shouldered old man make his way down the street. Otis was a friend as well as her protector. She shuddered to remember what her life had been like before he came along. He'd first stepped in to help her when a drunken cowboy had decided their card game was only a prelude to something more. Although she'd taken all of Otis's money, he'd been good-natured about it and had been quick to put the cowboy in his place. Somehow they'd just stayed together since then. Otis kept track of her winnings, and she'd trusted him implicitly. The Kansas Palace hadn't been just her dream, but Otis's as well. He was more a partner than a hired hand. She'd have to find some way to repay him for his loyalty.

Her attention was caught by a tall black-robed figure. Father Michael was making his way up the hill to his church. Now was the time to take him the rest of the money she'd collected for him, Kansas thought, getting to her feet. Without Otis's shuffling, grumbling presence she could move much faster. She'd be there and back before he even returned from the general store. Kansas hurried inside to collect her hat and the money for Father Michael's church.

The sun was already bearing down so, hot images shimmered before her eyes. The dusty street, lined with jerry-built stores and saloons, was empty save for a couple of horses hitched in front of the Bloody Guts Saloon. One swished his tail at the indolently buzzing flies and stomped a foot, sending up little puffs of dust. A desert wind, hot and dry, caught the disturbed dust and tossed it in the air, playfully swirling it into little eddies. It stung the eyes and cheeks.

Sweat quickly formed on Kansas's upper lip and at her temples, so despite her intentions she was forced to slow down. Ambling along at a more leisurely pace, she studied the town. It had changed dramatically since she'd come here. New streets were laid out and houses and shops quickly built along them. The spires of the unfinished Catholic church rose at one end of town.

High in the hills, the steep slopes were dotted with openings to hundreds of mines, some profitable, fulfilling their owners' wildest dreams, others barren holes that did no more than shelter their tired, discouraged miners from the elements. Echoing over the whole valley came the grinding, booming sound of the new mills that had been built along the river. Enterprising entrepreneurs had quickly forseen the problems of the miners in extracting the silver from the rock and soil and had devised a method to do so. Now, along with the whores, gamblers, and suppliers who benefited from the labor of the miners, other businesses had come to reap their share. Rumor had it that they were soon to have a bank in Virginia City. Reeny and the other girls had caught a glimpse of the new banker and his wife and daughter.

"Never even looked our way or acknowledged we existed!'' Reeny had sniffed in disdain. ''I've seen the likes of them before. They put on airs, but underneath they're just as common as the rest of us.'' Reeny had paused and pursed her lips wistfully. ''Of course, I reckon I'd put on airs, too, if I owned a gown like the one that daughter had on.''

Kansas skipped a step as she thought of the last order she'd sent back over the Sierras to San Francisco. She'd ordered the best and prettiest gown possible for Reeny. Now she was anticipating its arrival more than she was that of her own new wardrobe. Kansas was so caught up in her happy thoughts that she didn't notice where her footsteps had led her. Now, a man's harsh curse and whelp of pain as he was propelled from the Bloody Guts Saloon brought her up short. Normally she crossed the street rather than walk in front of the saloon. Now she hesitated, and remembering Otis's reprimand that she use caution, finally stepped into the dusty street.

''What's the matter, Kansas McKay?'' a voice called out, and she turned to see Quill Ramsey emerging from the squalid saloon.

He stood out from the rough-looking men around him. His jacket and waistcoat were impeccable. A black string tie was knotted at the collar of his white shirt. He was cleanly shaved and his blond hair was slicked back from its part. A faint whiff of flowery scent emanated from him, cloying and unpleasant in the dust-laden air.

He's too pretty to be a man, Kansas thought, then reminded herself not to be disarmed by his sleek good looks. Quill Ramsey was as dangerous as a rattlesnake. Her fingers groped for the reassurance of her derringer, but she'd taken it out of her bag to make room for the money she carried to Father Michael. Uneasily she backed up into the street.

''I don't want any trouble from you, Quill,'' she called. ''I'm just passing by on my way to church.''

Her words seemed to amuse him. He smiled at his men

and leisurely puffed his cigarette. Leaning against a post, he crossed one foot over the other and studied her from narrowed eyes. "Why would you expect trouble from me, Miss McKay?" he asked quietly, and Kansas had a sensation of a snake slithering into a coil, preparing to strike. "Perhaps you're feeling scared because you don't have your"—he paused and curled his lips in a smile of sorts—"bodyguard with you."

The men behind him snickered. "Bodyguard! Old Otis ain't good enough to be called a bodyguard."

"He suits me," Kansas said evenly. "You'd do well not to underestimate him."

"Don't try to scare me with an old man like that," Quill said.

"Let me get rid of him, boss," Farley said, easing his gun out of his holster meaningfully. His eyes were hard and eager, and dimly Kansas realized that Ramsey's hired hand enjoyed killing people.

"No!" she shouted. "You leave Otis alone. If any harm comes to him, Ramsey, I'll—I'll—"

"You'll what?" Ramsey sneered. He nodded to two of his men and they sprang forward to grasp Kansas's arms. She struggled in their hold, but couldn't free herself.

"Bring her here," Ramsey commanded, and the men half dragged, half propelled Kansas across the street to Ramsey. His eyes glittered with evil triumph as he watched her vain struggles.

"What will you do, huh, Miss Kansas McKay? Without your bodyguard, you're helpless." One manicured hand came out to grab a fistful of hair and hauled her face closer to his. "You've got something of mine," he spat out. "I want it back."

All humor had gone from his eyes, and Kansas saw cruelty there. For the first time, she felt afraid of Quill Ramsey.

"I don't know what you're talking about!" Kansas gasped, and gritted her teeth to keep from crying out. She

could see by the elated look on Quill's face that he was
taking a perverse pleasure in thinking he had her under his
control and was causing her pain.

"You know," he insisted, tightening his grip so she expected to see great clumps of her hair float to the ground at
any moment. Tears filled the corners of her eyes and she
squeezed her lids tight to keep from crying.

"I want my saloon back," he demanded. "Give me back
the deed and I might let you live."

Kansas believed his threat. Everything about Quill frightened her. He seemed to feel no ordinary restraints of de-
cency. There was no one to rescue her. She'd been a fool
not to listen to Otis, but she hadn't realized how deadly
Quill had become. His men ringed them, so no passerby
would readily discern her distress.

"I—I can't give you back what I don't have," Kansas
said in as soothing a tone as possible. "I don't own the
Silver Spur anymore."

"You don't own it?" Quill's eyes bulged in rage; his
handsome face twisted. He jerked Kansas's head up until
her face was just inches from his. She could feel the spittle
from his lips as he gasped out his demands. "What have
you done with it?"

Kansas twisted, trying to pull away, but Quill's two men
held her arms. "I—I lost it in a poker game," she lied.
"Who?"

"I—ow—I don't know. He—he was a stranger."

Quill's hand slashed the air. Kansas's head reeled from
the blow. With Quill's fist clamped in her hair, she couldn't
turn away. She took the full brunt of the blow, and it
seemed to the men watching that her slender white neck
might break under the reverberations. "You're lying!"
Quill shouted.

Suddenly a shot rang out. The porch post behind Quill's
head splintered. The bullet had missed him by inches. Quill

swung around, his face distorted with rage. His gaze collided with the broad figure of a man on horseback.

"What the—"

"Let her go," a deep voice commanded. Cole! Joy surged through Kansas so her knees turned weak and she no longer felt the pain in her head.

"Who says so?" Quill snarled.

"I do," Cole said quietly, but his tone was deadly.

The men who'd ringed the spectacle when a helpless woman was being abused now sidled backward out of the reach of the grim, towering figure of Cole Slater.

"Tell your men to let her go," Cole commanded in a louder voice, his hard gaze turning to the men who grasped Kansas's arms.

Quill Ramsey's hand was still knotted in her hair, but now, at the deadly challenge on Cole's face, he released her and stepped back. His eyes darted back and forth, assessing where his men were and how well covered he was. At a barely perceptible nod from Quill, his gunmen readied themselves, slinking behind horse troughs and wagons for shelter as they pulled their guns and waited.

Seeing Cole was well outnumbered, Quill put on a bold front. Pushing his coat behind his back, he freed his gun holster and spread his legs in a stance that was in itself an invitation to a gunfight.

"I'm not of a mind to, Slater," he said. "You're new to these parts, so you may not know that I rule this town. There's no sheriff, no law—only the law that I make. Right now, there's a law against men like you. I won't kill you if you turn around and ride out of town."

"Don't turn your back, Cole. He'll shoot you," Kansas cried, and one of the men wrenched her arm so viciously she was driven to her knees in the dust. Despite her resolve, a cry of pain tore from her throat and her head bowed. Her golden shimmering hair shielded her face from the onlookers, so none saw the tears of pain sliding down her cheek.

Cole guessed she was crying, and his fists knotted for a moment on the reins, then he forced himself to relax, forced a thin smile to his taut lips.

"Looks like we've reached an impasse," he said.

He threw one long leg over the pommel and, with his arms outspread for balance, well away from his holster, he slid almost playfully out of the saddle, landing in the dusty street on his feet. His horse shielded him from the gunslingers, who'd taken up positions across the street. In the same rolling motion, one hand cleared a long-barreled .45 from its holster.

The report was loud in the street. One man holding Kansas gasped and released her. Clasping his shoulder, he fell to the ground. While the onlookers gaped at the fallen man, Cole calmly reached for Quill, who'd recoiled at the first shot. Yanking Quill against him as a shield, Cole leisurely brought his gun up, letting the size and length of the barrel intimidate the gambler even before he placed the bore against his temple.

"Why don't you tell your man to let the lady go?" Cole said in that same quiet, deadly voice.

Sweat had popped out on Quill's brow, and his complexion had gone all red and mottled. Eyes rolling from the .45 to the man who stood holding Kansas, Quill bobbed his head, and Kansas felt herself released. She stood rubbing her wrist, her eyes contemptuous as she stared back at Ramsey. The shot had drawn the townsmen from the saloons and stores and now pounding footsteps could be heard.

"What the devil's going on?" Otis demanded. "Miss Kansas, are you all right?"

"Yes, I'm fine now, thanks to Mr. Slater," Kansas said, looking around the throng of people. Her head was tipped back proudly, her hair a tumble of curls down her back. "Quill Ramsey ordered his men to seize me and hold me against my will while he threatened me. We can't allow this to go on in Virginia City," she cried, looking around at the men and women who'd worked hard to make the town more than a raw mining camp. There was pride and expectation on their faces whenever they talked of Virginia City and what they hoped for her future. Now they muttered among themselves, helpless to fight against men like Quill Ramsey and the gunslingers he'd hired. "We need a sheriff . . . and law and order," Kansas cried, "otherwise this town will never grow."

Cole studied her proud carriage, noting the way the other townsmen listened to her words. Kansas, he realized, was not an ordinary town whore. She had spunk and ambition, and the men respected her. Cole felt a thrill of pride rush through him for her, then he thought of those same men coming to her room at night, and pride was replaced by rage.

"Otis, take care of Kansas," he ordered, and holstered his gun.

"Cole," Kansas cried, and hurried to him. Her face was urgent and she looked into his face. "Are you leaving town?"

"I'm riding out," he acknowledged, and saw a flicker of something in her clear gray eyes before it was quickly replaced by steely pride.

"Thank you for stopping to help me," she said, and her voice was husky. "Good-bye, Cole."

"Good-bye, Kansas."

No mention was made of their night together at the Kansas Palace, but it was there between them. The drunk-hazed memory of it had tormented Cole ever since, and standing before Kansas, he longed to drag her into his arms and kiss her sweet pink lips. But the men of the town stood in the street arguing. Quill Ramsey had sidled away and was talking quietly, furtively, to Farley.

Cole's eyes narrowed as he watched the two men. Quill glanced up and caught Cole's angry gaze, and the gambler's sleek features curved into a triumphant sneer. Cold fear washed over Cole, not for himself, but for the diminutive, spunky woman standing before him.

"We can't find a man brave enough to be sheriff," Otis was saying to the other men. "If'n I was fifteen years younger, I might take on the job, but I'm too old and too slow." Quill Ramsey and his men snickered loudly.

Cole gripped Kansas's shoulders and set her aside. Striding back to the knot of men, he faced the old timer. "Where's that badge, Otis?" he said, holding out his hand.

A grin spread over Otis's bewhiskered face. "By damn, I've got it right here," he said, digging into his pocket. He pulled out the metal badge and handed it to Cole.

Cole pinned the silver star on his shirt and turned to face Quill Ramsey and his gang. "Virginia City's got a sheriff now," he said evenly, "and there will be law and order."

Quill's face had gone ugly. Snapping his cheroot into the street, he turned his back and strode back into the Bloody Guts Saloon. Casting murderous, threatening glances at Cole and the men clustered around him, Ramsey's men followed.

"We're mighty grateful, mighty grateful, son," Otis cried, slapping Cole on the back. "We need a man like you to stand up to Quill Ramsey and his gang."

Cole raised his head and glanced at the spot where he'd left Kansas. But she was no longer there. Hair streaming behind her, skirts billowing, she was half running down the street, as if the devil himself were after her.

Kansas hurried down the street, her mission no longer to take money to Father Michael, but to escape Cole Slater and the fact that he was staying in Virginia City, after all. But try as she might, she couldn't outrun the memory of his kiss or his hard, masculine body covering hers, claiming hers passionately. Even now as the images of their sweat-slicked, plunging bodies plagued her thoughts, nerves and senses responded with a hot surge of desire that sent a blush to her cheeks and robbed her of breath. God help her, she wanted Cole Slater. She wanted him to stay here in Virginia City, she wanted him to come to her in the night—and he would. She had little doubt of that. It had been in that last searing look before he'd turned to Otis and the townsmen. He was staying because of her, and she was both thrilled and frightened at the prospect.

How could she continue an affair with him when he believed her a whore? How could she love and desire a man who'd taken her innocence in a drunken haze and not realized the taking? She felt defenseless against his accusations of her. Just as the shield of her virginity had been breached so, too, was her shield of resolve that had help her maintain that virginal state all these years. There had been men, kind men who'd touched her in some special way, men who'd desired her and wooed her, men who'd offered her marriage and given no thought to her tainted past, either as the daughter of a whore or as a gambling lady, but none of them had been Cole.

Kansas paused in the shade of a silver pine. She was high in the hills now, with the town below and the mountain and the blazing blue sky above. The scent of sagebrush was carried on a hot desert breeze. Kansas drew in a shaky breath and settled herself on a flat rock so she could look down at the town. Smoke rose from the blacksmith's shed, and she imagined the burly man drawing a horseshoe from the glowing embers of his fire and plunging it into the cooling water trough to temper it. Like that horseshoe, she'd been made to bend and had grown more resilient from it. She'd plunged into the fiery embers of Cole's passion—and the icy depths of his contempt—and now she should be stronger for it. But was she, when she sat here longing for his embrace?

Her restless gaze moved to the raw unpainted siding of

the boardinghouse and she wondered how Ellie and Mrs. Simpson were faring. Deliberately she turned her attention to the half-finished church, to the Kansas Palace with its fine high gables, and to the Silver Spur Saloon. Try as she might to busy her thoughts on the town and its occupants, she knew she was back where she'd started, thinking about Cole Slater and the fact that she loved him and always would.

"Oh, Cole," she moaned, and put her head on her knees as she fought back the tears of pain and humiliation she'd tried so hard not to shed ever since that night he'd made love to her. She'd been furious, and rightfully so, at his callous opinion of her. She'd vowed never to see him again, never, never to allow him to touch her, to kiss her, or to make love to her. That was easier to do when he wasn't around, but when he was here in Virginia City day after day, could she maintain her resolve?

Even now, she hungered for him. She longed to rush back down the hill just for another glimpse of his tall, rangy body. She shuddered, forcing down the ache that rose inside her. She was still that young girl back in Webster, she thought bitterly, still yearning after Cole Slater, waiting pitifully for any crumb of attention he might throw her way. . . . But not this time. Not this time. She'd struggled long and hard to break old ties, to change her own old way of thinking. No longer was she the helpless girl who must endure the taunts and misconception of others. She was a full-grown woman who'd worked hard to gain her independence and stand on her own two feet. Let Cole Slater think what he would of her, she knew what she was—and she had a right to be proud. She would soon show him she wasn't a woman of easy virtue. And although he was now the town sheriff and she a gambling lady, she carried as much prestige in town as he, perhaps more.

Still, he had stayed because of her. That was a certainty that grew deep inside her like some stubborn weed that flourished on the arid desert. Cole had stayed because he cared. Kansas raised her head, staring with luminous, joyful eyes down the hillside. Whatever mistaken notions he had about her, he cared for her, too. She would build on that. She'd tell him the truth about herself, make him understand he was the first man for her, the only man. Perhaps they still could find a way to each other. He'd wanted to marry her once. He'd loved her once . . . and must still. That was all that mattered. They'd work out the rest.

Her face was luminous as she hurried back down the hill, sending small stones rolling beneath her racing feet. Her hair was disheveled from her run-in with Quill and now it stuck to her sweaty nape and cheeks, but she took no time to push it away. She must find Cole. She had so much to tell him, so much to explain.

She regained the edge of town and hurried down the street. Ahead, she caught a glimpse of a tall, lanky figure on horseback. He'd paused to speak to someone in a fine carriage. Kansas guessed from Reeny's description the buggy belonged to the new banker. Cole tipped his hat and urged his horse into a gallop. Kansas's smile of anticipation faded and she opened her mouth to call out to him, but the stately carriage was drawing near and she had no wish to make a spectacle of herself. For the first time she gave some thought to her appearance and brushed at the yellow dust soiling her skirts. The carriage passed by and Kansas glanced up. As she caught a glimpse of the passengers, she gasped. The cloying dust seemed to settle in her nostrils and throat so the breath was choked from her. Her wide-eyed gaze met the equally startled gaze of Claire Howard. Then the carriage rolled past.

The dust swirled around Kansas, then slowly settled back to earth. Kansas walked back to the hotel on wooden legs. All her joy was gone, for now the memory of Cole Slater and Claire Howard dancing together overwhelmed her.

What a fool she'd been, once again, hoping like that

foolish young girl back in Webster, dreaming that Cole Slater could love her. Now she knew he'd stayed because of Claire Howard. Oh, he might come creeping in the night to Kansas's bed, the bed of a whore, but it was women like Claire Howard that men like Cole Slater married. Defeat was a bitter gall in her mouth.

Chapter 11

THE KANSAS PALACE was finished. With thick walls of stone cut from the mountains themselves, it sat in regal splender, its pristine whitewashed gables visible from the streets below. Curious people strolled by, pausing to study its elegant, uncluttered lines and imposing size. The Palace pleased them. Like the bank, the school, the church, and the large private houses going up on the other end of town, the Palace, by its very size and grandeur, signaled a new—more prosperous—era of the town's history. Furthermore, most of the miners had come to think of Kansas as one of their own. She might win their money, but she always did it fairly, and she softened the sting of their losses with a witty quip or a sweet smile that melted any lingering resentment. She'd also been known to loan a miner who'd been unwise enough to lose his grubstake enough money to start again. No man, woman, or child who knew Kansas McKay would go hungry for want of a friendly, helping hand.

Now those men who'd known her since she'd come to town, and in some instances before, reveled in her success. Talk and speculation about the Kansas Palace could be heard in every saloon. The miners anticipated something grand and unique, just like the Palace's owner. Kansas was determined not to disappoint them. Prudence was thrown to the wind as she sank her last dollar into the new gambling house.

Freight wagons rumbled over the mountain ranges from San Francisco bringing goods imported from the finest salons of Paris, London, Brussels, and the Orient. And no one was allowed to see what was in the crates and cartons that were unloaded and ushered inside. Only the women from the Silver Spur and Ellie had the privilege of helping Kansas to uncrate and arrange the furniture and rugs. Curtains of pure white Belgian lace appeared at the windows, a woven rattan rug was placed on the porch, but the rest of the house remained mysteriously closed. Good-naturedly the miners pumped Reeny and the other women about the Palace, and good-naturedly they accepted their admonitions to wait and see for themselves. Reeney and the others enjoyed being a part of the secret.

Caught up in the consuming task of furnishing the Palace, Kansas was preoccupied, but ever aware of Cole's presence. He seemed to be everywhere she looked. When she glanced up from a poker game at the Silver Spur, when she walked up the hill to St. Mary's Church, or when she lingered in the general store, Cole seemed always to be there, tipping his hat, his eyes soft and wary when he looked at her.

Virginia City wasn't big enough for both of them! Try as she might to ignore Cole's presence, he intruded on her days and nights, for when she'd sunk into bed, her body sore from the hard, unaccustomed work of readying the Palace and her mind fatigued from the long hours over the poker table, the image of his lean, tanned face and big-boned rangy body pressed in on her.

He'd made no effort to speak to her again since that day he rescued her from Quill Ramsey's tender mercies. Sometimes Kansas wondered if he even remembered having made love to her. Sometimes she wondered if it had been a dream, after all, a dream born of a desperate longing held too long in abeyance. Then she remembered the tenderness of her breasts the morning after and the blood-spotted petticoat. She would have known without all those things, for her body and senses, having once tasted the pleasures and passions Cole had shown her, now clamored for more.

Whenever she thought of his touch, a lanquid warmth stole over her and she often fell to daydreaming, so that Reeny and Ellie would nudge each other and whisper behind her back. Though they said nothing to her of their thoughts, she had only to look at their teasing, smiling eyes to know they'd guessed. She only buried her feelings deeper. She couldn't bear to be hurt more, and Cole's words, uttered as they were that night in a drunken haze, had wounded more deeply than all the taunts of her childhood. She was a woman now, her needs were more complex, her desires more urgent, her vulnerability more frightening. So each morning as she rose, heavy-eyed and tired from her sleepless night, she clamped on a resolve so ironclad it seemed surely nothing could undo it. So the days passed, and she began to breathe easier.

"Did you see what those freight wagons hauled up to the Palace today?" Everett Howell said one afternoon at the Silver Spur Saloon. He'd come in for supplies and stopped in to visit and have a drink or two. "That was just about the biggest, grandest bed I expect I've ever seen."

The other men nodded in acknowledgement and cast a quick glance at the tall man seated in the corner talking to Otis.

"Take it easy, Ev," one man warned under his breath. "Rumor has it the sheriff is ah . . . uh . . . interested in Miss Kansas."

"Shoot, that don't much matter. Nearly every man in town and them hills out there is interested in Miss Kansas."

I didn't see her standing still for him when he first came to town. She went hightailin' it right out the window to avoid him. No, sir, what Miss Kansas is lookin' for is a real man, like me.'' The men snickered at the young man's bragging, and he grinned good-naturedly.

"What do you figure a lil' ole girl like Miss Kansas is going to do in a bed that big?" Ev slapped his friend's shoulder. "Reckon she needs some company?"

His friend's answering grin was a little thin, but Ev didn't notice.

"Makes a man wonder what all he could do in a bed like that," the young miner went on. "Takes a special kind of man to fill up a bed like that. I'll bet it's got a feather mattress and two plump little pillows just like Miss Kansas's b—"

The other men at the bar sidled away as a long arm reached out and a fist gathered up the front of Ev Howell's shirt. Cole Slater's face was ugly mean as he stared down at the young miner. How many of the men lined up along the bar thought the way Ev did?

"You in for supplies, Ev?" he asked in a deceptively mild tone.

"Uh . . . yes, sir," Ev said. His eyes had gotten big. They rolled from one side to the other as he looked for help from his friends. He'd forgotten just how formidable the new sheriff could be.

"Well, son. I suggest you go on over to the general store and get what you need and get back out to your claim."

"Yes, sir."

"Don't you go up that hill to the Palace."

"N-no. I w-wasn't plannin' on it."

"Don't even look up there."

"N-no, sir."

"Don't even let your mind think about the Palace or anything in it."

"I—I won't, Sheriff." Ev shook his head vigorously.

"If your mind should happen to wander to the Palace and the furniture it has in it . . ." Cole released Ev's shirtfront and gently smoothed the collar. Ev swallowed hard enough to be heard by the other men. "If your mind should wander, Ev, think about the kitchen table."

"The kitchen table. I wi— That's good advice, sir." Ev blabbered. "I reckon I'd best get my supplies together." He sidled away, and when he was sure he was clear of Cole's long arms, he bolted out the door.

The other men guffawed until they saw Cole was watching them. Quickly they turned their gazes to their mugs. Grimly Cole stalked out of the saloon and stood on the porch, staring up at the Palace.

"Damn it to hell, Kansas, don't you know what you're stirring up down here?" he muttered under his breath. He'd wanted to kill Everett Howell. Only the young miner's pale, scared face had kept Cole from forcing him to draw. Cole wiped his hand over his face as if to clear away the anger. Swinging into his saddle, he headed his mount up into the hills, where he spent the rest of the day checking the outlying claims.

Kansas stood on the porch of the Palace and drew a deep breath. Wearily she hunched her shoulders high, then let them droop again. She was more tired than she'd ever been in her life, but the Palace was ready, at last. Each room gleamed with a special richness she'd envisioned. For all the expense and hard work, she wasn't disappointed with her new home. And a home it had become. Above the wide salons and gracious dining rooms were her private rooms, the place she could go to be alone when she felt the need. Besides the salons and parlors and dining room, the first floor also contained a kitchen, a breakfast room, and a small morning room, used by Kansas as an office, while at the top of the fine sweeping staircase were her bedroom, a dressing room, a private sitting room, guest rooms, and maids' rooms. All were carpeted and furnished. Even the cellars were completed and filled with fine imported wines from France, Italy, and Germany.

Kansas drew a deep breath of satisfaction and gazed out at the town. She should go bathe and change now; she must be a sight with her skirts tucked up and a rag tied around her hair. Her arms and hands were smudged with dirt and she reckoned her face was as well. Still she lingered, thinking back over the past few days and the task she'd completed with the help of Ellie and Reeny and the rest of the women.

"Pardon me, ma'am." A lazy, teasing voice broke through her thoughts. "I'm looking for the princess who lives in this fine palace."

"Cole." Kansas snatched the rag from her head and scrubbed at her face before thrusting it and the broom behind her. In her haste, her curls were dislodged and tumbled in glorious disarray around her shoulders. "I was just finishing some last-minute cleaning," she explained, not at all immune to his smile. "I don't look much like a princess, more like a scrubwoman."

"I don't agree," he said quietly, and Kansas stopped fussing with her rolled-up sleeves and glanced at him.

His face had gone somber, his teasing grin was gone, but his eyes swallowed her whole, picked her up and swirled her around like one of the dust eddies out on the desert. She felt all breathless and dizzy. She forgot her anger, forgot her resolve—and remembered only the magic of being held in his arms, of being caressed and loved by Cole Slater.

"It was good of you to stay in Virginia City and act as our sheriff," she said, seeking a bit of conversation to cover the flush he'd brought to her cheeks and the pounding to her heart. "Otis is mighty grateful."

"How about you, Kansas?" Cole asked quietly. "Are you happy I stayed?" He sat slouched in his saddle, one leg thrown over the saddle horn, his wide-brimmed hat pulled low, leaving his face in shadows. She caught the glint of gray as he studied her through narrowed eyes and awaited her answer.

"I—of course, I'm grateful, too, that we now have a sheriff," she fumbled, and looked down at the edge of the porch. One white knuckled hand grasped a pillar for support.

"That's not what I mean," Cole said, and slid off his horse.

While her mouth worked and no words came to ward him off, he strolled across the yellow dust and stood below her. Even with the elevation of the porch, she was not that much taller than he. She watched his gaze move up her body, pausing at her hips and breasts, and felt herself grow warm. With one step forward, she could rest her arms around his broad shoulders, pull him close so his face buried itself against her soft breasts. She stood holding her breath in the hot afternoon air, imagining just that, imagining her fingers twining themselves in his thick, dark hair, imagining his mouth opening and his teeth closing gently, urgently, over one nipple. What would the townspeople think if they drove by and saw her standing in full view on her porch allowing the town sheriff to suckle her right through her dimity bodice? Kansas sighed, letting go of the fantasy, pulling her old rigid aloofness around her.

"That was all I meant, Mr. Slater," she said crisply.

He stood puzzled at her change of moods. For a moment there, he thought he'd glimpsed a touch of the raw hunger that had driven him for three years. "Heard this was a gambling house, rather than a calico palace," he said, leaning one hand against the same pillar she gripped.

Kansas studied their two hands for a moment, acutely aware of the differences between them, man and woman differences. His hand was darkly tanned from his hours in the sunlight, hers was pale and slender, his large and callous, hers daintily small and smooth.

"Where you going to put the rest of your girls?"

"My girls?" Kansas repeated, puzzled. Then comprehension flooded her mind and her teeth gritted together in an effort not to rail at him.

"There won't be any other girls here," she said softly, her voice little more than a husky, intimate whisper. "Only me."

Cole looked startled. "You're getting out of the business then?" he asked softly. He didn't need to say which business, she knew all too well. Why must he persist in thinking the worst of her? she wondered bitterly. Why must he believe it inevitable that she follow in her mother's footsteps? Proudly she raised her chin and gazed over his head.

"No, I'm keeping some of my best customers," she said, and her words struck at him like a rawhide whip, so he turned away from her then and didn't see the bleak pain in her eyes. Kansas saw the full lips form into a thin, disapproving line and the flare of his nostrils as he sucked in air—and she read them all as a sign of his contempt for her and what he thought she was.

Perversely she put a hand on one hip and swayed suggestively. "I'm going to be very selective with my clientele . . . and very expensive. You probably won't be able to afford me on your sheriff's earnings, but I'll put in a word with Reeny and the girls." His jaw tightened. She could see the muscles flex beneath the smooth, tanned skin.

He turned to face her again, and the eyes that had danced with humor and sunshine and a hint of shimmering passion were now cold and flat with anger. "So you sell yourself for a fancy price now," he said in a quiet, even voice that struck a spark of fear within her. Before she knew what was happening one broad tanned hand shot out, grasped her arm, and jerked her forward.

She screamed and let go of the broom. It clattered to the porch as she scrambled for one instant to regain her footing, but Cole's grasp was unrelenting as he tumbled her down into his waiting arms. Bands of muscle, bone, and sinew wrapped around her, crushing her to his chest; his mouth settled on hers, hot and demanding. She felt his tongue against her lips forcing entry, then thrusting deep time and again until all thought of resistance was driven from her and she was clinging to him with all the fervor and desire of which she was capable. Dimly she realized the whole populace of Virginia City could ride up that hill and observe her in Cole Slater's embrace—and it mattered not one jot to her. This was where she wanted to be, caught in the churning power of his passion.

Cole kissed her thoroughly, until they were both breathless, then he raised his head and stared into her eyes. "Don't ever think I can't have you when I want you, Kansas, no matter how fancy the price," he bit out. Once more his lips settled on hers in a hard, branding kiss that said he would never be denied, then he released her so quickly she nearly fell to her knees in the dust.

Cole was already swinging into his saddle as she looked at him through tear-glazed eyes. What had happened between them was too painful, and undeniable. Cole knew it, too, for he sat on his horse gazing down at her as she crouched in the dust.

"I'll be back, Kansas," he promised, and rode away, leaving her aching with need for him.

"Damn you, Cole Slater, don't come back," she shouted after him.

Cole heard her cry, but didn't look back. She would never know how difficult it had been for him to leave her there. Kneeling in the dust, her hair tousled, her lips full and bruised from his kisses, her skirts crumpled around her, she'd looked earthy and sensuous. He'd wanted to climb off his horse and take her there, in the yellow dust of her front yard, but he'd guessed something about Kansas in her youth and knew it still applied today. She wanted to be respectable. Despite her past and her present, she longed to be a

lady of virtue instead of a soiled dove. Riding down the hill
he thought of all the things he'd heard about her here in
Virginia City. She was the first one to offer help, the first to
contribute to the town's needs. She'd built a reputation that
had nothing to do with being the town whore. He'd not do
anything to hurt that fragile image by taking her cheaply.
He'd do it her way, but by damn he'd be back—and he'd
beat to a pulp any man he learned had been with her in that
big bed. . . . Cole drove his heels into his mount's ribs and
galloped toward the new jail.

"Looks like the new sheriff's got hisself het up over
something," Otis said to Hugo Betts.

He watched the big man ride by, then grinned. Yessir,
Kansas could get anyone het up, but with Cole Slater it
seemed worse than usual.

Chapter 12

OPENING NIGHT AT the Palace was more successful than Kansas could ever have hoped for, but her encounter with Cole that afternoon had left her feeling edgy and morose. Ellie had taken time off from her job at the boardinghouse and come to help Kansas with last-minute details. Her commanding tones could be heard from the kitchen to the salons, where newly hired maids were putting out cut-glass bowls of sweetmeats and nuts, fine imported cigars, and gold-edged lead crystal ashtrays. Sparkling crystal, wine, and whiskey glasses sat at the ready on the sideboards, where silver buckets of ice-chilled bottles of the finest wine imported from France, Italy, and Germany sat. Irish whiskey, English gin, and Scotch were on hand, as were uniformed bartenders to serve them.

Gaming tables had been set up throughout the richly appointed salons. Opulent Turkish rugs, incandescent, two-tiered chandeliers, damask draperies, matching parlor sets with rich satin brocade coverings and wide-coiled spring seats at first awed the rough miners, then delighted them as they realized they'd been arranged for their own comfort.

Rules applied here just as they had in Kansas's room when she first came to Virginia City, and the men accepted without rancor that they mustn't put their boots on the fur-

niture or spit tobacco juice on the floor or—the most important rule of all—climb the stairs to the private rooms
above. There were no women here at the Palace, save those
who'd been hired to serve them food and drink. If a man
needed a woman for any other purpose, he knew to climb
back down the hill to the Silver Spur or one of the other
saloons specializing in such services. A man must bathe and
don a frock coat if he expected to gain entrance to the Palace
and, once inside, he was expected to behave himself as a
gentleman at all times. There was no distinction of class. A
lowly miner might sit elbow to elbow with a town dignitary,
and for a short while, as they enjoyed Kansas's expensive
cigars and smooth cognac over a game of cards or faro, they
shared a common bond. If a man grew hungry, he had only
to wander into one of the spacious dining rooms, where
mahogany tables, spread with fine white Irish linen, groaned
under a variety of food, and French chefs in splendid hats
offered their latest culinary efforts on plates of delicate English china.

In short, there was everything a man could want—save
that provided by the women of the saloons and cribs
below—and such needs were not discussed here. This was
a gentleman's club, a place to come and partake of fine
wine, food, and a little gambling. Here, even the lowliest
could enjoy the refinements of a gentleman for a little while.
The miners loved it; the town dignitaries welcomed such a
place, which offered them such diversions without the
bawdy stigma of the saloons. The Kansas Palace was a
resounding success.

"So why ain't you happy?" Ellie demanded when she
came upon Kansas looking pensively out the window.

Kansas shrugged a slim shoulder beneath the elegant silk
gown she wore and turned back to the salons. A quick
glance told her all was going well. Otis was mingling with
the guests, slapping men on the back, calling them by name,
refilling glasses. She should be happy, Kansas reminded

herself, but felt no lessening of the discontent that filled her. She had, she realized, been waiting all evening for Cole Slater to appear. She'd taken special care with her gown and hair, wanting him to see how beautiful she could be before she hurled her rejection into his face. Anger still simmered below the surface.

"He didn't come tonight, did he?" Ellie demanded, and with a start Kansas realized she hadn't answered the woman's first question.

Ellie seemed unperturbed. Snatching an empty wineglass from a Jelliff table of inlayed walnut and maple, she scrubbed at the lingering ring of moisture. "Men," she snorted, and Kansas wasn't sure if she was referring to the careless guest who'd left the glass behind or if she'd guessed that Kansas had waited expectantly for Cole Slater to show up. The Irish woman's next words assured her of the latter.

"Just like a man to come find you in sweaty cotton, but to never mind about seeing you in silks and satins," she muttered, casting a piercing glance at Kansas's flushed cheeks. "Never you mind, dearie. If he's like most men, he don't care if you have on anything at all."

"I don't know what you're talking about," Kansas said, mortified that Ellie might have guessed her need for Cole Slater.

"I'm sorry to say I saw you from the kitchen window this afternoon and I seen the way he done you, grabbing you and kissing you like you was a piece of baggage left for his use. . . . But I seen something else, Kansas, that you didn't. I seen his face, and I'm tellin' you that man is probably prowling the street down there, pickin' on some poor unsuspecting drunk when all he wants to do is be up here with you."

"You're wrong, Ellie," Kansas said, turning away from the woman with an impatient gesture. "Cole Slater is someone I knew in my past, but he means nothing to me now . . . nor I to him."

"I allus thought you was a right smart woman, Kansas McKay," Ellie snapped, "but if you believe that—or think to make me believe it—then you're dumber than dirt. I'll wager Cole Slater will be here before the night's out."

"You'll lose, Ellie," Kansas said, twisting her hands in front of her. "I have no desire to discuss Cole Slater further. I—I have guests to see to."

"You mark my words," Ellie mumbled, bearing the wineglass to the kitchen. "The bay leaves don't lie. I predicted he was near once before and I was right. Mark my words, he'll be here tonight."

Kansas stared after the frowsy woman. She really should tell Ellie she didn't need her anymore, that she should return to her job at the boardinghouse. Certainly Ellie didn't fit in with the elegant setting of the Kansas Palace, but Kansas hadn't the heart to send the woman away. Once again she turned to the window. She could see the lights in the saloons below. Was Cole there as Ellie had said, pining for her as she . . . ? But she wasn't pining for Cole. She flounced away from the window and strolled through the Palace salons, nodding graciously to her clients.

The evening seemed interminable—and each time the door opened to disclose still another customer, Kansas couldn't stop herself from looking, hoping to catch sight of a tall, rangy figure with broad shoulders, a broad grin, and touseled, sun-streaked hair. But Cole didn't come, and at last she stopped expecting him. He'd been an insufferable beast anyway. She should never speak to him again for the way he'd treated her.

The last card had been played, the last silver exchanged hands, the last droplet of wine poured and drank, and Otis tactfully but firmly had led the last customer to the door and bolted it firmly behind him.

"I'd say your fortune's made in this town, Miss Kansas," he said, loosening the string tie he'd valiantly worn all evening.

"Yes, the Palace was well received tonight," Kansas replied wearily. "Our receipts were better than anything I'd hoped for."

"The Palace'll soon pay for itself at this rate," Otis agreed. "If you don't need me anymore, Miss Kansas, I'm going to bed."

"Good night, Otis. We'll clean up tomorrow." Wearily Kansas watched Otis climb the stairs, wishing she could go up to her rooms and slide into her own soft bed, but she must lock away her receipts and see that the kitchen was cleared away and locked.

Gathering up the gold and pearl box that held the day's take, she made her way to the small room she'd claimed as her office, locked away the considerable amount of cash and silver, then, carrying a sheaf of bills with her, she turned to the kitchen. One more task to complete and she could go to bed and go over her bills before sleep claimed her. She had little hope of accomplishing much tonight, but at least she would have something to fill the lonely hours. She pulled the pins from her hair, letting the heavy gold mass tumble around her shoulders in disarray.

"Ah, mademoiselle, such a night," Andre Gage said when she entered the kitchen.

He was busy putting away the rest of the leftover food and securing the pantry. He'd laid aside his starched white coat and chef's hat, and she was struck by what a handsome distinguished-looking man he was. She stood watching him, grateful for his consideration and help.

"Your entrees were *beaucoup très bien*," she said, stumbling over her attempts at French. "The customers enjoyed them a great deal."

"*Mais, oui.*" Andre shrugged. "I must admit, mademoiselle, that when you first brought me here, I thought I was out of my element, a fish out of water, eh? But, ah, the Palace"—once again he rolled his eyes—"*c'est magnifique.*"

"Thank you, Andre," Kansas said, touched by the Frenchman's words. "You added a great deal to its success tonight—" She was interrupted by a knock at the front door. "See, a persistent customer." She laughed. "Good night, Andre."

"*Bonsoir*, mademoiselle," Andre called after her.

The imperious knock sounded again on the heavy oak door, this time more impatient and more demanding. Kansas swung the door open, prepared to give a tongue-lashing to the inconsiderate oaf on the other side. Cole Slater stood filling the doorway and, involuntarily, she stepped backward.

"Hello, Kansas," he said, rolling the brim of his hat between big suntanned hands.

She might have thought him nervous or uncertain if not for the arrogant tilt of his chin and the mocking challenge in his eyes. "I'm sorry, Cole," she said, drawing herself up proudly, "but you've come too late. We're closed."

"I didn't come to gamble," he said, brushing past her. He turned and his gaze pinned her. "You know why I've come."

Kansas felt the heat flare in her groin and spread outward, warming her, consuming her. She gritted her teeth, struggling to control the spiraling desire. Coolly she looked back at him. "I'm sorry, I—not tonight."

"What do you mean, not tonight?" Cole growled. His hat went sailing through the air, skidded across a marble tabletop, and landed on the plush rug.

While Kansas's nervous gaze had followed the flight of his hat, Cole had strode forward and now gripped her shoulders, pulling her forward. "After this afternoon, you knew I'd come," he said, shaking her slightly.

"After the abominable way you behaved this afternoon, Mr. Slater, I wasn't sure of anything as far as you're concerned. I'm afraid I haven't planned to receive you this evening, therefore you'll have to go."

She reached for the doorknob, but he pulled her roughly against his chest and lowered his head. He was going to kiss her, she realized, and tried to turn aside. His lips, hot and moist and hungry, landed on her cheek instead.

Cole seemed not to notice her resistance. Hungrily his lips slid along her jawline, his tongue blazing a hot path to the point of her chin. His mouth opened, and for one brief moment closed over the rounded point of her chin. Kansas shivered in his embrace, her lips parting to emit a moan. Cole's lips moved to cover hers, his tongue delving, demanding, dancing over hers with light feathery strokes that grew more urgent with each thrust.

When at last he released her, she was incapable of standing alone. She lay against his chest gasping in air. He gathered a handful of golden curls and held them to his face, drawing in the fragrance that was Kansas. His breath was hot against her cheek, his voice ragged as he whispered against her ear.

"Make me go away now, Kansas," he challenged, and part of her longed to hurl him through the door—while another part clung to him and whimpered, her hungry lips sliding across his rough jawline in search of his mouth.

"Miss Kansas, you forgot— Oh, *excusez-moi*," a voice said from the salon.

Cole's body stiffened as he raised his head and glared at the distinguished dark-haired man who stood in the doorway with the sheaf of forgotten bills clutched in his hand. Cole's quick, angry gaze took in the lack of a proper jacket, the missing shirt collar and tie, and the droopy suspenders, then he turned back to Kansas with her hair tumbling all down her back and onto her low-cut décolletage. His fingers bit into the soft flesh of her arms and once again he shook her, this time not so gently.

"Who is this?" he demanded. "Were you going to spend the evening with this man? Is he one of your infernal special clients?"

Anger swept through Kansas. How dare he talk to her this way? How dare he stalk in here and treat her as if she were a child caught in a wrongdoing? How dare he jump to such conclusions about her? She jerked free of his grasp, her magnificent hair flying around her in a silken mass. Her chin jutted high, her eyes were triumphant.

"Yes, Mr. Slater," she said sweetly, triumphantly. "This is what I've been trying to tell you. I can't be with you tonight. I already have a customer."

"*Mon Dieu,*" Andre gasped as Cole's savage glare settled on him once more. Anxiously the Frenchman backed up. "*Mais, non,* monsieur," he said placatingly.

"Get rid of him," Cole demanded, his glare on Kansas now. His lips were taut. A muscle twitched near his right eye. He looked furious and dangerous.

But Kansas was feeling furious herself. One eyebrow arched upward and her gray-green eyes spit fire. "I'm not of a mind to," she said.

"Then I'll do it for you," Cole said, and strode toward the Frenchman.

"Cole!" Kansas cried a warning, but he ignored her. His fists were clenched, his eyes narrowed, and he moved with feral like purpose.

"*Mais, non,*" Andre said placatingly, "I did not wish to disturb you, monsieur. I only meant to—"

"I know what you meant to do," Cole snarled, bunching the little man's shirt in one hand while he raised the other in the form of a large brown fist. Andre's eyes rolled in his head.

"Cole, no," Kansas cried, and launched herself on Cole, grabbing hold of the upraised arm. She could feel flexing muscles beneath her soft hands and was all too aware of how ineffectual she would be against such power.

Cole shook her loose, but she pinned herself against him, pitting her puny strength against his. In the struggle she heard cloth tearing as Andre wrenched free of Cole's clasp and scuttled back in the direction of the kitchen. Cole swiped Kansas aside as if she were a bee and ran after him. Kansas heard the back door open and slam back against the wall and rushed to the kitchen. Cole was standing in the open door, chest heaving, eyes fixed on something out in the yard.

"Keep running, you paperbacked coyote," he shouted after the departing figure of Kansas's cook. "Don't you ever come back here—or I'll shoot you so you'll never have need of a woman again."

Outraged, Kansas stood staring at him as if he were mad, then, slowly, laughter bubbled up in her. She'd just lost a chef she'd gone to great expense to get, yet she stood here laughing like a dolt.

At the sound of her giggle, Cole turned around and glared at her. "What's so all-fired funny?" he demanded.

"Nothing," Kansas said, pressing a hand to her lips to still any further sounds. But her eyes danced with laughter. She stared at Cole Slater and her heart was so full she thought it might burst, because one thing had become undeniably clear to her. For all the insults he'd hurled at her, Cole had given himself away. He was, she realized, jealous at the thought of any man touching her. And he couldn't be jealous if he didn't care for her.

Cole's fierce look turned sheepish, and he took a step forward. "Look, Kansas, I'm sorry about that. I just didn't want you to be with anyone but me tonight. I don't know how much money he was about to pay, but I'll pay you back." He dug in his pocket; he didn't see the hurt that crossed Kansas's face and was quickly replaced with a smile.

"It doesn't matter," she said. "Cole, I have something to tell you."

"I don't blame you if you want to cuss me out," he said. "I know I took liberties I had no right to. It's just that since this afternoon, I've thought of nothing else but being with you." He pulled out some crumbled bills and laid them on the kitchen table.

"Cole," Kansas said softly, gathering up the money and holding it out to him. Her face was luminous. "I'm not what you think I am. I'm not a whore. I never was. You were the first man I was ever with."

"Kansas . . ." Her name was a groan on his lips. "You don't have to do this. You don't have to pretend to an innocence that you don't have. These past days I've been thinking about all that's happened to you, and I don't blame you for what you've become."

"But Cole—" Kansas began.

One rough brown finger laid across her soft lips stilled her words. "I accept you for what you are, Kansas," he said. "And I don't think any less of you for it. Don't try to be something you aren't, not for me." His wide hands settled on her shoulders in a touch that was awkwardly masculine and endearingly gentle.

Kansas studied his earnest face and thought she'd never loved Cole Slater more than at this moment. One day she'd convince him of the truth of what she said, but not tonight. The time for talking was done. Now need clamored through her so she was left trembling and expectant.

"I'll be whatever you want me to be, Cole," she whispered, and wondered if he knew how much she surrendered with those words.

He took the money from her nerveless hands, then gathered her up in his arms and carried her back through the darkened salons to the great stairs leading upward.

"Tell me where to go," he ordered huskily, and she directed him through the darkened house to her room, where one of the maids had left a rose-colored lamp burning. It cast a soft glow on the man and woman. Cole carried Kansas to the big walnut bed that had occasioned such speculation in town. Tenderly he laid her on the counterpane, then knelt to take off her shoes. When she sat up to help, he pushed her back.

"I was too drunk the last time to appreciate you," he said raggedly. "This time I want to go slowly and savor every moment." He settled a slow, sensuous kiss on her mouth, then knelt again to loosen her shoes, then her silk hose.

Kansas felt the rough texture of his hand against her heated thigh and calf. A delicious languorous warmth ran through her. Then Cole was towering over her again, his hands tangling with the laces and dainty buttons of her gown. While he fumbled with the fastenings, she lazily unbuttoned his shirt, letting her hands dip inside to feel the soft mat of hair and the warm flesh and sinewy muscles beneath. Their lips meshed in long languorous kisses that increased in fervor. Cole's tongue delved deep, tasting the sweetness of her. She caught his full lower lip between her small white teeth and nibbled until he groaned low and deep in his chest. Impatiently she pushed the shirt over his shoulders and moved her hands to his pants.

They were both breathing heavily. Cole trailed kisses onto the full thrusting tops of her exposed breasts and pulled impatiently at the tight-fitting bodice. "Kansas," he gasped. "These fancy buttons confound me," he confessed, and her fingers left his pants and tore at the dainty fastenings of her gown. Cole stood before her, legs wide spread, lean stomach taut, and slowly unbuttoned his trousers.

Kansas paused at the laces that held her corset in place and stared as the coarse material slid down the muscular columns of his thighs. But as spectacular as his lean legs were, it was the hard, burgeoning column of his manhood that made her catch her breath. Her breasts thrust against the restraining material of her hateful gown and she wrenched the last buttons free, hearing them pop loose. Tomorrow she would look for them. Tonight was not the time to worry about such things. A man, all hot male, stood before her, his eyes crinkling as he laughed at her impatience, his big hands reaching for her.

He pulled her to her feet and miraculously she stood, though her knees felt as paperbacked as Cole had accused Andre's spine of being. He finished undressing her, languid gentleness forgotten in his growing need for her. At last her shift and petticoat lay on the floor at her feet and she stood naked before him. She watched his face as he lowered his gaze. She felt the searing heat of his glance. Tentatively he reached out a hand to gather the rounded weight of one breast. His thumb brushed across one taut nipple and she thought she might swoon, then he dipped his head and suckled as she'd wanted him to do that afternoon, and a yearning flared to a conflagration.

Her fingers buried themselves in his thick sun-kissed locks as she held him to her. His teeth nibbled, bringing delightful shivers of pleasure, then his tongue laved the nipple in case he'd unintentionally brought pain. Her knees buckled and she fell backward onto the bed, bringing him with her. She felt the full weight of him, and her body hummed with a music that was new and consuming.

In the end his resolve to take his time gave way to the clamoring need of their bodies and he took her, gently spreading her legs with his knee, pausing for one moment to insure himself she was ready, then thrusting into her with a long, piercing stroke that drove her slowly, irrevocably mad. She clasped her arms around him and wrapped her slender legs around his lean middle. His hands slid beneath her buttocks, lifting her, positioning her for the next thrust . . . and the next . . . until he moved over her with an increasing rhythm that brought a sheen of sweat to their bodies. They were riding faster than the wind, and soon they would surpass it. . . . Then they were falling down a great precipice, into a downy softness of utter and complete contentment.

Later, when they'd rested, they opened their eyes and

smiled at each other, hands reaching out as lovers do to touch a cheek, a breast, a temple, and then the fires started again, and they spent the night putting them out. Only near dawn, when Kansas lay spent and bruised and satiated, when Cole's dark head lay against her breasts, did she take time to think back over the night. A smile lit her face. It had been a night of revelations, for in the darkness of the night, when passion ran hot and liquid between them, Cole had cried out her name and declared his love. Kansas closed her eyes and slept contentedly.

But in the morning when she woke, Cole was gone—and his money lay on her dresser.

Chapter 13

VIRGINIA CITY WAS blossoming like a flower on the desert floor, and if Kansas didn't feel the same fulsomeness in her own life, she pushed the thought away and went on. While the Southern states were locked in an escalating war with the North, people of the Nevada Sierras had petitioned the government to become a territory. Finally their efforts had paid off and a new governor was appointed. Virginia City was quickly gaining a name for itself nationwide as a place of refinement and great wealth. An excitement pervaded the town that was different from the raw exuberance of earlier miners who'd struck it rich.

Even the face of the mountain was changing, for conglomerates were slowly buying up claims or taking over from miners who couldn't pay on their loans. Most miners were unable to finance the heavy equipment and manpower needed to dig the silver from the mountainside and have it hauled over miles of rough terrain to the Truckee river, where the silver could be washed from the blue clay that clung to it.

"Thanks a heap, Miss Kansas," Jeb Willard said, twisting his hat between his hands and glancing around the office nervously. Everything about the room was elegantly uncluttered yet disturbingly female. If he'd given it any thought at all, he would have expected just this kind of setting for Miss Kansas. She fit right in with the pastel satins and delicate chairs. Sunlight streamed through lace curtains and the yellow silk chair covering seemed to echo the rich warmth. Kansas looked like a spot of sunlight herself, with her honey-gold hair and pale yellow morning gown. It lay in creamy folds around her feet as she bent over a rosewood desk, her lower lip caught between dainty white teeth as she concentrated on the paper before her. She wrote quickly, dipping her pen often in a well of ink.

"I'm much obliged for what you're doing, Miss Kansas," the man said again, and shuffled his feet. He was uncomfortable taking help from a woman—even though he'd heard she'd done it for other men in trouble. Kansas sensed the discomfort in his voice and sent him a dazzling smile.

"I'm glad I could help. If it weren't for you and the rest of the miners I wouldn't be here myself. We have to help each other," she said, sprinkling some sand across the inked page. When the paper was dry she folded it in half and crossed the room to hand it to him. "Take this to the bank. It instructs Mr. Howard to transfer funds out of my account to pay your loan." She walked him to the front porch.

"Thank you, Miss Kansas. You're an angel of mercy. My wife and kids—well, they'll be mighty glad to hear we can hang on for a little while longer."

"How is Selma?" Kansas asked, thinking of the thin, quiet-faced woman and the two skinny boys who'd followed their father to the mines and worked beside him, their slender bodies straining under the heavy work.

"They're fine," Jeb said. A frown creased his brow. " 'Cept Selma; she's right tired-looking." He grinned, his tobacco-yellowed teeth flashing behind a ragged beard. "I reckon this'll cheer her up some. I got me a good claim here, Miss Kansas. I know it. I can smell it.'' One rough finger tapped his large nose and his eyes gleamed with such conviction Kansas could almost believe him—but she'd heard the boast once too often and had seen that same half-mad gleam in other men's eyes, so she set little store by it now. Yet she couldn't tell him her doubts.

"I tell you, Miss Kansas, when my mine strikes I'm going to buy Selma the prettiest gown you've ever seen—the kind like you wear. Maybe you can help me pick it out when the time comes. I want it to be real special 'cause Selma and the kids are special.'' The light on his face died away, and he looked sheepishly at the paper she'd given him. "I guess you must think I'm plumb crazy to be car-ryin' on like this.''

"No, I don't,'' Kansas said softly. "I think you have a dream for a better life—and your wife and family share that dream with you. That means more to a woman than any gown.''

He grinned again, pleased at her words. His thin shoulders seemed to straighten a little. "I'll pay you back,'' he said, with quiet dignity. "I swear when my strike comes in you'll get every penny back.''

"I know I will, Jeb,'' Kansas said. "I trust you.'' She looked him in the eye and held out her hand.

Hesitating only for a moment, Jeb shook hands with her, and Kansas couldn't help noting the thinness of his bones and flesh. Was he not getting enough to eat? she wondered sympathetically as she watched him walk down the hillside toward the bank.

"You're never going to get rich if you keep giving your money away,'' Ellie fussed at her elbow. "I never seen such a stream of people come aneedin' so bad.''

"As long as I have it to give, I will.'' Kansas turned from her contemplation of Jeb Willard and faced Ellie. "I'm rich enough now. I never ever expected to earn as much money as I have, and what good is it if I can't help someone?''

"You ought to save some for a rainy day," Ellie grumbled. "Better yet, buy yourself a sapphire."

"A sapphire?" Kansas asked cautiously, aware of Ellie's outspoken ways.

"Aye, a sapphire," Ellie snapped. "It sharpens the mind. You've become addlepated what with all these men traipsing up the hill to get your money."

"Don't they need you at Miss Simpson's boardinghouse today?" Kansas asked pointedly. More and more Ellie had begun to stay at the Palace.

"Not as much as you do," Ellie stated, and with a whisk of starched petticoats disappeared into the house.

"She's got a point, you know," Otis said. He'd been sprawled in a porch chair during all of Ellie's reprimand.

"Not you, too," Kansas groaned. "Ellie grows more sanctimonious every day, and now even you say I shouldn't offer help when I'm asked."

"I'm just sayin' some of them miners you help ain't ever goin' to make their mines work—and the bank is just going to end up takin' them over, anyway. You can't stop it, and you shouldn't be throwing your money after bad. The bank'll end up owning the Palace as well."

"I know." Kansas sighed, sinking onto the porch swing. "But Otis, Jeb Willard and his family work so hard, and their faces are so thin and their eyes so big and hungry-looking. Which reminds me. Would you go down to the general store and buy up a month's supply of provisions and send it out to his family?"

Otis studied her a moment and, fearing he meant to scold her more, she looked away. "You do beat all I've ever seen," he said, and got to his feet.

"Otis?" Kansas called, not wanting to have any kind of disagreement between them. "I've put aside enough money so that if anything were to happen to me or the Palace, you'd be taken care of in your old age."

Otis turned to face her then, and she saw a fierce kind of

warmth in his eyes. "It ain't money or the need for security that keeps me working for you, Miss Kansas," he said, and with a shock she realized that he really cared about her.

She'd never had anyone express affection for her, not even Cole. The words of endearment he murmured in the heat of passion didn't count in the light of day. If her father were alive and here this very moment, Kansas thought, automatically reaching for the gold locket around her neck, he would look at her just so, with mingled pride and approval and yes, love. Tears filled her eyes, and she had to pinch her lips together to keep from crying.

"Thank you, Otis," she whispered.

He nodded, uncomfortable with this intimacy between them. He'd seen the glint of tears in her eyes and it touched him even more than her generosity to a miner's family. She was just a kid wanting and needing someone to love her. He hobbled toward his horse, gruffly cursing his arthritis to cover his embarrassment.

"Otis!" Kansas cried. "Don't—don't make them feel needy when you give it to them. Tell them Jeb ordered the food for them."

"Yes, ma'am," he said, and swung into the saddle. He waited until he got halfway down the hill before he pulled out a bandanna and blew his nose. Then he headed for the general store, and from there up into the mountains to a mine where a skinny, worn-out woman and her kids were waiting to hear some good news from her man.

Kansas watched Otis ride away and stayed on the porch, pushing the swing idly with one foot. She should be writing letters. She'd been asked to write to James Nye, the newly appointed territorial governor, inviting him to Virginia City. A special committee had been formed whose sole purpose was to convince the governor that Virginia City was the best place for his government seat. Carson City seemed intent on the same purpose, so the race was on. Still, the tasks could wait for a time. The mountains lay saffron and brown in the distance and the sage on the desert below undulated gently in a rare breeze, like rolling waves on an ocean. This was a raw, harsh land, where only the strong survived. Yet it was beautiful beyond description. She wished Cole would ride by so she could share this view with him. But Cole only came at night, when the Palace was closed and the last customer had gone home. Then he came up the hill in the black night and she stood waiting for him, her arms out-flung, her lips and body ready for his embrace.

She sighed and sprang to her feet, restlessly pacing the porch from one end to the other, the spectacular view below forgotten. At first she'd waited for the night he'd come to her without money in his pockets. Surely a sheriff didn't draw that large a salary that he could afford a fancy lady every night, but a mine Cole worked with his partner had come in and it was rumored to be one of the richest. Good fortune seemed to touch them both except in matters of love.

No matter how often she'd vowed never to see Cole again, by nightfall she was wavering, her body aching with need for him. While she sat at the gaming tables, expertly dealing cards, placing bets, and maintaining her reputation as a lucky lady, her glance would flick to the little porcelain mantel clock that cheerfully chimed away the hours, but never fast enough to suit Kansas. She'd tried once more to explain to Cole about her true status, but impatiently he'd smothered her words with hungry kisses—and later left his money upon her dresser. Some mornings, waking with her body replete and sore from his lovemaking, she felt like weeping upon spying his money. Impatiently she raked it into a drawer, never counting it. One day she would give it all back to him and they would laugh together over his misunderstanding.

In the meantime, she took petty revenge upon him by claiming that some new practice of lovemaking, which left him groaning with delight, had been taught her by one of

her other "clients." On those occasions, Cole usually rose
with angry, glinting eyes, clenched jaws and, tossing some
money on her dresser, stormed down the hill. She would
stop such pretenses, she thought now. They'd grown too
painful for them both. Of late, Cole had come later, until at
times she'd almost given up on his coming at all, and when
he arrived, he reached for her with angry desperation, as if
driven to her despite himself.

Kansas's pacing stopped and she stood gripping the porch
railing. What was she to do? She sensed Cole and she were
reaching an impasse. Somehow she must convince him of
the truth of who and what she was. Not a whore, never that,
simply a woman in love. Tonight—tonight she would tell
him, and this time she'd make him believe her. Feeling
better, she went back to her office to write her letter to the
new governor.

The afternoon had grown hot as always. Kansas pinned a
wide-brimmed straw hat over her coifed curls to shade her
skin from the sun, then, taking up a market basket, she
walked down the hill to Fredericks' General Store. The
musty interior seemed cool after the unrelenting light of the
sun. A knot of ladies stood at one end of the counter, Claire
Howard and her mother among them. Kansas nodded pleasantly as she walked to the counter.

While waiting for Mr. Fredericks, she went over her list,
trying hard not to notice the silent stares the women had
fixed on her. She longed to turn around and engage them in
conversation, but sensed their disapproving air. She
couldn't bare to risk their rejection where Claire Howard
might witness it. Curiosity made her study the dark-haired
girl out of the corner of her eye. Claire was just as beautiful
as when Kansas had first seen her. Though she knew she
was dressed as well as any of the ladies in the store—and
had taken extra pains with her hair in the hopes she might

see Cole—Kansas felt intimidated by Claire's easy, assured air.

Such was the difference in breeding, Kansas thought. No matter how hard she tried, she could never get over being Molly McKay's daughter. Then pride stiffened her backbone. She'd come to think differently of her mother over the past few years. Now she could understand and pity the choices Molly had been forced to make. She wouldn't allow these snobbish women to make her feel ashamed.

Claire Howard's dark eyes were shiny and unblinking as they studied Kansas quite openly. Involuntarily Kansas raised her chin, sensing an unspoken challenge in the other girl. What had happened between Cole and her that they had never married, after all? Did Cole see Claire now? Did he court the beautiful girl by day—and climb the hill at night to spend his passion with Kansas?

"Afternoon, Miss Kansas. What can I do for you?" Jim Fredericks said, coming to wait on her. Kansas forced her troublesome thoughts away and smiled with her old sunniness.

"Good afternoon, Mr. Fredericks," she said. "I've got a letter to go out. Can it make the afternoon stage?"

"Sure thing," Fredericks said, taking the envelope from her. "Is this here the letter invitin' the new governor here?"

"Let's hope he accepts," she replied, and held out her list. "Ellie informs me we need these things."

"I'll get them for you right away," Fredericks assured her.

While she waited, Kansas wandered around the store looking at piles of dress goods, ribbons, pots and pans, shovels and picks, boots, and rough-twill pants among other things. She could feel the weight of the other women's glances and hear their whispered exclamations.

"I think it's just outrageous that the committee should allow a woman like that to be involved with the governor," one gray-haired woman declared. Her small pointed chin and faded blue eyes snapped spitefully.

"Now, Mama," Claire soothed. "Remember what the doctor said. You're not to upset yourself. You'll have a relapse."

"Letitia is right," another woman spoke up. "We want Virginia City represented by decent folks. What will the new governor think if he's greeted by a—a—" The words flitted through the self-righteous woman's mind and were surely uttered behind the sanctity of her closed doors, but she daren't say them here in public before her friends.

"I believe I've heard them called soiled doves, Mrs. Thompson," Claire said sweetly, but her dark eyes studied Kansas across the counters of dry goods. Kansas felt the old hurts bite deep, but she'd long since learned to hide the pain.

"Soiled doves!" Mrs. Thompson declared. "It's an insult to that homely bird to call them such." The woman's fat chin fairly quivered in her indignation.

"We must be tolerant of such creatures," Claire said smoothly. "After all, some of them only follow in the footsteps of their mothers. The cowboys call them calico queens." Her laughter, rich and cutting, filled the store. "I suppose they do serve a purpose for a certain kind of man who works the mines."

"How astute of you, Claire, to make such an observation," Kansas replied calmly, although inside she was seething. "How charitable of you to recognize that the men who dig the silver and gold out of the mines—so your father's bank grows richer—do indeed have needs as well."

"Well, I'm too much of a lady to continue this discussion of such men's baser needs. I'm sure women of your caliber do an adequate enough job so that we ladies aren't accosted on the street."

"Most of the miners you meet on the street are more gentlemenly than some of your husbands!" Kansas snapped. "Just because they wear rough clothes and have rough ways doesn't mean they're not good men."

"Yes—well, we can guess at your opinion of such men, Miss McKay, since you take their money."

"Yes, I take their money—and in return I give them an evening of relaxation and enjoyment." The women gasped.

"Don't talk to that foul woman anymore," Letitia Howard ordered her daughter. "She's shameless enough to brag about what she does before decent women. Look how she flaunts herself and that—that den of iniquity she calls a palace."

"Indeed, I am," Kansas said angrily. "And I'm sorry you have such a low opinion of my gambling house. Perhaps if you came up the hill some evening, you could see for yourself what the Palace is all about." Their shocked expressions spurred her on to recklessness. "After all, most of your husbands are up there every evening anyway."

"Oh . . ." Grace Thompson swooned, her plump body caught by thin, raillike Mary Wilson. While the women struggled to keep their friend erect, Kansas turned to Claire.

"The money I receive from the men is honestly earned, not stolen as your father does at the bank with his bank loans," she continued.

"How dare you!" Claire cried in outrage. "My father is an honest, respectable man."

Claire's face showed such distress at the accusations that Kansas almost took her words back, but the memory of Jeb Willard's haunted, drawn face was still too fresh in her memory.

"As honest as you were back in Webster? . . . When you told me you and Cole were about to be married?"

Claire's troubled expression changed to arrogance. "So that's what you're doing in this town," she sneered. "You're still trying to get Cole Slater." Claire advanced a step toward Kansas. Her face was bright with triumph and spite. "I threw Cole Slater over three years ago because of you. He begged me not to break our engagement. He said he didn't love you and never had. But I was too proud. I made a foolish mistake. Now Cole and I are together again. You'll never drive us apart again. He loves me more than ever."

"Is that why he climbs the hill every night to share my bed?" Kansas cried, wounded by the other girl's words and wanting to strike back.

Claire Howard's eyes barely flickered at Kansas's revelation. Quickly she covered her surprise and smiled with a superior air. "He may come to you at night, Kansas McKay, but when I'm his wife, he'll have no further need to relieve himself on a common whore!" Her words ended in a shriek.

"Claire!" her mother cried in shock. "Come. Say no more to this trollop. Mr. Fredericks"—Letitia Howard drew her small fragile body to full stature and fixed the hapless proprietor with a sharp eye—"decent folks of this town will not frequent your store as long as you allow trash like this to accost us. I expect you to attend to this matter, at once."

"Yes, ma'am," Jim Fredericks said lamely. He'd been amazed at what had transpired in his store and wasn't sure where to lay the blame. But he knew all too well where his loyalties must lie. Oliver Howard held a note on his store for the larger volume of inventory he'd begun to carry.

"Come ladies." Regally the little woman led the other ladies from the store.

Shuffling his feet in embarrassment, Fredericks cleared his throat. "I'm sorry, Miss Kansas," he said.

"No, Mr. Fredericks. It's I who owe you an apology. I should have ignored their comments. It's not as if I haven't heard them before."

"That's just it, Miss Kansas," Fredericks said. "I have to ask you not to come down here to my store again."

"Not come here?" Kansas echoed in dismay.

"I'm sorry," Fredericks murmured. "It's best if you go

to Norm Robert's store down on Maple Street. That's where the rest of the"—his face turned beet red—"girls go."

"Don't you mean soiled doves, Mr. Fredericks?" Kansas snapped, her hands tightening around the handle of her basket until her knuckles were white. When the shamefaced man made no reply, she continued in a quieter tone. "I'll send Otis down to settle my account with you. Good-bye, Mr. Fredericks."

"I'm sorry, Miss Kansas," Fredericks called after her. "I ain't got any choice."

Kansas gave no sign she'd heard. Her shoulders were stiff with anger as she left the store and made her way up the street toward the Palace. On impulse she turned into the Silver Spur to talk to Reeny. Reeny would soothe her hurt with a glass of lemonade, some good practical advice, and a little laughter. But Reeny was surprisingly grim.

"Have you heard about the Paiute?" she asked. "They're acting up again, threatening some of the outlying homesteads."

"I hadn't heard," Kansas said, watching Reeny's face.

She wasn't afraid of an Indian attack. They'd both been hearing such rumors ever since they came to Virginia City. Something else was bothering Reeny. "How are things going for you and the rest of the girls?" she prompted.

Reeny shrugged. "The town's changin'," she said, with a note of resignation. "Folks start get high falutin ideas about what's decent and proper and what ain't. That committee's already pushed some of the girls who work independent off Main Street and into cribs down on the back streets."

"The Citizens' Committee?" Kansas asked disbelievingly. "Reeny, I didn't know. Have they bothered the Silver Spur girls?"

"They've made threats to close us down." Reeny shrugged and refilled their glasses. "Just talk, I figure."

"I had no idea," Kansas said, gripping Reeny's arm.

"You have to believe I wouldn't turn on my friends like that."

"I didn't figure you would," Reeny said, but her smile was considerably warmer. "The question is what are we going to do?"

"We're going to the next committee meeting," Kansas said, slapping the table to emphasize her point. "You, too, Reeny."

"Not me!" The dance hall girl drew back.

"Why not?" Kansas demanded. "You're a business owner here in this town. You have a right to come and express your opinion."

"Excuse me, Miss Kansas," Ev Howell said. "Me and the boys couldn't help overhearing. Do we have a right to come to that there meeting and express our opinions on what we want for this town?"

"I don't see why not," Kansas declared. "It's men like you who've built this town, and you have a right to be a part of it. We all do, no matter what our choice of occupations. The meeting's tomorrow night at the new schoolhouse. Who all will be there?"

"Count me in. I'll be there," most of the lounging miners cried.

"I'll tell some of the boys up in Gold Creek. They'll want to be there, too," someone said, and there was a general exodus to the doors.

Kansas looked at Reeny and grinned. "They should never underestimate the power of a soiled dove," she said, raising her lemonade glass in a salute.

Reeny laughed. "Especially if Kansas McKay is leading them!"

Kansas went back to the Palace feeling considerably better. That night, a few of her old regulars, Harry Thompson and his friends, were missing from her tables, but there were always men waiting to fill empty seats, so she gave it little thought. After the Palace closed, she waited for Cole to come up the hill. He was far later than usual, and she'd almost given up on him. His face was set and angry when he finally arrived.

"Is something wrong?" she asked when he turned his mouth away from her kiss. His large hands set her aside impatiently. A feeling of dread coursed through her, but mingled with it was an old anger. Thoughtfully she watched him divest himself of his coat and gun holster. Without glancing at her, he sat down on the edge of the bed and started pulling off his boots.

"Perhaps we'd better talk first," she said, and he couldn't miss the tart edge to her voice. Her eyes locked with his in a defiant gesture that reminded him of the girl back in Webster. The image softened his expression and he almost smiled. Instead, he sighed and dropped his boot on the floor.

"Dammit, Kansas," he exploded, and she knew he'd been holding in his anger all afternoon. "A man doesn't like to have his private affairs discussed in a yelling match in the middle of town."

"Are you referring to the discussion Claire and I had this afternoon?" Kansas hedged.

"Discussion?" Cole looked at her in dismay. "From what I understand, it was little more than a cat fight."

"I didn't make it one," Kansas flared.

"I hardly think Claire is the sort to start something like that," Cole snapped, slamming his other boot to the floor. "The way I heard it, you went after her, Kansas . . . ready to pick a fight. You stood there gloating about my coming up here at night."

Dismay filled Kansas. She'd certainly been aware of Claire's designs on Cole, but she'd never stopped to think he might be aware of them as well. "What about you, Cole?" she asked quietly. "Do you have feelings for Claire?"

His expression changed. Masculine pride dictated who

asked such questions. His chin jutted out stubbornly and his eyes flashed. "You don't have the right to ask me a question like that," he sputtered in outrage.

"Why not?" Kansas demanded, her chin drawn up, her gray-green eyes spitting fire. "Because I'm not your wife? . . . Or because I'm a whore?"

"Both," he snapped. He sensed her slender body quivering in rage, and caution took hold of him. "Neither," he amended. "Dammit, Kansas, we're not talking about my feelings . . . we're talking about your behavior."

"Perhaps if it weren't for your feelings, we wouldn't have to talk about my behavior. You'd understand my side of it."

"Don't twist my words." Cole's voice had risen considerably.

"Don't shout at me," shouted Kansas.

"It seems the only way to be heard. You had no qualms this afternoon about shouting out to the whole town that I come up here every night."

"It wasn't like that," Kansas said lamely. Rubbing her arms absentmindedly, she paced the room. "At least, I didn't mean for it to be like that, but I was hurt by the things she and the other women said. They were just so smug about being proper ladies. Claire talked to me as if I were a whore. She even referred to me as a—a soiled dove."

"You are one," Cole answered. "The truth shouldn't have hurt you, Kansas."

"But that's not the truth," she flared. "I've tried to tell you all along, and you just won't listen."

"I've listened," Cole said, and his lips were tight with anger, "and I've observed, Kansas. You didn't earn the money for a place like this serving tea, or even that fancy food your French chef whips up. There's only one way for a woman like you to earn money in a mining town."

At first he spoke in a too quiet voice, but as he continued, his voice crescendoed until he was fairly shouting at her.

Kansas's hand flashed through the air, landing against his smooth jaw. His fist jerked upward and at first she thought he meant to strike her back, but he caught himself. The muscles in his jaw worked convulsively, his blue eyes glared at her.

"I've accepted you as you are," he said quietly. "There's no call for you to go gallivanting all over town kicking up a fuss over it. Make up your mind what you want, Kansas." His gaze was unwavering, intimidating, but she'd not allowed anyone to intimidate her in over three years. Pride dictated she not do so now.

"Get out," she spat. "I want you to get out. Go back to your fancy, proper lady, Claire Howard. Don't come up the hill to me again, ever."

Surprise flickered across his face, replaced by his own anger and pride. "All right, if that's what you want," he rasped out. Whirling he picked up his boots and headed for the door in his bare feet.

Tears were pouring down Kansas's face, and she couldn't seem to stop the weakness that took hold of her limbs so she trembled. Pride kept her erect—pride and a sense of being wronged. Once again Claire had lied, this time to Cole, and he had believed her. He'd taken her part against Kansas. The cut went too deep to bear. Blindly she followed him out on the landing.

"I mean it, Cole," she called as he ran down the stairs. "Don't come back here, not ever. I didn't want you to come in the first place. I let you make love to me because you paid the price, no other reason—"

The slam of the door cut off her torrent of words. The house lay silent around her and slowly Kansas sank to the landing, her slender hands gripping the curved balustrade.

"Cole. I love you," she whimpered. "Why can't you believe me?" She lay on the floor weeping until Ellie, wakened from her sleep by the shouting, came to help her rise and return to her bed.

"There, lambie, he'll be back. The first fight's always the worst."

"He'll never come back," Kansas sobbed, curled up in her misery. Her long hair fanned back on the pillow and she looked vulnerable and childlike in her plain gown.

"We'll have him back," Ellie said. "There are love potions we can brew that'll bring a man back faster'n a scalded cat can jump. You mark my word; we'll have him back in no time."

"I'm not sure I want him back, Ellie," Kansas whispered. "Not as long as he believes I'm a—" She paused, suddenly aware she might offend the well-meaning woman.

"What's that? A whore? Ain't nothing wrong with him believing that as long as he treats you like you're a lady. I thought he done that."

Kansas looked at Ellie and suddenly realized the woman had just touched the real reason for Kansas's outburst. She hadn't minded Cole believing her a fallen woman as long as he hadn't felt ashamed of her. Now, for the first time, Kansas realized Cole might be ashamed of his association with her—and the thought made her cry all over again.

Chapter 14

COLE DIDN'T COME back up the hill that night. Kansas crept from her bed and took up vigil by the window overlooking the town, hoping to see a tall, rangy shadow, but the road to the Palace remained empty. Near morning she fell into an uneasy sleep in the window seat, her legs curled beneath her, her head slumped against the curtained pane.

When Ellie came to wake her, Kansas rose all stiff and achey. It matched the way she felt inside, she thought dismally, and began her toiletry in preparation for the Citizens' Committee meeting that afternoon. It was being held in the schoolhouse, and the children were given a free afternoon.

Kansas made her way down the hill, she saw young boys scattering over rocky ledges to the upper end of the creek that fed the town, fishing poles in their hands. Girls had drawn lines in the dusty street in front of their houses and were playing games of hopscotch and jump rope. The streets seemed crowded with men and horses.

When Kansas reached the schoolhouse, she understood why. Ev Howell and the other miners had made good on their promise to be there. The small schoolhouse was packed, and still a large number of people milled on the steps and in the yard. They stood amiably discussing their ideas for the town's needs.

Reeny and the Silver Spur girls were present, as well as other saloon owners. Quill Ramsey and Rod Farley had just arrived and were pushing their way through with characteristic arrogance. Kansas caught a glimpse of Otis and felt better for his presence. Never again would she take Quill Ramsey and his threats lightly.

When Kansas climbed the steps to the schoolhouse, the miners parted deferentially, allowing her to walk to the front of the large schoolroom and take her place with the rest of the committee. Kansas looked around the room, nodding at the men and women she knew. Claire Howard and her mother were seated with Grace Thompson in the front row. Their lips pursed disapprovingly and they fussed with their skirts, arranging the folds just so. They were impervious in their superiority.

As the chairman, Oliver Howard, took up a ruler and tapped the desk, the room fell quiet. Clearing his throat, he nervously pulled at his tie. "We'll have to ask you men to clear the room now," he said. "We're ready to start the meeting."

"We have a right to be here." A burly miner stood up.

"This is not a town meeting, Lane," Howard said. "This is a committee meeting, and therefore closed to the public."

"Says who?" Another man rose. "If what this committee decides affects this town, then it affects us, too. We got a right to have our say."

"Not today, you haven't," Oliver Howard said. "Now I've asked Sheriff Slater to be here in case there's any trouble. I hope you boys'll leave quietly."

For the first time Kansas saw Cole lounging against one rough-hewn wall. His hat was pushed back, his eyes narrowed as he listened to the proceedings. Anger and disappointment filled her at the thought that he'd so callously joined with Oliver Howard and the other men who were planning only on the best policies for themselves. Trembling she rose to her feet and strove for a calm tone.

"I think we should allow everyone to stay," she said, and her words were greeted by clapping and cries of approval from the onlookers. "How can we on the committee possibly know what the rest of the town needs if we don't listen to what they have to say?" Cheering broke out.

Oliver Howard's face was livid. His blue eyes snapped with wrath. "Quiet," he ordered, and the miners and saloon girls fell silent. They waited respectfully, expectantly, but Howard's anger blinded him to that expectation. "This meeting is for responsible citizens who want to make this town a decent place to live, not for the likes of this rabble."

A growl, low and menacing, rose from the room. Again, Howard failed to sense the mood of the audience. "Furthermore," he said, turning to face Kansas, "it's indecent and immoral for a woman of your caliber to be on this committee, and I hereby relieve you of that position."

The growl changed to a roar as the men and women in the room voiced their outraged. As word of the proceedings passed back to the people waiting outdoors on the steps, the roar was echoed outside the small schoolhouse.

"A woman of my caliber?" Kansas echoed. "And just what kind of woman do you think I am?"

"Come now, Miss McKay. We all know you're a soiled dove!" Miles Thompson sneered.

Once again the crowd booed his attitude. "Miss Kansas ain't no soiled dove," one man cried. "She's a gilded dove!"

The men around him laughed and clapped their approval of his words. The interchange was passed back, and ripples of laughter coursed through the crowd.

Oliver Howard paused as the shouting continued. His blue eyes peered around the room and came back to Kansas. Not for the first time she noted the glint of frustration and fascination in his eyes as he gazed at her. She might almost have thought it lust if his expression hadn't changed swiftly. She must have been fooled by the play of shadows, she thought. Howard glanced at Cole for reassurance of his own safety, but Cole was studying the slim, blond-haired girl. His gaze was thoughtful, almost bemused. Perhaps he hadn't taken sides with Howard, after all, Kansas thought, and felt some of her anger toward him melt.

Otis stood up and raised his hands. He was well respected by both the townspeople and the miners. Everyone quieted down and order was restored.

"We can't accomplish nothing like this," Otis said, reprimanding both sides. "Seems like we both have the same goals in mind—to better this town so's the new governor will settle here. We'll need to work together."

"That's right," people called out in agreement, and Jim Fredericks and some of the other men on the committee nodded in agreement.

Once again Otis raised his hands for silence. "We need to address each issue raised today," he said. "It occurs to me, this committee is made up of men who volunteered, but maybe the town needs to have some say in who's on the committee. Maybe we ought to have a vote." Oliver Howard and Miles Thompson looked uneasy, but the rest of the room voiced their agreement.

"Well, first off, there's me," Otis declared. "If you folks don't want me on the committee, don't be afeered to say so. If you do—" The rest of his words were drowned out with shouts of approval. When the noise had quieted, Otis bobbed his head sheepishly. "I'm much obliged," he said. "The next one we're going to vote on is Mr. Howard." The room was stone quiet. "Now, before you make up your minds, let me remind you that Mr. Howard is the town banker. He's helped a lot of people here already."

"Yeah, relieved 'em of their mines, he did," someone called, and there was an angry muttering.

"But he done it according to the law," Otis pointed out.

"When you run a bank, you got to run things by the law, else you run the bank dry and then we're all out. We can't fault Mr. Howard 'cause we can't pay our loans."

"Yeah, but—"

Otis rapped the desk with the ruler. "We ain't here to discuss the legalities of loans," he said, and his bushy white eyebrows drew together so the men knew to drop that issue and attend to the business at hand. "Mr. Howard here wants to help the town, and he's an important citizen. Now who all wants to vote for Mr. Howard?"

Reluctant hands went up. A few at first, followed by more, until most of the room had indicated, albeit with reluctant grace, that Oliver Howard could continue on the committee.

"Next is Miles Thompson," Otis said, and pointed out the mill owner's attributes.

Once again the miners agreed. They needed Thompson's mill for their ore. The next two members were eliminated. Their gossipy wives and high-handed ways had already irritated the townspeople.

"Last, we got Kansas McKay," Otis began. "I don't need to tell you much about Miss Kansas."

As of one body, the miners got to their feet and voiced their acceptance. Kansas smiled, feeling somewhat vindicated for things Oliver Howard and his wife and daughter had said about her.

"That seems pretty unanimous," Otis decreed.

"Just a minute, old man," Quill Ramsey said, getting to his feet. "There's some of us here who feel Kansas McKay ought'n to be on the committee."

"All those opposed, please stand and signify," Otis declared, with barely concealed impatience.

Quill Ramsey's men, Claire Howard and her mother, and all the ladies who lived on Buchanan Street got to their feet. For one incongruous moment, Kansas felt like laughing. In their hatred for her, the women hadn't realized that now they'd allied themselves with the town's most notorious citizen.

"The ayes have it," Otis declared, and none could dispute his final say, for the number opposed were indeed few.

"If we're going to be proper and legal like with all this," Otis said, "I reckon we ought to ask if any of you have someone you want on the committee to represent you."

A burly miner, his hair freshly slicked to his head, his woolly beard bristling, stood. "We got Miss Kansas to represent us," he said. "I ain't ever seen anyone fairer-minded or more honest than she is. I say that's enough."

The rest of the men called out their approval.

"If that's the case then," Otis said, "I move that we get on with this here meetin'. Miss Kansas, maybe seein's how you're so well thought of by this town, I thought maybe you might like to take over."

Oliver Howard's face reddened, but he made no objections.

Kansas got to her feet and faced the crowd. She felt proud of their acceptance of her and couldn't resist one triumphant peek at Cole. Once again he had slumped against the wall, his hat shoved back, his long arms crossed over his chest, his eyes glinting with amusement. Kansas began the meeting, listening to the complaints and ideas of the townspeople, shop owners, saloon girls, and miners alike. She presented her ideas for a new opera house and advanced a plea for a bit of culture to be brought to Virginia City. The meeting ended on a high note, with everyone feeling they'd accomplished something.

As the people filed out of the cramped schoolhouse, Oliver Howard approached Kansas. "You did very well, Miss McKay," he said. "You have a way with people." His probing blue eyes studied her face, hair, and finally her figure. Kansas felt a flush of anger, but held her tongue.

"The men and women who've worked hard to make this town grow just want to be a part of its future growth," she said. "It's easy to work with people if you listen to what they want."

"That is *your* business, isn't it, giving people what they want?" he said snidely. Yet his restless gaze continued to roam over her face and bodice as if looking for some clue as to who she was. He made her feel uneasy. She was used to men desiring her, but she sensed a greater intensity in Howard.

"As I tried to explain to your wife and daughter yesterday afternoon, the Kansas Palace is not what you think it is," she began. "If any of you care to come and see for yourself, I'd more than welcome you."

"Would you, Miss McKay?" he asked, his voice grown low and silky.

"Yes, of course," she said, taken aback, "as I do all my customers. You might talk to Mr. Thompson and Ed Bishop. They've both been up in the evening."

"They have, have they?" Howard looked surprised. "I will indeed talk to them."

"Perhaps then your wife and Claire will see that I'm not—"

"Despite the esteem in which the town seems to hold you, Miss McKay," Howard said, "I must ask you not to discuss my wife and daughter—nor to accost them in the stores again should you see them."

"I'll be only too happy to accommodate you in this regard, Mr. Howard," Kansas snapped, turning her back on him and stepping down off the dais.

"Miss Kansas," Oliver called after her, and when she turned to face him, his smile was surprisingly friendly. "I plan to take you up on your invitation and visit your little Palace soon."

Kansas bit her lip, wanting to hurl back the same kind of insults she'd received, but she forced a smile. "I think you'll be pleasantly surprised when you do," she said graciously.

As she turned away, she glimpsed Cole Slater watching her, his brow furrowed in a frown, the light in his eyes flat and cold, as if he were angry. How well she'd come to read his moods over the years, she thought bleakly. Let him be angry with her; she had pride, too, and she wouldn't go to him in front of the whole town and risk his rejection.

"Well, we done good," Otis declared, following her into the sun-baked school yard.

"You were wonderful," Kansas praised him. "The meeting would have gone badly if not for you."

The old man beamed with pride. "That was a mighty generous pledge you made toward a new opry hall," Otis observed. "Ain't you feered one day you might run out of money?"

"You're starting to sound like Ellie!" Kansas scolded him, but her mind was on other things. Oliver Howard had crossed the school yard and introduced himself to Quill Ramsey. The two men stood in deep conversation for a few minutes, then the two of them shook hands with some warmth.

"Looks like Howard's found someone to his liking in town." Otis muttered at her shoulder. "I'd shore like to know what those two men have in common. Suppose we could use one of Ellie's potions to find out what it is?"

"You'd best be careful, Otis, before Ellie turns one of her love potions on you," Kansas teased. She was startled to see his face redden.

"I believe I'll stop off at the Silver Spur for a bit if you think you can get on up the hill by yourself," he said, and at her nod, he struck off down the street toward the saloon.

She had, Kansas realized in wonder, struck a nerve with Otis. So *that* was the way the wind blew! And all this time, Kansas thought Ellie was always at the Palace to help her. Kansas chuckled and walked up the hill. For the first time that day she felt lighthearted and confident that somehow she and Cole would work out their differences. They'd found each other after all those years apart . . . neither of them would let such a separation occur again.

Or would they? After the Palace closed, Kansas waited late into the night for Cole Slater to climb the hill to her, but he'd taken her at her word. He wasn't coming back. Was he even now being entertained in Claire Howard's drawing room? . . . Or worse yet, her bed? At last Kansas understood the torment Cole had endured at the thought of another man in her bed. She'd never tease him again—given the chance, that is. She only hoped it wasn't too late.

In spite of the meeting, the division between the town citizens remained clear. The dance hall girls, gamblers, and miners remained at one end of the town, while the bankers, mill and mine owners, and their families, remained sequestered behind the doors of their fine houses at the other end. Though Kansas caught a glimpse of Cole now and then walking along the street or drinking in the saloons, he never climbed the hill to the Palace.

One night as she sat with a flush hand, she overheard two men talking about the sheriff and the banker's daughter. Quickly she folded and excused herself. Swallowing her pride, she wandered closer, but the men were already talking about the latest new mine discovery. Frustrated, she lingered, hoping to hear something more, but she had only that single phrase to mull over.

Could it be true? she wondered sickly, pacing her bedroom until the impending sunrise stained the far horizon with pinks and reds. Kansas tried to hide her fears and go on as if nothing were wrong, but Ellie was too wise to be fooled.

"I got a potion that can bring him back quick as spit drying on a hot rock," she offered, but Kansas brushed aside the offer, donned her wide-brimmed bonnet, and set off down the hill, determined to find Cole and tell him she was sorry if that was what it took. In her haste, she'd taken no time to change from the plain cotton gown she normally wore during the daytime when she supervised the servants in cleaning and stocking the Palace for yet another evening. Her long golden tresses hung down her back, brushing the top of her hips as she walked. She wore no makeup or any of the fripperies normally worn by women, no matter at what end of the town they lived.

When she reached the main street, she hurried to the sheriff's office, but it was empty. She made her way along the street, pausing now and then to glance inside a saloon or barbershop or general store. Cole was nowhere to be found. Had he gone up into the hills to work the mine he shared with Tobias? she wondered. Perhaps it was just as well. Now that she was here, she wasn't sure what to say to him. She'd just drawn level with the bank when the door opened and Cole stepped out onto the plank walk. Tobias was with him.

"Well, we did it, partner," Cole was saying as he shook the old miner's hand.

"I never thought I'd live to see the day I'd have that much money in the bank," Tobias said, shaking his head in wonder. "I'm shore glad I run into you back there in them mountains. Hell, I'm glad those men didn't kill you, and I was able to nurse you back to health. You've been my lucky charm ever since."

"You're the one with a nose for silver," Cole said, throwing his arm around the old man affectionately.

She'd never seen Cole look handsomer. He wore a frock coat of brown wool and a white shirt that contrasted crisply with his tanned skin. His face was relaxed and smiling, his eyes crinkling at the corners. He looked sleek and rugged all at the same time, and her resentment melted away.

"You kept me from getting my nose shot off by that sidewinder, Farley," Tobias was saying. "Wouldn't have done me no good to have a silver mine if'n you hadn't bought the supplies like you did."

"Maybe we've been lucky for each other," Cole said.

He slapped the old man on the back and glanced up, catching sight of Kansas. Their gazes locked and Kansas felt the blood run through her veins, hot and pulsating. His smile faded, and his expression grew closed and guarded. For a moment she feared he meant to turn away from her.

"Cole," she gasped, "I have to talk to you."

He paused, his gaze moving over her face before coming to rest on her soft, trembling lips.

"All right," he said softly.

"I—"

"Cole, Daddy's so excited to have you as his new partner in the bank," Claire Howard trilled, sweeping out onto the narrow porch. Her full crinolined skirts took up most of the room, brushing against Cole's legs almost possessively. Claire was smiling up at him, her eyes alight with pleasure. There was an easy familiarity between them that hadn't been there before, and Kansas felt her knees nearly buckle. They were lovers; she was certain of it. She wanted to launch herself at Claire's smug face and scratch out the eyes that were too triumphant, too knowing.

"Why, hello, Kansas," Claire said, with feigned surprise, so Kansas was certain the girl had caught sight of Cole and her through the gold-lettered window. "What are you doing here?" Her bright, dark gaze darted from Kansas to Cole and back again.

"This is a bank, isn't it?" Kansas said. "I've come to make a deposit." She turned to Cole. "Congratulations on your new business venture."

"Thank you," Cole said stiffly.

"I presume my money will continue to be safe in your bank."

"Guaranteed," Cole snapped, his brows pulling down in annoyance.

Was he annoyed with her? Kansas wondered, and pulled her chin high.

"Well, I must be on my way," she said. "If you'll excuse me."

"Kansas," Cole said, but Claire linked her arm through his and tugged prettily, a merry little laugh tumbling from her lips.

"Cole, you must come to supper tonight and share the good news with Mama. You know what high regard she holds for you."

Gratefully Kansas heard no more as she stepped inside the bank. She dawdled, having no wish to encounter Claire and Cole again.

By the time she'd climbed the hill to the Palace, the hot sun and pent-up emotions had taken their toll, so she arrived in the kitchen red-faced and teary-eyed.

"Here now, dearie. What have you done to yourself?" Ellie fussed, handing her a glass of lemonade and laying a cool, damp cloth on her brow. "You came up that hill too fast. You always walk as if the devil hisself was after you."

"Oh, Ellie, it isn't that!" Kansas gasped, between long gulps of the fruit drink. Tears and sweat ran down her cheeks. "I've made such a mess of things. After all those years when we were lost to each other . . . and then as if by a miracle, we found each other again. Now, I've driven him away, and that Claire Howard," Kansas paused to grind her teeth together—"Claire Howard has him wrapped around her little finger like he was a puppy."

"You can't talk to a man like Cole Slater the way you did that night, dearie," Ellie advised. "You have to coddle 'em and act like you think they're so strong and smart. You have to make 'em think you need 'em."

"I do," Kansas wailed.

"Pshaw." Ellie made a face. "You're Kansas McKay. Look what you done here all by yourself! You just think you need him. But if you're set on having 'im back, I can help you. I've told you, there are potions—"

"Oh, Ellie," Kansas said wearily, "I've told you, I don't believe in such things."

"Wouldn't hurt you none to give it a try," Ellie insisted.

"Ellie," Kansas said, with some exasperation, drawing the wet cloth from her brow. Her nose wrinkled in disgust, and she held the cloth away from her. "What is this thing?" she demanded.

Ellie shrugged. "It's the dishrag."

Kansas dropped the cloth on the table and ran to the dry sink and dipped out enough water to splash over her face.

"It kin na hurt you," Ellie rebuked her, and fearing she'd hurt the well-meaning woman who'd become a friend, Kansas sighed and, taking up a fresh towel to dry her face, walked back to the table.

"What spell would you suggest?" she asked, and was gratified to see the hurt look on Ellie's round face replaced by a wide smile.

"First we'll do the salt spell," the Irish woman decreed. "Salt has magic powers that are strong." She shrugged. "If that doesn't work, we'll try the bay leaves."

"What do I have to do?" Kansas asked, hiding a smile.

"Throw this salt on the fire," Ellie said, pouring some of the fine powder into Kansas's hand and leading her to the wood-burning cookstove. "It'd be best if we was outside over a campfire, but this'll do." She took the lid off the firebox. "Now wait!" Her plump hand caught Kansas's before she could toss in the salt. "You sprinkle it in kind of easylike, and you chant after me."

Kansas pinched her lips together to keep from laughing and nodded in agreement. Ellie grasped her hand to guide it in a circle as the salt was spilled slowly from between Kansas's fingers.

"It is not the salt I wish to burn," Ellie intoned. "Repeat it," she hissed, and Kansas followed suit. "It is my lover's heart to turn." Again Kansas repeated the words. "That he may not rest or happy be, until he comes and speaks to me." Kansas looked at Ellie, whose eyes were wide and gleeful.

"We do this twice more," Ellie whispered, as if in the presence of great spirits.

Sorry now she'd agreed to this, but not knowing how to get out of it, Kansas obliged, scooping up another handful of salt and sprinkling it over the fire slowly, so as not to put out the flames. Ellie whispered it would have evil portents if they put out the fire in the middle of a spell. The last time through, Ellie's voice rose as if by the added volume she could call down the help of the spirits who would work the spell. Kansas imitated her dramatic chanting, starting to enjoy the childlike shenanigans. The last deep tones of the chant had no sooner died away than the door opened and Cole Slater stepped inside.

"Kansas," he said. "I've come so we can talk."

Ellie rolled her eyes significantly and smugly turned back to her kitchen chores. Nonplussed, Kansas stared at the leaping flames.

"What are you doing here?" Cole asked, coming further into the room. "Did I catch you when you're busy?"

"No." Kansas nodded and quickly replaced the round iron lid. "I'm glad you're here. Ellie, we'll be in the backyard if you need me."

"Yes, ma'am," Ellie said, with exaggerated meekness, but Kansas saw the glee on her face.

Ellie was convinced her spell had brought Cole up the hill to talk, and Kansas hadn't the heart to tell her the truth— that he had come because she'd asked to talk to him. "Bring us some lemonade, will you, Ellie?"

Silently she led Cole out the back door and to a swing that had been erected in a natural bower made by an overhanging rocky ledge. A lone straggly piñon tree struggled in the dry rocky soil nearby.

"Congratulations on becoming a partner in Oliver Howard's bank," she said, settling in the swing and spreading her skirts with fastidious care. "Somehow I don't see you as a banker."

"How do you see me, Kansas?" Cole asked, and the muscle in his jaw moved convulsively. He was as unnerved by their quarrel as she was.

Kansas glanced away, choosing her words carefully. "Oliver Howard has made loans to miners, using their claims as collateral, and when the miners can't pay the loans back, he takes the mines."

"That's good business," Cole said, and Kansas felt her heart sink.

"Yes, I suppose it is," she agreed, "except for the fact that he gives the loans too easily—to anyone who's vulnerable—and he never allows any extensions and—and sometimes those mines are on the verge of paying off, for want of a few days. Yes, what he's doing is legal, but it's not—"

"Ethical?"

Kansas glanced at him sharply. "Surely you know he wants you as his partner because of the fair and honest reputation you've earned in this town. People around here trust you. Howard is using that trust to reassure miners who might otherwise be wary of him."

"Everything you say might be true," Cole agreed. "But you've failed to look at the influence I might assert on Howard and the bank's policies. If I have any say, the miners will receive extensions on their loans, payments reduced until they can make good on their obligations. The miners might be better off with me as a partner at the bank."

Eyes shining, Kansas stared at him with growing wonder. She had underestimated Cole. "I'm sorry for doubting you," she said. "I should have known better."

"Yes, you should have." His grin was smug, gloating, impudent, and Kansas found herself grinning back. The old warmth was there between them again. Then she thought of Claire, and her grin faded.

"Cole, I have something I need to ask you."

"What is it?" Cole's voice was a husky half whisper,' and she knew he felt the same energy flowing between them. It had always been thus with them. "You can ask me anything."

"There you are, Miss Kansas!" a jovial voice called out. "Ellie tried to tell me you wasn't here, but I saw you walk up the hill not an hour ago and it reminded me I had some business with you." Jeb Willard stood in the yard, a big grin on his face.

Kansas saw Cole's flush of irritation. "I'm sorry, Jeb, I'm busy right now," Kansas said quickly. She sensed the mood between Cole and her had been broken.

"I'm sorry to interrupt you, Sheriff, but I got me a powerful need to see Miss Kansas here."

"That's all right," Cole said, picking up his hat. His expression was dark and tight with anger.

"Cole, don't go," Kansas pleaded.

"I wouldn't want to come between a man and his need," said Cole bitterly.

Pain spiraled through Kansas as she watched him stalk away. Then the old familiar frustration and anger claimed her. "Cole Slater, you—you pigheaded—" But Cole wasn't listening. He swung into his saddle, and the last thing he heard as he rode down the hill was Jeb Willard telling Kansas how pretty she looked with her hair hanging down.

Why hadn't *he* told her that? Cole wondered. He'd certainly thought it. He'd wanted to take her in his arms and just hold her, but she'd been more intent on talking about the bank and what his being a partner meant to the miners.

Biting her lips in vexation, Kansas turned to face her visitor. "What can I do for you, Jeb?" she asked, with a forced smile.

"I'm real sorry to bother you and the sheriff," Jeb said, unaware of the real relationship that existed between the two. "I just come from the bank and I wanted you to know what I done."

"What have you done?" Kansas asked, though her thoughts were still on the tall man riding down her hill. "Don't tell me you've decided to sell out your mine? If you needed more money for your loan, I could have come up with something."

"It ain't that, Miss Kansas," Jeb said quickly. "Selma and the boys and me've started finding a little silver here and there, enough to meet the bank payments, but not enough to pay you back yet."

"Don't worry about me," Kansas said. "You can pay me back when you strike it big."

"Yes, ma'am, I know what you said," Jeb said quickly. "It's just Mother and me figure it ain't fair to have you take all the risk. You didn't even ask me for anything for collateral. There ain't many what would a' done that. So the missus and me, we tried to figure a way to pay you back—and we made you a partner in our mine! I signed the papers at the bank today."

"Jeb, you can't do that," Kansas declared, all her attention claimed by the earnest miner. "You and your family have worked too hard to give up part of your mine."

"Without you, Miss Kansas, we wouldn't have a mine to work. It was real nice of you to send up the food for the wife and kids. I don't hardly know no other way to pay you back."

His words were so sincere, his expression so earnest, that Kansas was touched. Stepping forward, she placed her arms around his shoulders and pressed a quick, grateful kiss on his cheek. Jeb's face flamed bright red.

"Don't you be embarrassed that I kissed you, Jeb," she admonished. "Even if Selma saw us, she'd understand that I know no other way of saying thank-you for your thoughtfulness. But I can't take part of your mine. You may leave my name on it, if you wish, but I'll never take a penny more than the amount you borrowed from me.''

This time Jeb was so moved his Adam's apple worked spasmodically as he swallowed. He blinked his eyes rapidly to hold back the tears. ''I ain't ever met a lady like you, Miss Kansas,'' he said gruffly. ''No matter what rumors are said about you around town, you're more a lady than any of them fancy pieces at the other end of town.''

Kansas hugged him again and stepped away. She tried not to let him know how much his words had awakened old wounds. She'd known rumors abounded, and she'd chosen to ignore their existence in spite of their vicious nature. Now she acknowledged she had little chance of Cole believing her when such rumors were drifting through town. Who had started them? she wondered wearily. Who hated her so much?

Riding down the hill, Cole thought about those rumors. Hell, he'd never been one to listen to gossip before. Why was he letting it bother him now? Because it was about Kansas, and because he couldn't stand the thought of her with another man. He had a half a mind to ride back up the hill and throw Jeb Willard out and tell him to get back to his wife and kids where he belonged. How did Jeb come by the money to buy a woman like Kansas anyway?

Cole brought his horse to a halt and turned in the saddle to gaze back up the hill. He could see Kansas and Jeb silhouetted against the dun-colored backdrop of the mountains. Even as he watched, the two silhouettes merged into one. Cole narrowed his eyes against the sun's glare and waited. The two figures didn't break apart. Cole kicked his horse's belly with his heel and rode on down into town.

Chapter 15

COLE'S REFUSAL TO believe her innocence nearly drove Kansas to distraction. She found concentrating on anything else so hard her playing suffered. Suddenly, for the first time since its opening, the Palace began to show a loss.

"You can't last long like that, girlie," Otis said.

"My luck is down right now," Kansas said lamely.

"A gambler makes his own luck," Otis answered gruffly, and wandered out to the kitchen.

Kansas knew he spent time in the kitchen talking to Ellie of late. No doubt she would be the topic of conversation for them today. Impatiently she donned riding clothes and, filling a canteen and wrapping a biscuit for herself, set off for a ride. She needed to clear her head of Cole Slater, once and for all. Ever since he'd come to Virginia City, she'd thought of little else. He dominated her life in one way or another, and she'd endured more humiliation at his hands than she'd ever thought to do from anyone. Digging her heels into the horse's belly she rode him hard, heading north toward the Truckee River and angling east, away from the mills that disturbed the valley's tranquility with their constant pounding.

When the horse was lathered and his sides heaving, she

relented, feeling guilty that she'd pushed the beast so hard in the heat. Virginia City, the Palace, and Cole Slater were behind her now. She would let the beauty of the desert and mountains soothe her turbulent thoughts.

Gaining the edge of the river, Kansas alighted and let the horse drink while she took off her boots and cooled her feet in the muddy water. Lying back on a patch of sparse grass, she gazed up through the branches of a piñon tree to the flat blue of the cloudless sky.

The sound of hooves in the distance caused her to spring up. Her dreams of Cole had been so vivid that she half expected, half hoped to see him come galloping out of the foothills to find her. The expectant light in her eyes faded when she caught a glimpse of the horsemen in the distance. They came from different directions, a handful of men riding to meet a solitary horseman. Heat waves shimmered around them. Kansas blinked and strained to see. The man who rode at the head of the gang of horsemen was Quill Ramsey. Only he wore a hat and vest like that. No doubt, the man on his right was Rod Farley. Even from her place, Kansas could see the gunman's hand move nervously toward his holster, as if for reassurance. They rode to meet a man in a dark suit with a dark hat pulled low over his face. At first, Kansas didn't recognize Oliver Howard, then he raised his head to look around and his face was revealed.

There was something stealthy about this meeting, something that made Kansas feel uneasy, so she drew back behind the piñon tree and prayed the men wouldn't look toward the riverbank and see her horse. There was little cover. Sliding down on her belly so she could peer over the riverbank, Kansas watched as Oliver Howard and Quill Ramsey talked. What did the two men have in common? she wondered. And why did they need to ride way out here to talk?

Oliver Howard reached into his saddlebag and, bringing out a thick envelope, handed it to Quill. With a smirking grin, Quill looked inside. His grin died. "What are you trying to do, Howard?" he demanded.

His voice was loud and angry, so Kansas could hear his words, although not Howard's answer. Whatever he said angered Quill even more, and Farley pulled his gun. With an impatient gesture, Quill signaled him to put it away.

"If you don't trust me, Howard, how come you asked me to do this job?" he demanded.

Howard's hands fluttered placatingly and finally he reached into his saddlebag and pulled out another envelope. Quill fairly snatched it from his hands.

Bad choice, Kansas thought. Ramsey is not to be trusted. Suddenly she felt sorry for the banker for having entered into any arrangement with Quill Ramsey. Should she warn Cole? While she contemplated the problem, one of Quill's men rode forward and pointed toward the riverbank. Both men looked in Kansas's direction. They must have spotted her horse. A shiver of alarm passed over her, but she forced herself to hug the ground and not panic. They may not have noticed, but if she stood up, they surely would. Furthermore, how could she explain that she'd been spying on them? Instinctively she knew she was in a dangerous situation.

The men talked, looking up and down the riverbank, obviously looking for the rider of the horse. "Find him," she heard Quill order, "and when you do, kill him!"

A staccato of hoofbeats sounded on the dry desert floor. Kansas rolled down the riverbank until she was at the water's edge, then plunged into the muddy water. With long, desperate strokes, she swam downstream. Instinctively she dived when she heard the horses, praying the river was deep enough and muddy enough to hide her. She stayed down until her chest was aching for lack of air, then pushed up. The skirts of her riding suit tangled around her legs, threatening to pull her down again.

The men were upstream, near the piñon tree, searching

the riverbank for her. Kansas drew air into her lungs and dived again, going deep before stroking forward again. She swam underwater until, once again, a need for air drove her to the surface.

The men were riding back toward Quill Ramsey, holding her mount's reins behind. Kansas watched them go, fighting the urge to call out to them to leave her horse. She didn't want to spend a night out in the foothills, not with the stories of the Paiute and coyotes, but she feared she'd be safer than if she attracted the attention of Quill Ramsey's men. So she kept her silence, staying in the river until they had concluded their business and ridden off. Only when they were out of sight did she crawl out on the banks of the river and lay exhausted and cold, her chest heaving from exertion and fear.

The sun was dropping behind the mountain range. Soon it would be down altogether and the desert, which could be fatally hot during the day, would turn cold and inhospitable. Kansas's stomach rumbled and she was reminded that she hadn't taken time to eat breakfast and her biscuit and water were still in the saddlebag of her horse, no doubt on its way back to Virginia City. Well, she couldn't walk back to town tonight. She'd have to make the best of it.

She had no matches for a fire, so she tried rubbing two sticks together as she'd once heard the Indians did. The task was hopeless. Finally she gave up and huddled beneath the Piñon tree, watching the red-orange of sunset give way to the mauve-grays of twilight and finally to black. The desert was dark and mysterious and in the distance she heard a coyote's howl. Something slithered through the dry grass toward the riverbank and Kansas screamed. The sound was startlingly loud in the desert quiet. Kansas clamped her hand over her mouth to keep from making any more sounds.

For a long time the desert was unnaturally silent, then one by one the sounds of the night creatures returned as they emerged from hiding. Trembling with cold and fear, Kansas swallowed back her whimpers, her eyes enormous as she tried to discern objects in the dark. She was once again a little girl, whimpering in the frightening darkness of the toolshed. Only now the name she whispered was not that of her momma, but of Cole Slater.

Dawn came as suddenly to the desert as night had. It rose on the lip of the earth like some pale gray specter, swiftly followed by the glorious tinges of red and gold as the sun stained the sky with its color and warmth. Kansas slept, hunched against the piñon tree, hair streaming over her face until the first rays of the sun painted gold in her tresses and turned the muddy river into a thing of beauty. With a startled cry, she jerked and woke up.

At first her eyes were wide and blank as she looked around, then memory returned and, pushing back her hair, she got to her feet, wincing at the soreness in her limbs. Hopefully she looked around. There was no sign of her horse. Brushing at her clothes, Kansas glanced up one end of the river and down the other, then set out walking back to Virginia City. She'd follow the river for a spell, then set out across the foothills. No doubt by nightfall she'd be back at the Palace with Ellie and Otis making a fuss over her. They were probably sick with worry by now. In the reassuring light of day, Kansas felt confident she could find her way back.

"Something's happened to Miss Kansas," Otis said glumly. "She didn't come back last night."

"I wouldn't worry," Cole said. "She may have gone to spend the night with one of her special customers." He was unaware of the bitterness that tinged his words or the disgusted look Otis gave him.

"Miss Kansas wouldn'a done that," he said. "She'd'a been at the Palace last night. It—it ain't been doing so well lately, and I know she wouldn't 'ave gone off to do something else."

"You say the Palace isn't doing well?" Cole asked.

"Miss Kansas ain't workin' like she used to, and her earnin's 'ave been fallin' off. She's been worried. She wouldn't 'ave stayed away. I'm tellin' you something has happened." A note of alarm in the old man's voice struck an answering chord in Cole.

"Did she give you any hint where she was going when she left?" he asked.

Otis nodded his balding head thoughtfully. "Like I said, she was right worried about things. She seemed real fiddle-footed, restless like. She put on one of them outfits like women wear when they's going riding horseback and she left. Carl down at the stable said she took one of his horses. He seen it tied up over at the Bloody Guts Saloon, but when he asked about it, no one knew anything about it. The only thing is, yesterday afternoon Quill Ramsey and his men rode out—and this morning when Carl talked to 'em, he said they seemed real edgy, and then they rode out real quicklike."

"That doesn't mean they have anything to do with Kansas," Cole said, buckling on his gun belt.

"No, but when it comes to Quill Ramsey and his men, I got to assume the worst," Otis replied, following Cole as he took out a rifle and filled his pockets with shells. "I'm goin' with you."

"Get your horse and be ready in ten minutes," Cole ordered. "Bring extra bedrolls, canteens of water, and food. When we find her, she'll be hungry and thirsty."

Kansas had never been so hot. She must have walked for hours. The sun was straight up, its merciless rays beating down on her head with such intensity she felt as if she were being pounded into the hot sand. She couldn't last much longer like this. Her tongue felt thick and cottony from lack of water and her eyes ached from staring ahead into the white glare of sun and sand.

She'd left the Truckee River some miles back, thinking to

cut across the sand and reach the foothills sooner, but she'd lost track of the foothills in the glaring light and now she trudged along, concentrating only on putting one foot ahead of the other. She'd taken off her skirt and tied it over her head sometime ago, but it hadn't really helped. She'd heard of people dying in the desert. She'd heard of how their mouths dried out and the sun boiled their brains so they went mad with hallucinations.

When she first spied the horsemen on the horizon, she thought that was just what had happened to her. She was seeing a mirage, all shimmery and distorted. She stood still and rubbed her eyes and looked again—and finally accepted the fact that these horsemen were real.

"Wait!" she cried, running toward them, waving her arms. Tearing the shirt from her head she waved it. "Wait!" she screamed, but the horsemen were riding away from her and her voice came from her parched throat in a mere croak.

Kansas ran, trying to draw closer to the elusive horsemen, but the heat had taken its toll on her. The hot sand sucked at her feet, pulling her back, so within minutes she was forced to stop and bend over while her chest heaved air in with hoarse, strangled sobs. Nausea washed over her and she fell to her knees, retching dryly, for there was no moisture her body could give up. Her nostrils flared and panic tightened her chest. She feared she might pass out from the spasms that wracked her body. At last the retching stopped and she was able to breathe again.

She had to find shelter from the sun or she would die, Kansas thought dimly. Slowly, painfully, she dragged sagebrush together, ignoring the tears and pricks to the tender flesh of her arms from the dry desert plant. When she'd fashioned a shelter of sorts for herself, she spread her shirt and then her petticoat over the bushes to give herself more shade. Then she crawled underneath. There was barely room for her, but she was provided some relief from the hot sun. She lay quietly, forcing herself to breathe in the air in short, shallow pants. Finally she could feel her body relax.

She had no idea how long she lay there, drifting in and out of a comalike state. From the slant of the sun against her makeshift shelter, she guessed several hours had passed. She didn't know she wasn't alone anymore until she heard a horse snuffle. Lying perfectly still, Kansas listened. What caution made her wait, she couldn't say, but suddenly the image of Quill Ramsey's face twisted in rage came to her and she lay wondering if he and his men had returned. If they had, they'd kill her. She was sure of it, without knowing the why of such a deed. Somehow she guessed she'd witnessed something neither Quill nor Howard wanted known. Breath held, she waited for the horse to pass on by, willing to face the death the desert promised than that merited by Quill or one of his men.

"Kansas!" The sound of her name startled her. There was a desperate plea to it, an unspoken fear, an anguish that touched some chord deep inside her. "Kansas!" She heard the creak of leather, then her shirt and petticoat were ripped away from the sagebrush and through the sparse, dry branches she could see the image of a man, a face.

"Cole," she cried, and scooted from beneath the sagebrush.

"Kansas, thank God," Cole said, catching her against him. His hands were rough, impatient as they roamed over her back, her hips, her hair, as if testing to see that she was unhurt. "I was afraid I'd never find you," he muttered with relief against her cheek. "When I saw your tracks turn away from the river and head into the desert, I thought—" His arms tightened around her, crushing the breath from her, forcing a sound of protest from her dry, cracked lips.

"I'm sorry," he said, quickly releasing her. "Are you all right?" His hands continued to explore for themselves, running along her bare arms, touching her cheeks. His wild, worried gaze caught a glimpse of her cracked lips and he reached for his canteen and uncapped it.

Eagerly Kansas reached for the water container and carried it to her lips so quickly, the rim bumped against her teeth. Water, brackish and warm, flowed into her mouth and down her chin. It was the best water she'd ever tasted.

"Take it easy. You'll make yourself sick," Cole said, grabbing the canteen and pulling it away.

Mutely she reached for it, but he held it aloft with one hand, while the other reached for her and pulled her against him. Cradling her head against his chest, he allowed her sips of water until she was replete.

"Can you ride?" he asked, capping the canteen and replacing it around his saddle horn.

Silently Kansas nodded. Cole glanced at the sloping sun, one eyebrow going up in a dear and familiar manner as he considered their options.

"The sun'll be down soon. We'll go back to the river and camp there overnight." Taking out his rifle he aimed it skyward and fired once, twice, three times. "Otis is out looking for you, too." He explained. "This'll let him know you're found."

The thought of Otis and Cole searching for her throughout the long day touched something in Kansas. She put her hands over her face and bent over. Sobs, convulsive and hoarse, shook her slim shoulders. Cole sheathed his rifle and gathered her in his arms. His strong arm wrapped around her knees and he lifted her high, cradling her against his chest.

"It's all right, you're safe now," he murmured against her temple. He felt her body jerk in spasms with each sob as she sought to control her weeping.

"I—I was so scared," she whimpered. "When those horsemen rode by and I couldn't make them hear me, I was certain I would die out here."

"What horsemen?" Cole demanded, his expression fierce.

"I—I don't know. There were several of them, but they were too far away for me to attract their attention."

"Did they look like Indians?"

"N-no." Kansas shook her head. The movement sent pain kaleidoscoping through her head.

"Quill Ramsey's men," Cole said from between clenched teeth. "I'd bet on it."

"Ramsey?" Kansas whispered. Her face grew pale. "He and his men took my horse. I—I hid from them." Wrapped in the security of his arms, she told him everything she'd seen. Finally she raised her head from his shoulder and smiled tremulously. "I'm being a big baby about this. You can put me down now."

The corners of his eyes crinkled as he returned her smile and slowly he released her knees so her body slid down the length of his. Kansas held her breath and gazed up at him. Her long hair was caught in his hat, so it fanned against his cheek, binding them together like a golden web.

"Kansas," he groaned, and wrapped both arms around her, holding her protectively within their circle. His mouth descended to hers, his lips warm and firm against hers. But there was none of the hunger in this kiss, none of the urgency of past embraces. His touch was tender, possessive, and protective. He'd nearly lost her, and now he wanted only to reassure himself that she was real and safe in his arms. His kiss ended as sweetly as it had begun. Gently he helped her into her shirt, possessively he buttoned it, protectively he helped her onto his horse and swung up behind her. Cradling her in his arms, he set the horse into a sedate walk and headed toward the river. Kansas was surprised at how close it was. She'd been walking in circles, she realized, and felt grateful anew that Cole had looked for her. Dismounting, Cole reached up to help her down, pulling her close for a moment before leading her to a grassy mound and gently pushing her onto it.

"Stay here while I make camp," he ordered.

"I can help," Kansas said, starting to rise and follow, but he was back with a canteen and bedroll. He threw the bedroll to the ground and handed her the canteen.

"Rest," he ordered. "And sip slowly."

Gratefully Kansas sank back to the grassy knoll, suddenly grateful for his efficiency, for her knees were wobbly and her head light. Obeying Cole, she opened the canteen and sipped on the brackish water. Her body had been nearly depleted of liquid and she needed to replace it.

Cole unsaddled the horse and hobbled him nearby so he could graze on some sparse, dried sprigs of grass. Then he set about gathering wood and building a small fire. The sun had dipped below the distant ridge of mountains and its brilliant colors were quickly fading to twilight mauves and pinks.

Kansas rose and walked down to the river, then, already feeling the chill in the air from the approaching night, quickly stripped off her clothes and waded into the river to wash away the sweat and tears of her day in the desert. She'd been lucky, she realized, flopping over to float on her back while she stared at the lavender sky. How long would she have lasted if Cole hadn't found her?

Chills tingled along her shoulder blades and, turning over, she swam to warm herself. Suddenly she heard the splash of a large animal somewhere in the river. Frantically she looked toward shore for Cole, but he was nowhere in sight. No doubt he was gathering wood. Who knew how far away from the camp he had to look? She'd better go back to shore. But as her arms arched, white and fragile against the dark river, she heard the sound of the animal approaching.

"Cole!" she screamed, and began to thrash about wildly. She could hear the animal behind her. "Cole—" she yelled. Something had hold of her foot and was pulling her under. She rose to the surface coughing up river water and gasping for air.

"Cole!" she screamed again.

"You called?" he said from right behind her, and Kansas whirled, eyes wide, hair flying, sending rays of water arcing away from her head. They caught the last glow of twilight and fell to the glassy surface of the river.

"You!" She gasped, and swung her hand through the water, splashing him so he laughed and ducked away. Quickly she swam toward shore, but he was right behind her, his long, powerful arms lapping rhythmically until he was upon her. His arms wrapped around her, binding her to him as he lunged downward, carrying them both beneath the water. They surfaced, laughing and gasping in air.

Treading water, Kansas studied Cole's face. His dark hair was sleek against his head, his expression was relaxed and carefree, like that young boy she'd once known long ago. Yet his face wasn't that of a boy. It was a hard face, the handsome planes and angles weathered by the sun, the lines tempered by the steel of the man himself. Water dripped from his eyebrows and ran along his cheeks and her laughter died away as she reached out a hand and smoothed away the runnels of river water.

His face had grown serious as his hand came up to catch hers. Turning his cheek, he pressed a kiss in her palm. "We'd better get out now. Supper's ready. You must be starving."

"I am," she said, her voice low and throaty. He couldn't miss the invitation in her eyes. It had been weeks since their fight, and their need for each other was powerful. Cole took her hand and led her up the riverbank until they stood near the fire he'd built. His hands ran over her body, sluicing away the water, warming her so she no longer felt the night air. Kansas's hands trembled as they reached for Cole. The firelight gilded the angular curves of muscle and sinew, the commanding line of bone and flesh that made up Cole Slater. Yet for all her hands touched and wondered at, it was his face and eyes, the love light she found there, that captured her heart and mind.

"Oh, Cole, I love you." She sighed, and the sound was caught by a river breeze and wound around them, echoing in their heads like a thousand fiddles. Cole's mouth was moist and hot and demanding on hers. Her kiss answered in kind. He released her only long enough to spread the bedroll beside their campfire, then he reached for her, gathering her close, lowering her to the covers. He loomed over her, his shoulders blocking the starlight, and for one brief moment she remembered their first night of making love on the unfinished floor of the Palace. Pain, brief and sharp, flashed through her, then was gone, erased by the erotic brush of Cole's hand against her cheek, down her throat, and to the peak of her yearning breast. He lowered his head and took the burgeoning nipple of first one breast and then the other into his mouth, his teeth grazing the sensitive ends until she moaned with pleasure and arched her back. His questing mouth roamed lower over her flat, sleek belly, along the satiny planes of her thighs and lower. He kissed each toe, nibbled the arch of her instep, slid his lips along the smooth curve of her calf, and licked the soft secret places behind her knees . . . and when she lay quivering with desire, he parted her legs and plundered the soft, moist core of her womanhood until she arched her back and cried out her need of him in fulsome measure. Then and only then did he lower himself to her, his broad chest flattening her arching breasts, his slender whipcord hips pinning her own in place as his hard, moist sheath invaded and claimed her. Kansas wrapped her legs and arms around him, her body clinging and releasing in an age-old rhythm that carried them both over the edge to a special, passion-filled world, where their cries of release mingled.

Sated and spent, Kansas lay staring at the star-studded sky. Cole's limp body lay half over hers, but she bore his weight gladly, for it was only that which had held her to earth. Otherwise she would be floating through the dark sky, a soul lost forever in bright ecstasy, like the stars who burn too hot and must eventually die. She shivered slightly and Cole moved, drawing the cover up over them both before settling his cheek near her shoulder once more. His arms tightened around her possessively. Kansas smiled. She'd never been so happy in her life. There had been a special quality to Cole's lovemaking, as if he'd thrown aside all caution and given himself freely at last. Kansas sighed contentedly.

"Cole," she whispered.

"Ummmm!"

"I have to talk to you."

"Nnnmmmm!"

"Now," she insisted. "It's important."

"Nothing's that important."

"It is. There are rumors going around town, things being said about me. They simply aren't true. And the things you believe about me aren't true, either. I was a virgin that first night we were together, Cole. And there's never been another man, only you." Her words ended in a soft whisper that touched his very heart. He made no answer, and soon her breathing grew even and he knew she was asleep.

Carefully he sat up, tucking the bedroll around her, for the night had grown cold. He reached for his tobacco and rolled a cigarette, then sat smoking for a long time, staring into the flames and thinking of all the things that had happened between him and this woman. Even more, he thought of things to come. Sighing heavily he turned to her and gathered her limp sleeping form in his arms. He knew he was being selfish, but his need for her was too powerful. He planted light kisses on her temple, her delicate jaw, and the soft white column of her throat. She moaned a protest. His mouth swooped lower, closing over one perfectly shaped breast. She moaned again and opened her eyes, and when he would have pulled away, she pressed his head down, shuddering as once again his mouth claimed her nipples, suckling until her breath was heavy and moist against his ear. Now that he had her attention, he pulled away and stared down at her. She gazed at him through languorous, passion-glazed eyes.

"Don't tell me any more lies, Kansas," he said softly. "I don't need to hear them to know the kind of woman you are. I accept you as you are this moment, no matter what has gone before or what others say. Let's forget the past. It has no more hold on us. Only this moment between us is important. I love you, Kansas." His words washed over her like a warm caress. He loved her—and was prepared to love her even if the rumors had been true. What greater test of a man's love than this?

"Oh, Cole, I'm so happy," she said, and flung herself against him.

Her sweet mouth claimed his. She kissed his cheeks, his eyes and brow, his chin, that stubborn chin, the brown column of his throat. Her tongue rimmed his nipples and he shuddered. She laughed, intoxicated with a new sense of power as they grew hard, pebbly. Cole's arms closed around her, pinning her back against the bedroll, but she pushed at his chest.

"No," she cried. "It's my turn to love you."

She slipped from beneath him and pushed him back against the blankets. Her hands roamed freely over his body, touching, caressing, tickling, until he was rigid with desire. Then, grinning wickedly at him, she straddled his legs and bent low, letting her full breasts swing over the tip of his pulsing erection. He groaned, and she slid her satiny breasts along his shaft, then he felt her mouth soft and moist and he groaned. She was unrelenting, she was thorough. She delighted in giving him pleasure. How many men had known this ecstasy with her? he wondered briefly, then pushed the thought away. It wasn't worthy of either of them or this passion that flowed between them.

Kansas raised her head and smiled at him. Her face glowed with love.

Cole reached for her, to claim her at last, but she eluded him and moved forward so she straddled his hips. Her hair brushed his belly, tingling, erotic. She slid herself down on him, capturing his throbbing manhood, sheathing it in the warm cocoon of her womanhood. Sensuously she rotated her hips, and Cole's body arched upward to spear deeper into the joyous, pulsing warmth of Kansas McKay.

The sun was barely on the horizon when Cole was up and saddling his horse. He poured a cup of coffee and drank it, then poured a cup for Kansas and left it, along with a cold biscuit, on the grassy knoll nearby. When he'd stamped out the fire and broken camp save for the bedroll, he woke her.

"Good morning," she said, smiling and stretching before hooking her arms around his head and pulling him down for a kiss. Her skin was warm and smooth, her cheeks flushed. Dark smudges beneath each eye testified to their night of lovemaking. Cole savored the sweetness of her mouth, then pulled away.

"We'd better head back," he said rising. "I left some food out for you."

"Umm, I'm not even hungry," Kansas said, but she slid out of the bedroll and walked to the grassy knoll where he'd left the coffee.

She seemed unself-conscious about her nudity, and Cole couldn't help but stare at the sleek lines of her body. Hair as rich and ripe as new honey hung down her slender back, brushing the tops of her trim buttocks. Sleek, perfectly formed thighs tapered into shapely calves. She turned, coffee cup clasped but forgotten in her hand as she stared at a bird that had risen from the riverbank and soared overhead.

Cole saw the firm tapering breasts, the smooth skin molded over delicate bones. Below her narrow waist, hips flared slightly and hair as golden as that on her head coyly guarded the sweet form of her womanhood. Cole felt passion flare and turned away. He'd been unfair to make love to her last night. He should have left things as they were. Now he must only bring her more pain, and he had no other choice. He tightened the cinch on his horse, rolled the sleeping bag and stowed it, and when he looked again she'd dressed, even pulling on the petticoats she'd thrown over the sagebrush for shade.

"I'm ready," she said when he turned and saw her.

Her face was alight with love and happiness as she came toward him. He turned away and retightened the cinch.

"Is something wrong, Cole?" she asked, her expression darkening like a cloud passing over the face of the sun.

He couldn't avoid her eyes, they were too anxious. He couldn't avoid telling her what was to come.

"Have you changed your mind?" she teased. "Have you decided you don't love me?"

"I love you, Kansas," he said roughly, and forced himself to meet her gaze. He had to make her understand. "I meant every word I said last night, but I've already asked Claire Howard to be my wife."

Chapter 16

KANSAS STARED AT him openmouthed, horror growing on her face. "You'll have to tell her you love me now," she whispered, but there was less assurance in her words.

Cole shook his head and turned away. "I can't do that," he said. "I intend to stay engaged to Claire Howard."

"But why?" Kansas cried, coming to catch at his sleeve. "You don't love her. You love me."

"Love hasn't anything to do with it," Cole said, and for the hundredth time fiddled with the cinch.

"If love hasn't anything to do with it, then what does, Cole?" she asked, and waited for an answer.

But Cole couldn't tell her anything more. He remained silent, feeling her condemnation and helpless to say the very words that would turn it aside.

"You're marrying Claire because her father's a banker and they have money and she's a lady and I'm—I'm a—a whore, aren't you?"

He whirled to look at her then, a denial on his lips. He'd tell her the truth and everything else be damned. But her eyes had grown dark with misery. He saw his own anguish mirrored there.

"I hate you, Cole Slater," she spat out.

He knew the words were born out of her humiliation, but he let them stand. It was best this way, safer for him and for her. She may already have stumbled into more than she should know.

A cracking sound split the air and a splume of dust kicked up at his feet. Cole froze and studied the ground, looking for a lizard or some creature that might have caused the disturbance. His emotions and reflexes were still centered on the woman who stood at one side, her head raised like a startled deer about to bolt.

Cole's disorientation couldn't have lasted more than a heartbeat, but it seemed like a lifetime. As if in slow motion, his body pivoted toward Kansas. He took a long running step, his arms reaching for her, his mouth open to call a warning even while his mind screamed he was too late. His mind registered more gunshots. He saw the bullets dig into the riverbank, kicking up sand and pebbles, tearing chunks of wood from the lone piñon tree, piercing the slender, helpless body of a woman. Cole saw her eyes widen, saw her body jerk and go limp as she slowly slid to the ground.

"Kansas!" he cried, and ignoring the raining bullets, he crouched over her, his shaky hands reaching for a pulse. Her eyelids fluttered and the vein in her throat throbbed wildly. "Kansas," he whispered, almost crying. "You're hurt, baby. Don't move."

His quick fingers explored her body for wounds. Two bullets had hit her, one low in the side and the other high in the shoulder. Was it high enough to have missed her lungs? he wondered, and laid his head near her face to listen to her breathing. There was no gurgling sound, no sign of blood seeping into her lungs, choking off her breath. Helplessly he looked around. Blood was everywhere. He felt the sticky wetness of it against his hands and impotent fury washed through him. He had to get her back to town or she would die.

The bullets continued to fan over his head. Quickly he packed her wounds, pressing down to stop the bleeding. She lay still and unmoving, her face deathly white, her gold lashes curling against her pale cheek in defenseless surrender. This was so unlike Kansas, with her determined spunk and independence, that he nearly wept then, but bullets continued to *thunk* into the sandbank protecting them.

Baring his teeth in feral fury, Cole drew his gun and fired. He was like a madman, barely taking time to aim, hitting his target nonetheless. One man went down, slumping in his saddle with a cry, then falling to the hot sand. Another man's gun went flying and he cradled his arm against his chest. He wheeled his horse and galloped away.

"Come back here," Farley called, and when the hapless horseman refused to obey, Farley shot him in the back.

The other men, seeing what had happened to their comrade, pressed the attack. Cole fired his last bullet and wished for his rifle, which was still in its scabbard on the horse. In his concern for Kansas, he hadn't thought to grab it. Hurriedly he reloaded his pistol, automatically counting the bullets left in his belt.

One of the gunmen rode to the edge of the sand bluff and looked down at Cole, an evil grin on his face. Seeing the man raise his gun and sight down his barrel, Cole hurriedly snapped the cylinder into place, took aim, and fired. The pin fell on an empty chamber. The man on horseback smiled once more. Cole could see his finger tightening on the trigger. A gunshot rang out, and for a moment Cole stood waiting to feel the pain. Then the man in the saddle pitched sideways and tumbled down the embankment, coming to rest half in the river. A horse made a mad gallop toward the bank, and with fingers suddenly gone nerveless, Cole worked on his jammed gun. At last the cylinder was freed and in place and he raised the gun—just as Otis appeared over the embankment.

"Whooee!" the old man cried, dismounting and taking shelter behind the bank. "You got some angry visitors out there." He raised his head and got off a shot.

"Where the hell were you?" Cole demanded, aiming and firing himself. "I thought they'd already gotten you."

"Naw, when I heerd your shots last night and knowed Miss Kansas was safe, I just camped where I was. I figured I'd ride in this morning for breakfast. Guess I'm a little later than I expected."

He didn't tell Cole that he'd ridden in earlier and seen the two of them sleeping, their limbs entwined. Discreetly he'd ridden out again, deciding to hunt for a rabbit along the riverbank. He'd gone further than he'd intended, until the sound of the gunfight pulled him back. Now he cast a glance at Kansas, who lay to one side.

"This shore ain't like waking up in the Palace, is it, Miss . . . ?" He paused, seeing for the first time the unnatural stillness and the red stains on her shirt. "Oh, no!" he said, shaking his head.

"She's still alive, but we have to get her back to town," Cole said, and the two men looked at each other. As if of one accord, they readied their weapons and stood up. The bank shielded them from the chest down and they stood blazing away at the gunmen. In the face of their unrelenting fusillade, the gunmen turned and galloped away over the desert toward the foothills. Even Farley had to retreat.

Quickly Otis and Cole gathered up their horses and Cole mounted. Otis handed Kansas up to him and gingerly he settled her against his chest, trying to cradle her with his body as much as possible. He checked the rags he'd stuffed against her wounds and noted they were soaked and of little use.

"What about these other coyotes," Otis asked, looking around at the two dead men.

"Leave them for the buzzards," Cole said. "I need you to ride shotgun, in case Quill's men come back."

Otis stripped the bodies of their guns and ammunition and stepped up into his saddle. Cole nudged his mount into a walk. It would take them longer to get back to town, but he didn't want to risk jarring Kansas any more than he had to.

It was late afternoon before they reached Virginia City. People stopped and stared as the blood-soaked sheriff rode through the streets clutching a crumbled body, equally bloodied, and with glorious golden hair streaming behind. Whispers turned to cries of dismay, and a crowd followed them as they turned toward Doc Langley's house. The good doctor heard the commotion and came running to his front gate. His face registered shock as Cole carried Kansas inside.

"She's lost a lot of blood," Cole said bleakly. "You've got to help her."

Doc Langley saw the desperation in Cole's face and the clenching and unclenching of his fists. "Wait on the porch while I examine her," he ordered, and Otis took hold of Cole's arm and led him outside.

Slumping down on the step, Cole buried his head in his hands and thus he sat, oblivious to the curious crowd gathered at the gate or of the spectacle he made sitting there in his blood-drenched shirt. He sat without moving, barely breathing, way into the night. He knew only that behind that door, in the weak flickering lamplight, the doctor worked to save the only woman he loved.

Memories of Kansas's laughing face hovering over him as she made love to him—the sweetness of her kiss, the delicate sturdiness of her slim body, the sound of her voice, the smell and taste of her skin—all mocked him, tormented him so he could only crouch there as if caught in a spell.

Some time near midnight, the doctor came out onto the porch, stretched his cramped muscles, and lit his pipe. After he'd drawn a couple of puffs, he took pity on the man who sat staring up at him with deadened eyes. "I got the bullets out," he said. "There's not much more I can do. She's weak, and it's going to take some time before we know if she'll make it. You might as well go on home, son, and get some rest."

"I'll wait here," Cole said, and his voice was so steady and flat the doctor knew it would do little good to argue with him. Sighing, he went back inside and brought out a couple of blankets. Otis took one and wrapped it around Cole, then rolled himself in the other and stretched out on the wooden porch. It was going to be a long vigil, he guessed.

He was right. For two days, Kansas fought against the fever that threatened to claim her. The doctor fed her laudanum for the pain that made her cry out in her delirium and kept wet compresses on her forehead to help cool the fever. Other than that, there was little he could do. When at last she gave a whimper and opened her eyes, the doctor rushed to the front porch to tell the haggard-faced man who'd never left his post. Otis had brought him a fresh shirt. The doctor had given him food and drink, but other than sipping now and then on coffee, Cole had eaten nothing. The doctor was glad to have his patient recovering, if for no other reason than to ease the towering presence from his front porch.

"She's awake now," he said, looking at Cole. He seemed to have aged ten years in the past two days. Now the gray face brightened, the granite eyes softened with a look of hope that touched the doctor. "You can see her for a minute or two, no more."

Eagerly Cole climbed the stairs and walked through the doctor's office to the small bedroom in back. He paused in the doorway, savoring his first glimpse of the slight, pale figure in the large bed.

"Kansas," he said softly, and moved to the bed. Tears burned the back of his eyes and nose and he swallowed against the lump in his throat. One large brown hand took up her pale slender one. He felt the delicate bones beneath

the flesh and in a paroxysm of joy, he carried her limp hand
to his cheek. The golden eyelashes fluttered and, slowly, as
if the effort were too great to contemplate, Kansas turned
her head. She opened her eyes and stared at Cole's somber
face.

She swallowed, and with great effort spoke. At first, her
words were too hoarse to understand, but she kept trying,
and finally the words were clear enough to strike a chill in
Cole's heart. "Go away, Cole. I don't want to see you,"
she said. "Go away."

"Kansas, we have to talk," he said, kneeling beside the
bed and grasping her hand. "Those things I told you back
there at the river . . . I have to explain."

"Go away," she repeated, growing more agitated. "I
hate you. . . . Hate . . . Cole."

"You'd better leave, son," the doctor said kindly but
firmly. "It's not good to upset her right now."

Cole wiped at his cheeks with his hand and got to his feet.
"She will be all right?" he asked, staring down at her.

"She'll live," Langley said. "You'll have plenty of time
to straighten out whatever it is between you. Believe me,
son, now is not the time."

Cole nodded—and to Langley's relief left the room. Langley followed him out to the porch. "It wouldn't hurt you
any to go home and get yourself some food and rest."

Cole settled his hat on his head. "First, I've got some
unfinished business to take care of," he said, his hand settling on his gun. With a final nod he stepped down off the
porch and headed toward town, a deadly purpose obvious in
every line of his body. Langley sighed. Whoever the sheriff
was going after, the doctor had little doubt he would soon
be tending the man's remains.

"Cole, you ain't going to try to tangle with Farley and
them men now, are you?" Otis said, rushing after him.

Cole made no answer. Out into the sun-drenched street he
strode, his long legs moving swiftly toward the Bloody Guts

Saloon, where Farley and the rest of Quill's men sprawled at tables, drinking and gambling quietly. Since returning to Virginia City, they'd remained as inconspicuous as possible. Ramsey had railed against Farley for the whole affair, and some of the men still weren't sure if he was angry because they'd shot Kansas McKay when Cole Slater was there or because they'd failed to kill them both. So they waited, not sure what they waited for, but growing edgy with each passing hour and with each new report on Kansas.

The door flew inward and the men in the saloon looked up to see the light barred by the tall, broad-shouldered man wearing the sheriff's badge. Suddenly they understood what they'd been waiting for. It had been inevitable that Cole Slater would come after them. Otis was right behind him. Some of the men edged their chairs around, their hands surreptitiously checking their holsters for the reassuring presence of their guns. Cole took a few steps into the saloon and ran his gaze along the line of men at the bar. His eyes grew hard as they settled on Farley, seated at a table nearby.

"What can I do for you, Sheriff?" Quill Ramsey asked, coming to stand before Cole. A swaggering grin was pinned on his handsome face, but his eyes were wary.

"I've got no business with you, Ramsey," Cole said in a low voice, "unless you ordered your men to gun down a helpless unarmed woman."

Quill shrugged his shoulders with elegant nonchalance. "Why would I want a woman killed?" he asked, and waved a thin, ringed hand toward the saloon girls that sat at the tables. "I find women have far better uses."

"Then stand aside," Cole said. "It's your man Farley I'm after."

"Why would you want him, Sheriff?" Quill asked smoothly. "He couldn't have done what you accuse. He's been here at my saloon for the last three days."

Cole's eyebrows drew together in an intimidating scowl. "Maybe you'd better pay more attention to who's here and who's not," he growled. "Two days ago, Farley was at the Truckee River shooting down Kansas McKay. She never knew what hit her." Quill opened his mouth to make another protest, but Cole glared at him. "If you don't get out of my way, Ramsey, I'll shoot right through you," Cole said quietly, but his lip curled with contempt and Quill had little doubt he meant it. Quickly he moved aside.

Seeing he no longer had Quill to protect him, Farley jumped to his feet and pulled his gun. Chairs scraped against the wood floor as men scurried to get out of the line of fire. Before Farley had his gun leveled, Cole had reached for his, pulled and fired. Face twisted in an agony of disbelief, Farley's glazed eyes rolled in his head and he slumped to the floor. Several of his men made to draw their guns, but they paused with them half out of their holsters, uneasily eyeing the twin bores of Cole's and Otis's guns. Some of the miners, having heard how Kansas was gunned down, now drew their guns and lined up behind Cole and Otis. Quill's men faced a full barrage of guns. Quickly they holstered their guns and raised their hands.

Quill, seeing his gunmen surrender, quickly stepped to the front. "Sheriff, I want to thank you for ridding me of that scum. I had no idea he was firing on innocent people. I hired him to help me maintain order here at the Bloody Guts, but he got so he took things on himself, thought he was boss. I told him if there was one more incident I'd fire him, didn't I, boys?" Quill turned to his men, who quickly nodded their heads in agreement. "I'm sure grateful you've rid Virginia City of a man like Farley."

Cole took hold of Quill's collar and nearly lifted the man off his elegantly booted feet. "If I ever learn that you ordered Farley to go after Kansas McKay, I'll be back here so fast you won't have time to spit. Have you got that, Ramsey?"

Quill's face flushed an ugly red. Cole shook him slightly. "Yes, all right," he gasped. "You won't have any more trouble from me and my men." Cole released him and turned toward the door. Quill's men relaxed visibly, but their relief was premature. Cole whipped about and strolled to a man slouching down at one table. The man's thumb was tucked into his belt, his arm tight against his body. Cole stepped close, brushing against his shoulder. The man cursed and winced. Cole took hold of the back of the chair and yanked. The man spun out and landed on the floor. Still holding his arm and shoulder stiffly, he scrambled to his feet.

"Don't shoot," he cried, throwing his good hand high in the air. "I never aimed for the woman, I swear."

Cole's cold eyes bored into the frightened man. He wanted to kill him as he had Farley, and it showed in his eyes. The man licked his lips nervously and looked around the room for help. There seemed little. "It was Qu—" His words were cut off by the sharp report of a gun. The gunslinger slumped to the floor.

Cole swung around. Quill Ramsey stood at the bar, a smoking derringer still clasped in his hand.

"Like I told you, Sheriff. I never could stand a polecat killer who'd gun down a woman. Maybe now you'll believe me."

"I'm taking you in for murder, Quill. That man had surrendered. He was my prisoner."

"Why, Sheriff, he was about to gun you down. Didn't you see his other hand inching toward his gun? He was a mighty fast draw, Sheriff. He would have shot you dead while you were listening to his pretty story. Ain't that right, boys?"

"Yeah, I saw him reaching for his gun," one of Quill's men said, and the others echoed his claim.

"I saved your life, Sheriff. Now you're beholden to me." Quill grinned, one blond eyebrow raised mockingly.

"Don't cross my path again, Quill," Cole said. "There won't be a next time."

"You're welcome, Sheriff. I was glad I could help you out," Quill said blithely.

Cole's fist clenched in an effort to keep from hitting the gambler, but he forced himself to turn and walk out of the saloon. The rage still burned in him. Killing Farley wasn't enough. He wanted Quill and he'd get him. In the end he'd get him—and Oliver Howard as well. He thought of Kansas lying in the doctor's bed, her face pale and drawn as she fought for her life, and he remembered the words she'd cried out at him. He'd only brought her more hurt, when he'd meant to protect her. Well, now the cards were dealt. He'd play the hand the way it lay.

Three days later, as Kansas McKay was being moved back to her own bed in the Palace, the engagement of Cole Slater and Claire Howard was announced to the citizens of Virginia City.

"Hold still now. This'll cure you," Ellie said, with some exasperation. She'd been tending her cantankerous patient for several days, and the tempers of both patient and nurse were wearing thin.

"Not another one of your concoctions," Kansas protested, pushing aside the bowl filled with an obnoxious brew of dubious origin. "What's in here? Eye of newt and dried toad?"

"Make fun of me if you will, missy," Ellie sniffed, "but it's been me and my concoctions as you call 'em that's got you strong again." She bustled around fluffing Kansas's pillow and straightening the covers with the same determined efficiency that had maddened Kansas over the past few days.

Looking at the woman in the stiffly starched apron with her gray-streaked blond hair pulled into a severe bun at the back of her head, Kansas found it hard to believe that Ellie had once earned her living as a whore. The change had been dramatic in the year and a half since Kansas first came to

Virginia City and won the Silver Spur in a card game. No doubt, Miss Simpson's efforts at converting the fallen woman to a more Christian way of life had had some bearing on Ellie's miraculous change. Still, there existed enough of the superstitious, rebellious "soiled dove" to temper Miss Simpson's rigidity. Ellie might playact at being a self-righteous woman, but occasionally she slipped back into her old habits. Following the superstitious practices of her childhood was one of them. Charms and amulets had been hung on every bedpost. Brews made with plants gathered from God only knew where in the sparse Nevada soil were pressed on the patient. Kansas wasn't sure if she was getting better because of them or so she wouldn't have to swallow the noxious drinks. When she woke with ash leaves pressed to her bosom and Ellie chanting over her about a love returning, Kansas's patience snapped and she ordered all traces of Ellie's spells and potions to be cleared from the room.

"I was trying to help you get that man back that you mutter so much about in your dreams."

"Cole?" Kansas asked unthinkingly. Had he come to see her again, after all? She'd turned him away so many times in those first days. Now that she felt better, she almost regretted her actions.

"Cole Slater!" Ellie repeated in ominous exasperation. "What other man have you gone lovesick over?"

"I'm not lovesick, Ellie. I was shot by Quill Ramsey's men," Kansas reminded her.

"Humph!" Ellie rejoined, and left the room, confident that she'd had the last word. She was soon back with a sly look on her face, and Kansas was sure that the amulets she'd ordered out of the room were finding their way back in, slipped, no doubt, between the mattresses or under Kansas's neatly folded nightgowns in the bureau. Kansas sighed in resignation and leaned back against the freshly plumped pillows.

"Tell me what's been happening in town since I've been ill," she demanded, to sidetrack Ellie in her intentions.

"The Palace is losing money since you've been ill. Otis has done his best, but he ain't the gambler you are."

"Yes, he told me he's worried," she said. "Our bank loan is due, and he's not sure we have the money to make the payment. But something will happen. I'll be well soon."

"It won't be soon enough for the Palace," Ellie said grumpily. "Without you down there, the miners just aren't coming like they did. Oh, they come to wish you well. They still care about you, but without Kansas McKay, the Kansas Palace ain't nothing special to 'em."

"Tell me about the town," Kansas said, wanting to change the subject. She'd known for some time that the Palace was in trouble, but somehow she couldn't seem to worry about it. Her thoughts were too occupied with Cole. "Tell me about Cole Slater," she said in a soft voice. "Has he been back to see me?"

"Not after you turned him away so many times!" Ellie scoffed. "You can't treat a man like Cole Slater that way and expect him to come crawling back. He has his pride."

"And I have mine!" Kansas flared.

"Well, pride will be a poor comfort on a cold winter night, missy!" Ellie snapped back. "You might as well know. You're bound to find out, anyway. Oliver Howard announced his daughter's engagement to Cole Slater."

"Oh!" Kansas's voice was as small as she felt at this moment.

"I'm right sorry to be the one to tell you," Ellie said contritely. "But I figured better me to tell you in the privacy of your bedroom than to hear it out in the town someplace. There's been lots of buzzing about it. Some folks thought you and the sheriff were getting mighty close. Of course, that Claire and her mother are gloating all over town."

"Don't worry about it, Ellie. I knew it was going to

happen. Cole told me when he found me in the desert." Kansas forced a smile to lips that had gone pale. "Tell me some good news!"

Ellie saw the bloodless lips and sensed her pain. "If I really was a witch like some folks are hintin'," she muttered, "I'd cast such a spell on those Howards. I'd turn Claire's hair white and grow a wart on that uppity nose of hers."

Kansas laughed in spite of herself. "Ellie!"

"The new territorial governor's arrived," Ellie said obediently.

"I'm missing his visit," Kansas moaned.

"He asked after you. Said he'd enjoyed his correspondence with you and thanked you for the invitation to Virginia City. That put Letitia Howard's nose out of joint some, I can tell you. She's acting as the official hostess."

"She'll be good at it," Kansas said, and tried not to feel rancor.

"They're having a ball for the governor at the end of the week."

"A ball!" Kansas repeated, her face lighting up at the prospect.

"You needn't get yourself all atwitter. You ain't going. You ain't well enough."

"I'll be fine by then," Kansas argued. "Otis can take me." Something in Ellie's face made Kansas pause. "Or perhaps he was planning on taking someone else."

Ellie's face flamed with color. "Just you never mind," she snapped. "Neither Otis nor me is going. Who wants to go to an old ball anyhow?"

Kansas studied the other woman. Something in Ellie's face hadn't lined up with what she said. Silently she pondered the reason Otis and Ellie had decided not to attend—and slowly the only reason that could be came to her. If invitations had been sent out, none had come to Kansas. No wonder Ellie had hovered over her when she opened her mail, and no wonder her face had tightened each time in anger. Kansas was aware of the fierce loyalty Otis and Ellie held for her, and now she smiled, touched anew by their caring.

"Since I'm too ill to attend the ball myself," she said tentatively, "I really wish I had someone there to represent me. Won't you and Otis reconsider, Ellie? You'd be doing me a big favor."

"I don't much fancy going to a ball," Ellie said, raising her eyebrows and looking down her nose. Even her small finger had come out to poke the air in pseudogentility.

"Would you do it for me?" Kansas coaxed, and was rewarded with a gleam of eagerness in Ellie's eye before the woman pulled her habitual disapproving air about herself.

"I suppose if you need me to go, I could manage it," she conceded, then as if unable to contain herself another minute, she leaped to her feet. "I'd best see if I have a proper gown to wear to the ball."

Eyes aglow she whirled out of the room, and Kansas breathed a sigh of relief, certain that for a time she'd be free of Ellie's ministrations. If she had to swallow one more brew of unknown origin or endure any more amulets, she wouldn't be responsible for what happened. Yet, now that Ellie was gone, Kansas missed her fussing and bossing. No one could fluff the pillow just the way Ellie could. Kansas gave up and lay back, staring at her canopy. She was getting as bad as Ellie, fussing over minor things to avoid facing the really important ones.

Cole was truly going to marry Claire. Now that she faced that reality, Kansas felt a pain deep inside that was worse than anything she'd endured in the desert. Perhaps it would have been better if she had died there, she thought morosely, and wiped at the weak tears that spilled out the corners of her eyes and streamed down her temples and nose. For a time she felt overcome with the grief of losing

Cole a second time, but finally it began to lessen, and if she was never free of a dull ache, at least she could breathe again and begin to make plans.

Her thoughts went to the ball. Everyone would be there, everyone but her. She could well imagine people whispering behind their fans, laughing smugly at the thought that Claire had won Cole from that dreadful Kansas person. What kind of name was Kansas, anyway? Kansas wallowed in the pain of their imagined slights, for this pain was less than that brought by the knowledge of Claire and Cole together.

When her eyes were red and swollen from crying and her nose stuffed so she had to breathe through her mouth, she sat up, placed her feet on the floor, and looked out her window at the town below. Everyone would be at that ball for the governor. Even the notorious, shameless Kansas McKay!

With that settled, Kansas stood up and took her first tottering step since she'd been shot. She must move about every day to regain her strength, and she must find something special to wear to the ball.

The night of the ball was clear, with a breeze cooling the frenzied heat of the day. Down on Main Street, the saloons and cribs were at full roar. Prostitutes and miners went about business as usual. No invitations had been sent to these good citizens, and they gave it no thought whatsoever, although the people on the hill gave them a lot of thought. Efforts had been made to tone down the exuberant, brazen fleshpots that flourished in Virginia City, but the miners, tired from their dull lives digging like moles underground, wouldn't allow it. The Citizens' Committee finally decided it best to leave the saloons open to keep the riffraff satisfied and in their place. Special deputies had been hired, since Sheriff Slater would be attending the ball with his intended. But the deputies hadn't the knack the sheriff had for keeping boisterous men in hand, and now hoots and shouts and gunshots could be heard clear up the hillside, outside the best dwellings.

"Ruffians!" Letitia Howard stood at the window staring out past lace curtains. Her hands and teeth were clenched with equal intensity as she held back the expletive she'd heard on the street one day and longed now to utter. She was a lady, and no such word would ever escape her chaste lips.

"Mother?" Claire came into the room, and Letitia Howard turned and smiled at her daughter.

"You are truly beautiful, my dear," she said, holding out her hands to take Claire's. "You look like a bride already."

Claire's dark beauty was enhanced by the white lace dress she'd donned. Glossy blue-black curls bobbed over each ear. Her dark eyes were lustrous and gleaming.

Claire dimpled, her smile restrained and controlled as it should be. She'd been taught from a small child to be a lady, and her breeding was stamped in every line of her carriage and costume.

"This is a triumphant night for you, Claire," Letitia said. "You've borne the interference of that shameless woman well, and in the end you've prevailed."

"Yes, Mama," Claire said, clasping her hands together in excitement. It was the only outward show of emotion she would allow herself. Her dark eyes glowed with a light that should have flattered, but didn't for its spitefulness. "I think we'll have an early wedding, Mama," she said thoughtfully. "Then I can insist that Cole give up that dreadful job as sheriff. Once Papa has completed his plans here, we can leave this town, perhaps return East, where we can live among civilized people once more."

"Patience, child. Only a little while longer," Letitia cautioned. "Our guests are arriving." The two women turned, any vestige of their conversation erased in their bland expressions. Smiling graciously, they moved forward to greet the first of their guests. Tonight was to be the crowning social achievement in Virginia City.

Within an hour Letitia and Claire Howard could count their fete a success. Governor Nye was a handsome, charismatic man who charmed everyone he met. Cole was resplendent in a dark suit and stiff white shirt. Claire clung to his arm, smiling up at him bewitchingly, all too aware of the handsome couple they made. Imported wine, hauled over the Sierras, was served in crystal glasses and the candlelight shone on the ladies' pastel satin and lace gowns. Servants, silent and efficient, passed trays of whiskey to the men.

The orchestra, once hired to play at the Palace but out of work now that Kansas McKay was down, had been engaged for the evening. Its melodious strains floated over the chatter of voices and laughter. Some couples whirled about on the dance floor, while groups of people gathered around the edges to talk of the price of silver, the trouble with the Paiute Indians, the lengthening battle between the North and South, but most of all about impending statehood. An excitement pervaded the air. Nevada was no longer a beggar child of the Mormon's Utah Territory, but a territory in its own right, and soon they planned for it to be a state. Their petitions had already begun. Elation showed itself in the lilt of men's voices as they spoke of Nevada's future and in the solid front of agreement such sentiments occasioned.

Claire and Letitia Howard had just exchanged a conspiratorial glance of congratulations at their success. The band had taken a break and people milled about the dance floor chatting quietly. At the sound of a commotion they turned with avid faces toward the door.

"I'm so sorry to be late," a woman's high lilting voice cried gaily.

Claire Howard's face paled. Her mother's pinched mouth tightened even further as she stared with hate-filled eyes at the young blond woman who crossed the room. Kansas McKay had come to the governor's ball!

Chapter 17

"*M*ISS McKAY. I'M charmed," Governor James Nye
bowed low over her hand, then straightened.
With his eyes twinkling, he regarded her. "I feared I might
not meet the famous Kansas McKay, after all."

"I wasn't certain I'd be here myself," Kansas said, smiling sweetly at Letitia Howard.

"Well, I—ah—"

"Thank you so much for your invitation," Kansas said
quickly.

Letitia Howard's mouth clamped shut with a snap and
barely opened again to utter the required words of welcome.

"Ah, Governor, there are some important people here
who wish to speak to you," Claire said, coming to her
mother's rescue. "You will excuse us, won't you, Miss
McKay?"

"Oh, no," James Nye said, taking hold of Kansas's
hand. "I want Miss McKay to stay with me. I want to
hear her opinion on the Nevada Territory. You will be my
dinner partner, won't you, Kansas? I may call you Kansas, mayn't I?"

"Of course," Kansas said, walking beside him as she led
the way across the room to the people Claire had indicated.

Claire and Letitia stood where they were, each trying to

238

recover the aplomb they'd shown so easily before Kansas's arrival. "The shameless harlot!" Letitia ground out from between her teeth, and Claire supposed the name was well fitting, for Kansas had come dressed in a silk gown of such a vibrant pink as to be almost red. No genteel grays and pastels here. Her smooth shoulders were bare and her waist impossibly tiny above the flare of her hooped skirts. Even Claire had to admit she was glowingly beautiful. Her face, still pale from her ordeal, was hauntingly lovely. No wonder men flocked to her. Claire bit the inside of her lips out of pure vexation and hatred for the blond woman. "Oh, to have to receive such a scarlet woman in my home," Letitia Howard whined. "I think I'm going to swoon, Claire."

Claire stepped close to her mother and pinched her arm with considerable viciousness. "Don't you dare," she whispered. "I won't have everyone think she's defeated us. We'll put a good face on it. She'll find few women who'll speak to her."

But Kansas had little need to speak to the women who clustered around Letitia Howard gossiping behind their fans as she'd envisioned. James Nye had meant it when he said he wanted her opinions on Virginia City and the development of the territory. Keeping in mind many of the complaints she'd heard the miners make while visiting the Palace, she offered suggestions that soon had the governor nodding in agreement.

"Quite right, Kansas," he said. "Establishing law and order and setting up jails to house those who won't abide must be our first priority. We can't expect decent people to move here if they're in constant danger of being killed or robbed."

"Decent people?" Kansas echoed, thinking of Letitia Howard and the other good ladies of Virginia City who had harassed the saloon owners and their girls. "Perhaps what we need is less decent people and more of the kind who are willing to work hard and mind their own business!" These last words were uttered as Letitia Howard approached. Kansas saw the woman stiffen and her expression grow hard. "After all," Kansas continued, "Nevada Territory is big enough for everyone to find a place here, if we can just practice tolerance for one another."

"I think you're a bit of an idealist, Miss McKay," Nye said, chuckling slightly. "We haven't learned yet how to do that back East."

The other men joined him in laughter. Kansas felt no rancor. They weren't laughing at her. She smiled in agreement. "You have to admit though, Governor, that the West is nothing like the East. Perhaps we'll set new standards here that the people in the East will follow someday. After all, it takes a certain courage and steadfastness of character to endure out here. The West can either make or break a man or woman."

"I quite agree," Nye answered. "And it's obvious your spirit's not been broken. You're the embodiment of the new woman in the West, independent and strong-willed. With men and women like you and the others I've met out here, it's little wonder Virginia City has gained recognition in the East as well as abroad. They speak of her as a jewel of the West."

"And so she is," Kansas said, raising her glass. "Gentlemen, a toast to Virginia City."

Solemnly all the men raised their glasses to drink. Over the rim of her glass, Kansas's gaze collided with Cole's and she read pride in his glance. Behind him stood Claire, her body tense, her gaze pinned on Cole's face, and for a moment, Kansas thought she read fear on the other woman's eyes. Then she linked an arm through Cole's and turned a triumphant face to Kansas.

"Governor, dinner is prepared. Would you care to lead the way?" Letitia Howard said, her voice faint in the shallow quiet following the toast.

"Thank you, my good lady," Nye said, and taking Kansas's arm led the way through the wide French doors toward the dining hall.

Letitia Howard looked about uncertainly. She'd planned on sweeping into the hall on the governor's arm herself; now she must content herself with the bland company of Rose Wilson. With Claire's arm still clinging tightly, Cole followed behind, his gaze fixed on the gleaming gold curls of the governor's companion.

"Tell me, Kansas," Nye said halfway through supper. "What do you think of Nevada's role in this Civil War?"

Kansas put down her heavy silver fork and prepared to answer. All along the table, talk ceased and eyes turned to her. Carefully she picked her answer.

"If we're to become a state, it seems to me we must take on a certain mantle of responsibility for what occurs in other states, as well. This war has dragged on far too long already. Men who went away to war expected to return home in a matter of weeks, months at the most. Now with this General Lee leading the Southern troops, the South may never surrender. I think we must offer what aid we can to the North so the war will end quickly and judiciously. Enough men have been killed."

"Well spoken," Nye said, and other men nodded their heads in agreement. "But would you offer men or silver to the North?"

Kansas paused, knowing the rich silver mines had indeed captured the support of legislators back East. "Both," she said finally. "Whatever it takes. Why, if I were a man, I'd volunteer tomorrow."

Unconsciously her voice rang with conviction and every guest at the table heard. A round of enthusiastic applause sounded and, blushing slightly, Kansas sat back in her chair and looked at her plate.

James Nye's eyes gleamed with enjoyment as he took in the creamy skin with the faint flush on the cheekbones, the finely molded nose and lips, the wide luminous eyes with the gold-tipped lashes sweeping downward to hide her momentary shyness. He found her utterly appealing with her air of bold independence and unexpected demureness.

Kansas danced with nearly every man there. Her vivid dress and sultry blond beauty drew admiring male gazes and envious spiteful gazes of the women. Only Ellie, resplendent in a silver rose-hued gown with white lace about its sedate high neck and long sleeves, stopped to chat with Kansas—and even then it was to scold.

"It's bad enough you came at all," Ellie fussed, "but you needn't stay late. You're getting dark circles under your eyes and your face is pale. You need to rest."

But Kansas only laughed away her words and whirled away in a spirited dance with Samuel Clemens, who had come West with his brother, an assistant to Governor Nye.

"Will you work with the governor, as well?" Kansas asked the energetic, dark-eyed young man as he whirled her around the room.

"I've taken a job on the Territorial Enterprise. Perhaps you'll allow me to call on you."

"By all means," Kansas said gaily, catching a glimpse of Cole's thundercloud expression. He danced on by and Kansas threw back her head and laughed. She felt light and carefree. Let Cole marry his lady. She had no need of him—not when handsome men like Samuel Clemens and James Nye pressed their suit. But later she felt her heart skip a beat when Cole stood before her and claimed a dance. It would be the first time they ever danced together. The orchestra had swung into one of the lilting new tunes known as a waltz, and Kansas found herself falling into step with Cole as if they'd danced together forever. Over his shoulder she caught a glimpse of Claire Howard's stiff face as she whirled by on the arm of her father.

"Aren't you afraid your fiancée will be offended by your dancing with me, Mr. Slater?" she asked sweetly. Her eyes glowed with impish mischief and her pink lips curved in a mocking smile. He remembered her face as she bent over him at the river, her soft hands as she caressed him.

"How are you feeling, Kansas?" he asked softly. The caring tone of his voice unnerved her, but she remembered that he was engaged to Claire.

"Your solicitude is a bit misplaced, Mr. Slater," she said, keeping a hard edge to her voice. "You should be attending to your bride-to-be."

"I simply want to know that your wounds have healed properly," Cole said. "I tried often to see you after I brought you back."

"I saw no reason for our meeting again," Kansas said implacably. "You've made your choice clear. In the future, if you find yourself in need of female companionship other than your wife's, I suggest you try the girls down at the Silver Spur."

"Kansas, stop this bickering," Cole said urgently. He'd danced her to one side of the room and now, with a final whirl, he carried them into a narrow hall. The music spun around them, but their feet were still, their hearts beating in a wild rhythm. Cole's arm still imprisoned her waist. His fingers on her wrist felt the wild frantic beat of her pulse.

"Please take me back to the ballroom," she whispered.

"I can't leave with this between us. I must see you again, talk to you, make you understand."

"There's nothing to understand," she flared. "Everything is perfectly clear. You want Claire Howard and all she represents. Well, you have her—and no regrets on my part."

"You little liar," Cole whispered. He leaned forward, letting his hard body crush her against the wall. His mouth descended, but she turned her head away.

"I hate you, Cole Slater," she choked. "You can't have Claire Howard as your wife and come to me as your mistress. Now unhand me or I'll—"

"You'll what?" he asked, loosening his hold on her

waist. His eyes crinkled with humor. Kansas didn't dare meet his gaze. Her knees trembled and anger rose in her breast at her helplessness when she was with him.

"I'll shoot you myself," she snapped. "Why don't you go away, Cole Slater? Why don't you go join the army?"

"Is that what you want me to do, Kansas?" he asked. His strong fingers still gripped her wrist. "Would you grieve for me if I went away? What if I were to die?"

"Good," Kansas stormed. "I would pray every day you were gone that a reb bullet would pierce your black heart." She wrenched her hand free. "I wouldn't even cry for you." Angrily she stalked back to the dance.

Cole watched her go, seeing the proud tilt of her head. He longed to go after her and kiss away the stubborn set of her chin until she gasped in surrender and took back every harsh word she'd uttered. He'd hurt her pride, and she was entitled to her anger. He couldn't change things now. Other men were involved, and a cause that was bigger than any two people. Soon he'd tell her everything.

Wearily Cole returned to the ball and Claire's clinging hands.

"It's a shame, a shame to treat a man like that," Ellie muttered under her breath. "Cole Slater has pride, you know. Little wonder he went to that mewly faced Claire. You should try to be a little sweeter." She paused and looked at Kansas. "We could burn chicken feathers and try to win him back."

"I don't want him back!" Kansas snapped. "Claire's welcome to him."

"The way he carried on over you when you was wounded and no one thought you'd live . . ." Ellie shook her head.

Kansas quit her contemplation of a spider crawling along the ceiling molding and studied Ellie as if looking for some sign of deception. "Was he worried?" she asked, with feigned disinterest.

"The poor man sat on the Doc's front porch for three days until you opened your eyes. Never took time to eat or sleep, and the first words you say to him is 'go away'!" Ellie's scathing tone told Kansas exactly what she thought of such behavior. "After you sent him away like he was just an unwanted hired hand, he went down to the Bloody Guts and shot Farley dead. He faced all of Quill Ramsey's men alone. Well, except for Otis, which is help enough, I reckon."

"He only did his job as a sheriff," Kansás said.

"He could have been killed!"

"He wasn't."

"When're you going back down to the gaming tables? The Palace is suffering, you know." Ellie tried a different tack. "You can't just hide away up here in your room. Why, even the new governor's tried to see you."

"I've had a relapse, Ellie," Kansas said tiredly.

It was true. Ever since the ball she had been lethargic and had little interest in anything. She'd spent the last three days closed in her room, her mind drifting over nothing of importance. She'd found if she emptied her mind of all but the most mundane, she felt no pain. It was a state greatly to be desired.

"I reckon you ain't going down to the speeches and whatnot they're having today," Ellie said, dusting the fine mahogany dresser and bureau.

Pausing before the looking glass she caught the gleam of a diamond and ruby pendant resting against her ample bosom and stood admiring it. One day, she'd wear it at the throat of her wedding gown. That thought brought her back to the task at hand and she cast an exasperated glance at Kansas. She and Otis couldn't make plans as long as Kansas was so unsettled. Ellie could shake the prideful girl.

"There's going to be a parade before the new recruits leave for the war."

"That's nice."

"I hear tell they got about thirty men in all."

"Umm!"

"Course most of them signed up after the sheriff signed up hisself."

Kansas turned away from the window, where she'd been staring disconsolately down on the town. "Cole signed up to fight in the war?"

"Umm!" Ellie took her revenge.

"Are you sure?"

"Umm!"

"Ellie, how do you know? Did Otis tell you?"

"I disremember who told me!" Ellie feigned little interest. "It didn't seem all that important at the time." The brassy sound of music drifted through the window.

"Sounds like the band's playing. They must be finished with all the speechifying! Now comes the parade of the new recruits as they ride out of town."

"Ride out of town?" Kansas cried, leaping to her feet. "Ellie, why didn't you tell me? What good are burning chicken feathers and salt spells and charms if he's not here?" The last words were thrown over her shoulder as Kansas rushed down the stairs.

Ellie watched her go, a grin on her face. "She moves right smart for someone who ain't interested in Cole Slater," she cackled, and with some satisfaction went back to the kitchen.

Kansas took no time for a hat. She barreled down the hill, heedless of the hot sun on her hair and the sweat gathering along her lip. When she gained the sidewalk at the edge of town, she could see the mounted recruits some distance down the street, riding away from her. Unmindful of the people who stopped to stare at her, Kansas gathered up her skirts and ran pell-mell down the street. Soon she was on the edge of the crowd, impatiently pushing her way through. She could see Cole riding at the head of a group of men.

"Cole," she called, but her cry was lost in the brassy, off-key shrill of a trumpet. Frantically Kansas pushed against the bodies that pressed in on her. She had to get through. She had to speak to Cole.

"Cole," she cried again, and the people around her turned.

Claire Howard stood with her mother and father and the faces of all three registered their rage at her behavior, but she cared not one whit. She couldn't let Cole leave without knowing she hadn't meant all the hateful things she'd hurled at him. A tall, gray-haired man towered in front of her. "Otis," Kansas gasped. "Help me get through. I've got to talk to Cole."

Otis took one look at her expression and shouldered forward. "Make way," he called, and the cheering men and women moved aside good-naturedly for the aging and gentle giant.

Kansas gained the front edge of the crowd and impatiently tugged her skirts out of the way. Her legs churned, her knees flying high as she strained to reach Cole. At first the watching crowd laughed, then cheered her on. Hair streaming behind her, Kansas passed the rear guard as they cantered along.

"Cole!" she screamed, and at last he heard.

Reining in his mount, he turned in his saddle. He'd never looked so invincibly masculine. With one brown hand he pushed his wide-brimmed hat to the back of his head and grinned, waiting for her to come to him.

She arrived at the side of his horse, chest heaving, tendrils of hair sticking to her flushed face. "Cole, I didn't mean what I said at the ball," she gasped. "I don't want you to die."

He bent from the waist, reaching down to grasp her hand. He freed one stirrup and automatically her foot went to it. She felt herself pulled upward and she was pressed against his chest. His men cheered.

"Would you mind repeating that?" he asked huskily, his gaze intent on her mouth.

"I said I love you," Kansas cried. "And you love me, too. And I won't let Claire Howard have you. You and I belong to each other—"

The rest of her words were cut off by his kiss. Kansas threw her arms around his neck and returned his kiss fervently. Again the men around him cheered.

"Wait for me, Kansas McKay," he said, holding her tightly.

"I will!" she gulped. Tears glistened in her eyes. "Just come back to me, Cole Slater."

A final kiss and he was lowering her gently to the ground. His eyes were filled with promise. With a jaunty salute, he rode away and the cheering, laughing men followed him.

Kansas stood in the dust of the street watching until they were out of sight, then she turned toward the Palace. The band had dispersed, along with the rest of the crowd, and the street already carried an abandoned air. Claire Howard and her parents were nowhere in sight. Kansas gave them no thought whatsoever. She felt bereft, as if some part of herself had been torn away, yet the gleam in Cole's eyes as he'd asked her to wait for him, assuaged the ache.

Wearily Kansas made her way up the hill. A loneliness was seeping around her soul, and she knew she must bear it until Cole returned. Pray God he would return—and that no rebel bullet brought him down. The hateful words she'd hurled at him at the ball tormented her all the way up the hill.

Now came a time of waiting for Kansas. She prayed as she had never prayed before. As soon as she'd climbed the hill after Cole's leaving, she'd gone straight to Ellie and begged any amulet or spell that would ensure his safe return. Too nervous to stay in her room, imagining all sorts of tragedies, Kansas returned to the gaming tables.

The first night, word spread that Kansas was back, and

the miners flocked up the hill to the Palace. Kansas wished Otis were here, but he'd ridden into the mountains on some mysterious errand. That left only Ellie to worry and fuss over the loan. It was dismally overdue, and Ellie wondered if Kansas had returned too late.

The second night after Cole and the other recruits had left, the Palace was so packed that men stood in line to play at the gaming tables.

One of the maids came to whisper in her ear that she had a guest who wished to see her in private.

"Cole!" she murmured. He'd come back! "Tell him I'll be right there. If you'll excuse me, gentlemen, I must leave for a while."

She turned her winnings over to Ellie and hurried to the hall. Her expectant smile dipped when she saw the banker waiting to see her. Hiding her disappointment, she joined him.

"Mr. Howard," she said, holding out a hand graciously. He ignored it.

"I have something to say to you, Miss McKay." His handsome face was stern.

"Why don't we go back to my study for privacy," she offered, and led the way.

Once there, she steeled herself and turned to face him. She had an idea why he'd come. Surprisingly enough he took time to study the room she'd claimed for her private affairs. His sharp glance took in the delicately ornate desk, the silk-covered chaise, and the carved rosewood side chairs. He seemed surprised by the tasteful furnishings and the uncluttered elegance of the room. He turned to study Kansas with the same thoroughness. Deliberately she retained an outwardly calm facade, although his dark, shrewd gaze left her unsettled.

"If you've come about the bank loan . . ." she began, although she'd vowed not to be the first to speak.

"I've come about something else entirely," he said, and

seated himself upon a chair, taking care to arrange the knife crease of his trousers with precision. "Sit down, Miss Mc-Kay."

"I prefer to stand," she said stiffly, angered at his proprietary air.

"I've come to talk to you about Cole Slater."

"There's nothing to talk about," Kansas said.

"I'm happy you recognize that," Howard said. "He's engaged to my daughter. It will do you no good to continue to throw yourself in his path."

"I refuse to discuss this with you further," Kansas said, furious at his audacity.

"Would you prefer to discuss your delinquent loan with the bank?" Howard had leaped to his feet, and now he pressed close, intimidating her with his superior height. His face was harsh in the lamplight. "I thought not, Miss Mc-Kay." He smiled, visibly softening his features. "Now, there's no need for us to quarrel over this. If you have a fancy for Cole Slater, I urge you to put it aside. You might do well to choose some other benefactor." He paused, flashing a smile again. He was, Kansas realized dimly, a handsome man, but something about him made her uneasy. Now he ran a hand along the fleshy portion of her arm, pausing near her breast. "There are many men in this town, myself included, who would gladly claim that privilege."

Kansas's eyes widened. "Like you, there are many men in this town who are married—and I have no wish to take them to my bed." Her blunt words seemed to displease him. He frowned and drew back, took a step or two, then turned to face her again.

"Surely you aren't trying to tell me a woman of your . . . reputation has scruples, Miss McKay?"

"Scruples, morals, whatever you wish to call them," Kansas said, meeting his gaze steadily.

"A pity that such pristine morals don't apply to Cole Slater. He soon will be married. Then what will you do?"

"He won't marry your daughter. He can't. Not when he loves me. I know that must hurt you, for it's obvious you love your daughter, but you must accept the truth. Now please, I must return to my customers."

She tried to brush past him to the door, but his hand, hard and cold on her arm, caught her up short.

"Please, you're hurting me," she said. She was relieved to feel his grip loosen.

"I have no wish to hurt you, Kansas," he said softly, "but need I remind you, you are with a customer?"

Kansas stared at him in dawning comprehension. "I'm sorry, you misunderstand," she said, trying to pull away.

"Do I? Isn't this where you entertain your special customers, Kansas?" His voice had gone husky and thick with lust. One slim hand slid along her cheek and gripped her shoulder none too gently. "You remind me of a woman I once knew, except you far exceed her in beauty and intelligence. I've been watching you, Kansas. You're quite a woman. Smart as well as beautiful." His hand was kneading her shoulder. "The men like you. They like you a lot." His words ended in a hoarse whisper, and his hand slipped downward, cupping one breast.

Kansas jerked, trying to get away, but he held her fast. "Mr. Howard, you have the wrong idea about me," she cried.

"No, I have the right idea," he gasped. "I could love you, Kansas, better than Cole, better than any of those other men." His mouth descended to hers, hungry and salacious. In distaste, Kansas twisted away.

"Ah, Kansas," he gasped. "I have such a need for a woman like you. My wife is ill, delicate, you know what I mean. She hasn't been a wife to me in years, and even then she lay stiff as a board. But you. I've been imagining you beneath me, doing things to me, things decent women don't know about, but things we men love." He'd backed her toward the chaise lounge, and now he bent her slim body backward until she fell heavily, with him on top. His hands were everywhere.

"No," she cried, but he wasn't listening. His face was buried at the bodice of her gown. "No!" Kansas gasped, pushing against his shoulders.

"Ah, Molly, girl, don't fight me. I need you," he groaned, and his groping hands ripped at her bodice. Kansas screamed, but it went unheard in the noise of the busy casino. She'd chosen this room at the back of the house because of its privacy, and now that worked against her.

"Please, Mr. Howard," she cried, struggling within his grasp. Her hair had come undone and her bodice gaped. The gold locket she'd always worn tucked beneath the edge of her bodice spilled across her milky white breast.

Oliver Howard's teeth closed on one pink nipple and he suckled as if a man long starved. Kansas could feel his hard arousal against her leg.

"Molly . . . sweet, sweet, Molly," he crooned, and slobbered a kiss on her neck, then on her other breast.

Kansas lay stiff, horror washing over her as she heard his words. Impatiently he pushed aside the locket and bent to her white breast. She felt the stiff shock sweep through him and slowly, so slowly it seemed he'd stopped breathing; he raised his head and stared into her eyes. His fist had closed around the ornate gold locket and he jerked at it, causing the chain to bite against her tender nape.

"Where did you get this?" he roared, his eyes wild-looking.

"My—my mother gave it to me," she whispered. "it belonged to my father."

His face twisted into a fearsome, ugly mask. A quick yank and the delicate chain broke. Fear clogged her throat so she couldn't breathe, and she gasped. Her soft breast brushed his cheek, and he drew away as if touched by a brand.

Slowly, as if he'd aged years in minutes, he rose. Taking

the locket with him, he turned his back to her. "Cover yourself, woman," he cried, and took a step away.

With her gaze fixed on Oliver Howard, Kansas pulled a tasseled scarf from a table and wrapped it around her shoulders and breasts. Howard turned back to face her, his manner threatening as he towered over her.

"Who was your mother?"

"Molly McKay."

"McKay! I should have known, should have made the connection, but I haven't thought of her in years, not until I saw you." He paced the room. "I heard she'd died, a whore in some town somewhere."

"Yes. In Webster, Idaho," Kansas said flatly.

"Webster!" Howard crossed back to the chaise. "Who was your father?" he demanded. "And don't lie."

"I have no reason to lie," Kansas said. "I don't know who my father is. I only know he came West on the same wagon train with my mother, that he was very brave, and loved us both. He gave her that locket to give to me when I was—" She stopped, aware she was babbling, but even more aware of the effect her words were having on Oliver Howard.

"How old are you?" he asked weakly, as if afraid of the answer, but needing to know, anyway. Kansas told him and waited while he digested the information. Wearily he sank down on the foot of the chaise and looked at the locket, then raised his eyes.

Father and daughter studied each other over a chasm of years and stations in life. He was a banker, a pillar of society, she was a whore, a soiled dove, his illegitimate misgot. She read his acceptance of the truth they'd discovered and his rejection of it, all in the flicker of an eyelash. Despair filled her. All her life, she'd dreamed of someday finding her father, but not like this, never like this—and now she felt his rejection, his scorn, without his uttering a word.

He got to his feet, weaving slightly. He said no word, but one finger came up to point at her, as if to accuse and condemn her, then slowly, shakily, his hand lowered and, spinning on his heel, Oliver Howard left the study. He spoke to no man as he left the Palace and made his way down the hill to his house. His wife and daughter were in the parlor, their heads bent over needlework. Claire's dark head came up as he stood swaying drunkenly in the doorway.

"Papa?" she said tentatively, her fine dark brows raised.

"How old are you, Claire?" he asked in a voice that sounded old and hurt.

"Twenty-one, Papa," Claire replied.

"You knew that, Oliver," Letitia Howard said. "She was born the winter after we made the trip West."

"Twenty-one!" he whispered to himself. The same age as Kansas McKay.

Howard made no answer. He reeled down the hall and closed himself in his study, groping behind his law books for the bottle of whiskey he kept hidden from his wife.

"Papa?" Claire called, knocking on the study door, but he made no answer.

After a while she went away. He could hear her climbing the stairs to her bedroom, all chaste and girlish. What did Kansas McKay's bedroom look like? he wondered briefly, and clenched his fists in a frenzy of denial.

Through the night he sat thinking of his two daughters: Claire, protected and well bred, a daughter to make any father proud, and Kansas McKay, wanton, sensuous, a harlot, an abomination. When the sun rose, Oliver Howard left his study, stone-cold sober in spite of the empty whiskey bottle he left behind. He arrived early at his bank and began proceedings to foreclose on the Kansas Palace.

Chapter 18

DAWN ROSE, GRAY-FACED and sullen, blown by a hot, petulant wind that whistled down from the Sierras and battered the sprawling towns below. Picking up dust and sand from the streets, it scoured the buildings, pitting the fresh paint and digging deep into the wood, as if warning the inhabitants that nothing would last forever unless the elements decreed it so. Horses nickered in distress at their hitching posts, turning their rumps to the sting of sand. Miners pulled their neckerchiefs over their noses and settled their hat brims low. The townspeople stayed indoors, peering anxiously from their windows, childishly reassured when they glimpsed their neighbors' abode through the swirling yellowish haze.

Huddled in the broad window seat in her bedroom, Kansas watched the first light of dawn form on the horizon and, with the first rays of the sun, saw the first dust eddies whirling through the streets, gaining momentum as the sun climbed higher. The blowing sand distorted the sunlight, casting a strange foreboding light on the town and hillsides. She could hear the whine of the wind and the insidious cat-soft brush of sand against her windowpanes. The air was heavy with it, so even here breathing was harder. She felt weighted down by the day, and by what the night had revealed.

She had found her father, but he wasn't what she'd dreamed of. Oliver Howard would never protect her or smile on her lovingly. She'd seen the shame in his eyes. He wished she'd never been born. Automatically her hand reached for the locket, but he'd taken it from her, almost as if he'd wanted to take away every evidence of their kinship.

Kansas thought back to when Molly had given her the locket. It was the day Oliver Howard came to town. Molly had recognized him then! Kansas sat remembering Molly sitting before the mirror, studying herself, wanting to find that young girl she once had been and knowing if she presented herself to Howard as she was then, he would only scorn her. Yet, she'd given Kansas the locket, and for a moment had given her a loving picture of her father. For the first time, Kansas realized the kindness behind Molly's efforts that day, and she drew some comfort from it.

"Oh, Mama. Why did life have to be this way?" She sobbed, allowing the tears to come for the first time since her confrontation with Oliver Howard. She realized more fully now the pain Molly had borne. Perhaps Molly had grown callous and cruel at the end, treating Kansas with indifference most of the time. But once she'd been young and beautiful, too. Oliver Howard had said she reminded him of Molly.

Kansas stretched her cramped legs and rose, crossing to the mirror to study her reflection. Once Molly had looked like her—and loved as she did—but Oliver Howard had gone back to a woman of good background. Would Cole Slater do the same? The thought frightened her. Her knees gave way and she sank to the floor, pressing her cheek to the cool, smooth wood of her dresser.

She was more alone now than ever. Before, she'd carried the hope of someday finding her father, but that dream was gone, forever shattered. She had nothing left but the promise she'd read in Cole's eyes. Was she destined to lose that dream as well?

"Please, come back to me, Cole," she whispered. "I need you." The thought startled her. She'd prided herself on never needing anyone, but now she knew her life was inextricably tied to his—and God help her, she needed him near her, needed his love to sustain her. Kansas laid her head on the rich Turkish carpet on her bedroom floor and wept like a small, lonely child.

"This is where I leave you, boys," Cole said, drawing his horse off the trail. The recruits, some of them little more than boys, halted their mounts and sat regarding him.

"Sure wish you was going with us all the way, sir," one of them said.

"I wish I could, too, Soldier, but I'm needed here. If I can stop Quill and his men, I'll be doing my part to bring the war to a fast end. We'll be looking for you men back here as soon as it's over."

"Reckon your ruse'll work, Sheriff?" another man asked. "I mean, you don't know that the rebs are goin' ta rob the silver shipment."

"We know well enough," Cole said. "If I'm wrong, I may have to catch up with you." He smiled and saluted. Some of the men saluted back, and the line moved forward on down the trail. Cole watched them go, then turned back toward Virginia City. He had a hard day's ride before his rendezvous with Governor Nye.

About midafternoon, he realized someone was following him. He'd expected as much. A couple of the men who'd ridden out with the recruits hadn't looked the type to self-lessly offer their services to the army, at least not the Union Army. Cole had tried to engage them in conversation, asking where they were from, but they'd stayed tight-mouthed and uncommunicative. None of the other recruits seemed to know who they were, either. Now Cole tried to remember what he had noted about the men, the kind of horses they rode and the number of guns they'd carried.

He rode on for the better part of an hour before he found what he was looking for, a deep crevice that cut across the barren desert floor. He tied his horse and pack mule there out of sight and, keeping low, made his way back along the trail to a clump of mesquite. They wouldn't afford him much protection if bullets started flying. He lay on his belly and waited, his eyes straining. There were two of them, all right. One was looking straight ahead while the other studied the trail.

"I tell you, we lost him," one man said. "I ain't seen him up ahead for some time now."

"He's got to be up there," growled the other. "This here's the way he come." Their accents were more noticeable now that they weren't being so careful.

Cole let them ride on by, then got to his feet, his gun drawn. "You boys looking for me?"

They whirled in their saddles, automatically going for their guns.

"I wouldn't," Cole said tightly, drawing back the hammer on his weapon. They hesitated, their eyes hard and dangerous as they met his gaze.

"You boys mind telling me where you're headed? Last I knew, you were on your way to join the Union Army."

"We—we had second thoughts," one of them said. His name was Darrell, Cole remembered, but couldn't dredge up the name for the other. The man on the right fiddled with his reins. "We figured we'd just join up with you. Figured you could use some help."

"Nope, don't reckon I do. You boys would be better off to just ride on back to the others . . . unless you're Johnny Rebs."

The man on the right went for his gun first. Cole had known he would. He was too restless. Cole waited a split second, giving him a chance to clear his holster, then he fired. The man swayed in his saddle, a growing red splotch on his shoulder. His gun spun through the air and buried itself in the sand.

Darrell had taken time to aim, and Cole felt the fiery bite of a bullet grazing his arm. He fired, and Darrell fell to the ground. With a wild reb yell, the wounded man kneed his horse and rode at Cole. Cole rolled with the sweating animal's lunge and fell free of the hooves, but his gun was lost. Crouching, he looked around for his pistol. The rider had his rifle free now and aimed it. Cole threw himself sideways, rolling away from the spot where bullets kicked up the sand in angry little spurts. He came to a stop near the dead man, who still clutched his gun. A bullet creased his hat, but Cole's long arm was already reaching. He wrenched the gun from the lifeless hand and fired without aiming.

He saw their campfire long before he reached the rocky outcropping. His tense shoulders sagged in relief and weariness. Now he could put a name to the worry that had dogged his every step since the ambush by the men who'd trailed him. He'd feared someone might hold the governor hostage as an added safety measure. Now as he approached the camp and made out James Nye's elegant figure seated on the ground nearby, he breathed a sigh of relief.

"Ho, the camp," Cole called, and rode into the circle of firelight. The governor and his assistant were seated around the fire, holding tin cups of coffee.

Otis came to greet Cole, and another man took his horse, throwing his gear down near the fire. "We'd just about given up on you, son," Otis said, slapping him on the back and handing him a cup of black coffee.

"Two men followed me and tried to kill me," he said, squatting by the fire. His gaze met the governor's across the leaping flames.

"They aren't taking any chances, are they?" the governor asked. His blue eyes were bright with excitement. "I'd say you called this right, Slater. They're going to try for the silver.''

"Looks that way."

"I noticed a lot of strange new men in town the past few days," Otis said. "They didn't look much like miners—and they spent more time out in the streets than they did in the saloons.''

"Yeah, I noticed them, too," Cole grunted.

"Do you reckon they're Johnny Rebs?" Samuel Clemens asked, and Cole had to smile at the young reporter's attempt to talk like the old-timers.

"I reckon they are," he said.

"Do you think they suspect we're onto them?" Governor Nye asked, and his tone was more thoughtful.

"I think we've fooled them," Cole said. "Oliver Howard was positively euphoric about my going off to fight in the war. Of course, Claire helped that some when she started insisting I give up the job of sheriff."

"So now they think Virginia City and all its silver is just sitting there waiting to be plucked," Otis said.

James Nye was more introspective as he studied Cole's tight face. "I might wonder if it bothered you that your future father-in-law may be involved, but judging from the demonstration of a certain Miss Kansas McKay, I begin to ask myself if you ever intended to marry the banker's daughter?''

Cole gazed into the fire, seeing Kansas's eyes in its glow. Slowly he shook his head. "Once, I might have entertained notions of marrying her," he said, "but I can't remember when. My pa"—he paused, and Nye saw a flicker of pain cross the quiet man's face—"my pa wanted me to marry her. Oliver Howard's an old friend of his." Restlessly Cole straightened, a bemused grin on his face. "It was too late. I already knew Kansas."

"She's quite a woman, Slater. Congratulations."

"Thanks," Cole said, and threw the dregs of his coffee into the fire. The flames spat and hissed, then burned as brightly as before. "She's the one who saw Howard and Ramsey together. It was the first time I was able to put it all together. I knew Howard had something in mind, but I didn't know how he planned to carry it out."

"The president is eternally grateful to you, Mr. Slater. If the South succeeds in getting the silver, they can prolong the war for God knows how long."

"We'll see they don't," Cole said, setting aside his cup and rolling out his bedding. "I figure tomorrow is the day they'll strike. It'll soon be over."

Ellie brought her the paper, crisply white with the words written neatly in black ink. The bank was about to take over the Kansas Palace. She had three days to come up with the balance of the loan. Oliver Howard's signature sat heavy and punitive at the end of the document. Dry-eyed, Kansas stared at it, unable to comprehend. Her head was fuzzy from lack of sleep, her eyes puffy and red-rimmed from crying. In the past few weeks, she'd been so preoccupied over Cole, and then, while she was struggling to recover from her wounds, she'd given little thought to the Palace. Now as she stared at the paper that could take it away from her, she realized how much of herself she'd poured into it and how little she wanted to lose it. Seized with determination, she raced downstairs.

"Ellie, bring me all the money we have—even the food money—everything," she cried.

"My land, what is it?" Ellie cried, and Kansas showed her the paper. "I knew something bad was going to happen. I seen a crow fly over."

"We have no time for your omens now, Ellie," Kansas said. "Come and help me count this money."

It wasn't enough! She'd known it wouldn't be, but she

was the eternal optimist. Now that stubborn optimism sent her scurrying up the stairs to hastily don a suitable gown and hat.

"What are you going to do?" Ellie asked, puffing along behind her.

"I'm going to the bank to talk to Oliver Howard," Kansas said. "I'm going to make him give me more time. Thirty days and good luck and I can have the money I need."

"You'd have the money you needed now if you hadn't given so much of it away," Ellie grumbled.

"That doesn't matter, Ellie. Those people needed help. I'm sure they would have done the same for me if I'd needed it."

"You need it now," Ellie called after her, but Kansas didn't look back. She'd stepped out onto the porch and already the wind and dust had clogged her nostrils so she gasped for breath. Pressing a handkerchief to her nose and mouth, Kansas pushed out the gate and hurried down the hill, her skirts whipping in the wind.

Ellie watched her go, an idea forming. Kansas was right; if the miners and their families whom she'd helped knew she was in trouble, they would return the favor. It was up to Ellie to see they found out. She cast an eye at the yellow, dust-laden sky and, shrugging, reached for her hat and bag. Hurrying down the hill toward the Silver Spur, Ellie chuckled to herself. She was getting to be as much of a busybody as that sanctimonious Miss Simpson at the boardinghouse. Maybe after she saw Reeny she'd go around to the boardinghouse. Maybe she'd tell Miss Ada Simpson that she was getting married.

"I've come to see Mr. Howard," Kansas told the bank clerk. He was a small, nervous man with a thin mustache and a threadbare vest. He moved in quick jerky steps—and almost before Kansas had a chance to form what she meant to say to Oliver Howard he was back.

Nervously he cleared his throat. His brown eyes looked every place but at Kansas. "He says he can't see you now! Perhaps tomorrow!"

Outrage made Kansas nearly speechless. "You go back and tell him I won't leave this spot until he's granted me an appointment! He owes me that much."

Again the little man went to the office door and timidly knocked and entered. Again he returned. "He says he has nothing further to say to you. He asks you to leave the bank."

"Tell Mr. Howard that if he doesn't see me immediately I'll have a great deal to say—and I'll say it all standing right here in the middle of this bank!"

The office door flew open and the little man exited so quickly Kansas almost wondered if he'd been propelled by force, but Oliver Howard stepped into the bank lobby. Shock rippled through Kansas as she looked at him. His face was gray and unshaven, his eyes sunken. He marched to where Kansas was standing and grasped her arm. Alarmed, she glanced around, but there was no one else in the bank except her and the bank teller.

"Get out of my bank," Howard said roughly, almost pushing her toward the door.

"Mr. Howard, your bank threatens to foreclose on me in three days. I think I'm entitled to a little more time than that."

"Go home, Kansas McKay," Oliver Howard ordered. "And don't come back here. Not today."

"But—"

"Get out, I tell you. I don't want you here."

"You can't just foreclose on me without talking to me," Kansas exclaimed.

"We'll talk tomorrow. Now, go on home," Howard ordered. His eyes were bloodshot; specks of spittle formed on his lip. Nervously he licked them away, casting a quick glance at the door.

There's some reason he doesn't want me here now, Kansas thought. Indeed, Howard took hold of her arm and pushed her toward the door.

Suddenly the door flew inward, crashing against the wall, and two men entered, each wearing long coats, their hats pulled low. Bandannas covered the lower half of their faces. They brought up rifles and leveled them at the bank teller.

"Just be real careful about where you put your hands," one of the long-coated men said. "Get the money out of the safe."

Helplessly the nervous bank teller looked at Oliver Howard.

"Do as he says," Howard ordered. The bank teller scurried to do his bidding. Two more men came into the bank. One took up his station at the door, his rifle poised and ready, his gaze fixed on the street. They'd chosen well. Because of the wind, few people were on the street.

The other man, who seemed to be in charge, walked behind the cage and scraped all the money out of the till and stuffed it into his pockets.

"You've got your money, now get out," Oliver Howard said. He seemed strangely unafraid.

The leader laughed, a jeering, mocking sound. "Not until I've finished my business."

Howard's face flushed, but the man paid him no more attention. His eyes, cold blue and calculating beneath his hat brim, were fixed on Kansas. Her pulse thundered in her ears, and her eyes widened in recognition. Beneath the battered hat brim, Quill Ramsey's pale eyes gleamed with evil intent.

"I said get out. There's nothing more for you here," Howard snapped. A gun went off near the vault, and he spun around. The nervous little bank teller lay on the floor, a pool of blood spreading from beneath him.

"You fool!" Howard whirled back to face the lead robber. "I said there was to be no killing."

"We can't afford to have any witnesses," Ramsey said, pulling the concealing bandanna away from his face. His grin was chilling as he leveled his gun at Kansas. "None at all," he said, his soft words falling into the quiet space between her heartbeats. Looking into his face, Kansas knew she was going to die . . . and she thought of Cole. Would he ever learn of her fate? Clear across a continent, trapped in a bitter war, would he, too, face death as she did now? Quill drew back the hammer, savoring his triumphant moment.

"Cole!" Kansas whispered. His name was a prayer on her lips. One slim, pale hand fluttered to her heart. Her face was nearly white, her eyes enormous.

"No!" Oliver Howard roared, and stepped in front of her. "Get out, Ramsey. You've got your money. Finish the job as you were paid to do and no more killing, or by God I'll tell the sheriff myself who did this."

"Don't push me, old man," Quill snarled, leveling his gun at the banker, "or I'll have to quiet you—"

His words died away at the sound of galloping horses and shouts in the street.

"It's Slater and a posse," one of the men yelled from the front window.

Quill cursed. "It can't be. He's headed back East." He glared at Oliver Howard. "You double-crossed me, Howard," he snarled. "You only needed me and my men to help you steal the silver for the Confederates."

"I did my part," Howard said. "If you'd just robbed the bank and ridden out, you wouldn't be caught here."

"I'm not caught, not yet," Quill said, and brought up his gun and fired quickly. Kansas felt Howard's hand at the small of her back and she went reeling to one side. She fell against the wall and felt the breath leave her, then slid down to the floor. Oliver Howard fell to the floor beside her, his eyes wide with pain, his sleeve bloody. He closed his eyes and lay still, feigning unconsciousness. Quill Ramsey leaped through the door to Oliver's office. Kansas could hear the back door being flung open. The sound of gunfire and shattering glass drew her attention to the front of the bank. Quill's men were engaged in a gun battle with the posse in front. Bullets ricocheted around the bank. Kansas crouched down and held her breath. There was a sound of scurrying feet, then all was silent as the men left the bank the back way.

Oliver Howard opened his eyes and looked at her. "Have they gone?" he asked.

"I think so. Out the back way."

They lay still for a while, listening to the gunshots and horses galloping wildly. Then all was silent.

Lying beside Oliver Howard on the floor of the bank, Kansas drew a quivering breath. "You saved my life," she said softly. "You must not hate me, after all."

Oliver's expression grew rigid. A shutter dropped over his dark eyes. Slowly he got to his feet and helped Kansas up before answering.

"I have no cause to hate you, Miss McKay," he said stiffly, "just as I have no reason to love you."

"I don't ask that you love me," Kansas cried, stricken by his coldness.

"Are you all right in here?" Cole Slater stood in the doorway, surprise and puzzlement mingling in his gaze. It was obvious he'd overheard part of their conversation.

"Cole!" Kansas rushed across the room to him. His arms closed about her shoulders briefly, but she felt a reticence in him and drew away. Other men had crowded into the room.

"I thought you'd gone back East with the rest of the recruits," she cried wonderingly.

"That's what we wanted the town to think," Governor Nye said from the doorway. "Our ruse worked!" He glanced at Howard. "You've been wounded."

The banker shrugged dismissively. "It's superficial. Did you get Quill and his men?"

Cole shook his head. "They got away, but they dropped the money." He indicated the bag Otis had placed on the counter.

"We'd've been here sooner, if we hadn't had so dang much trouble with the silver shipment," Otis said.

"Silver?" Howard looked from one man to the other. "Did they get away?"

"Did who get away?" Cole asked quietly; his eyes narrowed as he studied the banker.

"Well—I—uh, Ramsey's men. You sounded as if you think they took the silver."

"We know they didn't." Cole paused. His measuring gaze was fixed on Oliver Howard's face as if to determine his complicity. "Ramsey and his men helped Confederate soldiers take the silver. The rebs hightailed it out of here, heading south. Ramsey rode into town to rob the bank."

"Whooee, he had a big day planned all right, but we was one step ahead of him," Otis said. His grin was wide and satisfied.

"But the men with the silver, did they get away?" Howard persisted.

"They tried, but they didn't get very far," Nye spoke up. "Slater had them pegged pretty well. Right now the Virginia City jail is filled with Johnny Rebs."

Howard's face looked gray.

"You want to tell me what happened here?" Cole asked.

Howard shook his head. "It should be obvious, Sheriff. Quill Ramsey came into the bank and tried to rob it."

"How did you know it was Quill?" Cole demanded. Obviously he considered Howard a suspect.

"I recognized him," Kansas said quickly. Cole pinned her with a flat gaze. For the first time, Kansas realized how unrelenting he could be. She flushed beneath his penetrating stare, and she was certain she looked as guilty as they suspected Howard of being.

"Is that everything that happened, Kansas?" he asked abruptly.

She paused, remembering the things she'd heard. She sensed the tension in Oliver Howard. "That's everything, Sheriff," she said softly.

Her gaze never wavered, but something in the still way she held herself gave her away. She's protecting him, Cole thought. He'd overheard part of their conversation, and now he wondered at its meaning.

"I suggest you go after Quill, Sheriff." Howard's voice was belligerent. "He's killed my teller."

"He won't get away with it," Cole said, and with a final sharp glance at Kansas, he stalked out of the bank. Kansas turned back to Oliver Howard, her expression stolid and unreadable, her luminous gray eyes dark with suppressed feeling.

Howard's features grew sharp as he met her censorious gaze. A muscle twitched in one cheek. "You needn't have lied for me," he said. "I was Southern born and bred. I'm not ashamed of trying to help my own kind."

She remained silent. Emotions warred within her like a flood-swollen river tumbling unchecked down a mountain pass. She stood battered and bruised on the shore, struggling not to be swept away by the muddy waters.

Only a fragile dam held the flood at bay.

"You needn't think this will convince me to claim you as my daughter," he sneered. His dark eyes held only contempt as his gaze raked over her. "You have no proof you are my daughter."

The dam broke and the water roared by her, but miraculously she was left standing, stronger than she was before. But something had been taken from her. She knew she could never reclaim it.

"You saved my life," she answered dully. "Now we're even."

"Just a minute, Miss McKay," he said briskly. She

paused, without looking back. "You have two days left to raise the money for your loan. Then the bank takes over the Palace."

Silently she opened the door, wanting only to flee this man she once would have proudly acknowledged as her father.

"Do you hear me, Kansas McKay!" he called after her. "I'm going to run you out of Virginia City. You can't stay here."

Kansas stepped out onto the porch. People were clustered in the street, talking and staring at the bodies of the two dead bank robbers. Without speaking to anyone, Kansas turned and made her way up the hill, Oliver Howard's voice ringing in her ears. She wasn't aware of the tears streaming down her face. She was grieving too deeply for the death of a father.

"Looks like Oliver Howard may wriggle out of this," Nye said, pouring Cole a neat shot of whiskey from the bottle on his washstand. They were in his hotel room, and he had discarded his denim trousers and jacket and was once again attired in a three-piece suit. He looked every inch the governor. "Kansas couldn't give you any information about what went on?"

Cole shook his head. "She says she can't." Skepticism was obvious in his tone.

"You don't believe her?" Nye asked, eyeing the sheriff.

Restlessly Cole got up to pace the room before answering, and Nye saw the sagging weariness in the big man. "I don't know what to believe," Cole said. "Right now, I'll just concentrate on finding Quill and hope he'll tell us what happened."

"This can't be easy," Nye said. "I understand Oliver Howard is an old friend of your father's."

Cole stood at the window staring down at the town. The posse was regrouping in the street below. They'd gathered fresh horses and restocked food and water. It was time to leave. Cole tossed back the whiskey, feeling it burn his throat. "Howard and my old man met in Missouri more than twenty years ago. They came out West on the Oregon Trail. I don't remember much about the trip. I was too little. My mother died on that trip." Quickly he reached for his hat, as if sorry he'd gone back and remembered that much.

"Cole," Nye said as he swung toward the door. Cole paused.

Nye's voice was soft with regret as he offered his next bit of information. "Rumors are going around town that Kansas took up with Howard after you left. Several people saw him up at the Palace. They say she left the gaming table and disappeared for the rest of the evening with him."

Cole's face was bleak. "I'm much obliged for your telling me. It explains a lot."

"Maybe, maybe not," Nye said. "Rumors are a most unreliable source, and your Kansas McKay doesn't strike me as an inconsistent woman."

"You're right, Governor. She's not . . . inconsistent as you've so delicately put it. She's doing exactly as she's done all along. Why else would a banker go to visit a town whore?"

Nye was startled at the harshness of his words, but before he could reply, Cole had quietly closed the door behind him. He had never heard violence so eloquently expressed before as in that carefully controlled closing of a door. Nye crossed to the window and stood staring down at the mounted posse. Cole Slater stalked out of the hotel and smoothly swung into his saddle. He said a few words to the rest of the men. They nodded, then followed him out of town at a full gallop. During the whole interchange there was not one doubt as to who was in charge. The men followed him without question.

Yet Nye sensed something was different about Cole, something in the stiff set of his shoulders. Watching the posse ride away, it came to the governor that the big man was wounded as surely as if someone had taken a gun and shot him. Sadly he shook his head. Nye liked Slater. He liked the quiet way he went about getting things done. Fleetingly he wondered if he could persuade Cole to join his staff. He had need of men like him.

The thought was dismissed almost as quickly. He had little doubt Cole would perform whatever duty was asked of him, but the big rawboned man didn't belong behind a desk. He was most comfortable out under the big sky. Like the land he sought to tame, Cole Slater was a man bigger than life. And the same was true of Kansas McKay. They belonged together. Sighing, the governor turned away from the window, sorry that he'd told Cole of the rumor. Thinking of everything he'd learned about Kansas McKay, James Nye believed the rumors were untrue, but the important thing was what Cole Slater believed.

Chapter 19

THE SHOCK OF all that happened stayed with Kansas in the days that followed. Try as she might to understand Oliver Howard's need to help the South, she couldn't get beyond the fact that he was willing to steal silver from the men who trusted him, men who spent their days like moles, burrowing into the dark recesses of the mountains. Her championship of the miners eroded any attempts to excuse her father. Her father! Kansas stood before her mirror trying the words, but they didn't sound right to her ear. She was Kansas McKay, fatherless bastard of a town whore. She'd never learned the finer points of duplicity and treachery practiced by those higher placed in society. Her innocence gave way to cynicism, and she saw its birthing in the thin, hard line of her soft, full lips and the knowing light in her eyes. Her face seemed distorted by this new emotion and she turned away, carrying her hurt with her as she crossed to her window and stared down at the town.

The Palace had become a prison to her, just as Moody's Saloon once had been. It didn't matter that she would lose it in two days time. She wanted only to ride away from this town and her failures here. But Cole would return soon, and she wanted to be here for his return. She tried not to think of the flare of suspicion that had hardened his features just before he rode away. He knew she'd lied about Oliver Howard and he would expect an explanation, but could she ever tell anyone that Howard was her father? She would have to admit his rejection of her as well—and finally, her disillusionment.

Would Cole understand? She remembered the boy she'd known back in Webster, his gentleness and strength. He would understand, and he'd help her through this just as he had so many times in the past. With new resolve, Kansas wiped her tears and turned toward the stairs.

It was time to tell Ellie that she was losing the Palace and soon all of them would be without a home. Otis was with the posse. Of everything she must do, this was the hardest. Ellie and Otis had been her friends. Now she must repay their loyalty with such bad news. The salons of the Palace were empty, the elegant rooms already cleaned and ready for that night's customers. Kansas turned to the kitchen, where she knew she'd find Ellie.

The sound of voices and laughter reached her and she paused in the doorway, taking in the scene before her. Several miners were crowded into the warm, homey room; their rough clothes and boisterous voices were a welcome contrast to the stark barrenness of the salons. Ellie had passed around glasses of champagne and the men sipped appreciatively, now and then slapping one another on the back in a paroxysm of satisfaction.

"What's the celebration?" Kansas asked, walking into the kitchen. "Has someone's claim come in?"

"You might say that," Ellie replied, and exchanged conspiratorial glances with the men. Some of them guffawed and glanced away, ducking their heads as if trying to hide big grins.

"I hope you don't mind we made use of the champagne—the best the house had to offer!" Although Ellie was asking permission, her manner implied she couldn't have cared less *what* Kansas had to say about it.

Kansas nodded, her glance going from one miner's face to another. "Not at all," she replied. "Just let me in on the good news."

"Shall we tell her, boys?" Tobias called, relenting a little. The old man's face was bright with pleasure. The men called their agreement, and Tobias, making himself their spokesman, snatched his hat off his head and cleared his throat with an air of formality.

"Well, Miss Kansas," he began, turning his hat in his knobby old hands. "We miners have seen how you looked out for us these past years, when we was tryin' to get our claims to payin' off."

Jeb Willard stepped forward. "You helped our wives and young'uns. Sent out food when we was on our last leg. And you never asked nothing in return."

"Yeah, you started that widows' fund—and when the town committee got too busy thinkin' about beautifyin' Virginia City and less about helpin' its people, you stepped in and stuck up for us."

"You even borrowed against the Palace to help some of us. We ain't ever had no one believe in us that much, Miss Kansas." The man choked up and stepped back, wiping at his eyes surreptitiously, as if embarrassed at his sudden show of emotion.

"So we figured it was time we done something back for you," Tobias said. "Where's that bag?" he demanded impatiently of the men behind him. Someone passed up a pouch while other men cleared a place on the table. With some show of ceremony, Tobias opened the drawstring bag and dumped the contents on the tabletop.

"We figured this is enough to pay off that loan at the bank and then some. If it ain't enough—well, we'll just get more."

At first, Kansas was speechless, staring at the pile of money. With open smiles of satisfaction, the men watched as she slowly walked to the table.

"I can't take your money," she said finally. "It wouldn't be fair. You've worked so hard for it."

"It ain't our money, Miss Kansas. It belongs to you. If'n you hadn't helped some of us we'd have moved on long ago. As it is, some of us stayed because of you and we've been lucky. We can't repay you enough for that."

"Besides, you'd just win it from us in poker, if we played you. So what's the difference?"

"The difference is that you make a choice to sit down and gamble," Kansas said, "and you have an equal chance to win money from me. But this"—she spread her arms toward the money—"to just give your money away . . ."

"We had a choice, Miss Kansas. It's a right smart choice to my way of thinkin'."

"Yeah!" another man reiterated. "You took a gamble on us and now it's paid off."

Wide-eyed, Kansas glanced around the room, noting the proud expressions of the miners. This meant a lot to them, she realized, and she would offend them if she didn't take their offering. "I don't know how to thank you," she said, tears streaming down her face.

"Aw, ain't no reason to cry," one man said. "Women are always cryin' over the least little thing." The men shuffled their feet uncomfortably and, clamping on their hats, began edging toward the door.

"No need to thank us, Miss Kansas. This is our way of showing our gratitude for all you done."

"Sure like to be there tomorrow when you take that there money down to old Howard. I'd like to see his face."

"Yep, he's shore goin' to be surprised some."

Their voices faded away and still Kansas stood beside the table, rivulets of silent tears streaking her cheeks. The sense of failure and rejection that had cut at her so deeply was gone. The gesture of the miners was a testimony to the high esteem she'd earned from them. Slowly Kansas raised her head and looked at Ellie.

"How did they know?" she asked softly.

Ellie flicked a dishrag and shrugged. "I'm sure I don't know,"she said. "I just happened to mention something about your trouble to Reeny down to the Silver Spur and some of the men were sittin' around. I can't help it if they overheard."

"Oh, Ellie, you are a wonder!" Kansas said warmly, and crossed the room to throw her arms around the Irish woman. Ellie's face flushed with pleasure.

"If I was ever of a mind to have a daughter, I reckon you'd be it," she said gruffly, then pushed Kansas away, although her face was still bright with affection. "You get your bonnet on and go on over to that bank and plunk that money down for that Howard fellow and come back here and tell me everything."

"Come with me, Ellie," Kansas cried, pulling the ties to her apron. "You can see for yourself."

"Ach! Ellie Mannion in a bank. Ain't one soul in my family ever set foot in a bank, ain't ever had a reason to."

"Well, you have reason to now," Kansas insisted, throwing her apron over a chair and reaching for her bonnet. Her face was glowing. "Oh, Ellie, isn't this a beautiful day?"

Failure was a dry, bitter taste in Cole's mouth, as acrid as the desert sand around him. He'd recovered the silver, captured most of the Confederate soldiers who had come after it, although their commanding officer had slipped away, and he'd recovered the bank money, but the one thing he'd wanted most, Quill Ramsey's capture, had eluded him. Now he and the men who'd ridden with him were returning to Virginia City. They'd spent long, exhausting days in the saddle tracking the elusive man. Who would have thought such a dandy could have the stamina and cunning to disappear like that? No doubt he was on his way to California, but they'd searched the mountain trails before turning eastward to track him through the desert. Except there had been no tracks. He'd disappeared as if the ground had opened and swallowed him down.

Behind the weary posse were two horses with their riders tied face down across their saddles. They'd never ride with Quill again, Cole thought grimly, and found little comfort. He was tired of the bloodshed, the blaze of guns, the whine of bullets past his head, and the boisterous, good-natured lawlessness of this silver town. He longed for the quiet solitude of a green Montana range. Lately he had a picture of himself riding herd on a bunch of cattle with the mountains rising in the distance like smoke against the horizon and a ranch house beckoning him at the end of the day. He could smell meat cooking and fresh bread as he pushed open the kitchen door, but there the dream stopped—because the woman at the stove wasn't Kansas. He could never place her in this dream of his.

Cole's thoughts turned back to the bank robbery and he wondered what had really happened there. Why had she lied to protect Oliver Howard? He remembered the snatches of conversation he'd heard between them. Howard had declared something about loving Kansas, and her answer had been an impassioned plea. If she loved the banker, why had she thrown herself at Cole in front of the whole town? He needed answers to questions that had tormented him these past days and nights.

A cloud of dust rose in the distance. Cole and the men watched it grow. "Whoever that is, he's in an almighty hurry," Otis observed dryly.

Cole nodded curtly. "He won't last long like that. He'll wind his horse fast in this heat."

"Seems like any fool'd know that," Otis scoffed.

"Unless—" The two men looked at each other.

"Let's go, men." Cole waved to the rest of the posse and they set out at a brisk gallop toward the cloud of dust.

The dust cloud was a lone horseman, and since he was hell-bent riding for them, they were certain he wasn't the quarry they sought. Concern etched their weary faces as they bent low over their tired mounts and urged them forward.

"Sheriff!" Carl Boss from the livery stable was shouting long before they drew abreast. He and his horse looked in bad shape.

"What's the matter, Boss?" Cole shouted.

"The Paiute—they've gone on the warpath," Carl gasped, his eyes comically round in his hound-dog face.

The men in the posse cursed.

"What's got them riled up now?" Cole asked.

"Rumors came back that Quill Ramsey and a couple of his men holed up in the Indian camp. They raped a couple of squaws, and when their men objected, Quill pulled a gun and shot 'em down without battin' an eyelash. He and his men rode out, but not before he burned some of their tee-pees. The Paiute are sore. They attacked and burned Welsh's Post. Now they threaten to do the same thing to Virginia City."

"All right, you men, let's ride," Cole called, swinging an arm to motion in the direction of town.

As if one body, the men kicked their tired horses into a ride every bit as desperate as Carl Boss's had been.

The town was in an uproar. No sooner had the bank been robbed than they were threatened by an Indian attack. Now all their fine plans for Virginia City seemed spurious in the face of losing their lives. As word spread, miners rode down from their claims and the big mines shut down, so the saloons were soon packed with armed, boisterous miners looking for a reason to shoot. As the men made their way down out of the mountains, they stopped off to warn friends and neighbors and soon discovered the warning had come too late for some. Old Tobias was one of the unlucky ones. His body was found on the side of the mountain, not far from where he'd made his first digging.

The wounded were loaded on empty ore wagons and

brought to town to be treated. The doctor's one room was soon overflowing, so wounded men lay on pallets outside on his porch and in the yard with the hot sun beating down on them.

When Kansas learned of the disaster, she hurried down to Dr. Langley's house and offered room at the Palace. With the help of the miners, the wounded were carried up the hill, where Ellie and Kansas had set up makeshift beds in the elegant salons. The kitchen that had once been manned by a French chef and had turned out the best of French cuisine now specialized in Irish stew as Ellie presided over large steaming pots. Kansas helped nurse the wounded men, sponging their brows to bring down fevers and spooning broth for those too weak and injured to do it for themselves. In between she sang them bawdy songs that would never be sung in drawing rooms or in the elegant Palace salons under normal conditions. But they made the men laugh and forget their pain for a time. With some she prayed, and for those who feared they might not recover, she wrote letters to long-forgotten relatives. Altogether she had twenty patients.

With the Palace closed down, she was soon running out of money for food and bandages, so Doc Langley approached the Citizens' Committee to ask for additional money. One afternoon, Kansas looked up from changing the bloody bandages of one of Jeb Willard's boys to find Oliver Howard standing in the entrance of the Palace. She hadn't seen him since the afternoon she'd paid off the bank loan, and even then nothing had been said. For a long moment he stared at her, then without a word turned and made his way down the hill. An hour later, food and bandages were delivered.

Kansas tried not to think about the man who had sent them. But some part of her rejoiced that the man she could never call father was not as immune to human suffering as she had suspected. Doggedly she and Ellie nursed the men, rarely taking time to rest or take sustenance themselves. Kansas hadn't had a bath in days, only taking time to wash her face and brush back her hair. She still wore the gown from the day before. Except for Reeny and the other girls of the Silver Spur, no one else had offered their services in nursing the miners.

"The posse's back," Ellie cried the next day as Kansas sat reading to a young miner whose wounds had festered. She feared he wasn't going to make it, but she remained cheerfully optimistic around him. Now she saw the faces of all the men brighten at Ellie's words. She understood how they felt. The whole town had lived under the threat of an Indian attack for days now. At least with the return of the posse they could look forward to some protection.

Kansas rose and hurried to the window. "Ellie, keep watch while I'm gone," she cried, and grabbing up a shawl to fling over her bloodstained gown, she ran down the hill.

Cole and Otis stood on the porch of the delivery store, talking to the milling miners. Kansas halted at the edge of the crowd, happy just to see him again. He looked exhausted. Deep creases marked his cheeks, and his eyes looked sunken. Even his broad shoulders sagged a bit, and she longed to take him up the hill and smother him with the care she'd given the miners these past few days. Instead, she stayed where she was, content just to know he was back and safe. Governor Nye stood on the porch beside him.

"All right, men," Cole said to the throng gathered about. His voice had a harsh edge that bespoke his weariness. "Rumor has it that the Paiute are headed this way. We're going to ride out and meet them. We've got fifty men coming from Carson City. If you ride with us, you'll follow some rules. We aren't going out there as some vigilante group to murder the first Indian we see. Although the Paiute are angry over what Quill and his men have done, it's a group of renegades who've been attacking the miners. We want to try and parley with the Indians before we do any shooting. Is that clear?"

Some of the men in the street looked at one another and

reluctantly nodded their heads. Others just stared at Cole, offering an unspoken challenge.

"We got twenty or thirty wounded men up there at the Palace," Sam Laxalt said, stepping forward. His jaw jutted belligerently. "We got about as many new graves down there in the cemetery, and not all of them are men. I ain't aimin' to mollycoddle the bloodthirsty savages."

"That's right," the other men cried.

Cole met the challenge unflinchingly. "And I'm not going to let this escalate into a full-scale Indian war," he said. "The first man who draws his gun and fires without orders will be shot down by me. If you can't abide by this rule, we don't want you. Go on back in the saloons and have a drink, or else stay here and protect the town."

The men mumbled among themselves, but it was obvious most of them intended to ride in the posse. Since they expected to intercept the Indians well away from town, Cole picked only a handful of men to stay behind for protection. Governor Nye stepped forward to say a prayer, and the men scattered to see to their gear.

Now, Kansas left her post and moved forward to speak to Cole. He saw her coming and met her halfway, pulling her into his arms. Kansas leaned against his lean, hard body, drawing in the familiar scent and warmth of him. Her head rested on his broad chest.

"We have to talk, you and I," he said roughly. She could feel his warm breath stirring her hair.

"I know," she said softly. "I have so much to tell you. Why didn't you tell me you weren't really going with the recruits? Didn't you trust me?"

His pause was too long, and she raised her head to look into his troubled eyes. "Kansas, what about Oliver Howard? What is he to you?"

He had every right to ask, but her emotions were too raw. She wasn't sure she could speak of it without crying, and she wouldn't do that in the middle of the street. "I—I can't tell you—not right now," she stammered, and saw his mouth tighten. He'd misunderstood. "When you come back, we'll—"

"The men are ready, Sheriff," Otis said from behind them.

Cole's gaze held hers a moment more, and she read the condemnation there. Without another word, he released her and stalked toward the horse tied at the post.

"Cole," she called, but her cry was lost in the impatient stamp of horses' hooves and equally impatient men set on avenging the deaths of their friends.

"Sheriff Slater," a voice called out, and Oliver Howard rode forward.

"What are you doing here, Howard?" Cole demanded.

"I'm riding with the posse," the banker declared.

Cole studied the older man. He could order him to stay behind and protect the town, but something about him made it plain he was intent on going. "All right," he finally agreed.

"Cole, no!" Two voices rang out with equal intensity. Claire Howard stood on one side of the street, her face pale with fear for her father. And on the other side of the street Kansas stood in her blood-splattered gown, her hair a tangled golden mass, her face equally pale.

Cole's face was grim, impassive, as he raised an arm and waved the posse forward. Spurring his horse, he rode out of town without a backward glance.

Standing on the boardwalk, Kansas stood gazing after him. She'd wanted to cry a final warning to him—that he mustn't trust Oliver Howard—but she'd been unable to. With the streets empty, she caught a glimpse of Claire Howard. The two women did not speak; each turned in opposite directions—one to make her way back to her pampered existence, the other to climb the hill and sit beside wounded men. Each of them prayed for the return of the men they loved.

Chapter 20

"**M**ISS KANSAS." AD Russell, one of the men left behind to protect the town, stood on her porch. "If you'd agree to it, ma'am, we'd like to bring everyone up here to the Palace until we know any danger to the town is over. We figure the Indians'll have a hard time burning down your stone walls and all."

"Of course," Kansas readily agreed. "I have rooms upstairs for some of the ladies, and we can turn over one of the parlors to them."

"Much obliged, ma'am," Ad said briefly, touching his hat brim before hurrying away.

In less than an hour all the women and children left in town were ushered up the hill and into the sinful halls of the Kansas Palace. Whores and dance hall girls mingled with the wives of bankers, mill owners, and the town's elite businessmen. Kansas stood on the front porch welcoming them all with equal graciousness. Claire Howard helped her mother up the porch steps and paused before Kansas. She looked distraught over her mother who seemed too weak to stand. Kansas hurried forward to take the trembling woman's other arm, but Letitia Howard jerked away from her. Kansas stepped back, her hands falling to her side.

"Welcome to my home," she said in an even tone.

"It's generous of you to let us take refuge here," said Claire, with grudging humility.

"I'm sure you would have done the same," Kansas answered quietly, and Claire Howard's head came up proudly. Both girls remembered the invitation that had not been sent for the ball.

Color stained Claire's cheeks. "This is something quite different, isn't it?" she said coldly, and swept by.

"No, I can't go in here," Letitia Howard protested as they neared the door.

"You must, Mother. Shhh, everyone is listening," Claire admonished her mother. The older woman grew quiet and they passed inside. Kansas knew that Ellie would lead them to one of the salons where tables had been removed and extra chairs placed. When the last of the women had made their way up the hill, Kansas hurried inside to help Ellie.

As she might have expected, the delicate ladies from the prominent side of town were clustered on one side of the parlor while Reeny and the rest of the saloon women settled on the other. Most of them had never seen the inside of the Palace, and now they gawked openly.

"Lordy, would you look at this," they cried. "I ain't seen anything this fancy since San Francisco."

"Don't it beat all?" they exclaimed, staring with wide-eyed wonder at the molding and frescoed ceiling.

The ladies on the other side of the room sniffed and looked down their noses disdainfully, yet Kansas had caught one or two of them surreptitiously fingering the fine damask of the draperies or examining the authenticity of a fine porcelain vase. She hid her grin.

"Where are the wounded men?" Reeny asked when they had tired of examining the decor. "Do you need some help with them?"

"Oh, yes," Kansas answered gratefully. "There's only Ellie and me to see to everything."

"You don't need to wait on us while we're here," Reeny

said, and the rest of the gaudily dressed women nodded in agreement.

"Could we have some tea here, please?" an imperious voice called from the other side of the room.

"Like I said, don't worry about us none. Now where are the men? We'll help feed and bath 'em."

The fancy women of Virginia City seemed happy to leave the repressive atmosphere of the parlor. They trooped through the house to the salon, where the men's faces brightened considerably upon seeing their new nurses. Some women made their way to the kitchen, where they drove Ellie crazy adding pinches of salt and pepper and various other seasonings to her pots of stew. But the hill ladies never left the parlor. They waited in martyred patience until tea was brought to them, then with much sniffing and lip-tightening they commented upon the quality of tea in such a place.

"I'm going to give them something to grumble about," Ellie said after delivering a plate of cakes and receiving no thanks.

"Ignore them, Ellie," Kansas said. "They won't be here long. Cole and the posse should have the Indians under control soon."

"They'd better," Ellie grouched. "I knew I should have put up a horseshoe to ward off the evil eye." She wrung her hands. "If only I had me some Saint John's wort like my grandmammy used . . ." The rest of her lament was lost as she entered the kitchen.

The afternoon was long. Kansas moved from the parlor, to the salon where the men lay, to the kitchen, seeing to everyone's needs, trying to foresee what would be needed later. Claire Howard and some of the other women had taken out needlework and now sat serenely stitching. Letitia Howard huddled on one end of a settee, her bright eyes feverish and slightly mad when she looked at Kansas. Now and then she shivered as with the ague. Kansas brought her

a coverlet for her knees, but she pushed it away. Gently
Claire replaced it.

"Mama, we must endure," she said. "We will triumph
in the end and soon we can return home. In the meantime,
we must remember we are ladies."

No word of thanks had been given to Kansas for her
trouble, and now she turned away, smarting at the deliberate insults of the women. "Let them go back to their homes
now, for all I care," she muttered to Ellie. "See how their
ladylike ways will protect them if the Indians come."

"I've got a potion working," Ellie whispered. "They'll
be gone soon, and they'll be sorry for the way they've
behaved."

"Oh, Ellie," Kansas said tiredly. "Potions won't cure
every ill of the earth. Besides, these ladies think they have
right on their side. You can't change their attitudes with a
bit of bay leaf or salt."

"Just you watch," Ellie said, and turned back to the
stove.

For a moment, watching the Irish woman bending over
her steaming pots, Kansas could almost believe she was a
witch, but Ellie's figure had grown too rotund, her round,
open face too good-humored to ever present a menace. With
her untidy, fading blond hair and wide blue eyes she looked
more like a cherub. Kansas giggled at the sudden image of
Ellie casting a spell while the "good" ladies of the town
cringed in terror. Feeling restored, she went on her rounds
again.

Late in the afternoon, the sound of gunfire came to them.
The women looked at each other in dismay. Some of the
ladies screamed, one swooned, while Reeny and her girls
paused in their administrations to the wounded men,
shrugged and made a joke, so the haunted, scared look on
the men's faces were replaced with relief. They'd lived
through one Indian attack. Now, wounded and with a house-
ful of women, they were worried.

Kansas and Ellie looked at each other as the gunfire continued, then faded away. "Ellie," Kansas said quietly, "let's close the shutters."

"My thoughts exactly," Ellie said, and the two of them made their way outside to the porches.

With as little fuss as possible, they closed and barred the shutters. Hurrying inside, Kansas fetched lanterns and candles and carried them to the parlor.

"I demand to know what's happening!" Claire Howard said when Kansas entered the darkened room.

"I'm sorry. I don't know what's happening," Kansas replied evenly. Her hands were steady as she lit the lamps and set them about.

"Why did you close the shutters?"

"It's something Ellie and I often do in the evenings," Kansas answered. "Supper will be ready soon, ladies. I hope you have a taste for Irish stew." She left the room without waiting for their reply.

"Miss Kansas," Ellie called from the doorway when she crossed the great entrance hall. "Come look." Kansas joined her on the front porch. Peering down on the town, she could see horsemen galloping madly through the streets.

"Is the posse back?" she asked, then gasped as a flickering torch cast light on a rider. "The Paiute. Quick, Ellie."

They hurried inside and closed the door. Reeny came to join them in the hall.

"What's wrong?" she asked, seeing their faces.

"Injuns!" Ellie said.

"Where are the lookouts?" Reeny asked. Her face went pale. "You don't think they've been killed? . . ."

"We'd better not depend on them protecting us," Kansas said. "Reeny, come help me. Otis has some guns in his room. Ellie, don't say anything to the other women. We don't want a panic."

Swiftly the two women headed for the stairs.

"Do you know how to use one of these things?" Reeny asked as they loaded a rifle and Kansas's small derringer. She was dismayed at the lack of weaponry. Otis had taken his new rifle and a brace of pistols with him.

"I've never used a rifle, but Otis showed me how to load one—and I'm a pretty good shot with the derringer."

"You're better off than me," Reeny confided. "I've never even held a gun in my hand." Kansas glanced at her in surprise. "Never needed to," Reeny explained. "There've always been men around to protect me."

"Well, this time, we're on our own," Kansas said. "Follow me."

The two women made their way to her room, where they looked down over the town. The Indians had stopped their aimless ransacking of the buildings and had remounted. Now they pointed up the hill at the Palace.

"They're coming," Kansas whispered. "Get ready! We won't fire unless they fire on us."

The mounted Indians rode up the hill, the sound of their horses like a death roar. Kansas heard the women scream below, but she flattened herself in the window seat and watched the oncoming Indians. When they reached the road in front of the Palace they paused, talking among themselves.

"What are they doing now?" Reeny whispered.

"Having a powwow," Kansas answered. "Hold your fire. They may just ride away."

"No such luck," Reeny said as the lead Indian raised his hand and drew a circle. Immediately his warriors kicked their ponies into motion and began circling the building. Sharp yips pierced the air, answered by the screaming women in the parlor.

"What a racket," Reeny cried.

"Noise won't hurt us," Kansas said, and tried not to think of the flower and vegetable garden being smashed beneath the horses' hooves.

Time and again the Indians rode around the house, whooping and shrieking. Finally they withdrew back to the road. At a command from their chief, they took out their rifles.

"Oh, no, they're getting serious," Kansas said, and tightened her grip on Otis's rifle.

Once again the Indians circled the building, this time raining bullets at the stone walls. For the most part, the bullets bounced off the walls or thudded into the thick wood of the shutters. Now and then one penetrated a crack and broke a glass or lantern in the parlor. At these times, the women below screamed with renewed intensity.

"I've got to do something to stop this," Kansas cried, and began firing at random into the circling Indians. She couldn't seem to hit anything, but she kept trying. Suddenly the large Indian who had seemed to be their leader rode into view. With sweating hands, Kansas sighted along the barrel and pulled the trigger. The Indian jerked, then sagged against his pony's neck. The men around him looked at the Palace in consternation, then sent a volley of shots against the front while others took their wounded leader and withdrew.

Kansas and Reeny huddled on the window seat while broken glass and bullets whizzed over their heads. From below stairs came a renewed screaming. The barrage of bullets stopped, and slowly Kansas and Reeny raised their heads and looked out. The Indians were gone, riding pell-mell down the hill and through town. Kansas breathed a sigh of relief, then stiffened.

"Something's burning," she cried, and leapt to her feet.

Reeny was right behind her as she raced downstairs. Ellie was coming from the kitchen.

"Something's afire!" she cried.

Kansas ran to the parlor and paused briefly to take in the scene. Flames licked at the thick Turkish carpet and engulfed the heavy damask drapes. The women were huddled in one corner, away from the fire. None had made a move to put it out. Kansas and Reeny rushed to the window to drag down the heavy drapes. Throwing them on the floor, they stamped on the flames to put out the fire. Ellie swatted at the carpet. In no time, the flames were out. The room was filled with smoke, the window frame and floor scorched.

Claire Howard sat with her arm around her mother, who seemed caught in a paroxysm of coughing. "My mother needs to lie down," she said.

Kansas bit back the rebuke she longed to hurl at the helpless women. Her shoulders sagged wearily as she looked around. "Open one of the shutters, Ellie," she said. "Let's air things out a little in here." Her gaze settled on Claire Howard and her mother. "You can bring her upstairs to my room. Reeny, give her a hand."

"Sure thing," Reeny said, and stepped forward, but Letitia Howard shrank away from the saloon girl. "Suit yourself." Reeny shrugged and walked away.

"Come this way," Kansas said, and led the way upstairs to her bedroom. Claire tried not to show her curiosity as she looked around at the richly appointed room.

"Oh, I couldn't!" Letitia Howard said as Claire led her toward the huge bed. "Who knows how many men she's entertained here!"

Kansas's lips compressed angrily. "There's been only one man in my bed, ever," she said. "You can believe that or not, I don't really care. But other than the servant's quarters, there is no other bed for you."

"How dare you speak to her like that? Especially after—" Claire bit her lips.

"Especially after what?" Kansas challenged. She was tired of the innuendoes and lies connected to her name.

"We've heard the rumors about you and—and my father," Claire hissed.

"Your father?" Kansas could only stare at the other girl

in dismay. In all her wildest dreams, she had never thought anyone would believe this.

"Claire!" Letitia Howard sagged against her daughter. Automatically Kansas stepped forward to help, but Claire shielded her mother with her own body.

"Don't touch her, you—you harlot," she cried. "You aren't good enough to touch her skirts."

In rigid silence Kansas waited as Claire lowered her mother to the bed and turned back to face her. "I suppose you had my father up here."

"I've never entertained your father in the fashion you mean," Kansas said, aware of the enormous strain the other girl must be under if she believed this of her father. Kansas stepped closer to the bed and looked at Letitia Howard. The older woman's breathing was shallow, but her eyes were bright and alert. "The rumors are untrue, Mrs. Howard," she said softly.

Letitia Howard's mouth twisted scornfully. "I know they're not true," she said. "I saw the pendant in my husband's hands. I saw his face. His past has come back to haunt him and he's ashamed. Ashamed, do you hear me?" She relaxed against the pillows, her head thrown back, her eyes blank and staring at the ceiling as if she were traveling a long way back in time.

"Molly McKay," she said scornfully. "She was nothing, a girl of no consequence, someone's maid who'd decided to go West for a better way of life. But these people take their own way of life with them. So I hired her. I was too delicate to handle all the chores of cooking. She was a lazy slut. I had to drive her all the time. She was a pretty thing at first. Every man on the train wanted her, Oliver, too. He thought I didn't know he was sneaking off to meet her at nights after everyone was asleep. At first I didn't mind it too much. I was a lady. I didn't care much for the animal needs of a man. But then something changed. I could tell he was thinking about her when he wasn't with her. He'd stare into the fire and kind of smile. Every time she passed by, he'd get a soft, weak look about him. I hated him for it. I hated her." Letitia Howard turned restlessly on the bed. Kansas stood transfixed, knowing she was hearing the real story of her father and mother. She could picture Molly, young and fresh-faced, alive with hope for a better future, working her way across country for an exacting woman like Letitia Howard and slipping away at night to meet Oliver Howard.

"I made her pay," Letitia said, and her mouth twisted with spite. "She never had a minute for herself. I knew she'd gotten herself with child long before she did. I found her puking out behind one of the wagons, and I knew. I didn't let up on her. I made her work twice as hard. I wanted that baby to die." Letitia turned her blazing gaze to Kansas. "I wanted you to die!"

"Mama!" Claire cried. Her fists were pressed to her mouth as she stared with dawning comprehension at her mother. With horror-stricken eyes she turned to Kansas.

"He was going to take her away when he found out she was pregnant," Letitia went on. "I heard them talking. She lay under the wagon, pretending to be sick, and he came to her, cradling her in his arms, like she was his child and crooning to her, words he'd never said to me. Well, I stopped them. I told him I was pregnant, too. What could he do? I was his wife. I needed him more than she ever did." Letitia chuckled feverishly. Her gnarled hands plucked at the covers. "He gave her a locket and some money and left her at one of the forts along the way." She turned to Kansas once more, her face shiny with triumph. "I made him choose—and he chose me." She laughed. "Of course, I wasn't really pregnant, and I had to submit myself to him to get myself pregnant, but he was my husband!"

Her words faded away in the quiet room and she began to snore. Claire stood as if made of stone. The only movement in the room was the curtain blowing in the breeze from the broken window.

"Claire, I'm sorry you had to hear this way," Kansas said softly.

"The locket Papa had," Claire said as if in a daze. "It came from you?"

"Yes." Kansas rubbed the back of her neck as if remembering the pain as he'd ripped it from her. "He hadn't known."

"And you made sure he found out," Claire said bitterly.

"No, it wasn't like that," Kansas said quickly. "I—I didn't know Oliver Howard was my father until that night he—he came to the Palace."

Claire's lips curled in contempt. "You lured him here."

"No!"

"Then you produced this—this locket. That proves nothing."

"It doesn't matter," Kansas said. "I don't expect anything from him or from you."

"From me?" Claire laughed. "Why should you expect anything from me?" Her tone was so ridiculing that Kansas couldn't resist.

"Because we're sisters," she said, quietly, and left the room, making her way down the stairs while from above Claire Howard forgot about being a lady and shrieked her anger and denial for one and all to hear.

"Lordy, I never heard such language," Ellie muttered, and shrugged. Ladies weren't such a mystery, after all.

Chapter 21

*T*HEY ENGAGED THE Paiute just as they'd given up and were returning to town. Riding over a ridge, they'd come face-to-face with the renegade band, who had seemed as startled as they. Dismounting, the men had scattered, taking shelter behind rocks and bluffs, whatever the land afforded. The Indians drew back, regrouped, and, rifles held ready, rode straight at the posse. The ensuing battle was fierce and short. When the smoke cleared, the renegade band retreated, their numbers decimated. Cole took stock of his men. Two were dead and three mortally wounded.

"Cole, Oliver Howard's wounded back there," Otis said, nodding toward an outcropping of rocks. "He wants to talk to you."

"What about?" Cole said, intent on getting his men on the move again.

"He wouldn't say, but he seemed real keen on it." Otis paused. "I don't figure he's going to make it."

Cole watched the old man amble away, then, sighing, he turned toward the rocks, where Oliver Howard was recanting all the sins of a lifetime and making his peace with God.

"The men are back!" Ellie sent up the cry and the women who'd spent the night weeping and praying crept out of their hiding places. Blinking against the brightness of the morning sun, they shielded their eyes and stared down the hill at the horsemen entering the town.

"It's the sheriff," they cried and ran down the hill, their dignity and fears forgotten in the joy of being alive.

Husbands gathered wives close, listening to their tangled accounts of the night's happenings. The bodies of those left behind to guard the town were discovered and grimly covered. Reeny and her girls told their story of how the women had survived and how Kansas had shot the renegade leader. Somberly the men crowded into saloons where whiskey was poured, and even the ladies from the hill forgot to be disapproving as they stood patiently waiting for their menfolks to finish their drinks and go home with them. Those whose husbands had been wounded carried them off to nurse and bully them back to health, and those whose husbands came back belly down over their saddles stood weeping in the streets.

Claire Howard came down the stairs at the Palace and stood staring at Kansas with hate-filled eyes. "I'll need some help in getting my mother back home," she said, and Kansas noted the dark circles under her eyes.

Impulsively she went to the foot of the stairs, placing her hand atop Claire's, where it lay on the newel post. "Your mother will be all right," she reassured her, remembering how the proud girl had sat by her mother's bed throughout the night.

Claire snatched her hand away. "I'm sure she will—as soon as I get her away from this house!"

"Claire . . ." Kansas tried again, gripping her hands tightly for control. "If we are never to be friends, could we at least try not to be enemies. We share the same father, and that's not the fault of either of us. I'll keep our secret if you want."

Claire turned back to Kansas, her eyes wary. "Can you give me your word on that?" she asked harshly.

"Yes, I give it gladly," Kansas said. "I have no desire

to hurt you or your family. Perhaps someday we can put the bitterness behind us and find a way to be friends.''

Claire's glance was scornful, her face sly as she forced a smile. ''Perhaps,'' she said, and Kansas's shoulders sagged in defeat, knowing the other girl's words were prompted from fear that she might yet reveal their kinship.

''Either way, I shan't go back on my word,'' Kansas said, and saw relief wash over Claire's face—to be quickly replaced with the stony snobbery it had always worn.

''Will you send for someone to help my mother?'' she asked, and regally climbed the stairs.

Otis rode up the hill to check on Kansas and Ellie and he had a couple of men bring the buggy around and load Letitia Howard in it for the short ride to her house. He kept to himself the news that would greet the Howard women once they reached home. Kansas stood on the porch, hugging her arms around herself in an effort to remain on her feet. Now that the Indian scare was behind them and all the women gone, fatigue and delayed fear were taking their toll. She wanted only to sink into her bed and sleep for a week, but first she had to see Cole, to tell him how much she loved him and how she'd prayed for his safety.

Her vigil was rewarded by the sight of a tall, rangy figure on horseback. Slowly Cole rode up the hill and brought his horse to a stop just short of the trampled flower beds. His face was grim and he swung his long legs over the saddle pommel and slid off.

''Hello, Kansas,'' he said, coming to stand on the bottom step. His eyes were level with hers.

''Cole,'' Kansas said, and threw her arms around him. She longed to feel his arms gather her close, but they remained at his side. ''Cole, what is it?'' she whispered, drawing back.

''Oliver Howard didn't make it,'' he said, watching her face go pale.

''Oh, no!'' she cried, and tears welled in her eyes.

She turned aside, as if not wanting him to see her pain, and he felt his own pain rip through his guts. He made no move to comfort her, and when her shoulders had stopped trembling and she had straightened once more, he dug into his pocket.

"He sent this to you." He held out the gold locket he'd seen her wear a hundred times before. "He said to tell you he was sorry—that given another time and place he could have loved you. He died before he could finish."

"I know what he meant to say," Kansas said quietly, and her eyes were luminous. They darkened as Cole stepped down off the step.

"Cole, wait!" she cried. "Why are you leaving like this? We have to talk."

He swung around to face her, the lean lines of his face hard and set. "I don't think there's much left to talk about."

"But there is."

"Oliver Howard was your lover, wasn't he?"

"No, he wasn't," Kansas cried. "I know what you must believe with all the rumors going around, but they aren't true. None of them are."

"You loved him!" Cole's voice was soft and ragged.

"I could have, given the chance." Kansas paused, remembering the pledge she'd made to Claire. "I can't tell you anything more. I promised someone I wouldn't. . . . Cole, wait!" she called when he swung around to leave. "Can't you have some faith in me?"

He stood beside his horse, his shoulders sagging, his head bowed, then slowly he raised his head and stared at her. "My faith is gone, Kansas. Good-bye." He mounted and rode away.

Kansas stood on the porch, gripping the locket until it bit into her hands, and watched through tear-bleared eyes as he disappeared down the hill. "How many times must I watch you leave me, Cole Slater?" she whispered fiercely. "How many times must I prove myself to you?"

She turned and staggered into the Palace, up the stairs, and into her room, where she fell face down on her bed. "These are the last tears I'll ever shed for you," she whispered. She felt dead inside.

The town had recovered from its traumatic experience. Quill Ramsey still hadn't been caught, although there were reports of him turning up in towns close by. To Kansas, it seemed Quill Ramsey was lying out there somewhere just waiting for her. She remembered the hate in his eyes that day in the bank when he'd vowed to exact revenge against her someday.

The Kansas Palace had reopened, although some of the windows remained boarded up from the Indian attack.

Kansas sent the gold locket that had belonged to Oliver Howard to his widow. It was like closing a window on a painful time in her life. Grimly she threw herself into her work, gambling recklessly. Miners still vied to gamble with Kansas McKay. She'd become something of a legend. A New York newspaper, writing of the attempted silver robbery and the importance of Nevada as a state, did a whole feature on Kansas McKay, the brave-hearted, generous soiled dove of Virginia City. Kansas no longer made any attempt to deny the things said about her. Only she and one man knew the truth about her innocence, and Cole Slater couldn't seem to remember or to care. Ellie had heard that he was still engaged to Claire. Kansas had thought the dull pain she carried deep inside couldn't get any worse, but at the thought of Cole marrying her half-sister, she feared her heart would truly break. She pulled her shredded pride about her and went on. Finally even the miners began to notice her heart wasn't in the cards anymore, and one by one they began to stay away.

James Nye had selected Carson City as his territorial capital, and the citizens of Virginia City had given up the notion of adding new fame and luster to their town. Past prejudices eased a bit. The opera house was completed and a well-known theatrical group scheduled to appear. Kansas sent for tickets for herself and Ellie and Otis. They'd discovered they had adjoining claims, and a big strike had been made on each. Otis and Ellie had decided to marry, and that evening would be a celebration.

The afternoon before the performance, Kansas and Ellie sat in the kitchen planning Ellie's new house.

"It's to be a grand thing," Ellie decreed. "Almost as grand as the Palace, with a long, winding staircase. I always had me a hankering to come sweeping down a long, curving staircase."

"One long, winding staircase," Kansas wrote down on her pad. "What else?"

"Well, I'd like two parlors and a ballroom and I want some of them fancy rugs like you have in the salon—Lands sake, who's that?" Ellie rose at the sound of a knock and hurried to the door. A young boy delivered a letter and scurried away.

"It's for you," Ellie said, handing it to Kansas.

Kansas took the note with trembling hands and tore it open. Quickly she scanned the handwritten page, then disbelievingly read it again.

"What is it, love?" Ellie asked, seeing Kansas's expression.

" 'Don't come to the theater tonight!' " Kansas read. " 'Decent folks don't want you there.' "

"Who would have sent something like this?" Ellie exploded. "Sounds like something those Howard women would do. I hear they're going to be there tonight. Well, if you can't go, I won't go, either."

"We've been through this before, haven't we, Ellie?" Kansas mused. "They didn't stop me before. I don't see any reason for them to do so now."

"Then you're going?" Ellie cried. "Good for you, girl. I'll make you an amulet to wear under your gown, so nothing they say or do can hurt you."

"Nothing can prevent them from hurting me," Kansas said softly. "I guess I'll never grow used to the cruelty, but I won't let them stop me."

"Otis and me'll be right there beside you, Kansas," Ellie said. "If anyone as much as looks down their nose at you, I'll put a spell on them."

Kansas grinned. "Would you do that for me?"

Ellie opened her mouth in surprise. Kansas had scoffed at her spells and potions for so long! Now she grinned back. "Just watch me," she said, and leaped to her feet.

"And Ellie, while you're at it . . . have you got any potions to bring back lost loves?"

Ellie knew she was teasing, but the underlying sadness in her eyes made her words sad and pitiful. "I'll try my best potion," she said softly. "It's bound to work."

Cole Slater handed Claire and her mother out of the carriage, then escorted them into the new opera hall. Claire looked especially lovely tonight in her pale gray, moire silk mourning gown. Her dark, shiny hair was coiled on top of her head and her long white neck looked graceful and fragile. Claire was an extraordinarily beautiful woman, he realized. But he still missed the earthy, sensuous beauty of Kansas. He found himself straining to catch glimpses of her in town and around the Silver Spur, but she hadn't come down the hill since the Indian attack. Her aloofness only seemed to add fuel to the gossip that swirled around her. Some claimed she was half mad with grief for her dead lover. Others claimed to have seen her walking the parapet of her roof by the light of the moon, looking for some sign of his return.

Cole knew these things were untrue, but he did nothing to dispel them. Kansas McKay was no longer his concern. He wasn't certain Claire Howard was, either, but they had the bank in which Cole had half interest in common, and somehow he'd just let things drift these past few weeks.

Now he guided the two women to their seats. Murmurs of sympathy rose from those around upon seeing the banker's widow. Letitia Howard was still dressed in black and clutched a lacy white handkerchief, which she pressed to her brow and lips now and then. She seemed to enjoy playing the role of the grieving widow, Cole noted. He seated himself behind the ladies and looked around.

The new theater was sumptuous, well in keeping with the town's growing reputation. Crystal chandeliers hung from a frescoed dome ceiling. Cherubs frolicked among curlicued moldings and heavy, wine-colored velvet draperies hung at the stage and around each box. Cole's gaze fixed on one box and he caught his breath. Kansas McKay, Otis, and Ellie had entered the box and were seating themselves. He couldn't tear his eyes away from Kansas. He hadn't seen her since the Indian attack, and now he felt the impact of her beauty like a blow to the stomach.

Her thick wheat-colored hair was gathered in a loose knot on top of her head while tendrils curled against her cheeks and slender nape. She had on the same vivid pink gown she'd worn at the governor's ball, and its brilliant color set roses blooming in her cheeks. Her shoulders were smooth and creamy, the rise of her full breasts above the low-cut neck inviting. Cole's hands clenched into fists. He remembered all too well the feel of that creamy skin beneath his hands. Slowly he became aware of the whispers around him.

"The hussy!" Grace Winslow hissed to Letitia Howard. The widow wore a martyred expression, but behind the pious air, Cole noticed a gleam of malice.

"How could she?" Claire demanded, her face twisted with rage. "I sent her a warning."

"A warning?" Cole echoed.

Claire glanced at him sharply, aware she may have revealed too much. Quickly she pulled her petulant features into a more pleasing array. She'd have to be careful for a little while longer, until she and Cole were married. She was all too aware that he still bore some feeling for Kansas.

"Yes, I sent her a note explaining Mother would be attending, that it was her first outing, and that under the circumstances, if she could refrain from appearing. . . ." Claire looked helpless and hurt. "After all, she must realize how distressful it is to my mother to be forced to sit in the same room with my father's . . . mistress." Claire dabbed at her eyes. "How could she flaunt herself like this?"

"How, indeed?" Cole said, and Claire was satisfied to see the anger and condemnation in his eyes.

The buzz had risen in the theater so the orchestra could no longer be heard. Kansas was aware everyone was looking at her and at Letitia Howard, who sat swooning in her box. Kansas had glanced at the Howard box only once. The sight of Cole Slater hovering over Claire had been too painful for a second look.

"Don't let them bother you, lovey," Ellie said, and Otis leaned over to pat her on the shoulder, his awkward vote of support. Kansas smiled at them wanly, wishing she hadn't come.

The whispers had grown to angry voices now, their sound filling the room. Letitia Howard was the brave widow of one of the town's prominent citizens. And although Kansas was a heroine herself—and a legend—it was one of which they were growing weary. Now they championed Letitia Howard, while those rough men and women who stood behind Kansas were not the sort to attend a play.

The time for the play to begin had come and gone. The manager had come on stage once to warn the audience they were about to begin, but no one had listened. This couldn't go on, Kansas thought. Who knew where it might end? Slowly she got to her feet and stepped to the edge of the box. Instantly the theater fell silent, as if all were holding their breath.

Kansas cast a quick glance at the Howard box. With a cruel, victorious smile, Claire linked an arm through Cole's and met Kansas's gaze, her eyes glittering. Kansas turned back to the audience.

"I know I'm not wanted here tonight," she said. "I received an anonymous note today warning me not to come."

Cole glanced at Claire, whose pale face blushed scarlet. He drew his arm away.

"But Virginia City is my town, too. I've helped build it, helped protect it, and you can't drive me away. There's room here for all of us, if we'll just practice a little tolerance. I have a right to be here."

No one said anything and, defeated, Kansas turned away. Taking up her shawl she made her way from the box. Otis and Ellie followed. The people in the theater cheered and clapped loudly. The sound followed Kansas from the theater and out onto the street.

"Are you all right, Miss Kansas?" Otis asked. "You want me to go in there and bust a few heads?"

Kansas smiled and shook her head. "We can't change their minds about me, Otis. Please don't let me spoil the evening for you and Ellie. Go on and have some supper. I'd just like to be alone for a while."

"All right, Miss Kansas. If you're sure," Otis said reluctantly.

"I'm sure," Kansas said, and turned up the street toward the Palace.

"I guess we showed that brazen hussy," Letitia Howard crowed. "She can't come down here with decent folks and pretend she's like the rest of us. She got just what she deserved." Her fingers fluttered restlessly with the gold locket at her throat. "She's no better than her mother."

Cole's head came up. "You knew Molly McKay?"

Letitia's voice was liquid with malice. "Oh, I knew the little slut, all right—chasing after my husband, making a fool out of me, trying to pass her bastard off as Oliver's."

"Mama, shhh!" Claire said nervously.

"When did you know Molly McKay, Mrs. Howard?" Cole asked softly. His eyes were narrowed and assessing.

"She was my personal maid when we came across the Oregon Trail," Letitia said. "But she wasn't much good. She didn't know the least thing about helping a lady. We had to leave her back there on the trail at one of the forts. You know she turned into a whore after she left us. She wasn't good for much else. Same way with that daughter of hers." Her hands gripped the locket, swinging it back and forth.

Cole leaned forward and gently disengaged the delicate locket from her grip. "Be careful, Mrs. Howard," he said sympathetically. "You'll break your pretty locket."

"Why, thank you," Letitia said, pleased at his attention. She simpered up at him, much as she had done to Oliver Howard when she was a young girl.

"Mama," Claire said, and Letitia noted the desperate edge to her daughter's voice and saw no reason for it. "I told you not to wear that locket."

"Why shouldn't I?" Letitia demanded petulantly. "It's mine. It was rightfully mine years ago." She turned back to Cole. "It belonged to my husband's mother, you know, and her grandmother brought it over from England."

"It's beautiful," Cole said, although he was no longer looking at Letitia Howard or her locket. He was staring at Claire—while all the things Kansas had said to him about her father fell into place.

"Cole . . ." Claire began.

"You knew, didn't you?" he said quietly. "All the time you knew, and you kept the lie going."

"No, no, Cole. What you're thinking is wrong. Papa couldn't possibly have fathered her." She lowered her voice and glanced around, fearful others might have heard. "It's all a lie that she made up. She sent that locket down to Mama, and Mama has it mixed up."

"It won't work, Claire," Cole said, getting to his feet.

Claire leaped up. "Go to her then. Have her for your mistress if you must, but marry me, Cole. Marry me, and together we'll own this town, the mills, the mines. I worked with my father. I know how he had planned to call in loans and take over the mines. You and I, Cole." Her hands reached for him, clinging and grasping.

Disgusted, Cole took hold of her wrists and pushed her away. "Kansas is more decent and good than you and your kind ever dreamed of being."

"Go to your slut, then!" Claire cried, unmindful of the faces turned to their box. "How long will she stay faithful to you? She's a whore, a soiled dove."

Cole laughed then. "The men called her the *gilded* dove, and I'll take my chances with her." Still chuckling, he left the box and ran down the stairs.

Her face tear-streaked, Claire stared around the quiet theater and was met with shocked stares. Even Letitia Howard stared at her as if she were a stranger. Everything she'd said had been heard, she realized. No one would ever bank with her now. She was finished in this town. Claire whimpered as she faced the ruin she'd brought on herself.

Cole hurried up the hill toward the Palace. Kansas had asked him to believe her, to have faith in her, but he'd turned away from her, willing to believe the worst. He'd done it time and again, he realized. Why? He curled his fists and felt like pounding his chest in anguish. Why had he chosen to believe everyone else but the woman he loved? She'd done what she must to survive, and he'd condemned her for it, and, although he'd professed not to care, he'd adopted the same attitude as the rest of the town. He'd reached the Palace now. The windows were

dark. The night breeze was sultry, the sky was filled with
a million stars . . . like that first night he'd made love to
her here at the Palace.

He bounded up the steps two at a time and knocked,
but no one answered. Pushing open the door he stepped
inside. Now that he was here, he wasn't sure how to convince Kansas how sorry he was. He wiped his sweaty
hands against his pants and stood in a patch of moonlight.
His thoughts turned once more to the night he'd found
Kansas.

He'd been furious, with a rage that had taken three
years of building, three years of refining in the whorehouses and saloons where he'd searched for her. When
he'd seen her in that dress—with all the men calling to her
good-naturedly, touching her—he'd gone crazy. Whiskey
and pent-up fury had driven him to follow her, but the
sweet reality of Kansas herself had gentled him when he
took her here on this very floor. Cole paused, memory
spilling through him. He relived that night, that moment.
He could hear her words denying his accusations, feel her
flesh beneath his fingers, taste her mouth. He felt the passion that had sent him plunging against her and the muffled cry of pain.

"Oh, God, forgive me, Kansas," he whispered. "You
were a virgin." He heard the cry again and clamped his
hands to his ears, sure he was meant to be tormented by it
the rest of his life. The cry became a scream, and Cole
straightened, his head turned toward the stairs. "Kansas,"
he cried, and sprinted up the stairs two at a time.

She was on the bed, a man bent over her. A knife blade
glinted in the moonlight and the white sheet beneath her
was red with blood. Cole threw himself across the room,
the momentum of his rock-hard body knocking the man to
the floor. Cole rolled free and rose, groping for the man
in the darkened room. His fist connected with flesh and he

felt a bone splinter. The man reeled backward, gripping his nose. Moonlight spilled through the window.

"Quill Ramsey," Cole grated out. "You've come back for me to kill you."

"Slater?" Quill said. "My quarrel ain't with you. I come back to get this whore. She took everything from me—my saloon, even the money from the bank. If it hadn't been for her, I'd be rich now, sitting somewhere in San Francisco."

"No, you wouldn't have, Ramsey," Cole grated. "I would have tracked you down to the end of the earth, if need be."

Quill stood gasping in air, then, with a howl, he launched himself at Cole. The two men fought, tumbling and vying for a hold that would allow one to finish off the other. Cole landed a punch on Quill's chin, and he went down. When he came up, he had his knife in his hand.

"Cole, look out," Kansas cried, and he ducked, then pushed up with his knees, his fists carrying the force of his big body behind them as they pounded Ramsey. The knife went flying and lodged against the fire irons and Ramsey followed. He carried a poker with him when he came at Cole. Cole put up an arm to ward off the blow and felt the iron strike his temple. The blow left him dazed. Above him, Ramsey laughed and leveled his gun at Cole. A shot rang out. Ramsey's face showed comic surprise, then he staggered toward the door, leaving a trail of blood behind him. Chest heaving, Cole followed.

Quill made it to the landing, then tumbled headfirst down the great winding staircase of the Kansas Palace. He landed on the marble floor below, his head twisted at an unnatural angle.

Cole hurried back to the bedroom. Kansas lay on the bed, clutching her side, a smoking derringer in one hand.

"Did he get away?"

Wearily Cole shook his head. "He's dead."

"He always did underestimate a woman," she mumbled, and fell forward.

"Kansas!" Cole rushed to her. He lifted the small, crumpled body and felt blood beneath his fingers.

"Oh, no, Kansas," he crooned, his strong fingers seeking and finding the thin thread of a pulse. He lit a lamp and examined the knife wound. Relief flooded through him when he saw the knife had merely grazed her side. "Kansas," he said gently, tapping her cheek. Her long lashes fluttered against her pale cheeks, then opened. Her clear gray eyes gazed at him. Cole felt his heart constrict with love for this woman.

"Will you marry me?" he asked huskily.

"Yes," Kansas whispered unhesitatingly. "But Cole, I have so many things to explain to you."

"I know it all, my sweet," he whispered, and looked around for something to bandage her wounds. A fine lawn petticoat lay nearby; with a few quick jerks he'd torn it into strips. His hands were gentle as he tended to her.

Kansas watched his face, taking in the strong features and the warm love she saw in his eyes. "I fear I may have died and gone to heaven after all," she whispered. "All my dreams seem to have come true."

Cole snatched her up and held her against him. "All your dreams will come true from now on, Kansas. I promise you," he said, and his voice shook with emotion. "I'm sorry, Kansas. Please, forgive me."

Her fingers twined in his thick hair. She was lightheaded with joy. "I forgive you with all my heart," she said softly. Cole's lips claimed hers, possessing her tomorrows as they had her yesterdays.

"Cole," she whispered when he had released her mouth and buried his face against her neck. "I want to leave Virginia City and go someplace where people don't know me. I know it sounds like running away, but I'm tired of trying to make people believe that I'm not a soiled dove."

"Will it bother you to leave behind all the glitter of the Palace? With me, you'll only be a rancher's wife."

"That sounds heavenly. Can we go tonight?" Her head was weary.

"In the morning, after you've rested," Cole said. "Sleep now, my little dove." His voice held a smile. He cradled her against his chest, and her eyelids fluttered shut.

"Tomorrow," she muttered thickly. "Tomorrow we go to . . ." Her voice trailed off.

"To Montana. We go to Montana," Cole said, thinking about the open range land there. Through the night he held her, sometimes half dozing, sometimes half dreaming of the ranch house he'd build and the blond wife who'd live there with him—and of the children they'd have. One day he'd tell them stories of their brave and legendary mother, but not at first. First, he'd be sure she was safe and happy. As he cradled the woman he loved, Cole felt the restless, driving fury that had dogged his steps leave him and he was finally at peace.

Before the dawn light had stained the peaks of the mountains, two figures slipped away from the Palace, mounted their horses, and rode away to the north. In the saddlebag of one were a cache of jewels and some silver coins. In the saddlebag of the other was a half interest in a mine that had played out soon after it was mined and the deed to a bank that would go bankrupt within weeks. Behind them, they left a boarded-up Palace, a silver badge, and a dead bank robber. When Ellie went to call on Kansas, she found blood-soaked sheets, a derringer, and a deed giving Otis and her the Palace.

The town speculated for a while on what had happened to Kansas McKay. Some thought she'd been killed by the same men who'd killed Quill Ramsey, some claimed she'd been carried off by his men. Most folks thought she was dead. The miners and Reeny and her girls held a funeral for Kansas McKay, but the ladies at the other end of town didn't come. They pulled down their shades as the mourners marched past.

In time, the folks of Virginia City didn't talk much about Kansas McKay. Other men and women came to town in search of their share of the Comstock Lode, and in return left their mark on the town's colorful history. Otis and Ellie built their own fine house down along the river, and folks flocked to the lively parties they gave. Ellie became the darling of Virginia City's better society with her quaint, humorous ways. The Kansas Palace stood boarded up and empty, but once in a while, men stumbling home late at night swore they saw a light in the window . . . and a girl sitting there brushing her long blond hair.

About the Author

Peggy Hanchar is a successful romance writer living in St. Louis, MO.

Capture The Romance
With
Jennifer Blake